DESTINY, TEXAS

DESTINY, TEXAS

BRETT COGBURN

PINNACLE BOOKS
Kensington Publishing Corp.
www.kensingtonbooks.com

PINNACLE BOOKS are published by

Kensington Publishing Corp.
119 West 40th Street
New York, NY 10018

All Kensington titles, imprints, and distributed lines are available at special quantity discounts for bulk purchases for sales promotions, premiums, fund-raising, educational, or institutional use. Special book excerpts or customized printings can also be created to fit specific needs. For details, write or phone the office of the Kensington sales manager: Kensington Publishing Corp., 119 West 40th Street, New York, NY 10018, attn: Sales Department; phone 1-800-221-2647.

PINNACLE BOOKS and the Pinnacle logo are Reg. U.S. Pat. & TM Off.

ISBN-13: 978-0-7860-3669-1
ISBN-10: 0-7860-3669-9

First printing: August 2015

10 9 8 7 6 5 4 3 2 1

Printed in the United States of America

First electronic edition: August 2015

ISBN-13: 978-0-7860-3670-7
ISBN-10: 0-7860-3670-2

PART I
HAMISH

Chapter One

Somewhere along the Little Wichita River,
100 miles beyond the frontier, state of Texas, 1866

Gunn and I rode the lead oxen, him on the big gray, and me
beside him with my scrawny legs dangling down either side
of the motley-colored steer Papa called Speck. Gunn had
his freckled nose wrinkled and his eyes squinted against the
far horizon like he always did, as if he were more than
twelve years old and leading the wagon train himself, as if
he could look into all that distance before us and see something that I couldn't. Gunn always thought he was bigger
than he was, and maybe that was because Papa doted on
him so.

It wasn't really a wagon train at all: just Mama's buggy,
two wagons, a Mexican cart, two milk cows, on one tailgate
a crate of fussy leghorn chickens that Mama insisted on
bringing, and Gunn's big yellow dog running in and out
amongst us all.

Old Ben was driving Mama to one side and out of the
dust, the brim of his big flop hat tugged down over his face,
shading his bushy gray eyebrows against the glare of the

sun. Ben was from back in the Alabama times. That's how I was already thinking about what we'd left . . . other times . . . before Texas . . . back before the war and before Papa came home half-dead and found what the Yankees did while he was gone. "Blackhearted Blue Bastards" are what Papa called them. Burned the big white house he built, stole Mama's silverware, broke her fine china, and carried off the split-rail fences for firewood. What they didn't eat or steal, they burned or ruined out of pure spite.

Everything changes, and a man can't stop it any more than he can stand in front of the wind and make it stop blowing. That's what Mama said. What she said didn't matter, because everybody cried some over our misfortune, except for Papa and Gunn. They never cried.

I looked behind us at the pale wagon tracks mashed into the spring grass and wildflowers until they faded and disappeared the way we had come, leading back to somewhere else, beyond some point of no return, to some other people that looked like us, our forgotten predecessors of a sort in a world we'd quit. Old things were fading and something new took their place. All around us there was nothing in sight that spoke of civilization and nothing to prove we might exist except those wagon tracks—just miles and miles of sky and nothing. You could see forever, like a promise or a threat. Nothing and everything, that was Texas for you.

I turned the other way and saw Papa riding back to us from the south. I knew it was him because nobody else sat a horse like that. And his horse was easy to spot, too—the same long-legged, harebrained Thoroughbred that used to carry him along the roads, trading cotton and seeing to the business of his plantation, and the same chestnut gelding that packed him along with General Forrest from Chicka-mauga to Brice's Cross Roads, where he got shot in the left leg by a Blue Bastard minié ball. Nobody rode Shiloh. He was a one-man horse, even if Papa would have tolerated anybody else on his back.

"Mama's fussing and wants to make evening camp in the shade," I said to Papa when he rode alongside us.

Papa scowled for an instant at Mama's buggy. She was fair skinned, wouldn't be caught outside without a hat or bonnet, and was used to waiting out the heat of the day on her porch swing or under the high ceilings of the house we used to live in. But Papa knew her buggy would follow along behind him, no matter if he decided we were going to travel past sundown and all night if he wanted to. Old Ben never failed Papa, and Papa didn't have to look behind him to know that Old Ben would be bringing Mama along. She could complain all she wanted about Papa's hard-headed, Scotsman ways.

"You boys get off of those oxen and get your rifles out of the wagon," Papa said. "Hurry up now."

Gunn bailed right off and ran for his gun. Me, I hesitated and looked a question at Papa.

"Do like I said." Papa's expression made it plain that he wasn't going to tell me again. "Smoke to the south."

I noticed for the first time the sooty column of smoke mixing with the cotton-white clouds in the distance and didn't ask any more questions. Smoke was bad. Things burned—things you missed. And then there were the Indians Old Ben had talked about all the time since we ferried our wagons across the Sabine River months and months ago. Indians were fierce; everyone said so.

Gunn was already inside the wagon and he handed me my gun. The Richmond musket was longer than I was, and I envied the short Maynard carbine that Papa had given my younger brother. It didn't look near so outsized or so silly in his hands when he carried it back to Papa.

"You men look to your weapons," Papa said to the four Mexicans he'd hired to come along with us. "That smoke might be something or it might be nothing."

Papa passed Old Ben a look and nodded when he saw that the black man already had his double-barreled shotgun propped up against the buggy's dashboard and the slab-sided Dance revolver that Papa had bought for him laid on his lap. Old Ben was a good shot, and there were those back before Texas that said Papa was mistaken to give a nigger a gun. But Papa took great pride in his own common sense and laughed at them and reminded us boys that a Scotsman must be practical above all, and that it made sense to give Old Ben a gun. Ben could be trusted, and from what we heard about the Texas frontier, I suppose Papa might have armed all his slaves if that Republican, Abraham Lincoln, hadn't taken them away from him.

I wasn't sure then exactly what a Republican was, but I knew they were as bad as those Blue Bastards. If you went to Texas you might get away from them, and Papa was dead set on that and making a new home for us. Once we got to Texas, men that he talked to along the trail said all the good cotton ground down south was taken. What's more, a carpet-bag (another word I aimed to find out about) governor and other "radicals" had beaten us to Texas. All bad things, but that didn't stop Papa. He said we'd go farther west than anyone else. Maybe there wouldn't be cotton ground there, but we would find other ways to make a living. No matter what, we would live like freemen and like a Dollarhyde should. I was young, but even then, I had an inkling of how stubborn we Dollarhydes were.

The rutted trail we followed left the prairie and entered a thick belt of low, scrubby oaks. Gunn and I walked to either side of the wagon, both of us eyeing the edge of the trail to either side of us. Indians might be anywhere, and

Texans said they stole children if they didn't cut out your guts and scalp you. Gunn and I had spent a great deal of time on imagining what terrible ways an Indian could hurt you. Mama made us quit if she heard us discussing Indian massacres. She said such talk would give us nightmares.

We soon came to another stretch of prairie barely visible through the timber ahead. The smoke climbing black into the sky was close by then, and Papa had us all stop and form up the wagons tight together. He put Mama, Baby Beth, and Juanita, José's wife, inside one of the wagons, and the Mexican men stood guard around it. We didn't know anything about Texas Indians at that time, or I don't think Papa would have been so foolish as to think his arrangements might help anything.

"You boys look out for your mother," Papa said while he waited for Old Ben to untie his saddle horse from the buggy and mount up.

We nodded fiercely but neither one of us had a clue. We just stood there and watched him and Ben ride off toward that smoke. The south breeze couldn't find its way through that thicket, and it was as hot as the dickens. The flies were bad and making the stock restless, the Mexicans looked nervous under their big hats, Baby Beth was crying inside the wagon, and neither Gunn nor I could see a thing of what had everyone so worried. Neither of us spoke Spanish, so we had a fair excuse when we took off after Papa, ignoring whatever orders or warnings those Mexicans were calling after us.

We knelt at the edge of the oak thicket, where we had a good view of the far prairie. There was about a mile of nothing but grass and prickly pears between where we were and where the river made a bend to the south. Not far from the riverbank were the ruins of some kind of settlement. Smoke was pouring from it, and at such a distance, the black silhouettes of what was left of the buildings looked charred.

The wind picked up hard enough to bend the grass, and a couple of white wagon tops down there stood out, billowing and snapping against their bow frames. I couldn't see anybody moving among the wagons, but the wind kept blowing the smoke across everything and made it hard to see. One thing was for sure. A ways out from those wagons, little stick figures of men on horseback were trotting back and forth. Occasionally they shouted or made strange, shrill cries, but nobody answered them.

"Indians," Gunn said.

I glanced at him, seeing how he had his carbine ready, and that his hands weren't shaking like mine. It would be like him to notice that, too, and remind me of it later.

"Comanche or Kiowa, I guess," I said.

"How do you know?"

"Because I'm smarter than you."

I might not shoot like Gunn, or get my pocketknife as sharp as he could, or decipher a deer's track from a hog's, but I read a sight more than he did. Hamish the reader, the bookish one, that was me. Papa was always on me to put down my books and quit lazing about and do something, but hadn't I been the only one to read Mr. Irving's book about what we could expect on the prairies? Gunn never read anything.

"See there," Gunn said with a quaver to his voice. "Papa's getting ready to fight."

Indeed, Papa had pulled up a couple of hundred yards from the besieged emigrants in those ruins. He was off his horse and kneeling with only his upper body sticking up out of the grass and his Sharps to his shoulder. Old Ben was dismounted, too, holding both horses by their bridle reins behind Papa.

"Man on foot can shoot steadier," Gunn added, like he had ever fought an Indian in his life.

"Papa doesn't have but one shot, and there looks to be a half dozen of them."

"Papa ain't scared."

No, Papa probably wasn't, but I was. And Gunn would have been, too, if he weren't such a fool for any kind of trouble.

The stick Indians finally noticed Papa, and after more milling around, they started toward him. I wanted to call out for him to run back to the timber, but the words wouldn't come.

The warriors came on in a wide skirmish line until I could make out the bright paint on their horses and on their own, burned-brown hides—strange hieroglyphics in blues and whites and yellows and reds. Their horses' legs surged through the waving grass, and the faint tinkling of the little hawk bells some of those braves had braided into their horses' manes barely reached my ears over the wind. Feathers, scalp locks, buffalo tails, and other trinkets dangled from the edges of their shields or from their weapons.

I've heard a lot of people, so-called pioneers, try and describe various plains tribes' war cries, but none of those imitations did the real thing justice—not even close. The shrill cries and whoops coming from those Indians made my bladder spasm, and all I wanted was to run or pee.

"Savages," Gunn said with awe in his voice, and more than a hint of admiration.

Papa waited and he waited, until one warrior fired off an old trade musket. The powder smoke from that musket hadn't even blown away when Papa shot him off his pony. That was the first man I ever saw killed.

Chapter Two

One of the Kiowa—for that's what they were—pulled up to gather his downed comrade while the rest of them kicked their horses to a run and came on. Papa never took his eyes off them while he set down the empty Sharps and stretched out an arm and an open palm behind him. The saddle horses were spooked from the gunshots, but Ben held on to them and handed Papa the shotgun. Papa leveled the 10-gauge and waited some more while those Kiowa came on through the grass.

The charging warriors split into two bunches a long rock's throw in front of Papa and passed to either side of him at a dead run, hiding behind their buffalo hide shields and hanging from the off side of their horses. Papa held his fire, unwilling to be baited into wasting his last rounds. Most guns back then didn't reload near quick enough. Maybe one of those Blue Bastard Spencers or Henry repeaters, but not a breechloader like Papa's Sharps. And especially not that old double-barreled shotgun Old Ben handed him.

Old Ben popped off a couple of shots with his Dance revolver, but missed, the frightened horses jerking him around too much to take good aim. The Kiowas' momentum carried them well past him and Papa, and they were almost to where Gunn and I waited by the time they pulled up to turn for another go. One of the Kiowa was having trouble with his horse, and it reared right in front of where we hunkered in the thicket. I heard the sound of Gunn's carbine cocking several seconds before it dawned on me what he was about to do. None of those Indians had a clue that we were so close to them, and I started to whisper to Gunn not to shoot right before he did.

That Maynard gun cracked and the Kiowa on the rearing horse tumbled off its back before the animal's front hooves even hit the ground—as if it had thrown him for a tumble, instead of Gunn's bullet boring a hole through his rib cage.

The remaining warriors turned to face the timber, and I rested that Richmond musket on an oak limb and eared its hammer back to full cock. Gunn was cussing like a grown man, and out of the corner of my eye I saw that he had his Maynard tipped open and was trying to find another cartridge and primer in his belt pouch. Two arrows hissed between us and rattled off the tree limbs, but that only made Gunn cuss worse—words that I didn't even know he knew. Papa didn't have anything on Gunn when it came to cussing.

I couldn't keep any of the Kiowa in my gun sights. They were milling and moving too fast, and my Richmond gun was too big and awkward for me to handle like I should. Something hit the tree trunk I was hiding behind, and flying bark and I don't know what else struck me full in the face. Guns began going off behind us, and our Mexican teamsters were coming through the brush to help us by the time I could see anything again.

The Kiowa were caught between us and Papa and Old

Ben and not liking it any. My eyes were still watering too badly to take aim and I never fired a shot. By the time Papa and Old Ben rode up, the Kiowa were retreating across the prairie, joined in the distance by the other one who had stopped to pick up the warrior Papa had killed.

Papa and Old Ben took some time looking me over to make sure that I hadn't been shot in the eye, and then some more time chewing out the Mexicans for leaving Mama alone in the thicket. Those two delays were an opportunity and excuse for Gunn to slip off. He was out in the grass by the time we spotted him.

Gunn was staring at the body when I walked up. The flies were already buzzing around where the dead Kiowa lay bent and crooked in the bloodstained grass. He would have been as tall as Papa if somebody had straightened him out.

"It's all right, Gunn," I said. "You did what you had to."

The Kiowa's face wouldn't let me look away. A fly crawled across one of his eyes, yet it remained wide open and unblinking. The dead warrior was all but naked except for a red strip of wool cloth covering his privates, and that breechclout was soaked were the Kiowa had spilled his bladder. The bits of gray intestine around the ugly bullet hole stood out starkly against his brown skin. The fly and the smell of guts and urine made me want to puke.

Papa and Old Ben rode up.

"From the look of you, I'm taking it that it was your shot that got him," Papa said.

Gunn nodded and looked away from the body.

"It's a hard thing there, especially as young as you are, and I hate it for you. But if it helps, that Indian would have done worse to you and yours."

I think it was Papa mentioning Gunn's age that made

Gunn say what he said next. He took it in mind to prove some point to us.

"Somebody let me borrow their knife," Gunn said.

"Whatcha want a knife for, young 'un?" Old Ben asked.

Gunn looked at him like he was daft. "I guess I ought to scalp him."

"You're going to what?" Papa asked, spurring his nervous horse to keep it close to the body.

Gunn clenched his lower lip in his teeth and stared defiantly at Papa with his bony chest puffed out, although his jaw trembled a little bit. I think he realized his big talk had backed him into a corner, but wasn't going to quit what he started and lose face.

"You was raised better than that," Old Ben said. "Civilized folks don't scalp people. No, they don't."

"Texicans do," Gunn said. "Man I talked to back in Fort Worth showed me his scalps. Every real Indian fighter has some."

"A man you talked to?" Papa asked.

"Said he was a Texas Ranger. Had two pistols and a knife as long as that." Gunn held his hands wide apart to approximate a very, very large knife—one of those down-scaled swords Texans called a Bowie, and good for anything from splitting wood and skinning buffalo to lopping off people's limbs. Texans are high on utilitarian, versatile weapons.

"Quit that foolish talk," Papa said.

Gunn had been avoiding looking at the dead Kiowa since I first walked up, but he had another glance and spotted the sheath knife in the Kiowa's belt. He took a deep breath, and then jerked it free with a quick tug.

Papa had used up the last of his patience, and I thought he was on the verge of snatching Gunn up and giving him what Old Ben called the "what for."

"The Indians need to know not to mess with us," Gunn said, oblivious to the limit he had pushed Papa to, or not caring. "They would see the scalp and know that this is Dollarhyde country. Not theirs."

"Dollarhyde country?"

"Our country," Gunn said.

"Where does he get this stuff?" Papa asked Old Ben with a little less frustration in his voice.

Old Ben shrugged and the two of them shared a look.

"Killing isn't something to be proud of, nor to be taken lightly," Papa said.

"Are we going to bury him, Papa?" I asked.

"That Indian's long past caring. Burying him or all the ceremony in the world won't make it any different," Papa said. "We'd best get the wagons to where those folks out there are holed up. They might need our help, and we can fort up with them if need be. More of those Indians are liable to come back for the body and catch us out here in the open."

"I hear they never leave one of their fallen after a fight if they can help it," Old Ben said.

"You two boys get yourselves back to the wagons," Papa said. "I'm about half a mind to tan you both for not staying where I put you."

Papa was done talking and already riding away, and even Gunn wasn't so stubborn as not to know what would happen if he argued anymore and didn't do as he was told. He threw one last glance at the dead Kiowa. Tough, maybe, but I noticed he gagged when he looked, and quickly turned his back on the sight.

"I bet you wish you had shot that Kioway," Gunn said to me as we followed behind Papa and Old Ben.

I didn't egg him on by answering him. What he wanted was to argue more.

"I'm going to be the best Indian fighter in Texas," he added. "You watch and see."

"You'd better put that Kiowa knife away before Mama sees it," I said. "She's going to be mad enough at Papa for leaving her in the brush."

He gave me another one of his defiant looks, but tucked the knife into his belt behind his back. "You're just jealous."

"Why don't you shut up?"

"You don't think I would have scalped that Indian, do you?"

"I wouldn't put anything past you."

"I can whip you any day." He shouldered into me and gained two steps on me while I regained my balance. "You know it."

Papa was looking over his shoulder at us, so I kept quiet.

"You may be older, but I can still whip you," Gunn said after a bit.

"Okay, you're the toughest."

"I'm going to be tougher than even Papa someday."

"Maybe, but I'm going to be smarter than both of you."

"You might be, at that. I wouldn't put it past you." Gunn found his hat where he had lost it at the edge of the woods. He picked it up and dusted it off and twirled it around in his hands. I could tell he was still thinking something over.

"I wouldn't have scalped that Indian," he finally said. "Not really. I was joshing."

"I know it."

"Never thought it would feel like that. Didn't feel like that when I pulled the trigger," he said. "You know when you're all excited and shoot a rabbit and then you walk up to it and feel kind of bad?"

"Yeah."

"It was like that, only way worse," he said. "Papa shot

one. You think he feels the same? He shot lots of men in the war."

Papa never talked about the war, and Mama said not to ask him. All the other boys back in Alabama bragged about what their fathers did in the war, but the only things we knew about Papa's service were bits and pieces we over-head from grown-ups when they didn't know we were around. Old Ben wouldn't even tell us anything, and said Papa had done things he wanted to forget. Him saying that only made us more curious.

"Try not to think on it and remember if we hadn't come to help, those Indians might have got him and Old Ben," I said.

"You weren't the one that shot him."

"Come on, you two," Papa called back to us. "And don't tell your mother that you were in the middle of that fight. She's most likely to find out anyway, but don't you say any-thing."

Papa put his horse to a trot, and I picked up my pace. I didn't want to miss what Mama had to say to him when he got back to the wagons, especially when she found out he had taken her boys into an Indian fight. Papa was right. You couldn't hide much from Mama.

Wouldn't you know it, but Gunn slipped off again. I was almost back to the wagons before he caught up to me. He was leading a blue roan Kiowa pony and smiling like he was the king of England. I compared the way he had looked only a bit before to the way he looked then, and it was like two different people. He was always moody and changed like the weather.

"My horse," he said.

I didn't argue any. I was too busy trying to hear what Papa and Old Ben were saying.

"Dollarhyde country," Papa said.

"That boy's something else. Kind of reminds me of you at times," Old Ben answered. "No offense meant."

"None taken," Papa said. "Dollarhyde country. That boy worries me, but I kind of like the sound of that."

Chapter Three

The emigrants were waiting for us behind their wagons or hidden in the ruins of the old settlement. Many of them were black with soot where they had been fighting to put out the fire in one of the half-collapsed buildings near their wagons. There were better than twenty of them: five men, their women, and a whole lot of big-eyed, snotty kids peeking out from behind them. They must have been unsure who we were, for it took Papa two shouts to get them to come out and talk to him.

"Thank the Lord for hearing our prayers," the oldest of the men said in a crackling voice when he walked up to Papa's horse. He was tall and thin and his hatless, his bald head was sunburned and spotted with peeling blisters. "Welcome."

Papa looked over the group a long time without speaking while he studied the remains of the settlement on either side of an overgrown, short stretch of street. There had once been ten or so buildings lining that street, but most of them had been burned to the ground years before. Only two shelters could be termed to be still standing. One of them was nothing more than some rickety log walls with a portion of caved-in roof hanging over it, still smoldering from the day's Indian raid, and the other was a half-completed sod structure those emigrants had been working on. Some charred, salvaged lumber was piled alongside it, as well as a stack of fresh-cut sod bricks and a moldboard plow.

Last, Papa's eyes landed on a brand-new sign nailed to a post beside the old man. DESTINY, TEXAS was painted on it in wavy, unsteady red letters.

"People back down the trail never mentioned a place by this name," Papa finally said.

"It wasn't what it was called before the war," the old man answered. "I mean, before all the people left it to the Indians."

"Looks like you're aiming to rebuild this town," Papa said.

"We were, indeed," the old man said. "A new name for a reborn place."

"Were? Changing your mind?"

"We're rethinking things. Praying on it. I don't know if God intended for men to live out here."

"Is this all of you?"

The old man turned to his people to pass somber looks between them, and then shook his head. "No, Brother Ezekiel and Brother George are out there on the prairie where they went to greet those Indians. Sister Josey, George's woman, went crazy when she saw what they did to George and took two arrows before we could drag her back."

"Mind if we camp here for the night?" Papa asked. "Could be, those Indians will come back."

The old man acted as if he didn't understand. But then again, it could have been the sun in his eyes. The Texas sun was hard on a man without the good sense to wear a hat.

We formed our wagons up in a square against the front

wall of the dilapidated log building after we put out the smoldering parts with handfuls of dirt, and Papa built a fire inside the log walls and under where the roof was missing. Mama sat in the shade, fussing over my baby sister while the wife of one of the Mexicans, Juanita was her name, started cooking us some supper. Juanita was young and pretty, but I soon tired of watching her and went to double-check that I had tied the horses securely, as Papa would hide me good if one of them got loose.

Papa was leaning against a wagon tailgate, puffing on his pipe and staring at those emigrants over by their own wagons. They were sitting in a circle on the ground, facing one another. Some of them were reading from Bibles, some of them had their heads bowed, and occasionally one of them would break into a hymn or quote some scripture.

"What kind of people are those?" I asked. "I've never seen church held like that."

"Quakers," Papa said. "Call themselves Friends, or some such like that. Gentlefolk."

"Papa, why would gentlefolk come out here?"

"Looking for a place they fit, I guess."

"They don't look like they fit."

Papa tapped his pipe on the heel of his palm to knock out the ashes and nodded at me. "No, they don't look it. My impression of this country is that it's going to require a scrapper."

"Mama says it's going to be hard out here. Living, I mean."

"Don't let things vex you. You're bad to be thinking instead of doing."

I was about to ask Papa more, but he was already looking over my shoulder at something else. I turned around and saw that Gunn was trying to get on the Kiowa pony he had claimed, but the crazy little paint kept either shying away from him before he could get close or dumping him on the ground as soon as he could get a belly across its back. Both of us could hear Gunn cussing, and from the way those Quakers were looking his way, they heard him, too.

"That boy is as stubborn as your mama," Papa said. "I guess I'll have to give him a whipping if she hears him talking like that."

"Gunn likes to fight," I said. "And he doesn't care about anything except what he wants to do."

"Gunn makes his mind up in a hurry. He'll take some hard licks because of it but he'll eventually learn." Papa walked off toward Gunn and his Kiowa pony. "That fool boy is going to get himself killed if he doesn't leave that horse alone."

Gunn came to bed a long time after sundown. He smelled like horse sweat, and I guessed he had kept after that Indian nag in the dark.

"Wake up, Hamish. You ain't going to believe this." Mama had told him over and over to quit saying "ain't," but it never did any good.

"Be quiet." It had taken me more than an hour to get to sleep, and I was cranky enough to punch him in the nose for disturbing my rest.

Earlier, Gunn just had to tell a story about a man he had heard about who was bitten by a big black centipede with orange, bony legs that crawled under his blankets. He said it rotted off the man's big toe where it bit him, and eventually a doctor had to amputate his whole leg. No matter how I checked around me and shook my blankets, I kept imagining creepy-crawlies all over me. It's hard to get to sleep when you're worrying about big black centipedes tickling their bony digits up your bare legs.

"Wake up."

I propped myself up on one elbow and saw that Papa was sitting at the fire on the other side of the building from us. What's more, Mama was next to him and Mama didn't like to stay up late. The man with the sunburned head was sitting across from them.

"Looks like they're trading," I said.

"They're trying to give Papa a kid," Gunn said. "Mama wants him, but Papa ain't having any of it."

Chapter Four

"Can you believe Papa gave them a horse for that little ole runt?" Gunn asked the next morning.

Mama had Beth in the crook of one elbow and the other arm around that boy, hugging him to her until he was half-hidden in her dress. He was thin and stared at us with big, dark-ringed eyes. His tangled blond hair stuck out every which way, no matter how Mama absently ran her fingers through it, as if she wanted him to make a good first impression on us.

"Looks like he's about to cry," Gunn said to me as we walked up.

"Boys, I want you to meet Joseph," Mama said. "He's going to live with us."

"What about his people?" I asked.

Mama glanced at the three fresh graves under a little oak beyond the Quakers' wagons. "The Kiowa took his folks, and none of the others are set up to help him. They've all got troubles of their own."

"More like they thought more of that nag of a mare," Gunn said under his breath. "Indians shot one of theirs, and they ain't going back where they came from without enough horses to pull their wagons."

"What's that?" Mama looked hard at Gunn.

"Nothing, Mama."

It wasn't even real daylight yet, but the Quakers were already preparing their wagons. Gunn was right; they were harnessing a plow mare that Papa had brought with us. She was so old that none of us understood why he had even brought her along. Her teeth were bad, you could count her ribs, and she hadn't been in harness since we left Alabama.

"Say hello to Hamish and Gunn," Mama said to that boy, pointing us out as she named us.

The boy didn't say anything and ducked his head.

"What did you say his name was?" Gunn asked.

"Joseph," Mama said.

Gunn whispered, "I think I'll call him Peckerhead."

"You two let Joseph ride the oxen with you if he wants. Get to know each other." Mama noticed Gunn wasn't paying any attention. "And mind your manners, Gunn Dollarhyde. I raised you better than that."

Joseph shuffled forward uncertainly, with Mama's hand gently pushing him. Snot shone on his upper lip and there were tear streaks down both dirty cheeks. He followed us, although we didn't say anything else to him until we were almost to our wagons.

"Mama ain't been right since she had Little Beth," Gunn said. "Papa even says so."

I considered that. Papa had told us more than once to go easy on her until she got better. Neither Gunn nor I was sure what was wrong with her but both of us knew that Mama had been better before Baby Beth and before the Blue Bastards burned us out. She would still read to us at night, cluck her tongue and tend to our scrapes and bruises, and occasionally pass us a sweet smile for no good reason we could see for it. But she was different. There was no denying that.

Mama was quieter, and cried sometimes for no reason we could see. She still smiled, but even her smile seemed a little sad at times. It was probably true that Papa was trying to coax her out of whatever funk she was in. That was the only reason I could see that Mama could talk him into trading for a Quaker boy.

Texas was the first and only place I ever saw where you could horse trade for a half-starved child as bony as a bag of sticks and with black-ringed eyes like a corn crib raccoon. Indians, sky, and burned-down towns in the middle of nowhere, plus kids for sale—I told myself not to be surprised at anything that happened next.

Papa was already in the saddle, and the Mexicans had our wagons ready. We came to the oxen and I jumped on the wagon tongue and climbed on Speck's back.

"Take your pick," I said to Joseph, pointing at the four oxen behind me.

"He can ride my steer if he wants to," Gunn said. "If he ain't scared."

"Isn't."

"What?"

"If he isn't scared. You aren't supposed to say 'ain't.' It isn't proper."

"Proper? You sound like Mama." Gunn spat in the dirt. He didn't chew tobacco but he was absolutely fond of spitting when he wanted to make a point. "Nobody talks like they do in those books you're always reading. Most times, real people are in too big of a hurry to worry about what words to use."

Joseph looked from one of us to the other with blank

eyes, and I was beginning to wonder if Gunn was right and the boy was a mute. I guessed he was maybe seven or eight years old. It was hard to tell.

"Are you going to walk?" I asked Gunn. We had come a lot of miles riding beside each other on those oxen, and as irritating as Gunn could be, I didn't like the thought of having to spend all day with a stranger that didn't or couldn't talk, and didn't have the sense to wipe his nose.

"I'm riding my horse," Gunn said.

"That Indian pony won't even let you get on him. Maybe you should try and trade him to the Quakers."

Gunn looked Joseph up and down and went to fetch his horse. "Don't think I will."

"Are you going to stare at me all day or will you climb up here?" I asked Joseph.

Joseph blinked, but didn't move.

"You don't talk much, do you?"

He blinked again and sniffled.

"Good, Gunn talks nonstop and half the time he's wrong. Maybe the muse will take you later in the morning, and we'll get to know each other."

Mama was bound to get upset if I left her mute behind, and I was still trying to figure out how to get him to talk when Gunn came around the back of the wagon. There was dust and bits of grass all over his back, and I knew that he had tried to mount the Kiowa pony behind the walls of the old building so that we couldn't see how things turned out.

I watched as he tied the roan to the corner of the wagon bed. "Threw you, didn't he?"

"Shut up."

Gunn's dog rubbed against Joseph's leg, and the boy reached down and put a hand on its head.

"Don't touch that dog. He bites," Gunn said. "His name is Killer."

Gunn really called the dog Reb, and that yellow skillet-licker never bit anybody. A rabbit could jump up right in front of old Reb and he might not notice it. The only way he could hurt you was to lick you to death or get under your feet and trip you.

No matter, Gunn loved that worthless mutt. Slept with him every night since we had been on the trail. Used to sneak him in his bed in the house before Texas, and let him under Mama's kitchen table and fed him scraps.

Joseph didn't pay any attention anyway, and continued to pet the dog absentmindedly.

"Sic 'im, Killer. Get 'im!" Gunn hissed through his teeth at the dog. "Attack!"

Reb only wagged his tail, and Joseph's expression didn't change.

"Get out of the way." Gunn shoved past Joseph and climbed up on the gray steer beside mine. His nose was trickling blood and he swiped at it with the back of his shirtsleeve. He was going to have a black eye.

"Papa says that Kiowa gelding probably never smelled a white man," I said.

"I'll ride him. You wait and see."

Papa was already a quarter of a mile west of camp, and Old Ben started Mama and the buggy after him. The two Mexicans who weren't handling Papa's other wagon were mounting their horses.

"Why doesn't Papa stay here?" I asked. "Looks like a place we could live."

"Papa said he'll know what we want when he sees it," Gunn said.

I turned to watch the Quakers' wagons rattling across

the grass in the opposite direction, and then looked again to the three fresh graves they had left behind. Papa had helped them bring in the bodies of their men the evening before. He wouldn't let me see what the Kiowa had done to them, even if I had wanted to.

I caught Joseph looking at those graves, too—both his parents gone to a Kiowa war party. "You better climb up here. Papa won't like it if we hold him up."

"I don't want to go," Joseph said, barely above a whisper.

"Did you hear that?" Gunn asked. "He talks like a Yankee. Little Blue Bastard Peckerhead."

Joseph did talk like a Yankee, and his voice quavered like he was about to cry. Mama should have let him ride in the buggy with her and Old Ben, or let Juanita watch him.

"Don't mind Gunn. He likes to talk rough. Thinks it makes him bigger," I said.

Gunn made a fist and held it out to me. "Keep talking."

"You ought to be nice to him. What if you were an orphan?"

Gunn scowled at me but then he noticed that Old Ben had stopped the buggy, and Mama was shading her eyes with the flat of her hand and watching us.

"All right, Peckerhead. Climb up here so I don't have to listen to Hamish whining anymore."

I got down and took Joseph by the arm and helped him up on the wagon tongue. I climbed back on Old Speck and nodded my chin at the other two yoke of oxen behind us. Joseph remained standing on the tongue between Gunn and me.

"I think he's off in the head," Gunn said. "We ought to put him up on the wagon seat."

I held out my arm, and Joseph took it after a bit and pulled himself up behind me. The other wagon was moving, and all six of our oxen leaned into their yokes and we lurched forward. Joseph wrapped his arms about my waist and hugged close to my back. Gunn noticed and spat on the ground again.

The wagons rattled across the prairie, ours in front following Old Ben and Mama, Juanita on the ground, prodding her two oxen and the cart along with a stick, and her husband coming behind her driving a four-up team of mules and the wagon carrying Mama's household stuff. The other two Mexican men split up and rode out some distance to either side of us. I guessed they were on the lookout for Indians.

"Papa is already out of sight," I said, scanning the distance for him. "How much farther do you think he'll take us?"

"Until he's sure there aren't any more politicians, and then that'll be far enough, I imagine."

According to Papa, politicians and lawyers were about as bad as Blue Bastards.

One of the chickens squawked in their cage on the tailgate, and Joseph hugged me tighter. I tried to ignore it.

"I'll be," Gunn said. "Thinks you're his mama. Peckerhead."

"Don't mind Gunn," I said to Joseph. "He isn't always like this."

"Those Indians scalped my daddy," Joseph whispered into my back.

"Wipe your nose."

Chapter Five

Our first Texas home was seven miles west of where we left the Quakers and about fifty yards from the Little Wichita River. It wasn't really a house at all, no more than that narrow, muddy strip of water was a real river. What we ended up with, instead of a house, was what Texans called a dugout soddy.

A man like Papa, I always imagined him riding down from a castle, like in all the history books I read. Named men, chiefs, and would-be conquerors on the rim of the world, they all had fortresses to show their power and to fend off all comers. Not to say that Papa was the kind to conquer the world, but, oh, he was the kind to be remembered; the kind that took hold of things and wrestled them until he'd done what he set out to do and lived by no one's rules except those he wrote himself. If Papa said it one time, he said it a thousand: the thing that he was most proud of was that he had never set himself to anything that he didn't finish. He hadn't yet told us exactly what he aimed to do in Texas, but he wouldn't rest until he'd stacked his own rocks and logs and dug his moat; left a mark for all to see that he was there and to be reckoned with.

Nothing then but a dirty little dugout—I guess empires, big or small, don't start out that way. Even Camelot was nothing but a pigpen before it shone with walls of marble. What I was coming to learn of Texas, the pigpen would stay with Camelot, and only the men were made of marble.

Papa and the Mexicans dug into the side of a little hill until they had an open-fronted square twenty feet deep and two wagon lengths wide. One of the Mexicans found a spot of ground not far away with enough of a hint of clay to hold it together, and with our moldboard plow they rolled up sheets of sod that were afterward cut into bricks, which became the front wall of our new house. The ridgepole and rafters were made from oak logs they cut and dragged up with a yoke of oxen. Old Ben split the logs with a sledge-hammer and wedges, and Papa hacked them to shape with a broadax and adze.

One of the wagons was torn apart and its planks used for roof decking, and Gunn and I helped the Mexicans, hauling dirt from their diggings up the hill in buckets and pouring it on the roof until there was a foot or more of earth over it. Papa had bought a brand-new cast-iron stove before we left East Texas, and they plumbed the stovepipe right up through the dirt roof. Old Ben hung a steer hide to serve as a front door, and the dugout was determined to be complete.

Mama camped for a week under the trees along the riverbank while the construction was going on, but I saw her often studying her soon-to-be new home. Once her furniture was inside, Papa brought her to stand before the dugout.

"I know it isn't much, but we can build something better later," Papa said when he tired of waiting for her to speak.

Mama started crying.

"I never said this was going to be easy," Papa added.

I watched Mama cry and knew she was thinking about

her house back in Alabama, with its white columns and a big porch lined with pretty flowers and her yard swing hanging under the limbs of an enormous oak. I had to admit, the dugout was a pitiful-looking thing. Papa saw a beginning, but Mama saw only a dirt hovel in the middle of nowhere. Papa was a man of big dreams, but I don't know what Mama dreamed. How two such different people decided to come together, I don't know.

Papa led her to the door and held back the steer hide, maybe hoping that once she saw her mahogany bed and her grandmother's dresser inside that she would realize that the dugout wasn't so bad. It could be that he didn't recognize how out of place Mama's fancy, heirloom furniture looked in such a crude room—a room not so nice as our root cellar had been back before Texas—and what he thought would comfort her only reminded her of all that she'd left behind, like rubbing salt in a wound.

She stepped inside and shifted Baby Beth to her other hip while she looked around. "It's like a cave."

It would take a few rains to pack the dirt on the roof, and a trickle of dust and powder poured through the roof decking overhead and onto her shoulder. She brushed it away and started to cry again.

"I want to go back," she said. "Argyle Dollarhyde, you take me back."

"Maybe once we get settled a little more I can go east to Gainesville or Fort Worth, or wherever it takes and get you a window or two," Papa said. "Windows in the front would let some light in."

Mama set Baby Beth on her bed and drew the blanket curtain Papa had rigged to block off the back end of the dugout that served as their bedroom. We could hear her bawling even after we went outside.

That night, Papa stayed out at the campfire in the front

yard, working on a big piece of rawhide. Come daylight, he was still working on it, and stayed at it until past noon. Then he knocked holes in the front wall to either side of the door, faced them with leftover wagon lumber, and tacked the pieces of the steer hide at the top over each new opening.

"See here," Papa said to me while he lifted one of the hides up from the bottom. "We can still shoot out of them if need be. I'll build some heavy shutters to go over them when I get the time."

He went inside and found Mama sitting on her bed, and he pointed at the pieces of hide. "Now you've got windows. They'll keep the weather out and still let a little sun in."

He had scraped the rawhide so thin that you could see the feeble glow of the sun through it. The crude windows did let enough light in to make it where you could see to work around the stove, if only barely. The rest of the room was still gloomy unless the steer-hide door and Papa's new windowpanes were tied out of the way, and even then, the back of the room was as dark as the bottom of a well.

Mama patted Papa on the shoulder. "It is better. I'll make do until we can build something else."

And then she started to cry again.

Papa hugged her with one arm. "It will be all right, Sarah."

Somebody outside was shouting like they were crazy, and Papa and I rushed out the door.

Gunn was up on the roof and pointing to the west, across the prairie dotted here and there with scattered mesquite. "Look!"

Papa saw something, and so did the Mexicans who had climbed up on top of one of our wagons for a better vantage point. I scampered up the side of the hill and got on the roof with Gunn.

"Do you see them?" he asked, still pointing and talking too loud.

How could I not? The whole horizon was dotted with shadowed beasts, the dust rising up beneath their hooves in a ghost cloud, and the raw red sunset smeared behind them as if they were born from a molten womb. There were hundreds of them.

"Real live buffalo," Gunn said. "Did you ever see anything like it?"

"No, I never."

I could hear the bulls grunting and see the spring calves bucking and playing and darting in and out around their mothers on the edge of the herd. I could feel them, even though they were a long rifle shot away. The presence felt ancient, and at the same time, like something new. Like the big, beating heart of the land was there in the smoky dust and the afterbirth of the dying sun, throbbing hot and strong and hard inside me—something right and pure.

I turned to look at Gunn again, and there was that same strange expression on his face that had been there when he first saw those Kiowa charging Papa on the prairie, as if he had found something he had been looking for, and as if the finding made him whole and happy.

Maybe it was the same look that other men had long before such as a boy like Gunn ever came to be. Men with flint-tipped spears and smoke-cured panther hides wrapped about their loins, hungry sons of Esau dancing before the flames to celebrate the coming of the herds, their tattooed and feathered soothsayers blowing bloodlust and sacrament through their bone flutes and pounding old magic from skin drums. Men before time scrawling charcoal dreams on sooty cave walls—mighty beasts that flicker and run in the torchlight, the shapes and signs of the gods' goodwill and the forms of the gods themselves. Vermilion-painted hand pressed into the stone with five proud, nimble fingers and a palm as red as blood itself, a sign left for all to see. Hunters and seekers were here, makers and destroyers, worshippers and slayers.

And even the likes of me knew then, like Gunn of the warrior heart, that Texas was a place like no other. And when I looked for him again, for that look on his face to confirm what I, too, felt, he was already off the roof and cutting around the corner of the house.

"Where are you going?" I asked, my eyes back on the panorama before me.

"To get my rifle," he called back. "Real, live buffalo."

I thought about getting my own gun, but then I heard Mama below me, crying again, and the buffalo song faded.

Chapter Six

"That'll take the starch out of him," Old Ben said. "Just you wait and see. Let him lay under that tarp in the hot sun, and it'll sweat the piss and vinegar out of him, sure as the world."

Old Ben was huffing and puffing, with both of his hands on his hips, sweat dripping off his chin, and looking at the form of Gunn's Kiowa pony under the wagon sheet. Papa and Old Ben had thrown the gelding, tied his feet, and covered him.

"I still think that's a way to ruin a good horse," Papa said. "Although I don't know if that animal qualifies as such."

"You let him lay there, boss man, and I promise you it'll take the devil outta him," Old Ben said. "Let him lay there all hot and bothered and to where he can't see nothin'. When we let him up he'll have a whole new attitude. Maybe, if he ain't pure outlaw."

"Some are," Papa said.

"Men, too," Old Ben said, taking a seat on a log we used for a couch at the fire pit in front of the house. "Lord, I'm gettin' too old to rassle horses."

"I guess we might go on a hunt tomorrow," Papa said.

"You mean a buffalo hunt?" Gunn chimed in. He'd been after Papa all day to let him go after one, ever since the first herd passed by our camp the evening before.

"We need to lay in some meat," Papa said. "Winters here are bound to be worse than what we're used to."

"How many buffalo do you reckon there are?" Gunn asked. "I bet there's a gajillion of them."

"Gajillion isn't a real number," I reminded him.

"There's a lot of them, son," Papa said to Gunn, and winked at me.

"That ain't all there is," Old Ben said.

"I saw a buck deer with great big antlers this morning when I was fetching water," Gunn said. "Had a hide as gray as a mouse and big ears, too."

Old Ben nodded. "All kinds of wild critters, but that ain't what I was talkin' about. Seen a lot of cattle running loose. Big old brindle and painted-hide thangs with the damnedest horns I ever saw."

All along the way west since we had left the Trinity River we'd spotted scattered groups of those big-horned cattle, so wild that they would throw up their tails and run off like a bounding deer at the sight of a man.

"Surprises me, too," Papa said, but he sounded like he had already been thinking on the matter. "I heard those stories about cattle so wild that early colonists in Texas used to hunt them like deer. To tell you the truth, I thought that was all only stories told by land speculators, or something long ago before Texas was taken from Mexico."

"Don't they belong to somebody?" I asked.

"Looks like they're wild to me," Papa said.

"Wild as a peach-orchard boar," Old Ben threw in.

"Maybe wandered off from somewhere east of here and multiplied over the years," Papa said. "I hear Texans take a hot iron and burn their ownership mark on every head of stock they claim. Mexicans, too."

"They burn Mexicans with hot irons?" I asked.

"No, the Mexicans are who taught them to brand cattle."

"I saw such marks on a few of those cows," Gunn said.

"Some," Papa answered. "But not on most of them."

"Maybe they belong to whoever built that abandoned town we passed," I said. "Or maybe somebody lost them and can't find them. That Quaker with the sunburned head said that all the people left this country when the war broke out. Maybe they were in such a hurry they left their cows."

Papa didn't answer me, but no more than I knew at that age, I could tell that he was working something around in his mind. Folks back in Alabama said Papa had a nose like a hound for sniffing out a profit.

"If they ain't marked, does that mean they belong to anybody that can catch them?" Gunn asked.

"What would you want with them?" I asked.

Papa looked at me and I had the feeling he was exasperated with me again, like he seemed to be most of the time.

Late in the afternoon Old Ben took the tarp off that Kiowa pony and let him up. The poor thing shook itself and snorted twice but stood quietly when Old Ben put a hand on him.

"You might get along better with him now," Old Ben said.

Gunn had borrowed a saddle from one of Papa's Mexican hands and he picked it up.

"Hold on there," Papa said. "I still think that horse is too much for you. Let one of the Mexicans gentle him."

Gunn looked heartbroken.

"All right, but don't say I didn't warn you."

The Kiowa pony stood surprisingly still for Old Ben to saddle him, and only humped his back a little and puffed his belly up when the cinch was tightened. All of the Mexican men gathered around to watch Gunn climb on the horse.

I saw Gunn swallow a big knot in his throat when Old Ben nodded at him, as if to say that Gunn had it to do.

"Go ahead, boy," Old Ben said.

Gunn squirmed himself up in the saddle while Old Ben rubbed his hands over the pony's near eye and whispered something to it to calm it. Gunn looked down at his leg and started to say something about the stirrups being way too long for him when the roan broke in two and started bucking like no horse I've ever seen. It farted and bawled and bucked, even after it threw Gunn ass over teakettle and planted his face in the dirt with a resounding thump. It pitched and fought and kicked at the cinch around its belly until it was so tired that its lungs were wheezing and its nostrils flared and pumped like bellows.

Gunn got up, dusting himself off and staring at his Kiowa pony standing there spraddle-legged and thinking about exploding again. I could tell Gunn was hurt and doing everything he could not to cry.

The Mexicans caught the horse after some trouble, considering that it broke into more halfhearted crow hops when it tried to dodge them. They led the roan back to Gunn, and he gave Old Ben another look, like climbing back in the middle of that storm was the last thing he wanted.

"You can't quit him now," Old Ben said.

"Finish what you start," Papa said.

Gunn tried again, but the roan threw him in two jumps. To make matters worse, it kicked him in the hip as it bucked past him.

I could tell Papa was going to make Gunn try a third time, but Mama showed up and gathered Gunn in her arms, checking him over for injuries. She gave Papa a hard look as she started back to the dugout with her arm around Gunn.

"Look at that," Old Ben said.

We all turned to see what he was looking at and found Joseph standing in front of that Kiowa bronc with his hand held out to its muzzle.

"Come away from there, Joseph," Papa said.

The roan was heaving and soaked in sweat, but I expected him to wheel away or start bucking again the moment Joseph got too close. There was a good chance it was going to jump right in the middle of that boy when it did.

"Joseph." Papa eased forward, wanting to get Joseph to safety but afraid if he moved too fast he would frighten the roan into another fit.

Joseph didn't even seem to recognize that Papa was talking to him. He took a short step forward and stretched his hand closer to the roan's black muzzle. I was still holding my breath when the roan stretched its neck and made contact with Joseph's hand. It flinched back, but soon reached its nose out again. Joseph smiled—the first time I saw him do that—and before long, he was working his way down the side of the horse and stroking its neck.

"You get back over here, boy," Papa said.

Joseph apparently heard Papa then, for he took up the hair hackamore rein and started our way. The roan followed along docilely behind him.

"Well, I'll be. The damned thing seems to like him," Papa said.

Old Ben was grinning from ear to ear. "Some folks have that way about them. Animals just can't keep away from them. Had a cousin like that. Old milk cow we had to tend to each morning wouldn't let none of the rest of us catch her without a hard time, but she would see that cousin of mine standing by the fence and come over for him to scratch her face. Followed him around like a dog when she could."

"He's beautiful," Joseph said when he handed the reins to Papa.

The Mexicans were holding a conversation in Spanish, and anything but English annoyed Papa to no end.

"What are you saying?" Papa asked, scowling.

José, Juanita's husband and a man who wore big spurs and professed to be a vaquero, answered him. "This boy, the *Güero huérfano*, I think someday he will be *un jinete*. *Un caballero*. A horseman."

Joseph smiled again while Papa's eyes measured him from the top of his tangled head to his bare feet.

"Can I have a horse like this someday?" Joseph asked.

"I hope when you're older you'll have sense enough not to want a horse like that," Papa said.

I happened to look toward the dugout, and Gunn was dragging along at the end of Mama's arm and looking back our way. I could tell he had heard everyone bragging on Joseph from the look on his face.

Chapter Seven

Mama read to us beside the campfire that night, the copy of Homer's *Iliad* propped open on her knees. Even Gunn's mood brightened. Tales of Achilles, the mighty Greek warrior, and his Myrmidons were one of the few of any kind of books he would sit still for.

The Mexicans nodded occasionally, whispering amongst themselves and enjoying the way Mama could read a story. At first, I enjoyed the evening as much as any of them, seeing visions of the great battlefield spread out before the walls of Troy and hearing the battle horns and the clash of weapons. But eventually my eyelids grew heavy and Mama noticed that. She closed the book and suggested it was well past time to go to bed.

"Turn in now. We've got a big day ahead of us," Papa said. The firelight flickering across his face and the arm that held his pipe propped on one knee made me think of how King Priam the Trojan must have looked down from his walls with all the worries of his kingdom upon him. "Tomorrow, we're going on a buffalo hunt."

It was too hot to suit us inside the dugout, and Gunn and I spread our blankets under a brush arbor Papa had built nearby. I squirmed myself into a comfortable position facing Gunn and the last thing I remembered before falling asleep was that he had taken his carbine to bed with him and was cuddled up with it like it was a puppy. Regular Achilles, that brother of mine.

Papa woke us well before daylight, the stars still twinkling in the sky when we crawled out of our blankets, rubbing our eyes and squinting against the campfire light. We barely had time to wolf down some leftover corn bread and chase it down with a swallow of water from Juanita's big clay jug hanging off a tree limb—an olla they call it down Texas way. The coolest, best water I ever drank came from one of those Mexican jugs hanging in the shade. I can still taste it now, cutting the dust and trickling down your throat like sweet nectar.

José was already up on his horse and he had two of the wagon mules bridled with blankets cinched over their backs for Gunn and me. Old Speck was rigged up in a single-yoke to José's little cart to haul back any meat we might take. Papa carried his Sharps laid across his saddle in front of him, but made us pack our rifles in the cart. Gunn didn't like that any, but Papa was already riding off into the darkness and we had to scamper up on those mules in a hurry for fear that he would change his mind and leave us behind. Old Ben stood by the fire in front of the dugout and waved us off, for Papa was leaving him behind to look out for Mama.

"You boys shoot straight and bring Old Ben back some buffler meat," he said. "I like the sound of saying I et some before I die."

"Why, you'll live to be a hundred. I'd guess you could

eat every buffalo in Texas by then," I called to him as I kicked my mule after Papa.

I don't know how Papa navigated through the dark, or if he just pointed us to the west and kept to a straight line, intending to take account of the country when the sun came up, wherever we happened to be by then. There weren't any roads west of us, or even a trail made by anything but wild game and Indians. We were better than seventy miles beyond the line of settlements that marked the frontier, and well into that country Texans called Comancheria. And at the time, I guess that there wasn't a better name for it. The Comanche and their Kiowa allies had kept that country to themselves for a long time. As we were learning, some settlers had tried before the war, but none of them could make a go of it out in the big empty.

Gunn and I rode to either side of Old Speck, intent on keeping him headed right, but that wasn't even needed. That old steer seemed perfectly content to follow Papa like a hound, and we did the same.

An hour after sunup all four of us were bellied down in the grass on top of a little hill, staring at a small herd of buffalo less than a hundred yards below. Our livestock was tied a ways off behind us.

"One of those old bulls is bound to be tough eating," Papa said to me. "Pick that yearling there closest to us."

"How come Hamish gets to shoot first?" Gunn whispered.

"Because he's the oldest," Papa hissed back at him.

"Don't worry," José said. "They won't run if your brother shoots straight."

For all the trouble Papa and José had made keeping us upwind of the herd, I still found it hard to believe that a gunshot wouldn't make the animals run off. José claimed to have hunted buffalo before, and Papa seemed willing to listen to him.

"Shoot low right behind the front leg," José said.

I tried to get my Richmond gun as steady as I could on the crossed set of sticks bound together with rawhide that José had made for me. Either the wind waving the grass was making my aim shaky, or it was me feeling Papa staring at me.

"Cock your hammer," Papa said.

My ears burned with shame. I was so nervous and intent on aiming that I didn't even have my gun ready to shoot.

"Take your time and make it count," Papa added.

Gunn was already propping his carbine up on his own shooting sticks beside me. "Hurry up, Hamish."

The Richmond musket Papa had given me was horribly inaccurate, and I knew that I needed to be dead-on with my aim to have a chance. The last thing I wanted was for Papa and Gunn to see me miss. I strained to keep my front sight on target until my right eye started to water.

"I'm going to shoot that bull with the big horns and head," Gunn said, regardless of Papa's instructions not to shoot the old bulls.

I could feel Papa willing me to shoot, and I squeezed the trigger. The recoil of the musket and the belch of smoke caused me to lose sight of my target for an instant, and the next I saw of the yearling it was lumbering into the midst of the herd stampeding away from our position.

"I think you shot too high," José said.

I knew that my aim had been poor the moment I shot and was about to agree with José when Gunn's Maynard cracked. He leapt to his feet as soon as he fired and shook his carbine over his head.

"Got him!" he shouted. "Lookee, Papa!"

I looked down the hill, and true to Gunn's word, a great bull, the biggest one I'd seen yet, slowly buckled its knees and crumpled to the ground.

"He never took a step," Gunn said.

"A fine shot," Papa said.

We went back to our stock and brought them over the hill to where Gunn's kill lay. José honed his knife on a large whetstone and then began showing Gunn how to skin a buffalo. He and Papa ran their knives around the bull's neck behind its skull and then split the animal open along its belly, tugging at the heavy hide and slicing it free and upward toward the backbone. They tied a rope from the back of the cart to the bull's hind leg on the underneath side and used Old Speck's power to slowly turn the huge beast onto his other side while they peeled away his hide. In that manner, they literally rolled the buffalo out of its skin until it lay there stark and white with bubbled and knife-nicked fat and connective tissue, the red flesh beneath already growing dull, from blood red to the color of burned clay.

The sun was already well up, and the flies buzzed around the carcass. Gunn made up for a lack of skill with enthusiasm and he was covered in blood and fat grease by the time they were halfway through.

Papa noticed me pouting when he finally took a break, and I feared that he also noticed I hadn't been doing much to help skin Gunn's kill. I tried to smile at him.

"I think you hit that yearling," he said. "Your musket isn't much, and I should have loaned you my Sharps."

I knew that Papa was only saying that to try and make me feel better. I had seen the disappointment written on his face when the yearling ran off.

"Let's go see if we can find him," Papa said.

I climbed up on my mule and rode beside him and Shiloh across the prairie, wishing that he would let the matter drop. We all knew that I had missed.

"Well, look there," Papa said after we had ridden about a quarter mile from the cart.

Before us, the yearling buffalo I had shot was struggling to get to its feet. Bloody slobber and froth hung in a string from its muzzle. It tried twice to get up, but fell back to the ground, facing us.

"Finish him." Papa was already off Shiloh and handed me his Sharps when I got down off the mule.

The poor yearling grunted loudly and made another try to run off. I cocked Papa's gun and did my best to keep a sight picture on its forehead. It was only a twenty-yard shot, but I feared I might miss again.

A gust of air issued from the buffalo's leathery lungs when the bullet busted through bone and into its brainpan. Its tongue hung lewdly out of the side of its mouth.

Papa took his gun and patted me between the shoulder blades when we walked up to the yearling. "You boys have done well. First hunt, and a buffalo for both of you."

My first bullet had struck the buffalo too high on its side, like José had predicted, and also well too far back. At best, I had managed a lung or paunch shot. I stared at the yearling's one eye I could see, the brown of it already fading to a milky film, and knew that I had made an extremely poor shot for such close range and the animal had suffered for it.

"We can tan both hides and you boys can use them for your beds," Papa said. "Or maybe you can get José to show you how to make a powder horn. There will come a day when you'll look back on such trophies and cherish them."

I nodded, although I didn't want any kind of trophy. I could understand Gunn being proud of his great bull, but not me with my yearling and his little horns and the two bullets it had taken me to kill him.

"How come it's got such a large skull?" I asked. Even the small yearling's head was so large as to be out of proportion with the rest of its body. To me, when standing, buffalo always looked as if they should tip over like a seesaw, with their nose hitting the ground and their back legs up in the air. Even the horns looked too small on such an overblown cranium, to the point where they appeared as an after-thought.

"Maybe it's because they aren't too smart," Papa said after a moment's thought. "God probably gave them that head to butt their way past anything that stumps them. Stubbornness can get you through sometimes when you can't figure a way around things."

"Kind of like Gunn, then?"

"Yes, you could put it that way. Gunn's head isn't that big but it might be as hard." Papa put a hand on my shoulder. "I'm proud of you boys. I think this Texas will be a good place for you."

"What about Mama and Baby Beth?"

Papa smiled, something he hadn't done much since the war, but a smile all the more special because of that. "For them, too. God knows what I would do without them."

And in that sad, strange, terrible path that life can some-times take, Papa got to find out. We all did. For once the meat and hides were loaded in the cart, and Old Speck was plodding back to camp, we hadn't gone three miles before we heard the gunshots. And later, we saw it like a stain in the sky to the east. Smoke again, billowing up in the distance from where our new dugout should stand. That god-awful, black, hellish smoke, like that feeling when you've just woken up from a nightmare and your guts are all twisted and your heart is beating out of sync. It seemed like our lives were marked with smoke, until we all should have smelled like brimstone and our tears turned to ashes.

Chapter Eight

Papa beat us there by a good bit, as nothing was going to keep up with Shiloh, especially not an oxcart and two boys on mules. José hung back with me and Gunn and the cart and tried to keep us from rushing forward once we got close. But we weren't having any of that. By the time we whipped our mules into camp Papa was already standing in the doorway of the dugout, his hands on each side of it, and his body shaking with misery and his head bowed as if he didn't have the strength to hold it up.

It wasn't the dugout that was burning. It was our last good wagon that smoldered with Old Ben's body lying next to it. Mama's new *casa grande*, the humble abode that was our squalid dugout, wasn't in ruins at all, for dirt doesn't burn, and Papa had built sturdily against such occasions. Other than the fact that one of the raiders had torn down the steer-hide door and Mama's things were scattered all over the yard, the dugout looked no different—squat and solid. The roof had even held, despite the pony tracks up the side of the hill where I could see that some buck had ridden on top of the roof. That dugout would have stood against storm and prairie fire, but it didn't do any good in the end. Instead of shelter, it was no more than a dirt box that held the worst of our fears and all of the loss we hoped against. I wondered if Papa knew that it was a tomb when he was building it.

"Dear God," Papa rasped. His knees buckled and only the great strength of his broad shoulders spanning the doorway kept him from falling.

Gunn and I ran forward, but he straightened quickly at the sound of our footsteps and whirled on us with his eyes lit up like a madman.

"Get back!" he snarled.

That's the only way I can describe it. Papa snarled like an animal—hurt and rage all mixed up together. More hurt and rage than I ever again saw in one human being—in anything.

Gunn and I froze, and Gunn let out something that sounded like a whimper—not as scary as Papa's sound, but horrible nonetheless. I looked past Papa's bulk into the dark confines of the dugout, in spite of how his eyes threatened and begged me not to. I saw Mama's bloody arm outstretched on the floor in the narrowing streak of light that spilled into the gloom on either side of Papa's shadow. Baby Beth's yellow, lace-edged blanket was crumpled in the dirt at the end of Mama's arm.

Gunn's whimper turned to a howl and he charged the door, but Papa wrapped him in his arms and carried him away. Gunn's little fists beat at Papa's chest, cursing at one moment and begging the next.

Papa reached out for me when he came past, but I staggered away. Everything in me told me that I needed to go closer and look farther into the dugout, but I couldn't, as if not seeing made it not so.

But there was no hiding from the sight of what they, those animals, had done to Old Ben. No shadows and walls hid him; nothing but the hot sun beating down and turning the black blood to a crust where it had seeped into the thirsty, cracked ground around him, staining the earth like rust. Naked, mutilated, and bloody—that's how they left you. No dignity, just a husk of shame and the pallor of pain frozen into your death mask.

I fell to the ground beside Old Ben and was still sitting there when José covered him with a blanket. Maybe I should have been the one to do that instead of sitting there so long. But I knew that there was nothing I could do for Old Ben, or at least nothing that would help him. That's why they did that to you, because nothing could fix you once you were like that. Not only dead, but maimed and tortured and bits of you cut away and left open to the world. Heaven or not, how do you ever get over that? Marked for life and beyond.

Old Ben, him that never asked for anything but a meal in his belly and a boy to tell his stories to. Him that went to look for Papa when Mama asked him to, and rode across Alabama to find Papa in a Confederate battlefield hospital, even though Old Ben had never been out of the county in his life and all the mad Southerners apt to string up a runaway slave. Took Papa away and cleaned the filth from his wounds, picked the maggots from his skin, and swore to God and to that rebel surgeon that he would shoot him down with his old shotgun before he would let them cut off Mr. Dollarhyde's leg. Doctored Papa and wrapped his wounds with poultices his mammy taught him to make and camped on the roadsides for weeks while Papa mended so they could make their way back home.

Old Ben once told Gunn and me how his father was a mighty chief and wise man in Africa across the water, and who hunted lions with nothing more than a spear. And how he was captured in a great battle and sold by his enemies to

Portuguese slave traders and sent to America on a great ship where many of his tribesmen died of disease and suffered lying like corpses chained belowdecks. Old Ben and his siblings never learned that old lion hunters' language, but they made up songs of their own. Sang them in the fields of my father. Taught them to Gunn and me. Praised the new god, and plowed and picked and chopped for the new masters: cotton, sugarcane, and tobacco. Said "yes, sir" and "yes, ma'am" and ducked their heads when the white folks came by. All the while, teaching Gunn and me how to catch a fat-bellied catfish down at the river with a switch cane pole, or how to patch the busted wing of the baby mockingbird we found fallen from the high limb of its nest.

I wished I had thanked him; I wished I could tell him how sorry I was for what happened to him.

José let out a cry of his own. Not a sad one, but a happy one. I wiped my eyes and looked to the edge of the timber and saw Juanita waving at her husband. They ran to each other while another of the Mexicans came cautiously out of the thicket behind her, his rifle held ready and his eyes spooked. I was shocked to see that anyone had survived.

While José and Juanita hugged and celebrated finding each other, Papa went past them at a brisk walk. The Mexican coming to meet him, Emilio I think he was called, looked ready to run at the first loud noise, shaken as we all were. Papa stopped ten feet from him, and they said things to each other that were too hushed and too far away for me to make out. And then Papa pulled his pistol and shot that man. Shot him in the head and dropped him where he had stood only seconds before.

I looked where Papa had left Gunn sitting under a tree. Our eyes met, and I wasn't sure that Gunn even realized that Papa had just shot one of his own employees.

"Coward," Papa said as he stood over his victim. "Let them at my family while you hid in the woods!"

Papa fired again into the body and kept firing until his revolver was empty. And I knew that Papa wasn't shooting the body—not in his mind. He was killing them that had done the thing, one by one, and blazing away in an attempt to kill all the misery filling him. It's a hell of a thing to see your father kill a man.

I helped José and Papa dig the graves while Gunn sat under the shade tree and rocked back and forth, hugging his chest with both arms. Juanita sat with him. Nobody knew what had happened to Joseph the orphan, but all of us were thinking the same thing but not saying it. The savages had taken him. Everyone on the frontier knew that the plains tribes were apt to kidnap young children and raise them as their own.

We dug only three graves, and I wondered if the reason we didn't dig a tiny one for Baby Beth was because the Kiowa had stolen her, too. Maybe she wasn't with Mama. Maybe there was a chance for her.

Papa went inside the dugout while I helped José lower Old Ben into the hole dug for him. We misguessed, or had already forgotten how tall Old Ben was, and had to fold him a little to get him to fit in his grave. We were about finished shoveling the dirt over him when Papa finally came out of the dugout at dusk. He was carrying Mama's body wrapped in blankets. José helped him set the load gently at the bottom of the grave. Mama was a little thing, and wrapped and padded like that, she didn't even make a sound when she settled there.

"I thought it best to bury them together, your mama and your sister," Papa said in one ragged, choking breath.

So there it was. No chance to dream of Baby Beth raised

among the heathens. Lost to us for a time, but still alive and waiting for us to come get her. No hope.

After we covered Mama and Baby Beth with earth, Juanita and José led me away. Those two had gathered what scattered goods the raiders didn't take, and I spent an hour picking up Mama's books slung all over the yard, while José buried Emilio. Some of the books were missing, and I didn't have a clue what an Indian would want with a book.

Juanita cooked us a meal. I ate because she told me to, spooning buffalo stew into my mouth without tasting it.

Gunn was beside me, still rocking back and forth and staring at where Papa stood beside the graves. I noticed that Gunn had somehow gotten Old Ben's Dance revolver, clutching it to his belly like it was holding in his guts. I don't know how the Kiowa overlooked it, or where Gunn found it.

Long after the sun went down and there were only the stars overhead and the dance of the campfire flames on the side of Juanita's cart, Papa's shadow marched across the yard and disappeared into the dugout. Shortly afterward, his bagpipes began to wail, low and quiet at first, and then louder until there was nothing else.

José and Juanita said nothing, looking at each other with big eyes and making the Catholic sign of the Cross upon their chests.

Mama had always laughed at Papa's love of bagpipes; said they were a highlander's instruments and Papa's people came from the lowlands. Papa himself might have been born in Scotland, but my grandparents brought him to South Carolina when he was still but a swaddling baby. Yet, he loved bagpipes anyway. Learned to play them long after he was grown and broke them out on occasion to play for us, no matter how much the dogs howled or Mama protested and laughed. Everyone agreed that Papa played them poorly and didn't know any lively tunes, but the song he played that night is still as plain to me now as if it were a song I already knew and not one from another time across the ocean. Sad, banshee instruments made for the heart-broken, that's what Mama called them, although Papa said that was the Irish in her talking. It was as if he jerked the sorrow from me and gave it a sound.

Mama. Nobody who knew her would have pictured her there, the belle of Montgomery County who young men had ridden for miles to court, and she who once sang and played her piano and recited poetry and tended her flowers, her laugh more alive than any sound on the earth. Who would I share stories with now? All the books we never read together. All the talks of learned things we would never have. Not a hug left from her on the whole turning of the earth. Lost to Texas. Gone like Baby Beth's cries, faded in an instant. Silence except for those damned awful bag-pipes that made me cry like the scared child I was.

The sound of hooves came through the thicket and José took up his gun. I noticed that he was shaking, thinking they had come back to finish us all.

Joseph shuffled into the firelight. He had lost one of his shoes somewhere, and he was even dirtier than he usually was, his blond hair tangled with twigs and bits of grass and the knees of his britches tore open to reveal his scraped knees. He was leading Gunn's Kiowa roan on the end of a rope and Gunn's yellow dog laid down at his feet when he stopped across the fire.

"I ran from them and then I hid under the creek bank," Joseph said, standing there looking at nothing in particular but the ground. "I thought they were going to kill me, too."

And then he looked up, right at Gunn. "I found your horse. He ran off in a thicket when they drove the rest of the stock away."

"Old Reb there, where did you find him?" I asked.

Joseph blinked and shrugged. "He hid with me."

Gunn rose and stepped over the fire, scattering sparks. He jerked the lead rope from Joseph's hand.

"You damned coward," Gunn said, glaring down at his dog.

Chapter Nine

Papa told us to saddle up the next morning while he went
to talk with José. They talked long enough that Gunn and I
were both sitting on our mules waiting for him. I noticed
that José and Juanita started to break camp and load their
cart as soon as Papa walked back over to us to saddle
Shiloh.

"Are we going back?" I asked.

Papa looked at me across Shiloh's saddle while he tightened his cinch. "Back where?"

"Alabama."

Gunn grunted and spat on the ground. Then he passed
a look to Papa, and it was as if I weren't there and the two
of them could read each other's thoughts. Papa grunted just
like Gunn when he swung up in the saddle.

"I've sent José and his wife on an errand," Papa said.
"We've got a chore to do."

I knew what chore he meant without asking. An eye
for an eye—that line has to be even older than the Bible for
Papa's breed. He would have lived by that law even if it
were never quoted to him. He could have written it himself.

Papa meant to follow whatever Indians raided us. José

said they were probably Kiowa or Comanche, but he wasn't sure. They left no evidence behind other than their pony tracks. There were tribes around us that we hadn't even heard about.

Gunn propped his carbine on his thigh as if to prove he was as determined as Papa to have his revenge. He had broken into howling again in the wee hours of the morning, and Papa had to pin him in his blankets and sleep with him hugged to his chest. But the craziness seemed to have spent itself, at least the loud part. Now he was crazy quiet. There is such a thing, I promise you. All you had to do was look at that hard, still face of his—Papa's, too—with those eyes burning like no little boy's you ever saw, and you knew things weren't right. Every kind of emotion was churning and cooking inside him, held back only by willpower. But like Papa, I think he found a way to channel all the hurt in him to one point of focus.

I, too, should have been filled with bloodlust, but I didn't feel much of anything. The wind was blowing, and the dust in my mouth kept making me remember the way Old Ben looked all cut up and Mama's bloody arm stretched so delicately and bloody across the floor of the dugout. Maybe we were all already dead and didn't know it yet.

"What about Joseph?" I asked.

Papa seemed to have forgotten about Joseph, but he quickly recovered. He turned Shiloh until he spotted the boy helping Juanita and José load the cart. "Hey, boy."

Joseph stared back at him.

"He doesn't have anything to ride," I reminded Papa.

"He ain't riding with me," Gunn said.

"Shut your mouth," Papa said. "Maybe I can get Juanita to take care of him."

But when Papa came back, Joseph was leading Gunn's Kiowa roan, and José had saddled the horse with Emilio's

saddle and tied a blanket behind the cantle and hung a
drinking gourd from the saddle horn.

"You ain't riding my horse," Gunn said.

"Then you ride him and I'll ride your mule." Joseph
looked down and scuffed the ground with one foot. He was
wearing Mexican boots that were way too big for him, and
I wondered if they, too, had belonged to Emilio, the one
that Papa had killed.

"I suppose you think you can ride him," Gunn said.

Before any of us could say anything else, Joseph pitched
his reins up on the roan's neck, stretched awkwardly to
poke a toe in the stirrup, grabbed a handful of saddle
strings, and climbed up on the horse hand over hand until
he was sitting in the saddle. The roan stood rock still while
he climbed him like a tree.

"Well, I'll be," Papa said.

Gunn grunted and turned his horse away so that he
didn't have to look at any of us.

I looked back as we were riding away. "Where did you
send José and Juanita, Papa?"

"I gave them your mama's silverware and her gold,"
Papa said. "They're going off to buy us more supplies."

The silverware and the handful of antique gold coins
had been a wedding gift from Mama's father. "Mama
would never sell those things."

Papa slowed Shiloh so that he could stare down at me on
my little mule. "No, she wouldn't."

"How do you know that José and Juanita will come
back?" I was thinking how Papa gunned down Emilio and
that José might be glad to get free of us.

"José will come back. He gave his word, and I believe
him."

Papa left me then, no matter how many more questions
I wanted to ask. He had already cut for sign earlier that

morning, and we picked up the trail of the Kiowa raiders across the Little Wichita and followed it north, mile after mile, day after day, winding through the choking hot oak thickets of the Cross Timbers and then west onto more open country that fronts the barren tableland of the Llano Estacado. Time and again, we lost the trail, but Papa wouldn't quit. How he intended to find Mama's murderers in such an expanse, or how he intended to deal with them with nothing but three boys, I don't know. I followed him only because there was nothing else to do.

Papa didn't talk, and Gunn didn't talk. Joseph didn't talk, either, maybe because none of us talked to him. I wondered what he thought of the mad family he had joined, but then again, he was an odd one himself and more than a little warped, like the rest of us.

Chapter Ten

"Is that them?" I asked. Papa had an old brass-tubed sea glass to spy on the Indian camp in the distance to the west, but I didn't have anything except for my own two eyes.

Papa lowered the spyglass and twisted his neck to look down the dry streambed to where Joseph was holding our mounts. "Have you boys checked the loads on your rifles?"

Gunn adjusted himself on his belly in the tall grass and shoved his carbine forward for Papa to see, as if that proved anything. I merely nodded at Papa, wondering what he had in mind. Although it was only a small camp of about seven lodges, I thought I had already counted at least five warriors and several women and children. The setting sun was in our faces, and it was hard to be sure of anything.

"We'll wait till morning," Papa said. "That will be best."

"How do we know it's them?" I asked.

"That's them, all right," Papa said. "That's your mama's good black buggy mare tied to that lodge. No mistaking that."

Indeed, it was Mama's mare. I'd have known her anywhere, and Papa would, too. General Forrest himself had given that mare to Mama as an anniversary present.

"Are they Kioway?" Gunn whispered.

"Maybe, but it don't matter." Papa put his spyglass to his eye again. "That's them that done it."

We watched the Indian camp until it was too dark to see, and then we went down the streambed to our horses and rode off to make a dry camp a good two miles away. Papa wouldn't let us have a fire, and it had been a day and a half since we'd eaten the last of a pronghorn buck Papa shot. We all settled for a drink of lukewarm, brackish water from our canteens and settled in for the night with nothing but sweaty horse blankets to cover us and our saddles for backrests. The coyotes started yammering at one another somewhere nearby, and we all sat quiet and listened to them until they quit.

"I know I'm asking a lot of you boys, but there's no helping it," Papa finally said.

There wasn't any moon to speak of, and I couldn't see him where he sat across from me.

"When the time comes, you think about your mama and your baby sister. Don't think about nothing but that when it comes time to pull a trigger." Papa took out his whetstone and began to sharpen his skinning knife. There was silence again between us, except for the sound of the steel grating back and forth along the length of that Arkansas stone.

I didn't sleep at all that night, and when the first gray light came I could see that Gunn was still awake, too. He was staring at me with his carbine already in his hands. If he was as scared as I was, he didn't tell me. Papa had already gone to saddle Shiloh before I had time to ask.

Once again, we left Joseph in the dry streambed to hold the horses. He didn't beg us not to leave him, but his crying said it without words.

"Buckle down, boy," Papa said to him and gave him a pat on the shoulder.

Papa led us through the grass toward the Indian camp and I looked back at Joseph as we climbed over the bank of the streambed. He looked so sad and abandoned that I would have known him for an orphan at first glance, even if I were a stranger. I guess he had no reason to expect us to return to him, having already lost both his real parents to Indians. So, I couldn't blame him for crying. Maybe Papa wouldn't judge him too harshly, either. Papa understood a lot more than he ever let us know.

We moved slowly, stooped over and stopping when Papa stopped, listening and studying the camp for any signs of early risers. The Indians had a herd of ponies—about thirty of them—a bowshot from their camp. We slipped to within sixty or seventy yards of it before Papa hunkered down on his heels and gave us our instructions.

"You two stay here. Those camp dogs are going to start barking when I get closer, and the first time you hear them I want you both to shoot a horse apiece," Papa said.

"Shoot horses?" I asked.

Gunn looked equally confused. "I want to go with you, Papa. Fight with you."

"Shoot the horses, then reload as fast as you can," Papa said more firmly. "As soon as those dogs find me, someone's going to come out of those lodges. When they hear you shooting their horses they're going to come running for you."

"And what are you going to do?" Gunn asked.

"I'll put myself to the side between you and the camp. Anybody that comes for the herd is going to have their attention focused your way and pass before me."

Gunn and I both nodded.

Papa noticed how I was shaking and rested his hand on my head. "Buckle down. Remember what they did to your mama, Baby Beth, and Old Ben."

"Yes, sir."

"I won't forget," Gunn added.

"Can I count on you to do like I said?" Papa asked.

I nodded again, trying to look fierce enough to make him believe me.

"Remember, keep your eyes peeled for a horse guard. From what I hear, there's liable to be a boy or two close by and keeping watch on the herd," Papa said. "Load quick once you shoot. The horses you don't down will run, and you be looking for men coming out of the camp after that. Take turns shooting so that both of you don't get caught empty at the same time. If things get bad, hightail it back to that gully and get Joseph and run."

"I won't run on you, Papa," Gunn said.

"You're both good boys," Papa smiled. "Give me Old Ben's revolver."

Gunn looked put out about giving up the Dance pistol but he handed it over anyway. Papa shoved it in his belt alongside the brass-framed Griswold he had carried since the war. He left us then, ghosting his way through the gloom toward the camp, but staying well to our right and out of our line of fire, should anyone come our way.

The Indians' conical, buffalo hide lodges, tepees they're called by some, were huddled together on a stretch of open country. Still, Papa was so stealthy moving through the morning that I had a hard time following him. I lost him for a bit when he neared the camp but finally spotted his head above a clump of yucca.

It was about then that the dogs started barking. Whether they smelled him or saw him, I don't know. What mattered is that they were loud, and Indians always have a lot of dogs around camp.

"Shoot, Hamish!" Gunn already had his Maynard

shouldered and was peering intently down its barrel at the horse herd.

I threw up my musket and took aim at a gray horse easy to pick out. The sun was just coming up and I could barely see my sights. Papa said we should think about Mama and Baby Beth when it came time to get mean, but I couldn't think of anything. I only knew that I didn't want to be there and I didn't want to shoot a horse or anything else. My hands gripped my gunstock so hard they shook.

Gunn's carbine boomed. I was determined to pull my own trigger, but it was as if it took more strength than my finger possessed. So small a thing, no more than a few pounds of pressure to set it off. I closed my eyes tight and fired.

In an instant, there were two horses down and thrashing and the rest of them were stampeding away from the camp. I fumbled with my shooting bag and took too long reloading. I was seating another ball home with my ramrod when Gunn shouted something at me.

An Indian was running toward us with a war club held in one of his pumping arms. He must have been guarding the horses and close by, exactly like Papa warned us, for he appeared out of nowhere. He fairly flew over the ground. Gunn had spilled his percussion caps on the ground and was digging around for one and couldn't shoot. About five more strides and that young brave would be in swinging distance of my brother. The problem was, I was directly behind Gunn and couldn't shoot without hitting him.

"Look out!" I shouted.

Gunn fell to his side and I was so scared I didn't even think to shoulder my gun. I fired from the hip and the running brave staggered and took a few more wobbling steps to crash atop Gunn.

Gunn kicked his way free and reared back with his carbine held like a club to smite his attacker. But the brave was all but dead, gargling and choking his last breaths and clutching at my loading stick protruding from his throat. I had been so excited that I had fired with my ramrod still in my barrel.

"Better load again," Gunn said, his voice shaking like a leaf on the wind.

I ran to the dying brave and closed my eyes and drew my ramrod free of his flesh. Up close, he was only a boy, no older than us. But death isn't particular about who it takes, and it's always ugly.

Gunn had found a cap to ready his gun but he waited for me to load again before he would shoot. If I was shaky earlier, I was even worse reloading the second time with Gunn watching me and a handful of Kiowa warriors charging toward us from the camp. They came on with the rising sun behind them, no more than silhouettes, and all the scarier because of that. Something whished through the air beside me, and it took another arrow burying in the grass beyond me for me to realize that they were already shooting at us.

I capped my musket and nodded at Gunn. He was too short to see above the grass and he stood to take better aim. I can still picture him there, standing with that Maynard pulled tight to his shoulder and his fierce face pressed against the stock. He aimed for what seemed like forever.

When his gun finally did go off, I didn't get to see if he hit or missed. I heard him grunt and then the carbine slipped from his grip and his knees buckled. He twisted away and clutched at his arm, and I saw the arrow buried in it.

I fired at the nearest warrior but was in too much of a hurry and missed. Gunn was moaning and I couldn't think straight with the enemy screaming at me and sure to be upon us in a matter of seconds.

And then Papa opened up with his Sharps. Those Indians were so intent on getting to Gunn and me that they ran right past Papa. He had them scattered in front of him like ducks in a shooting gallery. His first shot tumbled one of them and then he was standing up with a pistol in either hand.

All but one of the warriors was on foot and that one was running Mama's black mare straight at me with a long lance leveled at my chest. I intended to run but I'll be the first to admit that I froze. Just knelt there in the grass and waited for him to impale me.

People will tell you that a pistol isn't much good for shooting at any distance. And there are those who will say that a Griswold revolver was a cheap Confederate copy of a Navy Colt and more prone to blow up on you than to hit with any accuracy. Well, they never saw my Papa shoot, and his old Griswold must have been in fine feather that morning. Or else God smiled down on me.

Papa was at least seventy yards away, but he plucked that mounted warrior right off Mama's mare. It was so close a call that the mare had to leap over me to keep from trampling me, and her rider rolled into me as he hit the ground.

Taking Gunn's example, I clubbed at him with the barrel of my musket as I scooted away from him on the seat of my pants. I wouldn't have scrambled away from him any faster if he had been a rattlesnake thrown at my feet.

Soon, Gunn was there with me, both of us wailing away on that warrior. Maybe he was already dead from Papa's bullet, I don't know. I guess we did awful things to him before we ran out of breath and we were too tired to swing anymore. I'll use the excuse that we were scared and not thinking. Papa said that bad things happen in war, but I never knew what he meant before that morning.

Gunn stumbled to where he had dropped his gun while I fell to my knees heaving for air. Papa's pistol was still going off, and I watched as Gunn struggled to load his carbine with one arm.

"Load!" he said to me.

I don't remember doing as he said. It was as if I reloaded in a trance. Maybe that was because Papa had drilled us so on the way to Texas. Load and shoot; do it until you don't have to think about it. Ground the butt plate and tilt the barrel away from you to pour the powder from your horn, in case there was still an ember in the barrel that might touch off your powder and flash in your face. Cut a patch with your patch knife and lay it across the bore. Spit a round ball into your hand and set it on the patch. Forget the patch if you're in a hurry. The gun won't shoot as well that way, so be your own judge. Start the ball down the barrel, being careful not to snap your hickory rod until it's started far enough down the bore to go easy. Seat the ball all the way home and place a percussion cap on the nipple. Aim and fire.

Nothing to it, unless you're fourteen years old, you're under attack, your brother's shot and groaning like he's dying, and you're so scared that you've pissed your pants and would like more than anything to be somewhere else.

I didn't manage to shoot again before I realized that there was nothing left to shoot at. Gunn was groaning, and I was sure he had taken another arrow and would die any second. I started to him on hands and knees, but he held up his good arm to stop me.

"Help Papa," he managed to gasp, bile and slobber hanging from his chin and his eyes watering.

"Are you all right?" I was too shaken to realize what a stupid question that was until I had already asked it.

"Hurts like hell."

The arrow buried in his arm looked awful, and worse

was the way his arm hung so limply and lifelessly. I didn't know what to do for him.

"Come on." Gunn started toward the village. His jaw was quivering with pain, and I could hear his teeth chattering.

Papa was nowhere in sight, but his pistols were popping among the lodges.

The Indian woman was screaming something at Papa when we first walked among the lodges. She was half-twisted away from him with a baby's cradleboard held tight to her chest. Papa's pistols were holstered, and he held only a war club that he had picked up somewhere. The triangular, steel blade on it was covered in gore.

"Papa?" I called out.

We'd passed the scattered bodies of three warriors on our way into the camp—victims of Papa's unerring aim and his wrath. The body of an old man, almost as small as a child and wrinkled and withered and decrepit, lay at my feet. Papa had bashed his forehead in.

Papa didn't hear me, and the Indian woman screamed at him again with her back to her lodge wall. The club in Papa's hand reared back.

"No, Papa!"

The words hadn't even finished spilling from my mouth when the club came down and crumpled her to the ground with a sickening thud. Words have no power in a time like that. Again and again, the club rose and fell, timed perfectly with Papa's grunts of exertion. The baby she held squalled until Papa silenced it, too.

Papa hovered over the bodies, his shoulders slumped and his body heaving with exhaustion. While he stood there, another squaw dashed behind him, hoping to break free of the camp. Papa wheeled at the sound of her feet and grabbed at one of the pistols at his belt.

He tracked the running squaw with the barrel of his pistol, but the hammer snapped on an empty chamber, once, twice.

I stared at my father, thinking he was someone else—someone that I did not know.

Papa hurled the club at the squaw and struck her full between the shoulder blades, staggering her. Before I could call out to him again, he was already running after her. They disappeared behind one of the lodges.

I noticed the body of another squaw lying halfway in and halfway out of the doorway of one of the lodges. I looked to Gunn and found him sitting on the ground beside me, holding his wounded arm across him and rocking back and forth and muttering to himself.

"Papa's gone crazy," I said.

"You smell like piss," Gunn answered.

Yes, I'd wet my pants from fear. Pissed my pants and wasn't ashamed. Didn't give a damn. I was never going to shoot a gun as good as Papa. Never be as big and strong and sure as him. I was never going to be like Papa and didn't want to be.

There comes a time when we realize that our parents are actually two people—the characters we shape in our minds and claim in surety as our own, and those who they really are in spite of our assumptions—the real and what we make up because we want them to be that way. There was Papa, my father, and there was Argyle Dollarhyde, a man I did not know and might not ever know; a man who could kill effortlessly, women and children, bash their heads in with Stone Age weapons that he had never held before, yet fit his hand like old friends; chase after more of them, mad with the lust of the kill. Not me. For all the pain in me over losing Mama and Baby Beth, I couldn't find that much hate, only emptiness.

"I can't get up," Gunn said. "You go help Papa."

Help him? I could not. There was no help for any of us. Another squaw screamed somewhere outside the camp. We were all damned.

Chapter Eleven

Joseph led the horses into the Indian camp an hour later. He impressed me with that act. There was no way he could have known whether we lived or died from where we left him hidden in the streambed. For all he knew, the shooting and screaming he heard could have been the sound of our demise at the hand of the Kiowa. But he came anyway to find us. I wouldn't have. I would have taken that Kiowa roan and run for all he was worth.

We found Papa about midday. He was curled into a ball asleep in one of the lodges. Beside him were the bodies of another squaw and what we presumed was her mother, at least old enough to be. It was as if he had spent the last of his venom and then his body folded up and fell right there the instant he slew the last of them. I can't explain the contrast of the peaceful look on his face and the dried blood that coated him from head to toe. The only thing that wasn't relaxed about him were his hands. Clenched in one, as if someone might steal them, were a handful of bloody scalps. In the other was the war club.

He didn't say anything when I woke him. He stumbled from the lodge and squinted at the sun and stared at the bodies littering the grass as if seeing them for the first time. Then he spied Gunn lying on the buffalo robe I had taken for him from one of the lodges.

"How are you?" Papa asked as he knelt over Gunn and examined the arrow protruding from his thin arm.

"I've been better," Gunn rasped. Although he was in the shade of the wall of one of the tepees, beads of sweat still dotted his forehead, and his lips trembled so much that it was a wonder he could talk at all.

"Are you cold, son?"

"No, Papa. I just can't stop shaking."

"It's the pain," Papa said when he turned his head to me. "I've seen it before."

"He puked right after it happened and again about an hour ago," I said.

Papa nodded, as if he had seen that, too. I kept my eyes turned away from him, afraid that he would see how I recoiled from him.

"Fetch some hot water to bathe his wounds."

I did as Papa said and found water hanging in a bladder bag inside one of the lodges. I used a copper pot I plundered to heat the water.

By the time the water was ready, Papa had cut Gunn's shirtsleeve away. We bathed the skin around the arrow to better see the wound.

The tip of this arrowhead, perhaps at one time a bit of a barrel hoop or some German farmer's plow, hadn't gone all the way through the bend of Gunn's arm. Only the tip of it protruded from his triceps. Bits of bone and strings of tendon were pushed out of the wound.

As I learned later, the tribes of Texas had quickly learned to gather scrap metal during their raids on the white settlements and to shape that iron into blades for their weapons. There was no telling where the metal that pierced Gunn's flesh had come from, for it was said that the Comanche and Kiowa raided from Kansas down to the heart of Mexico.

"Hold him down," Papa said to Joseph and me. "Put your knees on his shoulder, Hamish, and Joseph, you sit on his legs."

Both of us did as he told us, and Gunn's eyes rolled wildly in their sockets when Papa gave the arrow a fierce yank. Twice more, Papa tried to pull the arrow out while Gunn bucked and groaned beneath us, but the shaft wouldn't come free.

"I'm afraid I'll break the arrowhead off in him," Papa said.

With that, he drew one of his pistols, held it by the barrel, and with the butt of it for a hammer drove the arrow through Gunn's arm. He snapped the arrow in two once the head of it broke free, and held up the two pieces before me. Gunn arched his back and kicked little Joseph, rolling him across the ground.

"There now. It's all over," Papa said and then flung the pieces of arrow away like they were serpents.

"Will he be all right?" I asked.

Papa was looking at Gunn when he nodded, but when he looked at me I could see that he was worried. He soon went off to be alone.

I washed Gunn's wound and bound it with makeshift bandages ripped from the shirtsleeve we cut off him. He couldn't move his arm, so Joseph helped me bind it to his chest with a sling made from the sleeve of an Indian hunting shirt we cut away. I had no clue if what I did was right, but Papa nodded at my handiwork when he came back. Apparently, he had gone to the nearby spring and stripped and washed himself, for he was clean of dried gore and he had traded his stained shirt for another.

"Something is stirring the dust out there," he said. "Looks like we'll soon have company."

I saw the dust cloud he was referring to. The country where we were was much more open than where we had settled, and you could see for miles in many places. It could have been buffalo moving out there in the distance, or it could have been men on horses.

"Kiowa?"

"Whoever it is, we'd best put some distance between us and them," Papa said.

Papa helped us get Gunn on his mule, and then tightened the cinch on Shiloh and got in the saddle. The buzzards were already circling overhead, and everywhere you looked there was death. I don't know how many of them Papa killed. Maybe nine, maybe ten or more, counting the one Gunn and I had done for. He never even looked around at his victims as we rode out of that Indian camp. It was as if he was blind to what he had done . . . what we had done.

"Sonny boy, I know you're hurting, but we need to ride hard," Papa said to Gunn.

Gunn looked about to fall from the mule's back at any second, but he nodded anyway. "I'll be all right."

"What about those horses?" Joseph pointed to the Kiowa ponies scattered a mile out of camp.

Papa, ever a practical-thinking man, had us gather those loose horses up and drive them before us, at least those that we could turn in with us in a hurry.

Papa spurred Shiloh up to a lope. "Gunn, you yell out if you need us to stop."

Gunn hunched over his wounded arm and with his teeth gritted kicked his mule up beside Papa. He looked down at the scalps tied to Papa's saddle strings and nodded.

And then Gunn looked at Joseph loping along beside him on that Kiowa roan. The orphan boy rode like he was born in a saddle, even though his feet in those outsized boots, made for a man three times his size, didn't even reach the stirrups.

By the time we were well on our way east, that dust cloud in the distance had turned into mirage shapes of men on horseback, their wavy, thin images distorted and rising from the ground like steam. If those were Kiowa, I didn't have any hope that we could outrun them.

I'll give it to Gunn, he hung in there and didn't beg to stop, not once. Shiloh usually could run all day and all night without breaking a sweat anywhere but under his saddle blanket, but he'd been too long without corn and he looked gaunt and less than himself after so long traveling and living on nothing but grass and too little water. Papa spoiled and pampered Shiloh, and that horse wasn't used to such hard living.

And nobody would call the mules Gunn and I rode racing Thoroughbreds. By evening, both of them couldn't be kicked out of a trot and threatened to balk or fall over and die.

Papa let us stop and rest for a couple of hours, and then he put Gunn and me on two of the gentlest-acting Kiowa ponies that he could catch. We rode through the night and didn't stop again until daylight. We would have moved on again after another break, but we couldn't get Gunn up. He was talking some, rambling on about dream things but not making sense, and his fevered eyes not seeing any of us.

We were sitting around him, fretting about what to do for him, when the riders appeared in the distance again. We couldn't do anything but stack our saddles and fort up behind them and wait for another fight to come to us.

Chapter Twelve

The riders following us turned out not to be Kiowa at all. Instead, they were a company of Texas Rangers on their way back to Parker County from pursuing a band of hostiles into the Tongue River breaks. To a man, they were as worn-looking as they were well armed. Their horses looked equally hard used and to have come a far piece.

"Captain Lucius Pike," the Ranger captain said as he dismounted with the rest of his men. He was a short, squatty man of middle age with the palest blue eyes I've ever seen.

"Argyle Dollarhyde, and these are my boys."

"Looks like that boy there is bad hurt."

"He took an arrow in the arm," Papa said, still keeping hold of his rifle and acting leery, no matter that our new arrivals claimed to be Texas lawmen.

"Best run a rag soaked in kerosene through that arrow hole," the captain said, clucking his tongue.

"We don't have any kerosene."

The captain must have seen the hard way Papa was looking back at him. "Not to be meddling in your business, but

I've had more than my share of experience with arrow wounds. The arrowhead wasn't hoop iron, was it?"

"Yes, it was."

"Did you get all of it out?"

"We did."

"Well, that's good. Hoop iron is bad to fester, and the blood poisoning is apt to set if you can't dig the head out right quick."

The other Rangers were already unsaddling their horses and staking them out, even though Papa hadn't invited them to do so. They looked like they were so tired that manners were liable to be the last thing on their minds.

"If you'll share a little bit of that water you're camped on, we'll share what grub we have with you and I'll see what I can do for that boy's wound," the captain said.

Papa looked at the little hole of brackish water in the bed of the creek we'd camped alongside—more mud and cattails than standing water. "I wouldn't refuse a man a drink."

"That's awful Christian of you. Thanks."

Gunn started babbling again. He was saying something about a big black Mexican eagle that was hovering over him and wanting to swoop down and carry him off. I looked up in the sky but couldn't see a thing except for the sun.

"What's that boy saying?" the captain asked.

"I think he's got a fever," Papa said.

"Already? That's a bad sign. Usually takes two or three days."

The captain knelt and began unwrapping Gunn's bandages while Papa stood over him. The rest of the Rangers threw their saddles on the ground and built a fire, no matter how hot the afternoon was.

"Is that a good idea?" Papa asked.

The captain paused his examination of Gunn's wound

long enough to look over his shoulder at his men. "Is it Indians seeing our fire that has you worried?"

"It is."

Gunn quit talking gibberish and moaned when the captain probed the wound with his fingers. The captain clucked his tongue again.

"That's what I thought," he said.

"You thought what?" Papa asked.

"His arm has to come off. The bone's busted all to hell and the poison has already set in," the captain said.

"You aren't going to cut my boy's arm off," Papa said.

"Then he'll die."

Papa looked from the captain to Gunn and back again, fear and anger written all over him.

"Be a shame, fine-looking boy like that," the captain said. "If you don't cut that arm off he won't last long."

"Thought you were a lawman and not a doctor."

"Doctor, no, but like I said, I've tended to a few wounds in my time. Snakebites, broken bones, colicky bellies, gyp water trots, and even an arrow or bullet wound or two."

"You let him tend to that boy, unless you can do better," one of the other Rangers said. "Captain Pike saved my life once when I had a bandit's bullet in my neck, and he might do the same for your boy."

"See this here?" the captain pressed on Gunn's wound and showed the yellow serum and fluid percolating from the hole. "He isn't going to use that arm ever again. Bone's busted past mending. You let the infection go farther and he'll die."

"Papa, don't let them take my arm," Gunn said. For an instant, his eyes were clear and he was all too aware of reality.

The captain saw Papa wavering. "It's got to come off."

The Ranger company went to gather more buffalo chips

for the fire. Wood was scarce out on those plains, and the sun-dried patties of dung left behind by the passing herds burned hot and bright.

"What do you want me to do?" Papa asked, setting aside his rifle and letting out a sigh that said he was resigned to what must happen.

"You talk to him. Pray over him if you're of a mind to, but for the most part, just hold him still and talk to him."

The captain squatted beside the fire and drew a skinning knife from his sheath and stuck it in the flames. He held his hat between his face and the heat while he sterilized the blade.

"No telling where this knife has been," he said as he pulled it out of the flames and studied the lightly blackened steel.

Papa knelt at Gunn's head. "Hamish, you come hold his legs."

The captain shook his head. "You might want to have one of my men do that. This won't be pretty."

"Hamish will do as he's told."

"Suit yourself."

One of the Rangers brought over a piece of leather he had cut off one of his saddle fenders. "Chew on this, boy."

Gunn went wild and fought against us, but the captain's hands on his chest and Papa's and my added weight kept him pinned.

"Don't let them, Papa," Gunn pleaded.

"Son, your arm is ruined. If we don't cut it off you'll die."

The Ranger that had brought the piece of harness leather handed his captain a bottle of whiskey. "That's the last sipping liquor in the company, Captain. I admit, I'm going to miss my evening constitutional, but it could be this boy could use it more than me."

The rest of the Rangers were cooking buffalo steaks

held over the fire on the ends of sticks they packed on their saddles for that purpose. Most of them acted as if nothing out of the ordinary was happening, but one of them was sitting with a pair of glasses on the end of his nose and a black Bible propped open on one knee.

"Have mercy upon me, O Lord, for I am weak," he read aloud. "O Lord, heal me, for my bones are vexed."

"That's nice of you to pray for him," Joseph said. "That's from the book of Psalms, isn't it?"

The Ranger, a tall thin man with a mustache that hung below his jawline, nodded. "I'll keep reading if you don't mind. Scripture might do some good, but mostly, my reading might cover up some of that boy's screaming."

No matter the piece of leather Papa put between Gunn's teeth, Gunn soon spit it out and commenced to scream like the skinny old Ranger had said he would. He screamed and he screamed while the captain cut.

"Return, O Lord, and deliver my soul. O save me for thy mercies' sake," the Bible-packing Ranger's twangy voice rose up with Gunn's cries of anguish.

Joseph joined in from memory. "For in death there is no remembrance of thee. In the grave, who shall give thee thanks?"

"Papa!" Gunn screamed until his voice went hoarse and faint.

I wished that he would pass out, but the captain had the arm off before Gunn finally went limp. His bony chest rising and falling ever so gently was the only thing that let me know he wasn't dead.

"I am weary with my groaning," the Ranger read on with Joseph's high voice slightly behind and out of sync.

The captain took up the whiskey bottle, pulled the cork with his teeth, and doused the bloody nub of Gunn's upper arm with the liquid. "We're lucky. The bone was busted so bad that there was nothing there to have to saw through."

"Oh God," Papa said.

"Stay steady, Mr. Dollarhyde. We're about done." The captain set aside the lower part of Gunn's arm. "Pinch off this vein for me, or he's going to bleed out."

"Mine eye is consumed because of grief. It waxeth old because of all mine enemies," read the Ranger.

"It waxeth old," repeated Joseph.

Papa's teeth grated together, but he didn't say anything else and helped where he could.

Once the captain had picked out the pieces of bone and anything else he could find that didn't belong, he doused the wound with whiskey again and asked for the needle and thread that one of the Rangers had brought up without even being asked for it. It was just an ordinary sewing needle with about two feet of thread hanging from it.

"What's that thread you're using?" Papa asked.

"Tail hairs from one of the horses," the captain answered. "Works pretty good in a pinch."

The Ranger captain sewed as carefully as a seamstress, making sure to cover the exposed bone and trimming flesh and adding a stitch here and there. "Trick is to leave some skin to fold back over the wound. I won't promise you that he won't have a bad scar."

When he was finished he stood to his feet and clucked his tongue, as I was beginning to think was his habit when he was pondering things.

"What next?" Papa asked.

It wasn't until then that I noticed that the Ranger with the Bible had quit reading from it, and that all the Ranger company were gathered around us looking at Gunn.

Captain Pike shrugged. "Nothing left to do but bind him up in some fresh, clean bandages and wait. Maybe he'll pull through and maybe he won't. He's out of our hands now."

"He's a tough boy," Papa said.

"I'm sure he is."

"Amen." The Ranger with the Bible slapped it shut.

"I'll pray for him," Joseph said.

I wanted to slap Joseph for that, and it shamed me.

The captain went to wash up while Papa and I bound Gunn's stump. I was carrying Baby Beth's lacy yellow blanket inside my shirt and I gave it to Papa for the new bandage. Papa gave me a strange look but used it anyway. Gunn's face was as pale as a sheet but he was still breathing regular.

"Hamish, you go on while I clean your brother up," Papa said.

I didn't know what he was talking about until it struck me how bad Gunn smelled. It took me a bit longer to realize that the pain of the surgery was so great that he had soiled himself.

"You take that and bury it." Papa jerked his head toward the remains of Gunn's left arm lying on ground beside him.

Captain Pike picked it up for me and carried it out from our camp. I took my knife and scooped a shallow hole in the sandy ground and we buried it there.

"I never expected this," I said, looking down at the fresh little mound at my feet.

The captain put his arm over my shoulders and started me back to camp. "You do your best to forget about this and be thankful your brother might live."

I sat with the Rangers at the fire, and one of them offered me a chunk of buffalo meat. But I didn't have any appetite, despite how long it had been since I had eaten. However, Gunn's surgery and the oppressive heat didn't seem to affect any of their appetites, and they ate like starving wolves.

Papa finally came to sit with us. He swiped at the sweat running off his face and looked to the captain. "Thank you."

"How's he doing?" the captain asked.

"I think he's sleeping."

"Make him drink some salt water as soon as you can. Good for the blood."

"Mix a little gunpowder in with it," one of the other Rangers added. "That always helps."

Several of the Rangers nodded their heads in agreement.

"Mr. Dollarhyde, I hope you don't mind my saying so, but this is an unusual bunch of Indian fighters you have with you." The captain pointed at Joseph and me with a jab of his thumb and then at Gunn lying on the grass behind us. "I'd be interested to hear your story."

"Kiowa hit our place. Killed my wife and my baby daughter."

The captain looked at each of his men, one and then the other around the fire. A few of them shook their heads, and a few of them gave Papa a look that I couldn't interpret other than that they seemed to be judging him in some way.

The captain cleared his throat. "Where was this at?"

"To the west of an abandoned settlement on a tributary of the Wichita, maybe another day's ride or so from here."

The captain nodded again. "Was a promising place at one time but there hasn't been any people there since not long after the war began. Comanche and Kiowa ran them off."

"It was Kiowa that hit us. At least that's what one of my hired hands believed."

"I'm pretty sure it was you and these boys that hit that village we passed a day ago to the north, or you wouldn't be driving a bunch of Indian ponies and your boy about to die from an arrow in his arm."

Papa had to get ahold on himself because he choked up. Maybe what we had done to Gunn was finally hitting him, or the rage over losing Mama was coming back. "We set in on their trail and had a fight with them when we found their village."

"Those weren't Kiowa you hit in that village. They were Wichitas."

"Wichitas?" Papa asked. "No matter, it was them. They had my wife's horse."

"That was a little hunting camp belonging to old Chief Big Belly."

"So?"

"You see, the Wichita normally live in grass lodges and farm most of the year. Corn and squash and beans and such. Spring and fall between crops, they take out tepees to do a little camping and hunt buffalo."

"Damn it, it was them!" Papa said loudly.

"I don't think so, Mr. Dollarhyde. The Wichita bands out here haven't bothered folks in twenty years, and old Big Belly's bunch has always been good friends with the white men. Me and my Rangers have visited with him many a time."

Papa stood, his right hand dangerously close to one of his pistols. "I don't like your tone, Captain."

The captain continued to stare at Papa calmly. "If your wife's horse was there I would imagine that the Wichita had traded for it from the Kiowa or Comanche that raided you. Those that done it might even have been the Comanche we were chasing."

"You lie."

Several of the Rangers stood to their feet.

"You ought to go easy with that war talk," one of them said.

Papa didn't seem to notice him, or any of the rest of

them, for that matter. His attention was on Captain Pike. "I trailed them."

"Are you a tracking man?" the captain asked. "You're obviously a fighter and maybe a military man in your past, but you don't seem like an old hand in this country. If you were, you wouldn't have drug these little boys along on an Indian hunt. Could be you lost the first trail and picked up Big Belly's tracks after that."

"They were the ones."

"Whether you're right or wrong, Mr. Dollarhyde, that doesn't explain why you killed the women and the little ones."

Papa was trembling.

"Don't you take a mind to try me, Mr. Dollarhyde. Don't be stupid. You keep that pistol in its holster, and me and my men will be on our way." The captain eased to his feet.

"I don't have to explain myself to you," Papa said.

The captain picked up his saddle but didn't immediately go to his horse. "If you're worried about us taking you in, rest easy. While it doesn't make me think much of you for doing what you did, I won't say I don't understand your situation."

Papa watched silently as the Rangers saddled their horses and mounted. They were almost ready to ride away before he spoke again. "You think you're better than me, don't you?"

The captain turned his horse back. "No, Mr. Dollarhyde, but what you did was wrong. There's some that say the only good Indian is a dead one, but old Big Belly was a decent sort, even if there isn't a court in Texas that would try you for killing him. I might shoot you on the spot here and now, or hang you if I could find a decent tree, but then I'd leave these boys without a father. And there's been enough bad in this country without adding to it."

"You don't know me."

The captain started away with his men but he threw back over his shoulder. "No, but I know what you did, and you do, too. I might not like it but I can live with it. The trouble is, can you?"

Chapter Thirteen

For the best part of the summer we slept on buffalo robes under a wagon tarp stretched over a rope strung between two trees. None of us would sleep in the dugout. Abandoned, it loomed over us as if it were one hundred feet tall. It was always there and catching your eye when you turned around, a burden that weighed more than earth and log, giving you pause, looming, accusing, reminding. The black eye of it, that dark doorway in the hillside, stared at us from dawn to dusk and never let us forget, no matter how hard we tried. I don't know why we didn't tear it down, but it became a scar that we all shared, as much as the stump of Gunn's lost arm.

I thought Gunn would die, at least at first. He looked so pitiful and frail on his buffalo robe, with his flesh drawn so tight over his ribs that you could count every one of them, and his skin so pale that it was almost translucent.

And weeks after the fever left him and his body began to mend and his strength return, he would still rarely leave the shade of our makeshift tent. He ate little, brooding and either staring at nothing or at the scarlet red and tender flesh of his healing wound with its knotted, puckered stitches crisscrossed in random patterns where the Ranger captain had sewn him together, making it up as he went, like a patchwork quilter with no plan in mind and nothing but odd-shaped scraps at hand.

But I don't think the pain and the loss of his arm were the only things that made Gunn so quiet. I feared that something besides his limb was cut away that day out on the prairie. A bit of him was gone and floated away on the wind.

Once, when Gunn did leave the tent, I found him down on the creek bank, clutching his stump and staring across the water at nothing but whatever lay out there to the west. I stood behind him for a long time, unsure if he even knew I was there, and was cautious about what I should, or could, say to him.

"Whatcha doing?"

It took Gunn a long time to answer. "Was thinking of drowning myself, but this sorry excuse for a river isn't deep enough."

That was the first thing he had said to me that was at all like the old Gunn I knew. I figured more small talk was in order.

"What kind of turtle do you think that is over there on that log?"

"Where did you leave me?" He kept his back to me, speaking as if he hadn't heard me.

"Leave you?"

"Where'd you bury it?"

I stammered and saw it as if it were happening all over again. It had been so light as I carried it, as if it weighed nothing. A poor little pale chicken wing that once was a boy's arm, and then it wasn't. There were times when I could still feel the coldness of it against my palms.

"Where'd you bury my arm?" Gunn had turned around and his eyes burned right through me.

I've never seen another person with eyes like Gunn's. You look at some of those pictures of Geronimo, Sitting Bull, or any of those old Indian chiefs, and maybe you'll know what I'm talking about.

"I don't know. If I could get back to that spring we camped at again I might find where I buried it, but I'm not sure." For some reason I was about to cry. "I stuck a buffalo rib bone into the ground to mark it."

"I can still feel it," Gunn said. "I never would have thought that. It's gone but it isn't gone. Papa says that's normal, but maybe if I could see it I wouldn't feel it anymore."

"Papa could take us back there."

"He don't want to go back there." He turned back to the river, lost again in whatever he had been looking at before I arrived.

I started back to camp and little things that Mama used to say kept coming back to me. Worries and troubles can be like a man astride a bad horse. I guess Gunn had his own devil horses to handle, and there was nothing to be done but to wait and see how he stood the ride.

"Bubba?" Gunn hadn't called me that in years, and his voice was only a whisper.

"What?"

"You shouldn't have left me out there."

Chapter Fourteen

It was near summer's end before José and Juanita returned. And they didn't come alone. There were four other Mexican families with them, women, kids, and all, traveling in a long train of big-wheeled *carretas*. The peeled cottonwood frames of their carts looked like strange skeletons rolling across the distance, the skinny oxen pulling them straining in their yokes, and the softwood axles screeching like demons.

Out to one side of the procession rode two handfuls of Mexican vaqueros driving a herd of horses before them. They were laughing, bold, wiry men under huge hats and wrapped in bright-colored wool serapes. The spoked rowels of their big spurs rattled in wooden stirrups hanging beneath the bellies of the long-maned, dish-faced little horses they rode.

It was soon revealed that José had traveled all the way south to the Rio Grande and the little village where he was born. There, he bought those ponies with Mama's treasure and convinced the entire village, by the presentation of such wealth, to come north with him to work for *Señor* Dollarhyde. José spoke of my Papa as *mi jefe, el patrón*, and all the other names poor Mexicans had of calling a man a big shot and to convince themselves that they should swear fealty to him.

At the time, I had no idea why Papa had purchased so many horses, but I assumed that José had brought his kin with him in order that we might have a settlement of sufficient size to fend off any Indian raids while we put in crops and tackled the building of homes. I should have known Papa had other plans, and that there wasn't going to be anything easy about them. Papa never was one to do anything by half measures.

First, he gave the men two weeks to throw together homes for their families, more shacks than anything— slim cedar and oak poles set into the ground on end to form walls, and mud dabbed between to fill in the cracks. "Jacales," the Mexicans called them—grass-thatched roofs and dirt floors coated in ox blood and tamped to the hardness of concrete. Joseph and I helped with the building of them, for Papa said any man who worked for him had to carry his weight. The thing about boys in Texas is that all of them want nothing more than to be considered men and will do anything to prove that they are.

As soon as the jacales were built, including one for us that became the new Dollarhyde headquarters, Papa gave us an afternoon off. And then we set in to gentling horses that didn't want to be gentled, and getting our gear ready to work.

In short, Papa had taken the notion that we were going into the cattle business. Two dollars a head was the going rate for a beef steer in Texas, but you would be lucky to find anyone with a dollar in their pocket, much less two, and much less anyone willing to spend it on a longhorn steer. The war hadn't left anyone in shape to buy much of anything, and most folks made do with what they could make themselves. Usually, they did without.

But Papa heard that there wasn't enough beef to feed the people back East. A fat steer would bring thirty to forty dollars there, and a railroad was building its way west across Kansas. It didn't matter if that railroad was about four hundred miles and a lot of rivers away from us. All that was needed were men with a little gumption and a herd to drive north.

Problem solved. There were more cattle running loose around us than you could shake a stick at, just ripe for the taking. And the men . . . well, Papa had gumption enough for ten men and was going to make me and my brothers into vaqueros—cowboys, folks later called us.

Chapter Fifteen

"There." José set the saddle down in the dust in front of our jacal. "I made it for you."

Gunn stood in the shadowed doorway, saying nothing and making no offer to come outside. He wouldn't even look at the saddle.

Joseph and I were already mounted with the rest of the crew. We soon forgot about work and watched intently.

And we weren't the only ones. One of the women tossing a pail of dishwater to the side of her door looked up and saw Gunn and José. Quick as that, she ran to the jacal next to hers, starting a chain reaction. In a matter of seconds everyone knew what was happening, and a half dozen feminine faces were peering out of their doorways or huddling together and whispering their predictions to one another. The kids followed the example of their mothers and quit their playing and peered from behind whatever cover they felt best suited their spying. You could have heard a pin drop.

"This should be interesting," Papa said beside me.

For an entire winter, Gunn had said little to anyone, would rarely look you in the eye, and steadily refused to join in the work, no matter how many subtle suggestions Papa or the rest of us made in that regard.

"It's a good saddle," José said.

Gunn finally gave in and glanced at the saddle. "Give it to somebody else that needs it."

"Your papa is right. Your arm is healed enough, and it's time you quit pouting and joined us."

"Are you like the rest of them and going to act like I ain't a cripple?" A little bit of the old Gunn and that anger he always packed inside him surfaced in his face. "Admit it. I have. It'll be easier on all of you."

José hefted the saddle again and held it in front of Gunn. "Your papa asked me to make this for you. Rafael and Hector helped me. Will you insult them by refusing their gift?"

"I appreciate it, but you wasted your time."

José looked to Papa and got a nod from him. One of the vaqueros rode forward, leading the Kiowa roan that Joseph had been riding for the past months. Several of the vaqueros had lent a hand gentling and training it. José took the horse by the bridle rein and pitched a blanket on its back and then settled the saddle there.

"Maybe you think that you can't ride," José said with his back to Gunn while he tightened the cinch. "But you have an arm left to handle a bridle and two good legs. There are men with less to work with."

"I'm not going to get on that horse."

José patted the seat of saddle and rested against the horse with that hand. He and Gunn stared at each other silently.

It was a good saddle that he leaned on, even if it didn't look like much. I know, for he or the other vaqueros had made me one like it. It was the kind of bare-bones rig that you could cobble together with what was on hand, with most of the white rawhide–covered saddletree showing except where a hair-on deer hide was laid over the seat for a pad, and the cinch rings for the single rigging made on Papa's blacksmith forge. Fancy, no, but stout and serviceable and made for men who handled cattle from the back of a horse. Those Mexican vaqueros had been building basically the same rig for two centuries.

The saddles we were used to riding back East either lacked a horn or had one so small and rigged so weakly that it was of little use when you had a rawhide riata tied to it on one end and a thousand-pound steer on the other. But the saddles that the vaqueros made had high forks and a great big saddle horn with a three-inch cap. It was like having a fence post in your lap.

It didn't matter what kind of saddle it was, because I knew how stubborn my brother could be. But then again, Papa was just as stubborn, and he rode Shiloh over there and dismounted.

"Gunn, you're going to get on that horse," Papa said.

"You can't make me."

Papa grabbed Gunn by his arm. "Son, I can. I've been too patient with you and it's time you quit moping around. Crying about it won't make it any better."

"I don't want to ride."

"You don't have any say in it. A Dollarhyde doesn't quit."

"What about what I think?"

Papa lifted Gunn and set him on the horse, ignoring Gunn's squirming and kicking.

"I don't care what you think," Papa said. "You grow up enough to get some sense and then maybe I'll listen to you."

"You won't always be the boss of me."

Papa looked up at him. "Time comes that you think you can do something about that, you come look me up. I'll run this family until then."

Papa and José went to either side of Gunn and unlaced

the stirrup leathers and fitted them to his leg length. When they were done, they jammed his feet in the stirrups and Papa slapped the roan on the top of the hip.

The horse took off in a scramble of sand and gravel, and Gunn nearly toppled from its back, falling over the saddle horn and clutching for the reins Papa had knotted together for him. The horse disappeared down the trail along the river and into the timber.

"Do you think he will be all right?" José asked Papa.

Papa climbed up on Shiloh and tugged his hat brim down. "He doesn't have a choice. This country won't give him one, and I won't, either."

Chapter Sixteen

It was the heat of the day when I noticed Gunn's horse standing riderless with its reins dragging the ground. The rest of the crew was scattered out at wide intervals, working through the mesquite brush to drive out whatever cattle were hiding there.

I feared the worst and put my horse to a trot and held up one arm across my face to shield it from the thorny tree limbs I was busting through. Gunn was wearing a white shirt, and that was the first thing I saw when I got closer. He was sprawled out on the ground next to a big clump of prickly pear.

I baled off my horse and knelt beside him. He pushed himself up on his elbow and squinted at me.

"Are you all right?"

"Hell, no. Do you think I would be laying here if I was?" He sounded bad, no matter how he tried to let on.

"Sleeping on the job, huh?" I noticed how pale he looked, and when I put my hand on his forehead his skin was clammy cold, no matter how warm the day was.

"I could use a drink."

I brought him my canteen and helped him hold it while he took a drink.

"Help me to the shade."

He was shaky, but got to his feet with my help. We made it to the nearest mesquite with high-enough limbs to get under, and he took a seat with his back to its trunk.

"Want another drink?"

He shook his head and pointed behind me. "Fetch my horse while I sit here a bit."

"I'm going to go get Papa."

He grabbed my elbow and tugged me back to him. "I said I would be all right once I sit a spell."

I noticed the dried blood soaked through his sleeve over the stump of his bad arm. I also noticed how his hand shook as it tried to hold me there.

"You aren't up to this yet," I said. "You need a little more time to heal up, that's all."

"Just got too hot. This brush holds the heat like an oven."

"Could happen to anybody." I knew that it wasn't only the heat. It was the second time in the last week I had found him where he had fallen off his horse.

Papa had been driving us hard. Fifteen hours a day in the saddle was tough on anyone, but especially for Gunn. He was still a shell of his former self, thin as a rail and hollow-cheeked—no way to be for the kind of work we were doing and the hot sun beating down on him.

"I can't believe I fell off," he said. "I started getting woozy and then the first thing you know, I hit the ground."

"You look as weak as a cat."

"I'm already feeling better."

"Liar."

"Get my horse."

I did as he asked, not because I thought it was a good thing, but to appease him and to keep him from trying to get up and get it himself. He held out his hand for the reins when I brought the horse, but I kept back from him.

"Why don't you sit there awhile longer?"

He took another sip from the canteen and then poured a little on top of his head. "That feels good. I think I cooked my brain."

"You never use it anyway."

He cocked his head, listening for the sound of the men working through the brush. "Somebody's going to see me like this."

"We all know that you're still mending."

"Easy for you to say. You didn't fall off your horse." He saw me looking at his stump. "Hand me my reins."

"I'm going to get Papa."

He crammed his hat back on his head and put his back against the tree and got his legs under him. He stood, putting his hand against the trunk to steady himself. "Don't make me have to knock some sense into you."

"You're in no shape to ride."

"I was riding when I fell off."

"You're going to kill yourself. At the least, I'll go with you back to camp. Rest up this afternoon and go at it again tomorrow, if you're up to it."

He lunged forward and snatched the reins out of my hand. "I'll quit when everyone else does."

I didn't think he could get on his horse, but he did. And he did look better than he had moments before.

"All I needed was some water. Got busy and forgot to drink enough."

I caught my horse and mounted, keeping a close eye on him. "You still look like death warmed over."

"You don't look any better. What's your excuse?"

"Killing yourself won't prove anything."

"To hell it wouldn't."

"Have it your way."

"Don't you tell Papa. Promise?"

"I won't tell him, but if I find you lying on the ground again I'm going to leave you there."

He started his horse through the brush in the direction of the drive, hunkered over his saddle swells a little and his hat brim bobbing as if he was having a hard time holding his chin up.

I watched him go and wished there was something that I could do to help him. Every day I watched him fight to learn how to do things with one arm—things boys with two good arms took for granted. All three of us, Gunn, Joseph, and I, were learning new skills when it came to handling cattle from horseback, but Gunn was working with one arm at a job that sometimes made you wish you had three. Gunn didn't like to think there was anything he couldn't do, and I knew he was afraid that Papa would leave him behind when we went north.

"Don't you tell Papa," he called out one more time.

Chapter Seventeen

*Spring 1867, Salt Creek Crossing
on the Red River, Texas, to Indian Territory*

"S*celoporus undulatus*, I think."

Gunn pulled his horse up and looked down at the little reptile I was pointing out, making a fair attempt at acting like he was interested. "Why don't you speak English?"

"Eastern fence lizard."

"All that smart talk make you feel good?"

"Latin is the language of science."

We had fallen back a hundred yards or so from the tail end of the herd, but the dust was still so thick you could barely see. Or breathe. Gunn had tied a piece of rag around his neck and he pulled it up over his nose until only his dark eyes showed beneath his hat. "No science to riding drag. No skill at all, or we wouldn't be back here. Just eating dust."

"Maybe I don't always intend to be riding drag."

"Me neither. I'm going to earn my way up to riding flank or I'm going to knock off one of those vaqueros and take his place."

"That isn't what I meant."

"Didn't suppose it was."

I coughed and squinted through the dust at the herd strung out in a long line before me, and then looked back across the river we had recently crossed. "We've barely been in Texas long enough to build a fire, and now Papa's taking us somewhere else."

"Papa's a driver and he ain't much for sitting still." Gunn hacked some phlegm up from his throat and leaned over and spat on the lizard. "We better get to driving ourselves. If we don't keep these drags moving Papa ain't ever going to make his next fortune."

"The longer we live in Texas, the worse you talk."

"Well, I'll keep talking like I like to talk, and you keep your nose in that grammar primer you're always holding over my head. You tell me if these old longhorns answer either one of us."

I looked to the herd strung out more than a mile in front of us, with Old Speck leading them with a cowbell clanging from his neck that Papa had tied there—2,223 bellowing longhorn steers, four years old and up, with their giant horns swinging with every stride, and every one of them with our $D brand six inches tall burned into their left rib cage. It might seem strange that I remember their number, but Papa was a stickler for an accurate count.

The world has never seen the likes of a Texas longhorn, before or since. More hoof and bone and horn and pure stubbornness than any other animal known to mankind, and a testament to the controversial theories those Englishmen, Darwin and Spencer, got everyone in such an uproar about. Descended from the original Spanish cattle brought to the New World, longhorns were a result of three hundred years of natural selection and survival of the fittest. What they couldn't outrun they outfought. Too tough and stringy to make a decent steak, they could make do with less and walk farther than anything short of a buffalo.

I let Gunn ride off before me, his thin legs pounding the sides of his tired horse, and his empty shirtsleeve pinned to his chest. He was still too skinny and his sun-bronzed cheeks too hollow, but he looked as hard as a piece of bull hide and wiry strong. Who was it that said Texas will either cure you or kill you?

Somebody shouted, and I looked to the edge of the herd and saw Joseph waving at us. He was helping our horse wrangler bring along our remuda, which was what the vaqueros called our herd of extra saddle horses. Each one of us had six horses in our string, so that we could rotate to fresh mounts as needed.

Joseph had taken to the vaquero life like a duck to water. Our Mexican teachers were wizards with those long braided rawhide riatas that they used to rope cattle, and Joseph, under their tutelage, packed his riata around every waking hour, roping anything and everything that had the misfortune to cross his path. From the chickens to my own feet, everything was fair game for him to practice with his favorite toy.

And as a horseman, we all knew from the first time he climbed up on that Kiowa roan that he was going to be one. He made everything he did from the saddle look easy.

I adjusted my own rope, hung from my saddle horn and resting coiled atop my right thigh. It was a waste for me to carry the thing, and I don't know why I did, unless it was because the loose tail of it was handy to wave around and keep the stragglers at the tail end of the herd, the drag, moving. It sure wasn't because of my skill with it. I was more apt to tangle myself up in it than I was to rope anything.

Ahead of the remuda was our wagon, loaded with our

bedrolls and supplies. Back in the early days, nobody had chuck wagons like you hear talk of. Some give Old John Blocker or Charlie Goodnight credit for being the first one to nail a grub box on the back of a wagon and take it north with a trail herd, but I don't know. All I know is that ours was simply a plain wagon. We were pretty poorly equipped, and looked nothing like most folks picture cowboys. Every one of us, except for Papa, was dressed like Mexican vaqueros with broad-brimmed, low-crowned sombreros, and our high-topped riding boots cobbled from ill-tanned leather by our ranch bootmaker. Cloth was so scarce that some of the men wore buckskin shirts. If a man had a pair of spurs, he traded for them or he braided his own rawhide quirt.

But those were the old days, before everyone and their brother decided they wanted to get in on the cattle business. The tricks of the trade were still being worked out.

The old Texas hands down in the brush country of South Texas didn't call gathering cattle a roundup. It was a "cow hunt." Men from the area would meet at a certain agreed-upon spot, bringing as many good cow horses as they could and their supplies loaded on a packhorse. They would drive the longhorns out of the brush where they could, sometimes baying them with packs of dogs, or moonlighting them on an open prairie in the middle of the mesquite and run them down and rope them. A large brush corral might be built to hold the gather while the men searched for more. As I've said before, a mossyhorn steer that had spent his life in the wild was a handful. Many a man and horse were gored or crippled racing through the thorny thickets in hot pursuit. You've never done anything until you've roped a 1,200-pound wild steer with horns six feet wide from the back of an 850-pound Texas pony. I don't know who was more outlaw, those longhorns or the men who went after them.

While we weren't in South Texas, we had gathered our trail herd in a similar way. Every day, Papa and José led the hands out, and together, we drove every head we could find back toward the ranch. Then we branded everything out in the open with no corrals, and men roping and throwing the cattle and others branding them and castrating the young bulls. By the time we were ready to drive north, in addition to the newly made steers big enough for market, Papa had his brand on some two thousand head of mixed stock, cows, calves, etc. All it took in those days for a man to become a rancher was a good roping arm and a string of horses. Stupid, stubborn grit and determination didn't hurt your chances, either.

We had crossed the Red River that day a little after noon, and only made five more miles before we bedded the herd and went into evening camp. Papa trusted to José, his *segundo*, and understood that the herd couldn't be pushed too hard. The sign of a good drover was to bring his herd to market in better flesh than when they left home. Every pound a steer lost was taking money out of your pocket. But none of us knew if anyone up in Kansas would buy our beef. The whole thing was a gamble.

José had assigned Gunn and me the first guard. The men were paired, and each pair stood roughly a two-hour watch on the herd, with the last guard starting the cattle grazing along the trail at daylight. The first guard was usually reserved for more senior men so that they didn't have to be woken in the middle of their sleep to stand their turn. I think Papa gave that guard to us because it was safer. Our herd was not yet trail broke, and apt to spook and run at the slightest provocation. But usually, if you could get them bedded calmly, any mischief was apt to happen after they had a chance to rest and chew their cud.

It was dark by the time I made my last slow ride around the bedded herd under the stars, and my relief rode out to take my place. I was usually too tired to do anything but wolf down my supper and fall in my bedroll, but we had company that night. A voice hailed our campfire from the dark, and after we invited him to come on in, a tall young man, maybe in his early twenties, on a hard-ridden horse trotted up and dismounted. He said something in Spanish to our cook that made him laugh, and then took the plate of food offered him and settled down on the wagon tongue across from Papa. Despite his friendly banter and Papa's offer to camp with us for the night, he seemed nervous and didn't unsaddle his horse.

I took the plate of beans and corn tortillas the cook handed me and sat on the ground close enough to Papa that I could hear what was being said.

"You look to have ridden far," Papa said to our guest.

"Not so far as that," the young man said. "But I aim to get out of this country as fast as I can and back down to Bee County where we've already got the Indians whipped."

"Indians?" Papa asked.

"The herd I was with ran on to them yesterday."

"Herd?"

"You didn't think you were the only one on the trail, did you?"

"We saw dust ahead of us yesterday," Papa answered between spoonfuls shoved from his plate. He was always businesslike about getting his meal finished and not much to talk during it. "Figured as much."

Our visitor was tackling his food even faster than Papa, as if he hadn't eaten in a long while, or he was in an awful big hurry to finish. He didn't bother with manners, and talked around the food stuffed in his cheek. "That's O. W. Wheeler's herd up ahead of you, and there's another bunch trailing east of us and two days ahead."

Papa looked put out. Much of his plan centered on being the first to reach the new market on the railhead. Competition was bound to lower the price of beef.

"That promoter up in Kansas has sent flyers all over Texas," the man said. "If you ask me, nobody knows a thing about this Abilene. Could be a bunch of hot air. This is the second time I've headed north with a herd, and neither time has worked out like it was supposed to."

"Second time?" Papa asked absentmindedly.

"Last fall I hired out with a crew to drive to Sedalia, Missouri. We were barely across the Neosho River when a bunch of farmers and their sheriff held us up with shotguns and turned us back. Those folks up there are dead set on keeping Texas cattle out of Missouri. Shot two of our lead steers and stampeded the rest. Arrested our trail boss and wouldn't turn him loose without we paid a fine. Ended up we scraped together seven dollars between us, and those squareheads took that and half our saddle horses to let him out of jail."

Papa grimaced. "I was thinking that if this Abilene place didn't turn out like it is supposed to be, we might cut to the east and drive to Missouri."

"They've got the whole damned state quarantined. Scared of Texas Fever. Who ever heard of that?"

"Texas Fever?"

"They say our cattle make theirs sick and die. Every steer in our herd was as healthy as can be. It's a racket, if you ask me. Damned Yankees got it out for boys in gray."

"Did you try this Abilene then, or did you turn back?"

"Weren't no Abilene last year. Not that we knew about." The man gestured with his empty plate and waited until the cook refilled it before going on. "Once we had our boss out of the calaboose, we heard a rumor that the Yankee soldiers might buy some beef at Fort Scott. A day south of there, we got held up again. That bunch weren't farmers. Regular herd cutters and holdup types. Border trash wanting us to pay a toll to go through their country. They tied one of our men to a tree and whipped him half to death with a switch. Texas Fever must not have been any concern of theirs, for they stole the whole herd. Us boys burned enough powder at 'em to keep them off of us, and rode south as soon as we could get our boss loose from that tree."

"You said you've been north two times," Papa said.

"This spring was to be my second trip. Slow learner, I guess, or I'm under some kind of curse. Old man Wheeler said we would be fine if we stayed west of those farmers and Jayhawkers. Has him one of those Joseph McCoy flyers he got off of some bottle peddler down in the brush, saying that there were stock pens and cattle buyers gonna be waiting on the railroad this spring and summer. All that may be, but the Indians don't give a hoot and a holler about no Kansas railroads."

"Indians?" Papa stood up and dusted off his pants.

"There's a big camp of them about seven miles north of you. They come up to us friendly-like, and we fed a few of them. But that wasn't enough. Before long they were making like they were mad and wanting more. Like to have been a big fight in our camp, but they had us outnumbered five to one and the boys kept their shooters in their holsters."

"And what became of your herd?"

"Oh, they stampeded us good. Rode through the herd and scattered them to hell and back. By the time we could gather them and move on, we were short fifty head. I guess those heathens will eat good this winter. Especially if you're bound and determined to drive past them."

"Any of your men hurt?"

"Nothing but hurt feelings." The man gave Papa a funny look. "I guess you're asking because you're wondering why I'm here."

"I am."

"Like I said, I'm done with this cattle drive business." He scrubbed his plate out with a handful of sand and pitched it in the wash barrel. "They want Texas cattle, let 'em build a railroad down here, and I'll be the first to help load their cars."

Papa followed the man to his horse. "You're welcome to pitch your blankets with us."

"No, I don't believe I will. Thanks for the grub."

"Safe traveling."

The man swung up on his horse at the edge of the firelight. "You boys be careful and sleep light. Those Kiowa were in a mood to lift hair."

"Kiowa, you say?" Papa's voice went hard.

"Yes, a mixed bunch of Kiowa and Comanche. Led by a tall young buck and an older one. That older one is the meanest son of a bitch in buckskins you ever saw. Little wrinkled-up fellow. Man with us that spoke a little of their jabber said they called him Lone Wolf. You meet him, you'll know who I'm talking about. Rides a yellow horse and wears two revolvers in his belt and a gold locket hanging from one of his braids."

"Gold locket?" Papa's hand grabbed ahold of the man's bridle.

"You know, the kind a woman wears. God bless the poor girl who he took that from."

"What did that locket look like? Was it shaped like a teardrop with a little ruby in the center?" Papa held on to the bridle, even though it was obvious the man was anxious to leave.

"I don't know. I didn't get that close of a look, and I had other worries, besides."

Papa seemed lost in his own thoughts.

"Mister, you let go of my bridle. I don't want any trouble with you, but I'm headed back to Texas."

Papa let go, and that man rode off into the night, the sound of his horse's hooves plain for only a bit as he headed toward the Salt Creek Crossing.

José went over to Papa. "We'd best cut to the east, *patrón*. See if we can slip past that Indian camp."

"Did you hear what that man said?" Papa's voice had a quaver to it.

"Do you want to fight Indians or do you want to get your cows to market?" José started to say something else, but hesitated. "We are only ten men, and there is no way we can fight Indians and handle this herd at the same time."

"We'll leave a few good men here with the herd, and the rest of us will go after those Kiowa."

"It won't work. You will lose your herd, and there are your *niños* to think about."

"Did you hear him? What that filthy Kiowa was wearing?"

José nodded. "Yes, I heard him."

"Are you saying you won't ride with me?"

"We will ride with you if that is what you want, but I ask you to think on this."

All eyes were on Papa. None of the vaqueros had hired on to fight Indians, but they were loyal to Papa for some reason unknown to me. Still, they were all looking at the ground and trying to act like they weren't hearing what was being said.

Joseph came and sat close to me, his hands working nervously at the rope in his hands. "Your papa will go after them, won't he?"

"Sssshh. Everything is going to be all right."

The problem was, I didn't believe a word I told him.

Chapter Eighteen

Papa was sitting on the wagon tongue staring at the campfire coals when I fell asleep, and he was still sitting there when Gunn shook me awake the next morning. I guess Papa wrestled with himself all night.

Until we had eaten our breakfast and saddled our horses none of us were sure what he would do. The herd had already drifted well to the north, and without instruction from Papa, we all fell to our trail positions. José took the point, and the herd was slowly swung to the northeast. Papa had saddled Shiloh that morning, which he didn't normally do when he intended to be handling cattle. The Thoroughbred was way too high-strung to be any good as a stock horse, and Papa usually saddled him only when he had a long trip to make or he was going to war.

He didn't even stop to pass the time of the morning with Gunn and me, or even to say good-bye when he rode past us. He stopped for a moment at the point of the herd to speak with José, and then we watched him until he disappeared to the north.

"He's going hunting those Kiowa," Gunn said to me.

"Yes."

"Do you think he'll come back?"

I was a little surprised that Gunn didn't seem bothered by Papa's decision. "Going off after those Kiowa isn't going to bring Mama back."

"That ain't what Papa's after."

"What is it then?"

"Revenge. Hurting them what have hurt you, and maybe for a little bit of time not feeling like you're helpless."

"And you? Don't you still want revenge?"

"I dreamed last night that I went with Papa and we came up on a camp of those Kiowa. They were all painted with ashes and their eyes and mouths outlined in soot, and there were clouds everywhere. You know, low down like fog, with things moving inside it. One of them was wearing something around his neck, and I went forward to see if it was Mama's necklace."

"Was it?"

"Yes and no. He had bones hanging from his neck—all kinds of them. He took hold of one of them and shook it in front of my face. It was my arm bone."

"How do you know it was yours?"

"Just did. He had it strung on a leather thong. Kept talking to me without his mouth moving, but I couldn't understand all he was telling me. Guess it was Kiowa talk."

"How could you dream in Kiowa if you don't speak it?"

"It was a dream, okay? He finally quit shaking my arm bone and one of the others handed him a skull that he showed to me. The top of it was busted out and he reached inside and pulled Mama's necklace from it."

"What did he say? The part you understood?"

"I don't want to talk about it."

"You're kidding me. You told me all of that, and then you say you don't want to talk about it anymore?"

"I shouldn't have told you what I did. You think I'm crazy or making this up, don't you?"

"We all have crazy dreams."

"Not like this one."

"It was only a dream."

"Then why are you bothering me about it?"

"Talk to that old man, Rodrigo. José says he can tell fortunes and interpret dreams."

"I already did this morning."

"What did he say?"

"Same thing I thought." Gunn turned his horse away and headed to the other side of the herd.

"What did he say?" I called after him.

"What I thought. It ain't worth it."

We stuffed grass in Old Speck's cowbell to keep it from clanging, swung well to the east for a day, and pushed the herd hard and never saw a sign of that Kiowa camp. There was no trail in those days, and José simply kept us pointed north, crossing rivers and creeks with no names known to us, blazing our way following the North Star. If there was a railroad up there somewhere we were bound to strike it.

The weather had been especially fine up until that point, but on the fifteenth evening since Papa left us, a big wind blew up from the south. Before long, the whole sky was a wall of low gray clouds with little smoky tendrils hanging below it and dancing around like wiggling worms. By the time we made camp, lightning was crackling and the thunder booming so loud it felt like the earth shook. The cattle were restless and wouldn't bed down, and José kept us all on guard. None of us really minded, for it began to rain so hard that we couldn't have slept anyway.

Somewhere around midnight, lightning struck a lone

cedar on the edge of the herd. The whole night was lit up, and before it went dark again I saw the shadows of dead cattle all around that tree and a staggering horse with an empty saddle.

That was all in the instant before the herd stampeded and my horse took off after them. You've never done anything until you've run a horse flat out in the dark with the rain coming down so hard it stings your face, and not knowing when you're going to find a hole or a gully that will send you end over end, either to get your fool neck broke or trampled to death by several thousand hooves.

You could feel the electricity in the air. I know that's probably not an educated way to say that, but it's the only thing that comes to mind. Sparks and little runners of lightning played across the cattle's backs as they ran, and twice I saw blue balls of fire on their horn tips.

There are those that will say that cowboys popped their pistols to turn a stampeding herd, but whoever started that tall tale didn't know a thing. Shooting off your popper is the last thing to calm a running bovine. The second thing you'll hear is how good hands could turn the herd back into itself until the run was broken and all the cattle were milling in confusion. I've seen that happen with a nervy man who knows his stuff, and a herd that was only half a mind to stampede. But with a stampede like we had that night, you don't do anything but run with them. Those steers were running so scared they were blind to anything, and there was nothing to do but stick with them and wait them out. Clench your teeth and keep your backside down in your saddle seat and pray that they don't run forever.

The horse I rode was a little black that I used only for my night horse. He was sure-footed and steady, and never once did I appreciate that more than when he carried me that night. The country was fairly open, but every drainage, branch, and gully was lined with cedars or elm and oak brush. Those steers didn't slow down for anything, and every time we busted through or sailed over one of those spots, with me clawing to stay in the saddle, I thanked the Lord that my black kept his feet.

We eventually hit a long stretch of rolling prairie, and I was shocked to discover that somehow I had ridden almost to the leaders. Lightning lit up the sky again, and I caught a quick glance of someone riding on the other side of the herd. It was little Joseph, swinging a blanket over his head, trying to turn the herd. He was riding a horse we called Crazy Man, a big gray that could outrun anything in our remuda. He belonged to Papa's string, and I don't know what Joseph was doing riding him.

We must have run for another mile or two. The rain slackened to a gentle downpour and the lightning was all in the distance. I had no clue where Joseph was, for it was too dark to see much of anything.

Sometime later, the herd slowed to a high lope, and then later to a trot. It might have been five minutes, it might have been half an hour, I don't know. My horse was heaving, but he kept along with the flow of the herd.

By daylight, I found myself with a small bunch of spent steers—maybe two hundred of them. There was nobody else in sight, and I didn't know where I was. I looked at the rising sun and took a guess which way was south. The steers were so tired that they gave me little trouble, more than content to walk, and some of them trying to lie down.

I soon saw something ahead of me in a wash. When I got closer I saw that it was Crazy Man's white belly that had caught my eye, and he was lying on his side in the gully in about six inches of running water. Joseph sat on the muddy bank above him, hatless and covered from head to toe in red clay.

"He never saw the gully," Joseph said in monotone. "We were falling before I even knew what hit us."

I studied how the horse lay. One of its front legs was broken until the bone showed and its head was twisted at an odd angle. "Looks like he broke his neck. At least he didn't suffer."

Joseph looked up at me. "He did. Took him a long time to die, and I didn't have a pistol to put him out of his misery."

"Climb up here behind me."

"What about my saddle?"

He was right. We might not ever find our way back to get it. I dismounted and slid down the gully to him. With both of us tugging and straining and digging, we managed to get the saddle out from under the horse. By then, we were both covered in mud.

It took Joseph two tries to climb out of the gully. The clay pulled his boot off once, and he had to slide back down the bank to retrieve it. We stacked Joseph's saddle on top of mine and walked beside my horse, doing our best to move the cattle in front of us on foot. Joseph was still holding that muddy boot in one hand, and the limp it gave him reminded me how comical we both must look.

We hadn't gone far when we began to meet stragglers from our crew, some of them bringing in more cattle. Gunn loped out to meet us.

"You don't look any worse for the wear," I said.

Gunn pulled his horse up and lifted one leg over his horse's withers and hooked the back of his knee on his saddle horn. There was a great big welt across his cheek that looked like a limb had slapped him in the face. The smile he tried to hide ended up as a smirk. "Hamish, Joseph, is that you? My horse almost spooked out from under me when he saw you. He thought he was about to be attacked by mud people."

"Funny."

"What happened to your horse, Peckerhead?"

"He tripped and fell and broke his neck," Joseph said.

"He was riding Crazy Man," I said.

"Who told you to ride him?" Gunn asked.

We all knew that Gunn had begged Papa to let him have that horse, but the gelding was a vicious bucker when you first stepped on him, and no kind of horse for a boy—no kind of horse for a one-armed boy was what Gunn probably thought Papa didn't say.

"I didn't ask. I thought it wouldn't hurt if I rode him easy," Joseph said. "Do you think he's going to be mad?"

"Papa?" Gunn said. "You'll be lucky if he doesn't give you to some farmer when we get up to Kansas."

"Don't listen to him," I said.

"Papa never wanted you," Gunn said. "She just felt sorry for you."

"Don't you bring Mama into this," I said.

"You forgive her if you want to."

"Forgive her? For what? Adopting Joseph?"

Gunn turned his back on me and rode off. Joseph was staring at me like he always did, with that look that I never could put my finger on.

"It's all right. I know I'm not your real brother."

"I told you not to listen to Gunn. He likes you. It's other stuff that's bothering him and he's taking it out on anybody he can."

"I never should have taken that horse."

"Papa will be mad when he comes back, but he'll get over it. I promise you I've done worse." It dawned on me then that I was assuming Papa would come back.

"Like your papa leaving and going after those Kiowa? I don't think he gets over things."

There it was again, that look he gave me. Who was this kid always staring with those big, wise eyes that didn't belong on his face? I started to tell him to forget about it, but I would have felt like a hypocrite. There were things I couldn't forget and never would—things so big that it was all I could do to hold them in. And all I had to talk to was a big-eyed kid who wouldn't understand any of it.

Chapter Nineteen

It took us two days to gather our herd again. Even then, we were short about thirty head, either missing or crippled during the run. Several of our horses were also lame, but it was the burial of the man that was struck by lightning that hit us the hardest.

After we buried him and rode our horses over the grave to pack the soil so that maybe the coyotes wouldn't dig him up, José drove a big stick at the head of the grave and hung the man's sombrero on it. I thought we would sing some hymns or someone would say a few words in eulogy, but they all seemed in a hurry to get as far from that place as possible. The vaqueros made the sign of the Cross and went to their horses without a word. I can't even remember that man's name that we left in the Indian Nations, but he was a good man. He had no wife or children or family that any of us knew, but he was a fair hand with a fiddle and kept us all entertained until he couldn't play anymore.

Another week went by, more rivers to swim and more places we had never seen, following the North Star. Gunn and I even got to ride scout ahead of the herd a couple of times and helped drive off the buffalo in our way.

We had it good, for not once did we hit high water at one of those river crossings, and we had Old Speck, gentle and sure, to lead our herd across. The rest of those steers fell in right behind him, trusting because he never hesitated, and following the dull ringing of that bell on his neck.

Gunn never liked it if we hit swimming water. I'd never thought about it until the first time it happened, but sitting in the saddle on a swimming horse or floating alongside it and letting it drag you across must have been a scary proposition for a boy with one arm. He used to swim like a fish, but that was before Texas.

On the morning of our twenty-fifth day on the trail we came across a set of wagon ruts baked into the hard ground and stretching into the distance ahead of us—the first sign of civilization we had seen in a long while. Trails always lead someplace, and that trail pointed due north to Kansas. All of us felt a little better for seeing it.

Later, we learned that the wagon trace we came across was made by a freighter and half-breed trader by the name of Chisolm. And things happened that day that kept us from dwelling on stuff like that, anyway. For it wasn't another mile up when we found Papa walking down the middle of those ruts with his saddle on his shoulder.

He had a bullet wound high on his chest that he had stuffed closed with a piece of his shirt, and the last two fingers on his left hand were gone, either torn away by another bullet or cut free with an arrowhead. He was so thirsty that he wouldn't put down the canteen that José offered him until he had drank most of it and poured the rest over his head.

"Where's Shiloh at?" I asked when I thought he looked like he was ready to talk.

"Gone."

That was all he said; nothing more, at least to me, about where he had been and what he had done. I knew not to ask again, for there were some things Papa wouldn't talk about. I guess he thought I wouldn't understand.

Chapter Twenty

That Joseph McCoy might have been a Blue Bastard Yankee, but he knew how to put a town on the map. He sent riders down into the Indian Nations to tell any herds they might meet about the new shipping point in Abilene and all the cattle buyers he had there waiting. I heard later that he went so far as hiring Texas cowboys to rope some buffalo for him, and he shipped those animals to Kansas City and Chicago to promote his business venture.

We were the second herd to arrive on the outskirts of the little town. Another herd bound for California had detoured there once they got word of the new market. It wasn't much of a town yet, and the pale oak planks of the new stock-yards they had built were the most noticeable thing, except for the three-story hotel McCoy had finished only weeks before.

Abilene means "city of the plains" if you read the Bible, and that part was true. Most of the few buildings were simple log cabins set along the banks of Mud Creek. I heard that stream used to be named after one of the town's early comers, but those abolitionists renamed it when that fellow joined the Confederacy at the start of the war.

We held our herd on grass as high as a horse's belly while Papa rode into town to see if there were really cattle buyers willing to spend Yankee gold on Texas steers. One thing Kansas had plenty of was grass. Grass like you've never seen.

Two men smoking big cigars and driving a new buggy soon came back with Papa and bought the entire herd for thirty-eight dollars a head. It all seemed too good to be true.

Being the promoter he was, that Joseph McCoy himself paid us a visit and talked Papa into cutting off a little bunch of steers and driving them right through town. Seems like McCoy had several newspapermen in town and wanted to show out for them and the local merchants.

We boys and half the crew got to go, and you would have thought we were riding in a parade, no matter that our clothes were about worn to rags and we looked like something the cat drug in. Gunn, he took the point on that little bunch of steers without asking or anybody telling him he could. He stared straight ahead, and with his empty shirtsleeve pinned up and the floppy brim of his oversized sombrero bobbing with each stride of his horse, he looked like some kind of raggedy boy revolutionary or bandito. People stared and a few of them were so rude as to point at him. I guess we were the first Texas men some of those Jayhawkers ever saw. Then again, my brother Gunn was one of a kind.

Even more of the crowd were impressed with Joseph, maybe because Gunn and I were at least three-quarters grown, while the sight of a half-pint kid sitting on a Texas bronc with his little legs barely long enough to hang below the saddle skirts and packing a fifty-foot rope in his hands like he was born with it was quite a novelty.

After we were through with our Wild West show, Papa let us boys and the other half of the crew see the sights in town while the rest of the men stayed with the herd and waited their turn. Some of the men got pretty drunk and lost most of their pay that first time in town. There weren't all the saloons that were there later, for it wasn't yet the trail town Helldorado it was to become. But there were still enough saloons and gaudy houses, and cardsharps and pimps who had gotten the word that dumb cowboys were about to hit the town in droves, to get a man in trouble.

Joseph and I made a round of the town and ended up buying a sackful of licorice and going down to the train tracks and laying stuff on the rails for the train wheels to crush. Gunn joined us later, and I smelled liquor on his breath. He staggered and tripped and ended up sitting on the train tracks.

"You're going to get squashed if a train comes along," Joseph said.

"I don't care," Gunn slurred. "Did you know they've got public girls in this town? Keep 'em in a tent."

Joseph looked at me.

"Gaudy girls, you fools," Gunn repeated.

"You wouldn't know what to do with a gaudy girl," I said.

"Well, let's go have a look, if you aren't too scared."

"You're too drunk to go anywhere."

"I only had three drinks. They said that much wouldn't hurt me. Said I ought to ease into it and practice up."

"Who said? Does Papa know you were in a saloon?"

"Wasn't in a saloon." Gunn's words were so slurred I could barely understand him. "They kicked me out, but Marco brought me a bottle out back. Said anyone that came up the trail was man enough to have a drink or two."

"Papa will have Marco's hide if he finds out. Marco isn't one of Papa's favorites anyway."

"I won't tell. Marco's nice to me."

"You ought not drink that stuff."

Gunn pulled a pint bottle about three-quarters full from

inside his shirt. He tugged the stopper with his teeth and spat it out. He took a quick pull at the liquor and grimaced and stuck the bottle out toward me. "Have a drink?"

"You don't have the sense God gave a goose. Don't you ever do what you're supposed to?"

"I tried that and it hurt. Have a drink."

"No."

"Chicken."

"You think I'm stupid enough to drink that stuff because you dare me?"

"Sissy. I double dare you."

I took the bottle from him and turned it up. For the life of me, I couldn't figure out why anyone would want to drink that stuff. The smell of that whiskey was enough to make you shiver. It was all I could do to keep from gagging, and it made my eyes water.

"That ain't how you do it. Watch." He took a pull again.

I counted two gulps and took three gulps myself. "Nothing to it," I said after I finished coughing. "Where did Joseph go?"

"Beats me."

We passed the bottle back and forth between us, glancing around from time to time to make sure nobody was watching us. The sun was down by the time we had almost finished the whiskey.

"Marco and some of the men told me that there's a girl they call Train Horn Sal. For a dollar she'll spread her legs for you, and for four bits she'll suck your goober," Gunn said.

"You're making that up." I couldn't help it that I giggled.

"That's what he said. How much money have you got left?"

I fumbled some coins out of my vest pocket but spilled

them and couldn't find them all in the dark. "Papa gave me five dollars, but I spent some of it on candy."

"Five dollars? That's what he gave me, but he paid the rest of the crew fifty dollars apiece."

"Yeah, but they hired on. We're just family."

"There's no way I ain't worth as much as a Mexican."

"What makes you think you're better? If it wasn't for those Mexicans we couldn't have got the herd here."

"Aw, I don't have anything against them, but they ain't like us."

"No, they aren't like us, but did Juanita or José ever hold that against you?"

"Papa said the Mexicans had Texas for two hundred years and didn't do a thing with it."

"Papa would have them picking cotton for him if we still grew cotton."

Gunn snickered. "Papa would have us picking cotton if he still grew cotton."

"I think I have three dollars left."

"Let's go find that train horn girl. Marco said she'll toot your horn until you can't take any more and teach you things they never taught you in school."

"I don't know . . ."

"Chicken. We could at least go peep inside that tent. Have us some fun. I bet she'll let you stick your finger in her belly button for cheap." Gunn made an attempt to get up, but fell back down on the seat of his pants.

"What happened to the moon?" I asked, lying down.

"What moon?"

"It was there a bit ago. Half a moon, for sure. Right up there."

"I can't see nothing."

"Me neither." I giggled again.

"What about that lantern light on the depot house? Can you see that?"

"I see two of them."

"I don't see but one." Gunn laughed like that was the funniest thing ever.

"I think I'm going to be sick. I . . ." My lunch spilled out of my mouth before I knew it, and I rolled over and retched some more. I was still dry heaving later when I thought Gunn was asleep.

"Hamish?"

"What?"

"Do you think any girl would look at me twice? I saw a farmer girl at the store, and she whispered something and pointed at me and her mama made her hush."

"I don't know. You're awful ugly."

"I'm talking about my arm."

"I don't think a girl would care about that."

"Those damned Kiowa."

I was too sick to think straight, much less answer him.

"Hamish?" he asked later.

"Leave me alone."

"Did you ever notice how pretty Juanita's skin is?"

I was seeing three lantern lights down at the depot house by then.

"You boys get up before a train runs over you," Papa's voice boomed out of the dark.

"Papa, you're going to pay me fifty dollars like the rest of the men," Gunn said.

Something grabbed me by the shirt collar and jerked me to my feet. Gunn was beside me, and we leaned on each other to stay upright.

"Who gave you the whiskey?" Papa asked and gave us a shake.

"I stole it," Gunn said. "Took my pistol and held up the saloon."

Papa kicked Gunn in the seat of the pants and sent him sprawling. "I ought to tan both of you. Get on now. We've got to load those steers at daylight."

"I'm sorry, Papa," I said.

Papa shoved us ahead of him. I don't remember how we got to where we had left our horses, or who saddled them.

"I don't think I can ride," I said.

"You'll ride," Papa said.

"Yeah, you're a Dollarhyde," Gunn snickered.

I heard Papa cuff him upside the head, and then we had to wait for Gunn to puke some before we could ride out of town.

"I don't care if I ever see that old town again," Gunn said, groaning like he was in agony.

Papa laughed. "What, and miss Train Horn Sal?"

Chapter Twenty-one

We cut out the first batch of steers the next morning and drove them over to the stockyards. They had a train of stock cars pulled off on a siding, and we helped load them out, twenty steers to a car. You'll hear some people refer to cowboys as cowpunchers, but nobody did back in the day. It's a dude term that nobody on the range ever used. Some city joker must have seen men urging and poking cattle through the chutes with a prod at some stockyards or load-out ramp, and coined the term.

Fact is, I never heard anybody use the word "cowboy" until later. If any dude had dared call one of my papa's men a boy he might have gotten a dose of lead poisoning or seen the business end of a knife. If it weren't for my brothers and me that year, there wouldn't have been any boys on a cattle drive. Trail driving might have been a business for young men, but the key word is "men." Down Texas way, we called ourselves "hands," or some down south even referred to themselves as "vaqueros," not differentiating between themselves and their Mexican counterparts in the trade. But I guess everything has to have a name, and somewhere along the way, the name "cowboy" stuck.

We turned the rest of the herd that was still out on grass over to the buyers' men, and our whole crew headed for town again en masse. That poor town never knew what hit it. Our Mexican vaqueros had been pretty reserved their first outing in town when they went in shifts, but with all of them together to egg one another on and the camaraderie of the other trail crew in town, it didn't take long for things to get a little rowdy. Abilene didn't even have a town marshal, as if those Kansas yokels didn't have a clue how much pent-up need to celebrate was packed in a man who had been weeks or months on the trail.

Some of the other trail crew's men decided to make a run on their horses through town, popping their pistols and yelling like wild Indians. Most of the good people of Abilene decided it was a good time to retreat indoors and fuss between themselves about the uncivilized nature of Texas cowboys. It wouldn't have mattered if I told them we Dollarhydes were from Alabama, for to them, we were still unreconstructed rebels, and Papa never hid it that he wore the gray during the war. And despite the abolitionist tendencies of those Jayhawkers, most of them turned their noses up at our Mexican vaqueros and thought of them even worse than they did us. Hypocrites, if you ask me.

The trail drivers pretty much had their way with the town, even though they didn't harm anyone or tear up anything . . . much. Papa and the other trail boss eventually gathered them up and calmed them down, and for the rest of our stay they behaved pretty decent.

Papa paid for new clothes for all three of us boys, and brand-new hats and boots. We went over to the cabin that some Irish woman had set up as a bathhouse and then paid a visit to the local barber before we put on our new duds. Other than a bath in the river, it was the first time I'd been close to clean since we left Texas. As soon as we walked out of the barbershop we all had a good laugh at one another. The sides of our heads were peeled so short that it looked like somebody had whitewashed them. That barber wasn't much at his trade, if you ask me, and I don't think he left any of us more than three hairs on the top of our heads—sheared us like sheep.

There was a man in town that would take your picture for two dollars, and Papa marched us down to the hotel. The photographer was a portly man with round spectacles perched on his nose and a grizzled goatee. He was also a man who took his business very seriously, no matter that he operated from town to town out of the back of a dilapidated buggy pulled by a one-eyed mule, and no matter that his studio was nothing more than an imitation Persian rug hung across one wall of his hotel room.

"You will not have your photograph taken, Herr Dollarhyde?" the photographer asked in a thick Swedish accent.

Papa was usually a friendly man, but he looked at the Swede with obvious contempt. "I hear you took pictures during the war."

"*Ja*, I did. And I sold them to Brady. Maybe you see some of them? Have you been to New York?"

"I saw some of them."

The Swede must have noticed Papa's scowl, and he pointed at Papa's rebel cavalry hat. "I see that you were in the war."

"I was."

"Will you go over there with your younglings and let me make your photograph?"

"You just make a picture of the boys."

"Maybe you think I wear the blue? No? I assure you that I only took photographs. I don't shoot at nobody. Never fought you Johnny Rebels."

"You photographed the bodies, didn't you? Drove around

the battlefields after the fighting was over and took pictures, even though the dead couldn't give you their leave."

"It was a noble undertaking, Herr Dollarhyde. History. Such a struggle should not be forgotten, no matter which side you were on."

"To hell it shouldn't. Take the boys' picture."

The photographer squinted over his glasses at Papa and then quickly went about his business. He studied me before he dug in a trunk of props and produced a fringed buckskin hunting coat of the kind that some of the Indians wore. "I think this will fit you. You are a tall boy."

"You want me to wear that?"

"*Ja*, you are a man of the West, no? This make you look tough and all the *unger damer* will swoon when they see you in this." The Swede looked over his shoulder and winked at Papa.

"All the damn what?" Gunn asked.

"The young ladies."

"I'm not wearing that silly thing," I said, and saw Papa nod his approval from the other side of the room.

"Give it to me," Gunn said. "I'll wear it."

The Swede sat me in a chair with Gunn and Joseph posed slightly behind and to either side of me. I took my hat off and tried to finger comb my hair, but the Swede complained, so that I put it back on.

"No, no, you keep the hat. And this is for the little guy." The Swede had Joseph hold a rusty old musket by the barrel in front of him, butt plate resting on the floor. Joseph looked askance at it, but kept it. We might have been boys, but none of us would have been caught dead owning such an antique piece of junk.

Gunn dug in the trunk on his own and without asking the Swede. He came out with a silk sash and pair of white, beaded buckskin gauntlets with fringe down the cuffs. He quickly wrapped the sash around his waist and stuffed his Dance pistol in it, along with one of the gloves. He put the other glove on his hand and rested it on the back of my chair.

"Good. You look dangerous and romantic," the Swede said.

"You look silly," I said.

Joseph giggled and Gunn elbowed me in the shoulder.

The Swede ducked under his camera hood until he was satisfied we were in focus. "You younglings will have to be very still."

As soon as he was done tinkering with the window curtains to let enough light in the room, he went into the closet and came out with a wooden tray containing the film plate and slid it into the camera. He stood beside the camera and smiled at us with his hand on the cap of the brass-tubed lens.

"This picture will be no goot if vee don't hold the still." He removed the lens cap with a flourish and began to count off seconds out loud. "*En, två, tre, fyra, fem . . .*"

I caught myself holding my breath and my eyes began to water from fear of blinking.

"You can breathe, youngling," the Swede said. "But be still. *Sex, sju, åtta, nio, tio . . .*"

After what seemed like an eternity, he placed the cap back on the lens. "There, vee are done."

I heard Joseph suck in a big breath as I did.

"Let me see it," Gunn said.

"It will take a moment." The Swede took his film box back into the closet and wasn't in there very long. He came back out holding the little tin plate gingerly. "Be careful not to touch the photograph. It will smudge and scratch very easily until I put the varnish on."

We had a big laugh looking at the photo, and Papa came

over and joined in. Joseph and I looked like we were scared to death, or so somber as to be at a funeral. But it was Gunn's image that was the funniest. Not only did he have his Great White Scout outfit on, but for some reason, his chin was tilted up like he really thought he was somebody.

"Where did you come up with that pose?" Papa asked. "I never knew you were such a dandy."

Gunn growled something under his breath and stomped out of the room.

"You come back in an hour and I will have your photograph ready for you," the Swede said and winked at me. "Then you can show it to your sweetheart, no?"

Papa stepped between us and gave the man his pay. I wanted to stay and learn more about how the Swede developed his photographs. The smell of chemicals and all the labeled bottles and gadgets intrigued me.

But Papa guided us out of the hotel before I could ask any questions. Joseph ran into Gunn's back on the boardwalk.

"Watch out, Peckerhead," Gunn said.

I thought Papa would scold him, but Papa's attention was elsewhere. A man in a fancy suit was coming down the boardwalk to us with a frown on his face, and the county sheriff was with him. It was plain to see that some kind of trouble was brewing and Papa was at the center of it.

Chapter Twenty-two

"**M**r. Dollarhyde, I would like to speak with you," the man in the suit said.

"You're speaking to me."

"There's no call to act unfriendly," the sheriff said.

I could see that lawman was paying special attention to Papa's rebel hat. He seemed pretty proud of his badge, although I wondered where he had been an hour or two earlier when Papa's men were running wild.

"Excuse me. Please allow me to introduce myself." The man in the suit was even taller than Papa, slender and narrow in the shoulder, and with the look of a banker or bookkeeper about him. He held out his hand to Papa. "I'm Clayton Lowe."

Papa shook his hand. "Pleased to meet you. What can I do for you?"

That made the Clayton fellow stammer a little bit. "I was hoping we could discuss the cattle you drove here."

"What for?"

Clayton and the sheriff passed a look between them

before Clayton continued, "Are you a Southern man, Mr. Dollarhyde?"

"You know good and well that I am. What business of yours is that, anyway?"

Clayton held up his hands, palms outward. "No offense intended. It's just that I happened to be of the opposite persuasion doing the War of the Rebellion."

Papa stood up a little straighter. "I say we let bygones be bygones, unless you are looking for trouble."

"Not at all. I was going to explain that due to some difficulties I experienced during the onset of the war, I was forced to leave my home in Cooke County, Texas."

"The rebels down there hung forty Union Leaguers," the sheriff said.

"And what side were you on?" Papa asked the sheriff.

The sheriff stood a little straighter, exactly like Papa had earlier, although Papa was a tall man and the top of the lawman's head barely cleared Papa's chin.

"Ninth Minnesota Volunteer Infantry," the sheriff said.

"I remember you boys at Brice's Cross Roads," Papa said.

The sheriff's mouth went tight. "And were you at Fort Pillow, too?"

"I was."

"They gave us badges to commemorate those poor black soldiers you massacred."

"That's a damned lie, but we picked up a few of those badges you Yankees dropped when we chased you back to Memphis."

I thought that sheriff was going to grab his pistol, and townspeople that had overheard Papa's words in passing stopped and gave him hard looks. Kansas was no place for a rebel.

Clayton Lowe stepped between Papa and the sheriff. "I didn't wish to rehash sore spots from the war."

"Then what do you want?" Papa asked.

"As I said before, due to hard feelings in Texas toward those of us with Federal sympathies, I was forced to retire to Kansas for the duration of the war. And as it was, I was also forced to leave many of my holdings behind."

"And?"

"I understand it that you have settled in what was once Clay County, and that you gathered and drove your herd from there?"

"You are correct."

Clayton looked uneasier, if possible, than he had when he first approached us. "Please don't take this wrong, but might I ask to see your tally book to check what steers carrying my brand I might be owed compensation for?"

"Are you calling me a thief?"

"No, not at all. Sometimes when gathering range cattle, it is easier to gather everything and settle with the rightful owners later for any of their cattle you may have gathered. Minus your expenses and profit, of course. I would say that any steers of mine that you may have sold were worth ten dollars in Texas. That still leaves you a handsome profit."

"Those were maverick steers."

"Yes, but you must understand the difficulties that the war presented. We men of Montague and Cooke Counties had long run our herds where you have settled, but were forced to abandon our seed cattle due to difficulties such as my own, or because of the Comanche raids. The stock you gathered must, in part, stem from my efforts and considerable investments."

From his vest pocket Papa pulled the tally book in which he kept our herd count. He did it so fast that the sheriff took a quick step backward. Papa held the tally book in front of

Clayton's face. "I left Texas with over two thousand steers. Every one of them was at least five years old and they wear no brand but my own," he said.

"Yes, but you must understand that . . ."

"You show me one of those steers wearing your brand and I'll pay you the going market rate for them."

"It's a matter of principle, sir. You are taking advantage of the efforts and misfortune of others. I know for a fact that several Confederate widows have interests in the range cattle in your area. You wouldn't rob from the mouths of widows, would you?" Clayton turned and played to the crowd.

A group of Papa's vaqueros passed by and heard the commotion. They formed a half ring outside of us.

Papa took a deep breath. "Mr. . . ."

"Lowe," Clayton said.

"Mr. Lowe, if you mention me robbing or stealing one more time, I shall take great offense. So much so that I would suggest you arm yourself," Papa said. "When I came to my home in Texas I saw no Confederate widows or Union Leaguer ranchers. All I found was wild cattle without brands, and nobody to claim them but the Indians, which I've fought to get these cattle to market. When you speak for others, I think you are speaking for yourself and hoping to play me for a fool."

"So, you won't listen to reason?"

"You want cattle, Mr. Lowe, you by God come to Texas and get them."

Clayton jerked down on both of his coat lapels to straighten them. "Rest assured, Mr. Dollarhyde, I will not be bullied and I will use the full recourse of the law. You haven't heard the last of this matter."

* * *

Papa opened an account in a Kansas City bank and deposited a draft for forty thousand dollars there. The other forty thousand left over he took in coin, and after we loaded out with supplies at the Frontier Store, he put that coin under the wagon seat in a strongbox. I drove the wagon, sitting above that fortune all the way back to Texas, with a span of six mules in front of me, and Speck, our oxen and lead steer, tied to the wagon bed.

"Papa, I want to go to school," I said our first day on the trail south.

"You've been to school." Papa kept his eyes straight ahead.

"I mean I want to go to college. Mama and I talked about it some before . . ."

"Son, that may seem like a lot of money there beneath you, but there's a thousand things we need to spend it on if we're to keep at this business."

"You aim to do this again?"

"Next year we will take two herds up the trail, if not more, and I'm going to need your help."

I started to tell Papa that he had plenty of help, but bit my tongue. "What about the next year? Could I go to college then, once we finish the drives?"

"You want to leave me and your brother? Gunn relies on you. You steady him some."

"Papa, there are all kinds of things I don't know, things I want to see and do."

"Son, I like stories and history as much as you do, but for the life of me, I can't see how you could live with your nose poked in a book."

"Look at those rain clouds building. Wouldn't you like to know what makes it rain? What are those clouds made of ?"

Papa shook his head. "Wouldn't help me a lick. Seeing them is enough to tell me I ought to put my oilcloth on or look for high ground to make camp. It's still going to rain, whether I know why or not."

"I want to be . . . something else. I don't know what it is yet, but something."

Those pale blue eyes of Papa's searched me for whatever failing he could find. "Maybe next year. We'll see."

At least I had some new books. Papa met an immigrant headed west on the Smoky Hill Trail and needing to lighten his load. He bought me the naturalist Thomas Nuttall's *Genera of North American Plants* and a well-worn copy of Plutarch's *Lives of the Noble Grecians and Romans*. The plant taxonomy book intrigued me greatly, and I could read aloud Plutarch's stories of Alexander the Great and other famous ancient rulers to the men around the campfire. They were always high on stories with swords and bold deeds. Many a time I've heard cowboys and vaqueros who couldn't sign their own name argue for days about some story I had read them, debating the decisions and actions of a ruler born thousand of years before.

"Papa?" I asked a little farther down the trail.

"What?"

"Do you think that man back in Abilene, that Lowe fellow, will cause us trouble?"

Papa scoffed. "No, son, he struck me as the kind that's all talk. Forget about him."

It wasn't the first time that I didn't agree with Papa.

Chapter Twenty-three

1869

Papa said that if the army would show up and kill all the Indians that the country would fill up with people in a hurry. The 6th U.S. Cavalry moved onto the site of the abandoned Butterfield stage station at Buffalo Springs fifteen miles south of us, and a few rawhide settlers started a little settlement around the temporary post. We all waited to see if the soldiers could catch any Indians, much less outfight them. They didn't have much luck.

Papa and José loaded a packhorse in late winter and left to go buy cattle in South Texas. When Papa returned in early summer, he had purchased two mixed herds of cows and calves, and paid trail crews to deliver them to us. He also purchased seven hundred Mexican steers, taking delivery of them at Laredo on the Texas side of the Rio Grande and hiring another trail crew to drive them to Kansas.

He paid nine dollars a head for those wet steers, and minus a dollar a day average in expenses for the trail crew and the fluctuations of the market, we stood to make a good profit. Papa drilled the importance of our financial ledgers into us, and said that any business idea that couldn't prove out on paper wasn't worth tackling. Gunn acted like he listened but never really paid any attention to the numbers. That left me to keep Papa's books.

Gambling with the last dollar we made to make the next, that was how things went. Indians stealing our stock. Ledger books and dollar columns. Drought and rain. High prices and low. Profits and expenses on the hoof. Hurt cowboys and lame horses. But those aren't what I remembered most about that year.

When Papa came back to the ranch he was alone. At first, we thought he had left José with one of the trail crews, but that wasn't the case at all. José drowned while swimming a flooded creek to cross a herd somewhere in that way down part of Texas. Juanita wore a black dress for weeks.

I guess her mourning makes what I did all the more shameful, but it's no wonder that I thought about her so much. I was sixteen, without a girl near my age anywhere around. There were times when I lay awake at night, thinking of her, even when José was still alive. In the hot time of the year the sweat would stick her dress to her and you couldn't help but notice. And then I saw her one day, wading in the river with her skirt gathered up about her knees. Legs so long and smooth and brown, and making you wonder about that dress lifting higher.

I was doing my best to draw a picture of a little yellow bird—*Spinus tristis,* a goldfinch, I believed—perched on a mesquite limb, but the wind was blowing my last sheet of paper all over the place, and I was almost too tired to hold my charcoal pencil, anyway. Papa was working us from sunup to sundown, and every muscle in my body was sore. Besides, I had little knack for art and was never going to be the next Audubon. But the thought that I might sketch what I saw, along with my observations, and send them back East for publishing like Audubon or Nuttall excited me immensely. I never told anyone about my plans to become a famous naturalist.

The brush grew thick to either side of the pathway leading down to the river, and Juanita walked right past me without seeing me. She had a laundry basket under one arm. Without being quite sure of my intentions, I kept to cover and paralleled her course.

Maybe it was only the devious curiosity of a growing boy or a weakness for temptation on my part. She was pretty and she was young—not much older than myself. Nineteen, maybe, but it was hard to tell and she never said. There were times when she flashed a smile at me and I felt my face and neck flushing with embarrassment.

It was an exceptionally hot morning, even though the sun was barely on the rise. The gnats and flies flittered and swarmed over the river in a cloud, and a big blue heron stretched its neck and flew farther down the river. The Little Wichita was spotty at best, dry for great stretches in the wrong times of the year, and we used a particularly large pothole at the foot of the pathway for gathering drinking water, doing our laundry, and watering the stock. But Juanita didn't stop there. She turned upriver and went out of sight.

I cast a look behind me to see if anyone else was coming along, but nobody was stirring among the jacales, except for Mama's white chickens scratching and clucking beneath the tree limb they had roosted in. Papa was a hard driver, but it was his habit to give his men Sundays off. Nothing but the saddle horses lifting their heads and flaring their nostrils above the pole corral saw Juanita and me slip down to the river.

There was another, smaller pothole up the river where the water ran clearer. By the time I reached a vantage point on the high bank above it, Juanita had already removed her blouse and was standing knee-deep where the water spilled lazily over a rocky shoal at the head of the pothole, with her skirt tucked into her belt to shorten it. Her black hair was already wet and she was working soap into it.

I stirred uncomfortably in the brush and accidentally crunched the gravel under my feet. She never heard me, and continued her bath, wading in a little deeper downstream and dunking her head underwater to rinse it, bent at the waist and the vertebrae in her backbone showing through the tight crease of her back.

I watched the swing of her hair and then how it draped across her chest, down to those swaying breasts, so large above her tiny waist, and the brown nipples turned slightly outward and hard and risen. I tugged at my pants and fought the urge to take hold of myself.

I thought of the story Gunn told me of the whore in Abilene who would suck you for fifty cents. As preposterous and unrealistic as the thought of any woman being willing to do such a thing was, I immediately imagined Juanita doing that to me. And she didn't do it because I paid her. She did it because she wanted to, without me asking.

I squinted my eyes tightly to shake away the vision, and lurched to my feet. The first thing that I saw was Gunn's face across the river. I don't think he saw me. He had climbed a blackjack tree and was perched in a fork, staring intently at Juanita—no easy task for someone with one arm, but Gunn could always climb like a monkey.

For some reason, the sight of Gunn shamed me and it also made me mad at him. Jealous, I guess. I quickly started back to the house, but froze when I had taken no more than a step or two. Somebody else was coming down the riverbank on my side.

It was Papa. He had his pistol belt hung over one shoulder and a smile on his face. I couldn't move without him hearing or seeing me, so I hunkered down again and watched.

I thought Juanita would shout to him in modest warning or shriek at the sight of him. But she didn't. Instead, her smile matched his and she went to the creek bank to meet him. He kissed her and sat down and let her pull his boots off and then his shirt. When one of her breasts brushed his face he kissed it, too, and then she stepped back from him, still facing him, and unbuckled her belt and let her skirt fall to the ground.

I glanced across the river before I fled, and Gunn was gone from his tree. I plunged through the brush blindly and only stopped once I reached open ground not far from the house. Gunn showed up and he was wet to the waist from wading the river.

Neither of us said anything about what we saw. Not to each other and not to Papa.

There was no conspiracy on our part, or at least Gunn and I never planned it or discussed it. Through our own individual efforts we went about the business of making sure Papa didn't get any time alone with Juanita after that. Call it silly if you want to. If Papa left where we were working the range, one of us slipped off with him. If one of us saw those two wander off in the same direction, we went, too.

On several occasions, Papa asked why we were so quiet around him, but we mumbled some excuse and found a reason to be elsewhere. That lasted about a month until we took delivery of the first cow herd up from the south. As soon as that herd was scattered where Papa wanted them and the trail crew paid off and sent back where they came from, I woke in my bedroll that night and noticed Papa was gone. It was still an hour before daylight and we were all going to ride into the headquarters at the same time that next morning. Gunn woke when I went to saddle my horse, and so did the others.

"Where's Papa?" I asked one of the men.

He rubbed his eyes and squinted at the stars overhead. "I don't know. Last night he said maybe he would ride in early. Something about his leg aching and he had left his liniment at the house."

Gunn and his damned Kiowa roan were hard to keep up with, but I hung with him and we quickly covered the ten miles to home. Papa wasn't at the house, but we ground-tied our horses in front of it so that he would know we were there if he saw them. I imagined the frown on his face when he realized his plans were foiled.

Gunn went to check on Juanita's jacal while I prepared to cook us steaks on the fire pit in front of the house. I barely had a fire built when he came back.

"She's gone."

"She'll be around here somewhere," I said.

I left our steaks uncooked and we slipped through the morning light, walking amongst the jacales and then checking the barn. We were on our way back from checking the river when we heard the sounds coming from inside the dugout. That dugout—where else?

We climbed the hill and approached it from above, standing at the edge of the roof. Inside, Papa grunted like an old bull and Juanita moaned.

"This is the third time I've hated him." Gunn didn't whisper. "I don't give a damn if he hears me."

Papa grunted and Juanita panted things to him in Spanish, while Gunn and I stood on the roof and watched the sun coming up.

"We should have torn it down a long time ago." Gunn stomped the roof. "It would serve him right if we caved it in on top of him this instant."

"I'm leaving. Maybe not right now, but the first chance I get."

Gunn nodded. "Figured as much."

"What about you? Why don't you come with me?"

"No, I belong here."

I waved my hand before us, motioning at the "out there"—places I saw as more of the same, but that made Gunn want to saddle a horse and go see them. "There? What's out there? You go find you a mountain or the tallest bluff you can climb and jump off it. Nobody would ever know. Nobody would even hear you hit the ground."

"I like that."

"Not me. Are you going to stay with him? Texas is big enough that you don't have to put up with him."

"He couldn't make me leave."

"He's spitting on Mama."

"He won't let you leave. Why do you think he didn't let you go off to college? He might as well put his brand on us like he does those longhorns."

"He can't stop me."

"What'll you do for money? You've told me yourself what college costs."

"I'll find a way."

"You're as stubborn as I am."

"He's making me that way."

We hadn't noticed that the dugout was quiet. Papa lurched out the door, tucking his shirt in and twisting around to see us on the roof.

"You boys come down here," he said.

We did as we were told, although we took our time about it. Joseph and the rest of the crew were riding in, and Papa made us stay there until he could wave Joseph over. Juanita came from the dugout, looking down at the ground and patting at her hair and straightening her dress.

Papa put his arm around her waist. "I never thought I raised such a bunch of sneaks."

Gunn and I bore the brunt of his hard look.

"José is barely in the ground," Gunn said, as defiant as ever.

I couldn't tell how shocked or surprised Joseph was by being called into the middle of such a mess, for he stayed on his horse and made a show of fiddling with his saddle strings.

"Juanita and I are going to be married. Like it or not, get that through your thick heads," Papa said. "You'll get used to it in time, or you will damned sure keep your mouths shut about it. No more sneaking around or glaring at me and acting like children."

"I hate you," I said.

"Saying that to my face would have been better than what you've been doing. Think I haven't noticed? At least I could have respected you," Papa said.

"She ain't my mama," Gunn said.

"And she doesn't have to be," Papa said. "The real world doesn't always work out like you want it to. Sometimes it hurts and sometimes you can't do a thing to change it. You're not little boys. Act like it."

I was having trouble breathing and couldn't say anything else.

"All right, Juanita and I are going to go tell the men. The company chaplain is riding up from Buffalo Springs next Sunday. I've invited some other people from down there and we'll kill a steer and celebrate some."

"Celebrate what?" Gunn asked.

"My wedding. And you'll smile and act like you're happy about it," Papa said.

Papa took Juanita's arm and went to meet the vaqueros. She raised her head and attempted a smile aimed at us, but didn't quite manage it. I hated her, too.

Papa didn't have any friends at Buffalo Springs. He disliked the Union cavalry stationed there and more than once he had told us how those settlers and homesteaders weren't much but a bunch of dirt-poor rawhiders and white trash, more apt to steal and butcher your beef than they were to farm or make a go of it. But that didn't matter. He wanted to show off and they were the only people around and the only way he could play the big man like he used to before Texas at those parties he held when all the planters showed up to drink his whiskey and tell him what a fine plantation he had. Now he could show his neighbors what a ranch he was building and impress them with the fact that he, a man almost forty with his hair turning gray and his belly starting to hang over his belt, could marry a pretty young thing like Juanita.

I turned to Gunn and he was already looking at me.

"I'm going," I said. "I don't know how or when, but I'm going. It might take me a while, but there are places where he doesn't matter."

Chapter Twenty-four

1871

You might think my brother was always an outlaw at heart, but it was Papa that made him so in truth, or at least gave him his start. You take a wild boy to begin with and you put him in every kind of jam imaginable, you're going to end up with a wild young man. You could say the start of it was when he brought us to Texas, or even when he took us hunting Indians when we were far too young for such. But me, I think it was that day on Holliday Creek, south of the Big Wichita. Papa and his damned ranch and his plans and schemes.

We were putting together a herd and readying for another drive north to the railroad when somebody said there were riders coming from the east. Papa acted like he was surprised when he saw who it was, but I wasn't. I hadn't forgotten Clayton Lowe, and he had struck me as the kind of man that wouldn't let a thing lie.

He was riding with three other men. One of them was a big-bearded fellow with a sour look to him, and another was that Ranger captain who cut off Gunn's arm years before. The third of the trio was a black man, sitting on a flea-bitten gray nag behind the others. All of them were armed, and what's more, all of them were wearing badges.

"Mr. Dollarhyde," Clayton said when he rode up to where we stood, dismounted and resting our horses.

He looked the same as I remembered him—ten-dollar suit and a neatly shaped, short-brimmed hat on his head. He was riding a high-stepping black, gaited mare, and you didn't see many gaited horses around in those days, at least not out West. It was a fancy horse for a fancy man in a banker's hat.

"You're a long way from Kansas, Lowe," Papa said, and then turned his attention to the Ranger. "Hello, Captain Pike. How are things with the Rangers?"

"There ain't Rangers anymore. You know that. Hasn't been since after the war." Pike pulled his makings out and began to build a cigarette.

Clayton Lowe tapped the badge on the breast of his coat. "State Police, Mr. Dollarhyde."

The State Police and Governor Davis were the talk of Texas, even though we didn't hear much news out in the boondocks. A lot of Texans said Davis got mad when the Confederate government wouldn't have him and joined up with the Union and became a general. But those saying that were mostly Democrats and Southern men. When the Republicans took over after the war, Davis was elected as governor.

Things were bad in Texas then, with the Rangers disbanded and outlaws running wild, and the bad blood on the part of most of those who had been on the losing side of the war. Davis tried to get Texas broken up into several smaller states, but couldn't swing it. Next thing he did was form the State Police, and those officers declared martial law in several towns or counties and levied heavy fines and taxes, supposedly to cover the cost of the men they sent to enforce it. Democrats said the State Police were a bunch of ne'er-do-wells and former slaves out to get their revenge through extortion and high-handed ways. I don't know if the State Police did any good, but in fairness, anybody who hired black men for police officers wasn't going to be spoken of highly by men like my Papa.

"Didn't take you for a lawman," Papa said.

Clayton smiled. "Duly appointed by Governor Davis as a lieutenant for Montague County."

"You aren't in Montague County."

"My jurisdiction is anywhere in Texas."

"What brings you here, Lowe? I'm sure you didn't ride all this way to pass the time of day, and as you can see, I have work to do."

"It's your work that interests us," the bearded man said.

"If you're still claiming I stole your cattle, I assure you there is nothing here that isn't mine," Papa said.

"We'll be the judge of what you've put your brand on," the bearded man said and spurred his horse forward.

Maybe he did it on accident, or maybe he aimed his horse at Papa on purpose. No matter, he was mistaken if he thought Papa would step out of the way. Instead, Papa jerked off his hat and swatted it at the horse's nose. It shied away and the bearded man had to grab leather to keep from falling off.

A couple of Papa's vaqueros were riding in from the herd and Captain Pike was quicker to notice them than the other policemen were. "Ride easy, men."

The bearded man got his horse pulled up and tugged at the pistol on his hip.

Before Papa could go for his own gun, Gunn took two steps past him and pointed his Dance at the bearded man. He practiced with that thing as much as Papa would let him and as much as we could stand him blazing away and making a racket shooting at tin cans around the head-quarters. He was a fine shot, even though the pistol was so worn out that he had to roll the cylinder on his thigh after he cocked it and before each shot to make sure the next chamber was lined up with the barrel. I saw a little tremble in Gunn's jaw, but his gun hand was steady as a rock.

"You hold on, Moon!" Clayton shouted at the bearded man. "Listen to me!"

The bearded man let go of his gun butt. "Pa, I don't have to take that off any man."

Clayton pointed his finger at Papa. "Tell your boy to holster his gun."

Papa kept his hand on his own pistol and nodded at the bearded one, Moon. "You teach your man some manners."

"Do as he says, Mr. Dollarhyde, before we all end up in a killing," Captain Pike said—I still thought of him as a Ranger captain, although he was no such thing anymore. He seemed the calmest man on the scene and kept his voice low and fiddled with his cigarette as if nothing were happening.

The black man dressed like a farmer tried to move his horse out wide of us. He had a new Joslyn rimfire rifle across his saddle swells and two Remington pistols strapped around the middle of his overalls.

"Tell that man to stay where he is," Papa said.

"Zeke, you stop," Clayton said.

The black man pulled up. "You're the boss, but say the word and I'll bust a cap on him. Teach him some respect the only way you can with his kind."

"You mind your mouth," Papa said.

"You don't do the telling," Zeke said. His rifle, laid like it was across his saddle, was pointed right at Papa.

"Show him your badge, Zeke," Clayton said.

The black man grinned, but not funny-like, and tapped

the badge pinned to one gallus of his overalls. "Had me enough of your kind. Ain't listening to you no more. The governor done swore me in, and you've got to do what I says."

"Is that so?" Papa asked.

Zeke nodded. "State's paying me wages and mileage. Sold me a rifle gun and a good horse on credit till I can work it off."

Papa spat in the dirt, just like Gunn was apt to do. "Man through here a while back told me how your bunch operates. Bullies and thieves working for a bunch of low-down carpetbaggers."

"That's a damned lie," the bearded one called Moon said.

"Shut up, son," Clayton said to him.

Papa was still eyeing that black man. "Sold you a horse and gun on credit, huh?"

"Seventy dollars for this here horse and fifty dollars for this gun," the black man said.

"And how much for that badge you're packing?"

"Three dollars."

"Well, pat yourself on the back. Your lieutenant here sold you a ten-dollar crow bait and a rifle that cost maybe thirty. They'll probably fire you as soon as you work off your bill. Hire them some other like you so they can make some more money."

"You can't talk to me like that. I'm the law now."

"Slave, weren't you? All filled up with yourself since they gave you that badge? Going to get some evens on us white folks?"

"You keep talking. We find you with stolen cattle, we're going to hang you."

"Shut up, Zeke!" Clayton said.

"Captain Pike, I wouldn't think you would run around with such men as these," Papa said.

The former Ranger lit his cigarette and squinted through its smoke at Papa. "Man's got to work, and they're the only game in town."

"Listen, Dollarhyde. We're going to look your herd over, like it or not," Clayton said. "If everything looks on the up-and-up we'll ride out of here without another word. If we find something questionable, we'll impound your herd until the courts can work it out."

"Like hell you will," Papa said.

"Have your son put down his gun," Clayton said.

"Mr. Dollarhyde, this isn't worth the trouble you're about to cause yourself," Captain Pike said. "Let the lieutenant here look at your herd."

Papa twisted around and looked at his vaqueros sitting their horses fifty yards behind us. "Any of these men take one more step toward our herd, you shoot them down."

"Papa!" I said. I knew that there wasn't a single steer in that herd that wasn't wearing only our brand or that we didn't have a bill of sale for. It wouldn't hurt for Clayton and his men to look at them.

"Shush, Hamish. Pull your gun," Papa said and slid his own out of its holster. He held it hanging beside his leg.

"Do you understand you're resisting duly appointed officers of the law?" Clayton asked.

"This pistol doesn't give a shit who you are, nor what jackleg politician gave you the right to steal," Papa said.

Clayton was so mad he sprayed spit with the next thing he said. "You'll not take that herd north without our inspection. There are men in Jacksboro who have the same claims as I do."

"Go get them."

"I'll put the army on you. Don't think I won't."

"Don't let them buffalo you, Pa," Moon said. "I ain't scared of this man or his bunch of greasers."

"What about me?" Gunn asked, his pistol still pointing at Moon. "You scared of me?"

"How about this, Mr. Dollarhyde?" Captain Pike asked. "What say you ride into Jacksboro with us? Tell your side of things to the judge there. If it's like you say it is, you can drive your herd, no more questions asked."

"Trust to some carpetbag judge? I've heard the only way a Southerner can get justice out of the new court system is to line their pockets with a bribe," Papa said.

"You'll get a fair shake," Clayton said.

"A fair shake? Word's out on your State Police. Seems like most of your prisoners get shot trying to escape," Papa threw back at him. "Or do you call it resisting arrest?"

"You have my word," Captain Pike said. "Nobody is going to shoot you. You can even keep your guns."

Papa looked at me and I saw the gleam in his eyes like he had when he thought he had outsmarted you. "Let me think on it some."

"Make up your mind now," Clayton said.

"I need to talk to my men about it," Papa said. "They're liable to make trouble if I go off with you without explaining it."

"Zeke and Moon will go with you back to the herd," Clayton said.

"Let him talk to his men alone, Lieutenant," Captain Pike said. "We aren't in any hurry."

Clayton argued some, but finally gave in.

"What happened to your arm?" Moon asked Gunn.

"Fell asleep in a snowstorm and the wolves gnawed it off." Gunn holstered his pistol and started for his horse.

"I get my chance, I'm going to break off your other arm and feed it to you."

Gunn never gave Moon the courtesy of looking back at him. He put a toe in the stirrup and swung on his horse and followed Papa and me back to where our men waited. I twisted around in the saddle in time to see that Moon lift his rifle and almost point it at us, but Captain Pike rode up beside him and knocked it down. They were still having words when Papa gave us all our instructions.

"I'm going with them to Jacksboro," Papa said. "Hamish, you're the oldest, so you'll be in charge of the herd. Take Gunn and Joseph with you. I don't want any of you around if worse comes to worst and those carpetbaggers show up at the ranch."

"Okay, Papa," I said.

"You listen to your men. They know more about driving a trail herd than you do, no matter what you think," Papa said.

"Trail herd?"

"Yes. As soon as I'm out of sight you start this herd for Abilene. You'll have at least two days head start on anybody that comes after you. Maybe more. You push hard and when you get north of Rush Springs you hide the stock in the Cross Timbers."

"Why's he in charge?" Gunn asked.

Papa ignored him. "You lay over for a month. Drift the herd a little west and let them graze until things calm down. Come fall, you go on to market. I'll meet you in Kansas or send word if it's safe to come back here."

"What about you, Papa?" I asked. "I don't like the look of those policemen."

"You worry about this herd. Let me take care of myself," Papa said. "Can I count on you boys?"

We both nodded.

Papa rode off with those policemen, but when he did he had six vaqueros riding around him. The rest of us started the herd north that evening—a little short of a thousand head of steers, and me in charge of it.

"Don't get to thinking you're my boss," Gunn said as he passed by me.

"Do you think Papa will be all right?"

"Papa is safe. Any one of our men he took with him would bury those policemen and never tell a soul."

He was right. We had other worries besides Papa.

And I should have been worried. That judge in Jacksboro called out the 6th Cavalry from Fort Richardson and put them on our trail, and twenty or so of those Union League Texans who had moved back home from hiding out in Kansas formed a posse and joined them.

Chapter Twenty-five

"You sure this is the way you want it?" Gunn asked.

I stared at the steps leading up into the passenger car and clutched my valise in my hand. The planks on the depot porch creaked under my feet. "I told you I was leaving."

"Going to be a college man, huh?" He flipped his cigarette butt at the train in front of us.

"I'm not stealing."

Gunn eyed my valise, as if he could see right through it to the wad of money bound tightly with a piece of string and tucked neatly inside my one change of clothes.

"He won't see it that way, and he won't ever forgive you for it."

"It's what I have to do."

"How long does college take?" You would have never guessed Gunn was only seventeen. He was already taller than Papa, blond, knife-edged and lean as a whip, and always with that far-off look to him. Maybe it was that his eyes were older.

"Whenever I get my degree."

"And then what?"

I shrugged. "I'll play it by ear."

Gunn nodded at my valise. "I guess it's right that you have your share."

"I don't know that it's right, but it's what I'm doing."

"All right, but if you take that you don't have any stake in the ranch. You're selling out your interest."

"Meaning it's yours when Papa is gone?"

"That's what I mean. I'm the one staying." Gunn cleared his throat. "It's been a long summer."

"That it has."

We had spent the whole summer hiding out in the Indian Nations, not knowing if the army or some posse was going to show up at any time or be waiting ahead of us when we finally drove north. Papa wasn't in Abilene that fall when we finally straggled in with the herd, but he had a rider waiting for us there to tell us he was okay and not locked up in the Jacksboro jail. He had taken a stage down to the capital at Austin and hired him a big shot lawyer that also happened to be a prominent state senator. After that, the State Police were told to lay off us until the case was worked out in the courts.

Papa had the money to hire a good lawyer. I know, because the cattle market was booming. Gunn and I brought that herd in so fat and prime that cattle buyers fairly fought one another over them, and I sent eighteen thousand dollars to Papa's Kansas City bank account. He would have had more, but I kept twenty thousand for myself—the same twenty thousand that had Gunn eyeing my valise.

"Gunn?"

"What?"

"Being mad at the world won't do anything but cause you more problems."

"Got an answer for everything, don't you?"

"No. Wish I did."

"I ain't you, and it might be that you aren't as smart as

you think you are. Might be you with most of the problems. You're the one running."

The engineer was already stoking the firebox full of coal, and smoke was pouring from the locomotive's stack. I brushed my hand down the lapel of my frock coat, feeling a little awkward in my new suit, but proud, too.

"I don't know how you stand wearing that getup," Gunn said.

"How do I look?" I adjusted the bowler hat on my head and stared down at the black-polished shoes on my feet.

"Like you're ready for your burial or a church service, take your pick."

I unbuckled my gun belt and pulled my holstered Remington Army from under my coat. I wrapped the belt around the pistol, making a bundle, and handed it to Gunn. "You can have it. Sell it if you want to."

"That's a lot of cash you're carrying to go without a gun," he said.

"I'll make do."

"You're going to feel naked without this on your hip." He held my pistol before him and hefted it up and down, as if weighing it.

"I don't intend on wearing one of those again."

"All aboard!" the conductor shouted.

"I guess this is it," Gunn said.

"So long, brother. You take care of Joseph." I held out my hand to shake with him, but he was already walking away.

I don't know if he heard me. I took a seat next to the window and watched Abilene disappear through the glass, the coal smoke floating past the train as wispy as my dreams.

PART II
JOSEPH

Chapter Twenty-six

1874

Some folks think I'm a Dollarhyde because I took their last name. That isn't true, at least by blood, but they did adopt me and I haven't thought of myself as anything but one of them in years. You would think that people would notice that I'm six inches shorter than those long, tall devils that I grew up with. Too much short Dutchman bred in me, if you ask my brothers. Gunn was the worst to ride me, but he didn't mean anything by it. It was just his way.

Papa—I thought of him that way, even though he wasn't my real father, although I never called him anything but Mr. Dollarhyde. I don't know that he would have minded if I called him Papa, but I never tried. Mr. Dollarhyde was what everyone called him, for he was a man who required your respect. A hard man, yes, but a man that bore listening to. I didn't always understand him, but he taught me most of what I know and never treated me anything but square. Not many would have taken me in, and I don't know why he did.

Anyway, it was Papa who sent me with Gunn. Having

me with Gunn eased Papa's mind, I think. Not that Gunn was a wanted man anymore. None of us were.

The former adjutant general of the State Police thought it a good idea to run off with thirty-seven thousand dollars of the state's funds, and after that, the legislature decided it was a good idea to do away with the State Police. That meant that the little black book of wanted men they put us in for running off with that herd didn't matter anymore.

That wasn't what worried Papa. It was because Gunn had a way of finding trouble. And there was the fact that Hamish left us. He rarely showed it, but Papa thought the world of his two boys—his real sons. He kept it hid as best he could, but Hamish leaving hit him hard. He told us that Hamish was a thief who took money the ranch badly needed, but it was his heart that was hurt more than his purse. Oh, he loved a profit, but his greatest pride was in his sons and the name he gave them. Not many know that, for he was a man hard to get to know.

They were all like that—all three of them tearing each other or tearing at themselves. I remember when we lost Mrs. Dollarhyde. Not the new Mrs. Dollarhyde, but the older one the Kiowa killed. Hamish and Gunn, they never got over that. Papa, neither, although he was the kind built to carry whatever burdens life loaded him with. I wonder sometimes if they hadn't been hoping the Kiowa would kill them all when they took me with them on their vengeance trail. Such men never know a day's peace until you lay them below the ground. If it hadn't have been the loss of Mrs. Dollarhyde, it would have been something else. They always had to have a fight, whether it was something that got in their way or something they imagined got in their way. Everything on the turning of the earth is made a certain way, dobbed together like a ball of mud between your hands. That's the way they were made.

They often tease me for being so quiet, but I can't help it. It was hard to get a word in edgewise, even when I wanted to, for none of them were ever ones to hold back their opinions. There were times I wanted to tell them that they should be glad they still had each other, but I didn't. Maybe I should have spoken up a time or two, for I could have told them what it's like to lose everyone you love.

No matter, I'm a Dollarhyde now. They gave me their name, and we don't talk about what's eating us. Admitting a weakness is the same as being weak.

When I caught up to Gunn he had stopped his horse on the edge of town next to the sign. It was the same sign that had been there when the Kiowa took my first family. The same old red letters painted on the same old piece of scrap lumber: *DESTINY, TEXAS.* Only the town had changed. In place of the burned-out ruins of the old settlement there was now a scattering of log cabins, sod-bricked shacks, and a few frame houses lining a narrow, short stretch of street, with a general store and trading post at the far end. Stacks of buffalo hides taller than a man on horseback made a wall of their own on our end of the street.

"Sons a bitches," Gunn said to nobody in particular.

I didn't even know if he had heard me ride up. "Who?"

"Those damned hiders."

I had to agree with him, even if I refrained from profanity. Men had come down from the north that spring—men with wagons and a crew to skin and one to shoot. Buffalo runners, some of them called themselves. We called them hiders.

Buffalo hides were bringing three dollars apiece, and the slaughter was on. You would come across a place where some shooter had made his stand with a big bore single-shot rifle propped on a set of shooting sticks and a sack of hand-loaded cartridges laid beside him. Everywhere you went, dead buffalo. Little bunches, big bunches, carcasses everywhere, the bubbly white fat of them where their hides were peeled away standing out on the prairie like bloody mounds of snow in the brown grass. I've never seen anything as indignant or as sad as what they did to those animals left to rot under the sun. The blowflies were so bad along the river that year that you had to strain your coffee before you could drink it, and you could smell the kill sites from a quarter a mile away, or farther when the wind was right. The lobo wolves and coyotes were thicker than I ever saw them, feasting and gorging themselves on scavenged meals.

"Damn shame the Indians don't wipe them out," Gunn said.

I knew he didn't mean the buffalo. "They've tried, but it's a losing battle."

That very summer, a mixed band of Comanche and Kiowa had cornered twenty-eight buffalo hunters up in the Panhandle. Adobe Walls they called it, but it was nothing more than a couple of hide town trading posts, with a sod saloon and a few outbuildings. More in the name than there was in the place. They say there was anywhere from three hundred to a thousand of those mad Indians, but they weren't any match for marksmen holed up with good guns—repeating Henrys, Spencers, and Winchesters for close work, and Sharps and Remington big bores that could knock over a bull buffalo at better than a quarter a mile away.

Some Comanche medicine man convinced those Indians that he could make them bulletproof, but a man by the name of Billy Dixon took aim with his bull-barreled Sharps at one of them over a mile away and tipped him over with his first shot. It was undoubtedly a lucky piece of shooting, but it was big medicine and enough to make those Indians decide to fight another day.

Other than killing a hunter or two here and there or raiding some supply train or lonely outpost, the southern plains tribes couldn't do much to slow the slaughter of their livelihood. The Kiowa were mostly held in a reservation in the Indian Nations, ever since General Sherman arrested some of their big chiefs and sent them off to prison. Only a few scattered, mixed bands of Comanche, Kiowa, and Southern Cheyenne made up the hostiles that wouldn't submit to the army and the reservation system.

You still had to keep your eye out for raiding parties, but it wasn't anything like when we first came west. Other than a few cattle run off from the ranch and one of our hands running his horse to death fleeing from a hunting party he ran across, we hadn't had much trouble out of the Indians in the last year. With the army hot after them, most of the tribes were hanging close to the edge of the river breaks and canyon country up in the Panhandle or farther west in the dry country.

I still couldn't sleep well at night, especially when the moon was full and the Indians were bound to be raiding. He might have joshed me some, but Gunn never told anyone how I used to crawl under my bed in our jacal and pull the covers over my head. Maybe it was because we all had nightmares those first few years on the ranch and were prone to call out in our sleep.

"Shit," Gunn said. "I wish there was someplace else to have a drink."

"We could ride to Buffalo Springs or down to Jacksboro."

"I'd die of thirst before then."

Gunn kicked his horse up and I followed him. There were several freight wagons along the street and men loading out hides or unloading powder, lead, and other supplies freighted in from the East. Many of them stopped their work to stare at us, recognizing the brands on our horses. None of the looks they gave us were anything close to friendly.

Months before, Papa had found one of our steers shot dead and he blamed it on some vagrant buffalo hunter, whether that was true or not. And then a prairie fire burned over a third of our range. Papa blamed that, too, on some hunter careless with his campfire. After that, he gave all his riders instructions to run off any hide men they saw on the range we claimed. The word had gotten around, and we weren't the most loved people among the hiders.

Gunn ignored them and rode on. The hitching rails in front of the lone saloon were filled up with tied horses.

"Let's go on to the store," Gunn said. "Maybe there won't be so many of these stinking sons a bitches in there."

"I think you wanted to ride in here just to thumb your nose at them," I said.

Gunn didn't answer me.

Clayton Lowe was standing on the porch when we loosened our cinches in front of the store. The sign above him proclaimed him as the proprietor, and mayor of Destiny.

"Good afternoon," he said.

"Fuck off, Lowe." Gunn shouldered past him.

I nodded at Clayton, hoping to take some of the sting out of Gunn's words as I followed him inside.

Clayton had a little watering hole in the back of his trading post. There were a couple of hide hunters outfitting themselves, but nobody was sampling the whiskey. Clayton filled his customers' orders and then went behind the sanded plank that served as his bar and rested both of his hands on it and looked from one of us to the other. "What will it be?"

"Like you've got more than one choice," Gunn said. "You could poison wolves with the stuff you sell."

"Take it easy," I said under my breath to Gunn.

Clayton seemed like he didn't hear Gunn, or was willing to ignore it. I don't know why he didn't leave Gunn alone. It was obvious that Gunn was in one of his quarrelsome moods, and bad blood between the Lowes and the Dollarhydes wasn't ever going to go away.

But Clayton was a man who liked to pick at a thing, and he poured us both a drink and then one for himself. "I hear the cattle market is awful this year."

"It's been better," Gunn said.

"Last year's financial panic hasn't righted itself yet," Clayton said. "I hear your daddy sold at a loss last summer— two herds that he practically had to give away up in Kansas."

"I bet that broke your heart," Gunn said after he downed his drink.

"You've been listening to your daddy too much. I don't hold any grudges against you Dollarhydes."

"To hell you don't." Gunn slapped down his money and reached for the bottle himself and poured another drink.

"Keep your money. It's on the house."

Gunn left his money on the bar and looked at me and then at the full glass of whiskey in front of me that I hadn't touched. "You going to drink that?"

He knew the answer to that without me telling him, but I answered anyway. "I'll pass."

"Still the good Quaker boy, huh?" Gunn tossed down my whiskey. "Sin or not, a little whiskey is about the only thing that makes some days tolerable."

Clayton made a show of wiping the bar with a rag, and butted in when he saw that I wasn't going to argue with Gunn. "I don't bear you any ill will, Gunn, or the rest of your family."

"Can't say the same," Gunn said.

Another group of hide hunters came through the front door. By the loud way they talked, it was plain that they had been in the saloon next door. One of them walked over and slapped Gunn on the back.

"Is there room here for one more? I've got money in my pocket and a man-sized thirst." The hunter wore a filthy army coat stained with blood and grease, and his finger-nails were black. He reeked like he was rotten. "I've been skinning for Frank Mayer. Best rifle shot in the world. Took better 'n sixty buffalo in one stand last week. Like to wore us out trying to keep up with him."

"Get your hand off of me," Gunn said, still staring at the wall behind the bar. "You smell like old guts."

"Excuse me?" the man said. If he hadn't been drunk he would have noticed that Gunn was looking for a fight.

Gunn reached for his pistol at his waist. He did it slowly, and the hider didn't notice until he heard the sound of the hammer cocking below the bar and out of sight.

The buffalo hunter backed up two steps while he looked to see if his friends knew what was going on. "That's a hell of a thing for you to be looking for trouble, especially a one-armed cripple."

The hider's hand inched up for the skinning knife on his belt, and the others were easing through the shelves of goods, trying to come at us from more than one angle.

"There will be no trouble in here," Clayton said. "Not in my store."

"Well then, let's all be friends." Gunn drew his pistol, uncocked it, and slammed it down on the bar top. He downed another whiskey and wiped his mouth with the back of his hand. "As soon as the sons a bitches take a bath I'll buy all three of them a drink."

I don't know why Gunn got like that. He was polite to

everyone most of the time, but if you crossed him, or he was drinking, it was best to walk easy around him. The problem was, his drinking had gotten worse since Hamish left.

I looked at the pistol Gunn had left lying on the bar. It was a brand-new .45 cartridge Colt that he had picked up in Newton to replace his old Dance the year before. The chunk of blued and case-hardened steel lay there on the bar like an unspoken oath, the tiny ruby eyes in the serpent engraved into the ivory grips glowing like coals—a Peacemaker, folks out West had taken to calling such Colts. They said God didn't make all men equal, but Colonel Colt did. I never saw anything peaceful about such a weapon, no matter what anyone might call it. A man with one of those can send his enemies straight to Hell, but he had better be careful or he can send himself right along to the same place if he isn't careful. The Devil's right hand is what people of the Good Book used to call them.

Clayton pulled a shotgun from under the bar and backed himself against his stock of whiskey. He didn't point the gun at anyone in particular, leaving it pointed at the ceiling. "I said there will be no fighting in here."

The hiders started out the door, but the one who had tried to drink with us hung back. "This ain't over, cripple."

Gunn smirked over his whiskey glass.

"You Dollarhydes," Clayton said when the hiders were gone. He set his shotgun in the corner and took a seat on a stool. "Think you're really something, don't you? Better than everyone else. I would throw the both of you out of here, but those hide hunters you insulted are likely to be waiting outside. Maybe they'll cool off and go to the saloon. A few more drinks and they might forget about you."

"Let them wait for me if they want to," Gunn said. "I ain't worried about them."

"I wouldn't be so anxious to cross those hunters. Your father already has them mad enough."

"Our line riders keep most of the buffalo run off the ranch, and there's nothing for the hiders to hunt," I said, but neither of them seemed to have heard me.

"It's our range," Gunn said.

"Your range?" Clayton asked.

"You tend to your town, and we'll tend to our ranch."

"That's a mighty big swath of country you're talking about. And you wonder why people like these hide hunters are mad? Why, that's enough country for lots of folks."

"Let it lie."

Clayton ignored Gunn's warning. "How about you show me the deed to this ranch of yours? That country west of the Cross Timbers you're claiming is open range. State land."

"Not as long as we're there. We don't claim what we can't keep."

Moon Lowe came through the door before Clayton could say whatever he was about to add. The younger brother, Prince, came in right behind him. Prince was close to my age, maybe seventeen. He was slim like his daddy, a sharp dresser, and nothing like that Moon. The rumor was that Moon had a different mother, but I don't know that for certain.

Moon was as stout as an ox, with big meaty fists and stubby arms as big around as my legs. Word was that he had killed at least two men. I didn't doubt that, for Moon struck me as a mean man.

It was obvious that he had been hunting buffalo, for he held a Sharps .40-90 in the crook of his left elbow, with a Vollmer telescopic sight mounted on the barrel. I could see that black man that traipsed around with him, Zeke, staring through the front window at us. You would think a Union man like Clayton would let a black man in his store, but it wasn't so, even if that black man had once worn a badge for him.

"Look what we have here," Moon said. "The Dollarhyde boys."

"Been hunting buffalo, have you?" I asked, for I knew that whatever Gunn would say would probably start a fight. You could talk to Clayton, as long as you kept in mind he was scheming on how he could get the best of you while he was smiling. But Moon, you simply tried to stay clear of him. Putting him and Gunn in the same room was like dropping a match in a pile of black powder.

"Yep, got Prince and Zeke skinning," Moon said.

"I wouldn't have thought you three were smart enough to skin a buffalo," Gunn said under his breath.

"What's that?" Moon asked.

Gunn looked at Clayton. "Are you going to give me my change?"

Clayton made change from his apron, and Gunn holstered his pistol and we headed for the door.

"I guess old man Dollarhyde can't find anybody full grown to work for him," Moon said to me.

I'm short and I know it, and wasn't about to let the likes of him get my goat. "Come on, Gunn."

Gunn stopped at the door. Zeke was standing just outside, blocking our way.

"There are two of our steers penned down there at the end of the street," Gunn said. "You wouldn't know anything about that, would you, Moon?"

"We've been hunting all week." Prince's voice was kind of high-pitched.

"I guess they penned themselves," Gunn said.

Clayton came across the room. "Man through here last week sold those steers to our blacksmith. You go find him to talk about it."

"I'm talking to you," Gunn said. "This is your town, ain't it?"

"The blacksmith's a man of short temper and liable to cause us trouble we don't want."

"All I see are two of our steers, and somebody did a damned poor job of trying to burn over our brands."

"You're young and you need to learn to be careful with your talk," Clayton said. "You make enemies where you don't have to. Give me time to talk it over with the blacksmith and I'm sure something can be worked out. If he won't listen, we have a county judge here now that can hear your case."

Gunn looked at Zeke in the door. "Are you going to get out of my way, or do I have to move you?"

Zeke stood there breathing through his mouth until he looked over Gunn's shoulder and finally moved. I didn't see it, but I imagine Moon gave him the okay.

"Rebel scum." Moon kept his voice quiet when he said it, but we still heard him.

I looked back behind us without turning around and saw that both the Lowe brothers and Zeke had followed us as far as the porch steps. Zeke already had one of his Remingtons halfway out of its holster and Moon had that buffalo gun cocked and propped on his hip. Only Prince didn't have a gun ready, but he scared me most. He had crazy eyes.

I was the only one who didn't have a gun. Sometimes, I kept one of those '66 Winchester carbines in a saddle boot, the one with that pretty brass receiver, but it got in the way when I needed to use my rope. It made Papa mad that I didn't carry a gun and he rarely forgot to remind me that some Indian was going to catch me one day and lift my hair. But he never said anything about how dangerous it might be to ride around with Gunn without proper armament.

"They've got us set up," I said to Gunn.

"You ride up the street and turn those steers loose," he said. "I don't care who tells you to stop, you go ahead and do it."

"You ain't turning those steers loose," Moon said. "You don't ride the high and mighty here."

Gunn turned around to face him; faced all three of them without flinching or acting like he gave a damn. "You go on, Joseph. Do like I said."

I got on my horse and started down the street, expecting to be shot at any second. Those hiders and freighters stopped what they were doing and watched me ride past them, and none of them looking friendly. And I saw other townsfolk peering out their windows or doorways.

The steers in question were penned in a three-rail corral, and the gate was tied shut with wire, top and bottom. I was going to have to get off my horse to undo it, and the thought of losing my one means of rapid escape didn't set well with my breakfast—if I had eaten any breakfast. I stopped short of the corral and looked back up the street. Gunn wasn't looking at me and was keeping his attention on the three on the store porch. From a distance and the way he was standing, it looked like he had them treed instead of it being the other way around. Gunn didn't back up for anybody, especially not when the whiskey had him.

"Don't open that gate," someone said beside me.

I had stopped in front of a lumber-framed house. It was also the only thing with any paint on it other than some of the wagons lining the street. Its yellow clapboard and white window trimming seemed too bright and tidy for such a rough settlement.

"Did you hear me?" The girl was standing in an open window looking at me.

"You startled me some," I said, and then regained my composure. "Those are our cows."

She was a pretty thing. "That won't matter. They're going to shoot you the instant you lay hand to that gate. Shoot your brother, too."

"How do you know?"

"I heard them talking about it when they saw you riding in." She had freckles on her nose and the prettiest blue eyes you ever saw. Did you ever notice that all the girls in those songs they sing have blue eyes?

"Hey, cowboy," a man called out to me from under the awning of the blacksmith shed. "I've got a bill of sale for those steers."

"I'd like to see that," I said.

The man stepped to the edge of the roof and far enough into the sunlight that I could see him better. He was shirtless and hairy where his leather apron didn't cover him, and patting a shop hammer in the palm of his hand. He was bigger and sweatier than any man I'd ever seen. The blacksmith, I assumed.

"Here's your bill of sale." He hefted the hammer to make sure I saw it.

Several of the other men around laughed at that. Those that didn't look like they were on his side were at least hanging around to see what was going to happen—see some fool, runt cowboy get knocked out of the saddle by a hammer or a bullet.

"Moon sold him those steers," the girl said. She seemed as nervous as I was and kept looking back up the street at the store.

"How do you know that?"

"I ought to. He's my brother."

I should have known the house belonged to Clayton.

"You listen to me," she said. "Leave them and don't come back. You're too cute to get shot over some old cows."

I wished it were that easy. Whether I opened that gate or

not, I was still in a pickle. Gunn wasn't going to leave it be. Not him. You have to stick with your brother, but sometimes Gunn made that a hard proposition. At times, being his enemy might have been as easy as being his friend.

I started my horse forward.

"I didn't think you would listen," she said. "Pa said you Dollarhydes were stubborn."

"He's my brother." I stopped in front of the gate and dismounted.

"You're treading on thin ice, cowboy." The blacksmith was already coming for me.

I had my hand on the gate and the blacksmith had that hammer reared back when I heard a horse running down the street. It was Gunn coming hell-bent for leather. That blacksmith was big, but the horse didn't even slow down when it hit him. Gunn pulled up hard and rolled his pony back the way he had come and ran over the blacksmith again at a trot. When he was finished, the blacksmith was lying on the ground moaning and cursing, and likely had some broken bones.

All that running back and forth had Gunn's horse stirred up, and he spun it around in a circle to hold it in place, glaring at everyone watching him. "These are Dollarhyde steers and we're taking them. Next time we find stolen cattle here we'll burn this whole town down!"

I couldn't believe somebody hadn't shot us yet. The gate fought me some, and it took me entirely too long to open it. I bailed on my horse and dove him in the corral and drove those steers out of town at a fast clip, while Gunn hung back to get us clear. I pulled up once I thought I was out of rifle range, but I'd heard too many tales about how some of those hide hunters could shoot. I could still see Gunn, and that meant somebody could be looking at me through one of those telescopic sights.

Gunn backed his horse for the first fifty yards out of town, unwilling to turn his back on any of them. When he finally did turn around I thought he would dig his spurs into his horse and run like he was going to a fire. But not Gunn. Oh, no. He wasn't about to let any of them think they worried him. He came on toward me at a leisurely walk, as if he didn't have a care in the world.

When we were finally out of sight of that place we pulled up. Riding out of there felt like it took a hundred times as long as it did going in.

"You're either crazy, or the coolest man I've ever seen," I said. "Or are you that drunk?"

"That bunch ain't anything to worry about." He started making a cigarette.

I noticed that his hand was shaking and I pointed to it. "Not a worry in the world, huh?"

He grinned at me and licked his cigarette paper. "I admit, they had my attention there for a bit."

Chapter Twenty-seven

The Indians called him Bad Hand, probably because he had a couple of his fingers shot off in the Civil War. Colonel Ranald S. Mackenzie was the only Yankee Papa ever had much use for and the only officer in the entire U.S. Army that knew the first thing about fighting Indians (again, Papa's opinion).

The colonel would stop at the ranch from time to time during one of his patrols or expeditions during the Indian Wars. All in all, he spent about seven years fighting Indians in Texas for General William Tecumseh Sherman, the same Yankee that Papa said burned half of Georgia during the war. Papa may have been fond of Colonel Mackenzie, but he would spit on the ground any time he said General Sherman's name.

Sherman didn't put on any airs about how he thought the Indians ought to be handled. You killed their buffalo to make their bellies empty and kept troops in the field to never give them a minute's rest. And those that wouldn't give it up and go to the reservation, you found in their winter camps and either destroyed their supplies or put them to sword and pistol.

Sword and fire. Bad Hand Mackenzie was General Sherman's sword and the troops they kept in the field were his matches. All in the name of progress and civilization.

White farmers wanted to homestead that country, and cattlemen like us wanted the grass. Buffalo and the Indians were the only things standing in the way, but Sharps buffalo guns and soldiers like Mackenzie were working on that. There wasn't anything pretty about it, but that's the way it was—bloody war, plain and simple.

I don't know who started hating who first, the white man hating the Indians or the Indians hating the white man. Some say those Plains tribes made a living of war, but I never saw that my own were any less warlike. Raw deals all the way around, no matter what color your skin was.

I was only a button when I lost my first parents, but they gave me a start in the Good Book. Says in there that Jesus will forgive any kind of sin, but we've got a lot to be forgiven for. And that goes for red man and white man alike. So much killing when we should have been busy living.

Like I said, Papa and Colonel Mackenzie got along like old friends. The colonel would soothe Papa by telling him how many Indians his soldiers had killed, and Papa would commend him and report any Indian movements that our cowboys had observed. After that, they would enjoy a little brandy on the porch and tell stories.

By that time, Papa had built what people in our country called the "big house." He had the lumber hauled in all the way from Gainesville, and a crew of carpenters from there built him the prettiest white two-story house you ever saw. It didn't have big porch pillars like the home he told about in Alabama, but it did have a porch all the way across the front of it. That porch was where Papa and the colonel liked to sit and drink their brandy and talk.

The colonel was leading two companies of cavalry

troopers back to Fort Richardson when he rode up that day. Their horses looked like death warmed over and the troops didn't look much better themselves. A few of them were wearing bandages, and the majority of them had a swollen cheekbone from the kick of those old straight-stocked Springfield needle guns they carried.

"You look like you found a fight," Papa said to the colonel.

"We got them this time," was all Mackenzie said until someone took his horse and he and Papa went up to the porch.

Juanita brought them a bottle of brandy and then disappeared inside the house. She was a friendly woman, but had little interest in their talk of war.

Mackenzie was carrying something and he handed it to Papa when he took his chair. "That's for you."

"Where did you get this?" Papa asked.

"One of my men cut it out of a Kiowa shield," Mackenzie said. "I understand that they sometimes stuff them between the bull hide for more protection."

It was nothing but a little book that Papa held on his knee, but I saw that his eyes watered up. He finally thumbed the book open and looked at something inside the front cover. I looked over his shoulder and saw an inscription written in a neat and decidedly feminine hand.

My dearest Argyle,
  I hope these poems will comfort you in the lonely
hours. May God keep you safe from harm in this
time of war. Thinking of you and longing for the day
you return to me.

  Love,
  Sarah

  June 15, 1863

I didn't know the first Mrs. Dollarhyde long, but the sight of that handwriting gave me a warm feeling—faint memories of tender hands and a soft smile. I could tell the book gave Papa memories, too.

Mackenzie worked on his brandy, allowing Papa time to gather himself. I took a chair at the far end of the porch, giving them some room but wanting to be close enough to hear what was said.

"I captured a Mexican trader this time. Comanchero that said he could show me the big canyon where the hostiles make winter camp," Mackenzie said.

Papa looked up at him. "And?"

"Two days into those river breaks, he got too scared to guide me any farther. Was afraid of what the Indians would do to him if they ever caught him out on the plains again and knew he gave away their secret," Mackenzie swirled his brandy around in his glass.

"Those Comancheros are worse than the Indians," Papa said. "Trading whiskey and beads and guns for stolen horses and cattle and white women."

Mackenzie nodded and gave a cold chuckle. "I had the men hang that old thief from a wagon tongue until he decided to talk again. Sent the Tonkawas scouting the way he said and they found that canyon. We hit those hostiles hard. Caught them sleeping."

"Who did you catch?"

"Don't know for sure. It was a big canyon with little camps scattered at the head of it. Comanche, Cheyenne, Kiowa. According the Tonkawa and some of the captives, Quanah, Red War Bonnet, Poor Buffalo, other big medicine types were there."

"Lone Wolf?"

"The old one or the young one? There are two that go by that name."

"The older one. Did you get him?" Papa asked.

"He was there, but we didn't get him. He's too cagey and retreated up the canyon walls on the other side and made it hot for us from there," Mackenzie said. "We didn't get many of them at all, but we ran them out of that canyon and burned their lodges and winter supplies. Captured their horses, too."

"Quanah, you said? Big Comanche?"

"That's him—half-breed son of that Parker woman the Rangers took back years ago. We didn't get him, either."

"I think I saw him once," Papa said. "He and Lone Wolf were together. Crazy brave and the best rider I ever saw. Cornered me in a buffalo wallow on the Washita."

I leaned closer to make sure I heard Papa.

"You were lucky," Mackenzie said. "We found that Ranger's skull in one of those canyon camps. You heard about that, didn't you? Lone Wolf's boys cut off that Ranger's head after the Lost Valley fight. Would have killed the whole Ranger company if the 10th Cavalry hadn't showed up and saved them."

"Negros make poor soldiers, if you ask me."

"I've commanded them and found them to be steady men if given sound leadership and proper training," Mackenzie said.

I think that's why Papa liked talking to him. Mackenzie was one of the few men who would argue with him.

Papa straightened his achy leg in front of him and read-justed himself in his chair. "Well, I didn't have anybody to save me. Not even buffalo soldiers. Didn't have anything but my Sharps breechloader and a Colt revolving rifle I borrowed from one of my vaqueros. Those Indians had killed my horse, so I forted up behind him and did my best."

"Like I said, you were lucky."

"Damned fool is what I was."

"When I first came out here everyone told me how you took on a whole Kiowa camp after they killed your wife and shot off your boy's arm," Mackenzie said. "It's getting dark and that's a story I wouldn't mind hearing."

Papa downed another glass and stared grim-faced at the colonel. Juanita came out on the porch and announced that supper was on the table. The colonel was hungry after coming so many miles, but I don't think Papa would have answered him, even if Juanita hadn't interrupted them with her good cooking.

Chapter Twenty-eight

1876

The brown gelding had about quit bucking when Gunn came out of the bunkhouse and walked over and hung his arm over the top rail of the corral. He wouldn't sleep in the big house.

He and his trail crew had ridden in late the night before. He was three hours late getting up, and from the look of him, the weeks' ride back from Dodge City hadn't totally cured him of the Kansas hangover he was nursing.

Gunn squinted at me. "You about got the rough rode off of him?"

The brown came to a stop, still quivering a little with fear and trying to watch me out of the backs of its eyes. I leaned forward slightly and rubbed its neck with my free hand, cautious and wary, should it explode again. "This one isn't so bad. I think he'll make a good horse."

"How can you tell? Looks like he's still of a mind to buck you off."

Everyone has a rightful place. You know, that place where you fit; where the world is perfect and all things balance and you know you belong. I can't explain all I understood about a horse, or how I came to that understanding. I couldn't explain it to Gunn, and didn't try.

"I take it your trip went well?" I asked.

"We got them delivered, and that's about all the good I can say," Gunn said. "Worst trip I've taken. That trader Papa bought those steers off of must have spent a year to find so many soured, crazy critters. I think the whole damned herd was made up of bunch-quitters and outlaws. I knew it when I first saw where a couple of them had raw eyelids and the rope scars where they had been hobbled."

Before cattle were worth anything in Texas, older, outlaw cattle down in the brush country between the Nueces and the Rio Grande were able to avoid captivity. Nobody wanted to fool with them when there were younger, better beeves that could be handled with a lot less trouble. But as prices rose and every Tom, Dick, and Harry in Texas wanted to get in on the business, they began to comb the brush for anything with horns and hooves they could put together for a herd.

Many of those outlaws were past veterans of other attempts to gather them, and holding them with a herd was next to impossible. A tactic that some of those brush country boys had developed was to rope and throw those brutes and sew their eyelids shut with twine. Blind, the animal's only comfort was the sense of others of its kind around it, and in that manner it would cling to the herd. Eventually, the stitches would be removed when the cowboys thought the animal was trail broke.

Another technique was to yoke a wild steer to a gentle ox, or to hobble a front leg to its own neck. After a time of tugging and fighting to no avail, the steer might give up the fighting spirit and decide it was content to go where it was pointed.

But no matter how you handled such cattle, they were never going to be gentle. It was like trying to herd mountain lions.

Nobody who knew anything wanted any part of handling such a herd, but the market was better that year, and Papa wanted to drive more to market than we had the numbers for. That meant he was buying steers wherever he could get them and counting on turning a profit in Kansas.

Gunn went south to take charge of one of the herds, and I stayed at the ranch to take delivery of the new breeding stock Papa had bought. By then, according to our books, we were running twenty thousand head of cattle on our range. Papa said that in another year or two we would produce enough beef to avoid having to middleman other people's stock, and could put four herds of our own up the trail every year. He spent half the spring riding from San Antonio to the border looking for bargains and trying to put trail herds together.

Gunn scraped at the stubble of whiskers on his chin. "It stormed the first two weeks on the trail, and the damned things ran on us the first and the second night. And it all went downhill from there. By then, they had the habit and were looking for something to spook at. You couldn't hold them for anything when they were of a mind to run. Had a big run up north of the Cimarron. There were five herds waiting for the river to go down so they could cross, and when our bunch stampeded that night it took all the others with it, mixing them together something awful. We spent three days sorting and trying to put our herds right again."

I didn't hear what else he had to say, for something spooked the gelding I was sitting on. It clamped its tail and bolted three running strides before it broke into pitching again. Its first jump was a big one.

The brown sunfished twice, twisting at the hips in midair

and rolling his belly and kicking out with both hind legs. The braided grass hackamore reins bit into my hand as he fought to bury his head between his front legs. But I was right in the middle. Like I said, there's a balance to all things, and even in such a storm, I had found the middle of my saddle, and nothing that brown could do was going to put me off-kilter. I wish all things were as easy. Some things don't seem to have a middle.

The brown stopped in a cloud of dust with his head jammed against the fence, and Gunn laughed. He had a good laugh.

"I thought they rarely bucked with you," he said. "You're always fussing about how we rough break a colt."

"There are some horses that you can do everything wrong with and it's all still easy, and some that you can do everything right with and they have to learn things the hard way. If they ever learn."

"You don't sound like you're talking only about horses," Gunn said. "Spit out what you've got to say. Don't beat around the bush."

"Never mind. Papa's coming."

Gunn twisted his neck to look in the direction of the big house. "He's probably coming down here to tell you how to handle that colt."

The brown had freed up a little and I moved him around the corral, letting him go where he would, and only gently taking a little pull on one rein or the other, here and there, to show him the beginnings of how to give to the pull of the hackamore bosal resting on his nose.

Papa was leaning on the fence not far from Gunn by the time I called my session with the brown to an end and dismounted and slipped my cinch. By then, Papa and Gunn were already arguing.

"Where were you this morning?" Papa asked. "I could have used you. This ranch doesn't run itself."

Gunn never looked at Papa, and kept squinting in my direction, studying the brown as if he had never seen a horse unsaddled. After a long wait, he ducked his head and spat between the fence rails. "I didn't ride in until midnight. Figured I was due a late getup."

Papa grunted. "I didn't get here until late myself. Rode all the way in from San Antonio in three days. You didn't see me sleeping in when there is work to be done."

"I ain't you."

"Where's your tally book?" Papa asked.

Gunn reached into his vest pocket and produced a tattered little notebook that he sailed at Papa with a flick of his wrist.

Papa caught it and spent several minutes poring over it. Papa was a stickler about his trail bosses keeping accurate head counts on their herds, recording any losses, and making a log entry of every day's events on the trail. Most of his men complained that they hired on to handle cattle and not write books.

"You lost fifteen head?" Papa asked with a scowl.

"And three more crippled that didn't bring more than the price of their hides," Gunn said.

"Why is it that you lost twice what the other two men I sent up the trail with herds did?"

"Maybe because you didn't send them with the junk you sent me with."

"You've got all kinds of excuses, don't you? I asked you if you could handle that herd, and you told me you could."

Gunn reached into his pocket again and pulled out a scrap of yellow paper. He held it up so that Papa could see it. "Your money's in the bank, and here's the draft. You made seven dollars a head on those steers, so I don't know what all this complaining is about."

"Money doesn't mean anything to you, does it? At a glance, I'd say your wagon expenses were half again what the other men incurred."

"That herd made money, and there isn't a son of a bitch that would work for you that could have brought them through any better. I feed my men well and don't scrimp when it comes to groceries. You treat a man right and he'll do what you ask him without complaint."

"I hear you had whiskey in camp. You know I don't allow that."

"You can hear anything."

"Why did you stay so long in Dodge? You should have been back here to help Joseph two weeks ago."

"Took me a while to find a buyer for the saddle horses. You're the one who told me to make sure I sold them if I could. You don't snap your fingers and find a buyer for sixty head of horses."

"How many head have we taken north this year? Last year?" Papa's face was turning red like it did when he was getting worked up. "What's our loss on the trail for this year? What's it costing me to pay the men? Ranch improvements? Total expenses?"

Gunn adjusted his hat on his head and stared at the brown some more.

"You don't know, do you?" Papa asked. "What about the grass this year? Are you worried that we've had half the rain we normally get? Thought about where we need to move our stock to make sure they get through the year like they should?"

"I'm sure you've got opinions about all of that."

"Son, I can hire all the cowboys I want. They're a dim a dozen."

best to ride him to a standstill. If you were lucky, after a month's rides you ended up with a half-wild horse that would only try to buck you off once a day, would paw you on top of the head on its worst day, and might not kill you if you never let down your guard.

"We've been doing a good business selling our strings, and I think we can get more money out of them if they're better than usual," I said. "A horse that's trained is bound to be worth more than one that only tolerates somebody on his back."

"You, too?" Papa put his hands on his hips. "Now you're telling me about the horse business?"

"You would listen if you weren't so stubborn," Gunn said. "Joseph's string is the best in the country. I'd give two hundred a head for any one of them, and I ain't the only one."

"And it takes him two years to turn out a broke horse. I can hire men who can turn out twenty horses a month my way and they'll bring thirty dollars a head. Who makes the most profit?"

Gunn started back to the bunkhouse.

"Where are you going?" Papa asked.

"To lose you some more money."

"I've got a job for you two."

Gunn stopped and turned around.

"You boys get a couple of hands and ride over to Destiny. I've got a little herd waiting there and I want you to bring them in."

"Can't whoever you bought them from bring them in?" Gunn asked.

"No, his horse kicked him and broke his leg. He's laid up at the hotel."

"No need for good horses, is there?" Gunn looked at me with a bitter smirk on his mouth.

"You don't make a dime unless some damn ⟨...⟩ take a herd up the trail for you."

"Yes, but that's all a cowboy does. I'm asking yo⟨...⟩ a cowman. Be a businessman. Get your head in the ⟨...⟩ and take a hold. Quit thinking about Kansas whore⟨...⟩ how you can throw away your pay at a card table once ⟨...⟩ hit town like every other fool that works for me."

"We've made a fortune."

"A fortune? How much money have we got in the ban⟨...⟩ How much? I lost twenty thousand last year on the thre⟨...⟩ herds we trailed north."

"You should have held those herds until the spring and waited for the market to pick back up. Others did."

"Oh, now you're telling me about the market? And what ⟨...⟩ paid the bills while I waited?"

"You sent me to deliver a herd, and I delivered it."

"If you would spend half the time learning the business side of things as you do riding off every evening to find yourself a good time I wouldn't have so many worries," Papa said. "I didn't build this ranch to lose it."

"Whose ranch, Papa?" Gunn said. "Whose? Yours? I'v⟨...⟩ been right here every step of the way."

Papa didn't have an answer or he had gotten too mad ⟨...⟩ argue the matter anymore. He turned his wrath on me.

"Joseph, you take too long with those horses. I'd pr⟨...⟩ you hand the breaking over to the men, but don't co⟨...⟩ and pamper those animals so much if you're boun⟨...⟩ determined to earn your keep as a bronc buster. The⟨...⟩ more important things that you can be doing inst⟨...⟩ spending all morning working with a thirty-dollar ⟨...⟩

I knew how Papa thought a horse should be bro⟨...⟩ roped him and snubbed him to a post and fought ⟨...⟩ until you could get a saddle on him. Then some th⟨...⟩ dollar-a-month brave fool climbed on his back a⟨...⟩

"Do like I said. I sunk a lot of money in this bunch," Papa said. "And stay out of the saloon. I want you back here this evening so I can look them over."

"We'll try not to lose any on the way back." Gunn held his hand out, waiting.

Papa handed him back his tally book. "Your hand-writing is terrible."

"I'd buy a new pencil, but I don't know if we have the money."

Papa grabbed me by the arm when I went past him. "You make sure he does like I told him."

"Yes, sir."

I don't know why I said that. Gunn did what he was of a mind to do, just like Papa. The only thing you could do was to pray and try to survive the storm. Neither one of them had any balance.

Chapter Twenty-nine

"What the hell are those?" Gunn asked.

"I don't know," I said.

"They're Herefords," the dried-up, little cow trader sitting in the buckboard beside us said. He hawked a wad of phlegm and tobacco juice over the side and then propped his crutch and his splinted leg up on the buggy's dashboard. "English cattle. Your father paid me two hundred dollars a head for these bulls. Outbid three other buyers for them."

Gunn and I studied the short, squatty yearling bulls in front of us. There were ten of them and they all looked almost identical. They were a rich red color with bald or freckled faces and more white hair on their throats, bellies, and their tail switches. They had pale, curved horns no longer than your forearm. To men used to looking at long-legged, rangy longhorns, the yearlings before us looked like some child's awkward, disproportional drawing of what a cow looked like.

Several passersby also stopped to look. Nobody had ever seen cattle like those.

"I don't know what that says for Papa," Gunn said.

"Look at the beef they carry," the cow trader said. "No

longhorn ever packed that much on his frame. People want to eat tender, fat meat, and a longhorn is little better than a stringy jackrabbit on the hoof."

"The fat little things' legs are too short to go anywhere," Gunn said. "How do you think we could get one of those up the trail to Kansas?"

"Won't be any trail drives before long. They're already talking about bringing the railroad to Destiny," the man said. "You're looking at the future."

"The future?" Gunn asked.

"Herefords will fatten and be ready for butchering in two years. Nobody back East wants to eat tough longhorn beef when they can eat one of these. No more waiting for the times when there's a beef shortage and a longhorn might sell for a profit. No more handling four- and five-year-old steers that are more horn and hoof and meanness than anything."

"You've got a lot of big ideas," Gunn said. "No wonder you and Papa get along."

The cow trader squinted one eye to fight the sun in his face. "You listen to your father, and you might even listen to me. I was following longhorns up the trail when you were still on the tit. Times are changing and a man had best be in on the ground floor."

"There aren't but ten of them. What's he going to do with them?" I asked.

The little man turned to me. "He'll turn out these bulls and let them cross with your longhorns. Given time, they'll improve your herd."

Gunn laughed. "Hey, Joseph, can you imagine one of these fatties taking on one of our bulls for the rights to the ladies?"

I couldn't help but giggle, and I hoped I didn't offend the seller. "Folks have tried roan Durhams for years, but they don't do well turned out on open range. Don't milk well when it turns hot and dry, and the wolves play hell with their calves. They're farmer cows that need to be shut up in a pen and the corn shook out for them every day."

The man nodded. "These are different than those short-horns. You wait and see."

"What I'll wait for is Papa going broke buying two-hundred-dollar bulls," Gunn said. "It will be worth the trouble to say I told him so."

"Tell your father that I'll be out to the ranch in a day or so," the man said, giving us a look like we were foolish children. "The doc here wants to keep an eye on my leg for a while longer. Says I'm too old and don't mend like I used to." He snorted through his nose.

"We'll tell him." I started my horse forward to open the corral and let the bulls out. We had two more hands with us, and driving ten yearling bulls a few miles to the ranch was going to make for a boring, easy evening.

"Hold on there, Joseph," Gunn said. "What's your hurry? Those bulls aren't going anywhere."

Somebody had forked the bulls a mound of hay and their water trough was full. They stared back at me with contented, gentle eyes. Fat and sassy.

Gunn pointed down the street. "Wouldn't hurt to check the mail and get a bite to eat. Maybe have a toddy or two and see the sights."

I knew it was useless to argue with him.

Regardless of what he said, there weren't many sights in Destiny, but the little town was still growing. The hiders had wiped out the buffalo to the point that there wasn't any profit in it. It was a rare occasion to see a straggling bunch anymore and the stacks of hides that had once lined the street were gone. A few of the buffalo hunters remained, but they had all gone on to other habits. There were some of them that had taken to farming at the edge of town and some that had put in small businesses. A larger part of them hung around to get drunk and lament the days when the buffalo were as thick as flies.

That's not to say that Destiny was nothing but a bunch of cast-off hiders. The country was filling up in the past few years. There were now lots of other ranchers with cattle on the range, and there were several patches of oats and corn showing north of town, tended by newcomers who had homesteaded a chunk of state ground. The town sported three saloons, a hotel and restaurant, stockyards, wagon shop, and a genuine cigar and tobacco store. And Clayton Lowe's general store still sat at the head of the street, right across from his yellow house.

"I could use a haircut if they've found a barber," I said. I was twenty years old and had never had my hair cut by other than one of the vaquero's wives.

We left the bulls and Gunn made a beeline for the nearest saloon. The bright green and yellow sign over it proclaimed it the LAST CHANCE FOR GOOD WHISKEY IN TEXAS.

Gunn dismounted and threw a loose wrap of one rein around the hitching post. He stopped on the boardwalk and turned to me when I didn't follow. "Still determined to have a haircut instead of a toddy?"

I nodded.

"Suit yourself. You know where to find me."

I hadn't ridden much farther down the street when I saw her sweeping off her front porch. She was even prettier than the last time I had seen her. I pulled up, making a show of studying the sky and wondering what to say.

"I thought you had forgotten me," she said. "What has it been? A month?"

"Three weeks. I've been awful busy."

"Excuses, excuses." Cindy Lowe wasn't but a snip of a

girl. Not more than a hundred pounds soaking wet, with freckles across her nose and curly hair that wouldn't stay where she pinned it. But she had a wit as quick as the snap of a steel trap and seemed to love nothing more than deviling me. It's hard to think ahead and have the right answers ready when it comes to women. No matter, I'd been coming to town to see her off and on for a good while.

"It's the truth," I said.

Her eyes were mischievous, but no matter how she teased me, I saw her throw a cautious glance across the street. "My brothers are gone, but Mama and Daddy are over there tending the store. Don't you hang around here too long."

"Excuses, excuses," I said.

"Joseph Dollarhyde, you know my daddy would strap me and you both if he knew you were sparking me."

I shifted uneasily in the saddle and cast my own glance at the store. Then I looked at the saloon that Gunn had disappeared into. Clayton Lowe seeing me might not be as bad as Gunn doing the same.

"Meet me at the river where we met last time," she said and disappeared inside the house.

I wished I had time for a bath and that haircut. Cindy always smelled so sweet. But I wasn't going to keep her waiting. She had opinions on lots of things and was temperamental at times and apt to give me an earful if I kept her waiting.

There was a pretty little spot in a grove of trees on the riverbank not a half mile from town. I barely had time to tie my horse and stomp the kinks out of my legs before Cindy came through the trees with a skip in her step and a smile on her face.

"Let's go wading in the river." The frank way she had of looking me in the eye always made me nervous, and her suggestion caused me to stammer instead of answering her.

"What? You ask me to sneak off with you, but then you're all of sudden too shy to talk?"

"It's just that . . ."

"Gosh, you're acting like I said we ought to strip naked and go skinny-dipping or something." A pout formed on her mouth.

"Somebody might see us."

"Wading in the creek?"

"Yeah."

"I promise not to hike my dress up too high. Surely, if someone sees my calves they won't die of shock."

"I guess so." It was always later when I noticed that Cindy made up all the rules and I pretty much did what she wanted.

"My, but you're an exciting one." She gave me a teasing frown and then sat down and plucked off her shoes.

By the time I got out of my boots and rolled up my pants legs she was already wading in the shallows with her dress hiked up to her knees. I took a look around to make sure nobody was around and then joined her.

"Ooo, the water feels good," she said.

"It's been a hot one today."

"Is that all you've got to say to a girl? Talk about the weather?"

"You stymie me some. Every time I get set with what I want to say to you, you throw me off-kilter."

Instead of answering me, she shrieked and nearly knocked me over, splashing her way to the bank. She turned around once she was back on dry land and pointed behind me. "Snake!"

It was definitely a snake slithering along on top of the water, and a big old cottonmouth at that—nasty, ill-tempered serpents and poisonous to boot. For all of that, it didn't seem intent on biting us, and swam slowly by me.

"Why don't you shoot him?" she asked. "Moon shoots their heads off without me having to ask."

I waded toward her and made an exaggerated showing of looking at my waistline and shrugging.

"I don't know what I'm going to do with you," she said.

"How's that?" I sat down on the riverbank beside her.

"I think you're the only cowboy in Texas that doesn't wear a gun."

"I never had a cow shoot at me."

"You're sweet, but there isn't any way that this is going to work."

"Us? Why, I like you something fierce."

"I know you do, but how's a man who doesn't carry a gun, doesn't cuss, and blushes at the sight of my calves ever going to deal with my family? Sweetness and kind gestures don't work too well on them."

"I guess we'll have to ease them into the notion of me."

"Daddy would have a conniption fit if he knew I was seeing a Dollarhyde. And Argyle Dollarhyde would rather spit on a Lowe than talk to one of us," she said. "I don't think you have the fight in you it would take, and me, well, I don't know if I've got the nerve to keep seeing you on the sly."

"I'd fight for you, if it came to that."

"Oh yeah? Is that why you're so willing to sneak off every time I suggest it? I haven't seen you anxious to tell my daddy or yours that you're sweet on me."

She was right, but that didn't make it any easier to take. If only things weren't so bad between our families. Papa had never forgiven Clayton Lowe for his actions with the State Police and trying to impound our cattle, and Lowe let it be known to anyone that would listen how Papa got his start in the cattle business by swinging a big loop and not being too particular whose cattle he roped.

"Don't look so sad." She laid a hand on my forearm.

"You can't help it, no more than either of us can help it that we have two stubborn fools for fathers."

I jumped to my feet. "All right, let's go tell your father now. And then we'll go tell Mr. Dollarhyde. They'll have to like it or lump it."

She stood slowly, ending up with her little pug nose not an inch from mine. "That easy, huh?"

"I'm no coward."

"No? You know what my daddy is liable to do, and worse if Moon's around."

"I won't fight Moon if I don't have to."

"He won't give you a choice."

"I'd hate it if it came to that."

She giggled, and a rush of anger built in me and I could feel the red crawling up my neck and flushing my face. "Go ahead and laugh at me. You do think I'm a coward, don't you?"

She giggled again and somehow she was even closer to me. She must have been chewing on a candy stick not too long before, for her breath smelled like peppermint.

"So brave, yet you haven't kissed me yet. Not in all the times I've gone out to meet you."

"I . . ."

She raised up on her tiptoes and put both hands on my chest to balance herself. "Kiss me." Her eyes were already squinted shut.

I gave her a quick, unsure peck, never feeling so awkward in my entire life. I intended to have another go at it to make up for the way I bungled it, but she was already running down the creek bank toward town, leaving me standing there at a loss. She never looked back at me, not once. That girl could really run.

Chapter Thirty

"If I didn't know you better, Quaker boy, I'd say you've found a sweetheart. You've got that dreamy, fevered look about you," Gunn said.

"Hmmph," I grunted. The yearling Hereford bulls were lazy and not apt to scatter, but I spurred my horse forward anyway, pretending like I needed to knock one of those bulls back into the line of our drive.

"I wouldn't have thought it." Gunn gave a long whistle. "There I was, drinking rotgut and wasting a perfectly good evening, and the little saint managed to find some feminine company where I thought there wasn't any. What did you do, find some farmer's daughter?"

Sometimes I could ignore him and he would give it up, but not that time.

"Who was it? Was it that blacksmith's wife? She's fat and ugly, but she'd do in a pinch. Especially for a first time," Gunn said. "I hear she used to sell herself to an occasional hider when her husband's business was slow."

I should have let Gunn believe that. It would have been better. Gunn might have been crude and rowdy, but he wasn't dumb.

"Don't tell me you did what I'm thinking. Tell me you aren't sparking that Lowe girl."

My lack of denial was as good as telling him he was right. I was prepared to fight him if it came to that, and I was sure it would. Gunn hated Clayton Lowe worse than Papa did.

"You better not let Papa find out," he said. "He'll disown you."

It shocked me how easy he took it. "She's a good girl."

"I bet."

"What are you meaning?" I rode my horse back to him. "I didn't like the sound of that."

"Don't crawl up my back. You've got yourself enough trouble as it is."

"Let me handle my own business."

"Fine. Can't say as I blame you. She's a cute little button and about the only thing around here. Even if she is a Lowe."

"I'll figure it out. Papa's going to hit the sky when I tell him, but maybe it will blow over."

"Don't count on it. But I'll at least be glad that someone else is on his bad side."

"I'm grown. He can't tell me everything to do."

"Don't you know he slapped his brand on you the instant we picked you up from that Quaker wagon train?"

"I don't think he thinks that."

"Papa don't turn loose of what he thinks is his, and the only way he thinks is right is his way."

"I'll get him to listen. I just need time to think of the right words. Maybe if he met Cindy."

"She'd still be a Lowe, and Papa has as much use for a Lowe as he has for a rattlesnake." Gunn pulled his horse up and he was staring at something in the distance. "No use for a Lowe at all. It's one of his better qualities."

"I said I would figure it out."

"Well, you watch out for Moon Lowe."

We'd come south of the trail we normally took back to the ranch, and I hadn't ridden through there since the spring before during roundup. I saw the trickle of chimney smoke that Gunn was seeing, and we hadn't gone half a mile more when we could make out the little log cabin tucked into a swale between two low hills. I knew it hadn't been there the year before, and the logs it was made from were still white and fresh where they had been peeled. A set of hog pens and a brush horse corral lay alongside the cabin.

We passed close enough that I could make out the man standing in the doorway of that cabin watching us. It was Moon Lowe, and that Zeke came around the corner and stood by him, shading his eyes from the sun and staring at us until we passed.

"That cabin's two miles inside our line," Gunn said.

With more ranchers moving into the country, Papa had long before decided to build a series of line camps around the boundaries of the range we claimed. A rider was assigned to each camp to ride our boundaries and keep our stock on their home range and turn back anyone else's cattle.

"Papa ain't going to tolerate that," Gunn said. "He'll have a fit when he finds out."

"Moon Lowe isn't going to like it, either."

Chapter Thirty-one

There had been a time when most of the Dollarhyde ranch hands were Mexican vaqueros and most of them married. But as the country settled up that wasn't the case. The feel of the ranch changed along with the times.

The cluster of jacales still stood, where most of the vaqueros lived, but most of the hands hired in the last few years were young, Anglo bachelors. Because of that, Papa had built a long bunkhouse. You might say two populations existed on the ranch, one centered around the jacales, which was a village of its own, full of women and children, and one centered around the bunkhouse. The jacal village lay about a half mile from the headquarters, and the ranch hands had taken to calling it "Rancho Poquito," the little ranch. The bunkhouse was a stone's throw from the barn. Except when it came to work, the hands from those two locations rarely spent time together.

There were places in Texas where Mexicans and gringos mixed like oil and water, especially close to the border, but it was more subtle on the $D. Oh, there were some of the boys in the bunkhouse who didn't hide it that they thought they were better than a bunch of greasers, and there were some of the vaqueros who had the story handed down to them of how the mean old gringos stole Texas from their ancestors. What held it all together was the fact that Argyle Dollarhyde didn't care who you were.

He treated everyone equally good or equally bad. He expected every man on the ranch to work whatever hours he put them to for thirty-five dollars a month. It was menial pay for menial work, but everyone suffered the same. Furthermore, he would personally chew out any man on the payroll or send him packing when he was displeased with their work, no matter what color your skin was.

On the opposite end, there had been more than once when he gave a man an advance in pay, whether it was to bail some dumb Anglo cowboys out of jail after a drinking spree or paying a doctor to deliver one of the vaquero's babies. It wasn't perfect, but nobody complained, at least where the old man could hear them.

No matter, we had more hands than ever—enough to run the ranch and enough to finish about any kind of a fight. Right then it was fighting men Papa needed. Funny how men who work like slaves for thirty-five a month were ready to go to war the second Papa told them to grab their guns and saddle their horses. Some used to call that riding for the brand, and Hamish used to call that feudalism, whatever that is. All I know is that Papa's men would do about anything he put them to. Even the bickerers and the complainers wouldn't hear anything bad spoken by an outsider about the $D. There was pride that went with being a Dollarhyde hand, and it was kind of like a family. You might gripe about your family, but you would beat the snot out of anyone outside the family that said one foul word about it.

Papa didn't brag about it, but I knew he was proud of how the men followed his lead. That's the trouble with being strong like that; it's a lot easier to fight without thinking when you're sure you'll win.

Papa took the news about Moon Lowe's homestead about like we thought he would, and when we rode out of headquarters we were twenty-five men strong, armed to the teeth, and Papa leading us hell-bent for leather. Papa didn't like the Lowes, and as a result, every man riding for him didn't like them and was willing to burn them out as a matter of principle.

Moon must have known we were coming for by the time we got there, he and Zeke were forted up inside that little cabin. They had shutters latched over the few windows and had parked a wagon in front of the door for a barricade.

"Papa, I would be careful if I rode any closer," Gunn said.

We sat our horses in a long line on top of the hill over-looking the homestead. Those that knew Moon, or of him, looked to Papa uneasily. They would charge hell with a bucket of water if Papa asked them to, but the thought of riding several hundred yards across open prairie with Moon and Zeke looking down the barrels of their buffalo guns was enough to give you a sour stomach.

"He built here to cause trouble. He's testing me, or his father is," Papa said. "We let him squat inside our range and more and more of his kind will flood in until we don't have enough good land to graze a herd of goats."

"You're right, but digging them out of there isn't going to be easy," Gunn said.

"Moon Lowe is a cattle-thieving son of a bitch to boot," Papa added.

"Nobody has ever proved that," I said, garnering a scold-ing look from both Papa and Gunn.

"I know a rat when I see one, without having somebody show me his tail," Papa said.

"It's time we ran him out of the country," Gunn said. "Let me handle it."

"Moon Lowe, do you hear me?" Papa shouted.

"I hear you," Moon's voice sounded from within the cabin.

"I want to talk with you."

"You brought an awful lot of guns just to talk."

Papa shoved his Sharps down in his saddle scabbard and scowled down the hill. Most of the men had long since swapped out such guns for lever-action cartridge repeaters like Winchesters and Whitneys. Papa also had a .44 Smith & Wesson on his hip and his old Griswold cap-and-ball tucked in behind his belt buckle. He'd come loaded for bear, but I was glad to see that it looked like he was going to try and talk to Moon first.

Papa nudged his horse forward. There were those that didn't like his hard ways, but anybody who saw him that day couldn't deny that he was a brave man. His hair may have been going gray and his belly a little heavier than it once had been, but he rode down that hill without flinching, even though that no-good Moon Lowe and his partner were as nervous as cats on a hot tin roof and apt to shoot instead of talk.

Gunn didn't let Papa's horse take three steps before he spurred up even with him. The last thing I wanted to do was to ride down there, but I couldn't let Papa and Gunn go without me. It seemed like I had been traipsing after those two for as long as I could remember. Some things don't give you a choice. If there was one thing the Dollarhydes had in spades, it was pride and expectations. Living up to them was the hard part.

Gunn was cocksure enough to smile at me when I caught up. "Good to see that you could join us."

Papa glanced at me and I could tell he noticed that I

wasn't packing a gun. "Joseph, you'd best hang back with our men."

"No offense, but I'll ride it out with you, Mr. Dollarhyde," I said.

"I'm not questioning your courage," he said. "I want you back there in case that Moon opens up on me. If he does, I want you to promise me that you'll make sure our boys hang his sorry ass and burn that two-by-twice outfit of his to the ground."

"Don't you come any farther!" Moon shouted at us.

"I want to talk things over with you," Papa said.

"To hell you do!"

"You remember what I said," Papa hissed quietly at me.

"The men will do what you want whether I'm back there with them or not." I kept my horse walking beside his. Gunn rode on the other side of him. We went three abreast down that hill.

"That's far enough," Moon said.

We pulled up about a hundred yards in front of the cabin. I could barely make out Moon lying on his belly under that wagon with his Sharps buffalo gun resting across a sack of Arbuckle coffee. He had what looked like a jug of whiskey beside him.

"You've built your cabin on Dollarhyde ground," Papa said.

"I filed with the state for this claim," Moon replied. "You don't own a bit of it."

"You knew my lines. We've run cattle and claimed this country since long before you showed up."

"Get gone. I'm warning you."

"Moon, I'm trying to give you a chance. There won't be any squatting on my range."

"You've got about ten seconds, Dollarhyde, to get your old ass back up that hill or I'm going to start shooting."

"I'll plug him for you, just say the word," Zeke's voice carried to us. A rifle barrel was sticking out between a pair of the window shutters where the voice came from.

"I'll burn you out," Papa said. "Don't push me."

A gun bellowed. I don't know if it was Moon or Zeke that shot, but the bullet spanged off the hardpan to one side of Papa's horse and it reared and made a wild jump. All three of us put the spurs to our horses and fled the way we had come. Gunn had dropped the reins over his saddle horn and was thumbing his Colt at the cabin behind us. I heard Zeke laughing when we finally topped over the hill out of sight of them.

"Next time I won't aim low," Moon's shout barely carried to us.

Our hands gathered their horses around Papa, some of them leaning over their saddle swells, afraid that they might be skylined over the top of the hill.

"How are we going to smoke those two out?" Gunn asked. "Wait till dark?"

"Riders coming," one of the men said.

Papa's horse was still nervous from the gunshots and the race back to cover, but he managed to quiet it and pulled his binoculars from their case and aimed them to the east.

"Who is it?" the same man asked.

"Look's like Clayton Lowe and a handful of his freighters and maybe a few of those hiders that hang around his store," Papa said.

"That's Prince riding beside his daddy, if I'm not mistaken," Gunn said. His eyesight was a wonder, for the riders coming still had to be a mile away. "He must have been here when Joseph and I rode by the first time and rode to get help after we were gone."

"If we let them get to that cabin it's going to be a hell of a fight," somebody said.

"It's going to be a hell of a fight no matter what," Gunn said.

"This is getting out of hand," I said. "We can't open up on Clayton for no reason."

"No reason?" Papa threw me a dirty look, but I could tell he was thinking the same thing. "I should have shot him years ago when I had a better excuse."

"Maybe we ought to let things settle down and come back later," I said. "Maybe they will listen to reason then."

Papa's perturbed look changed to something sly. "We're not licked yet."

An hour later, Papa had half our men sitting in scattered gun pits dug along the top of the ridge. All the cowboys looked grim, but I don't know if that was because they had to dig holes with nothing but their sheath knives, or because they knew what was coming. Papa had those of us riding back to the ranch leave our rifles and ammunition with those we were leaving behind in the gun pits.

"Don't shoot unless they try to come up the hill," Papa said. "We'll be back come morning."

"What's Papa planning?" I asked Gunn.

Gunn shrugged. "I don't know, but I wouldn't bet against him."

Chapter Thirty-two

There were two big double-freight wagons sitting in the ranch yard when we rode in at dusk. They had been there when we brought Papa's Hereford bulls home, but I paid them little mind and didn't have a clue what was in them.

After a short night's sleep, Papa gathered us all in front of the bunkhouse. Oxen were already yoked to those wagons, and the freighters that brought them looked ready to travel.

"What are they doing?" Gunn asked.

"They're coming with us," Papa said. "If I can't root Moon Lowe out, I'll make sure he doesn't move another inch into our ground."

"What's in those wagons?" I asked. I couldn't see anything for the tarps tied down over the wagon beds.

Papa smiled a wolf smile. "Something I ordered a few months ago. Couldn't have got here at a better time."

It was only five miles to Moon's homestead, and we were there before the sun was good and up. Our men were still manning their gun pits, but were glad to see us.

"Who all is down there now?" Papa questioned one of our cowboys.

"Clayton, Prince, and seven more men armed to the teeth."

"Did they give you any trouble?"

"No, I think their plan is to fort up and wait for us to come."

"Let 'em wait."

The hill we were on was shaped more like a long, low ridge running north to south on the west side of the dip the cabin lay in. Papa sent one of the freight rigs to the north with instructions and had the other one roll along the back-side of the hill headed south. The freighters and our cowboys began pitching out rolls of wire and fence posts at increments.

"What kind of wire did you say that was?" I asked, examining a roll of it. It was twisted, galvanized wire with a two-prong barb every so often along its length.

"Barbed wire," Papa said. "They've been using it some down in South Texas. I ordered it intending on fencing in a big pasture for those new bulls and some of my best cows, but now I've found a better use for it."

"What?"

"I'm going to fence from the Little Wichita as far south as that wire will go. There won't be one more squatter come along that won't see where our boundaries are."

"You're going to build a fence right in front of that bunch over the hill."

"I intend to send a message."

Our men didn't like work that couldn't be done from the back of a horse, but they kept to it because Papa said that was the way it was going to be. It wasn't much of a fence— three strands of wire stretched tight with a team and single-tree, with cedar, mesquite, and oak fence posts set thirty feet apart. All that first day, from dawn until dusk, we dug postholes and stretched wire and took turns manning our gun pits and keeping an eye on Moon's cabin. More of Papa's men had ridden in from the line camps, and we put a guard on the fencing crew. From time to time, Moon or some of his bunch yelled out at us. They could hear the commotion and ongoing work, but couldn't see what we were doing over the hill. We didn't bother to answer them.

Clayton Lowe rode alone up the hill the next morning. I'll give him that much. He wasn't the coward Papa and Gunn thought him to be.

He stopped that fancy gaited horse of his and waited for Papa to have the first word. He studied the fence while he tried to wait Papa out. Finally, he decided he was going to have to start the talking.

"Moon filed on that state land fair and square. As legal as legal can be," Clayton said. "That's the law."

"Best thing you can do is have him pack up and go back where he came from," Papa said. "He does that, and I'll pretend he didn't shoot at me."

"If he had shot at you, you wouldn't be here. He was only warning you."

"You see that fence there? There's a warning for you. Any more of you decide to claim what's mine, my men are going to have orders to shoot you the instant you cross that fence."

"You can't fence in what isn't rightly yours. You're a squatter as much as anybody ever was. Claiming everything in sight whether it's yours or not."

"You try to take it from me. I fought for this place when nobody wanted it, and I'll fight for it now."

Clayton swallowed his anger and took a deep breath. "It's going to take a lot of wire to fence everything you claim."

"I'll buy more. Before I'm through, I'll have six bull-tight strands stretched around it all."

"We keep what we claim, Lowe," Gunn said. "Just like I told you before."

"Your fence cuts across the west end of Moon's claim," Clayton said.

"Tell him to restake his claim," Papa said, pointing to the east. "He's got all of that to choose from."

Clayton sighed like a tired horse come to rest. "I've tried, Dollarhyde. Tried to get along with you. Tried to reason with you, but it never works."

"Best thing you can do is to stick to your own. Tend that town of yours and your freighting business. I don't begrudge you that."

"You aren't the only ones around here. This country's filling up. They're saying that maybe the railroad will reach here from Fort Worth in a few years. Clay County is reorganized and we're the county seat. We've got a telegraph and a county sheriff now."

"Then you ought to be happy. Leave the grass to me."

"The new people are going to see you for what you really are—a high-handed bully and grabber. We're getting civilized and the law won't put up with the way you operate."

"I'm the law on my land, and I'll take care of my own."

"You're starting a fight you can't win. No good can come of it."

"I don't lose, Lowe. Don't know how."

"We'll see what the state has to say about your fence when I talk to the judge. Maybe he won't have the same opinion about you laying siege to my son's homestead and fencing off state land."

"You tell that boy of yours that the next time I suspect he's been stealing my cows I'm going to hunt him down and hang his fat ass from the first tree I come across."

"I'll kill you first."

I noticed the nickel-plated belly gun tucked into Clayton's waist and the way his hand was trembling. I thought for a second that he was about to draw on Papa.

Papa pushed his horse forward until he was beside Clayton, their legs almost touching. "I'm here, right now. Why don't you start killing?"

Clayton tried to hold Papa's hard stare, but he couldn't. He looked next to the Dollarhyde hands gathered around him, and every man of them gave him a look almost as cold as Papa's.

"Don't push me too far." Clayton turned his horse and rode back to Moon's cabin.

"If I had one bit of backshooter bred in me I'd plink him off his horse right now. Save somebody else the trouble," Gunn said. "I still think we ought to ride down there tonight and finish this thing. Those Lowes are going to be a thorn in our sides as long as we let them hang around."

"I'll handle Clayton Lowe," Papa said.

"He'll do like he said," I threw in. "He's going to complain to that judge as soon as he can. You can bet on that."

Papa gave me that sly smile again. "Two can play at that. If he wants to hire lawyers, then we'll hire our own. If he thinks his politician cronies are going to help him, well then, we'll buy us one or two."

"It would be easier and cheaper to shoot him," Gunn said. "And I thought you hated lawyers and politicians."

"Fight fire with fire, I say."

Chapter Thirty-three

Papa put some of the men to cutting more fence posts and left for Austin the next day. We didn't see him for a month, but when he finally returned he brought more wagonloads of barbed wire and a land agent with him.

I don't understand all the legal shenanigans that went on to make the state land situation like it was, but in a nutshell, Texas made up her own homestead rules. Somehow, Texas had managed to keep its land when it was annexed into the Union. As such, the various Federal homestead acts didn't apply in the Lone Star State. Mixed among a 160-acre state homestead act for the general citizens of the state were old Spanish land grants and colony grants from the days when Mexico ruled, headrights for the veterans of the Texas Revolution, homestead laws for Confederate veterans, and the list went on. Couple that with the fact that the government coffers were generally busted from as far back as the Republic days, and that Texas had always sold or traded land to pay its bills or to get improvements it couldn't afford. Railroads were granted large rights-of-way, far in excess of what they needed to lay tracks. Other companies built projects for the state government in exchange for land certificates. Those land certificates were bought and sold and traded hands until sometimes it was hard to say who owned what.

The land agent Papa brought with him worked for some firm out of Sherman, Texas. His company had certificates for three hundred thousand acres of land, and he and Papa sat up half the night dickering. They were at it again late the next morning on the front porch of the big house when Gunn and I joined them.

"A dollar and a half an acre? Are you kidding me?" Gunn asked.

"Hush," Papa said.

The land agent, instead of a lawyer or bookkeeper type like I suspected, was a burly brute with a beard halfway to his belly and the look of a man who knew hard work. Come to find out, he had made a fortune in the freighting and construction business, and had bought land certificates to trade on when he could get them on the cheap. Not only was he a partner in the firm, he was also one of its salesmen and surveyors.

"Times are changing. When the railroad gets here it will bring people wanting land. We've already sold to the cattlemen surrounding you. The only reason they aren't buying some of your ground is out of respect and courtesy, and because you're the biggest operator in these parts," the land agent said.

"If they won't try and take it from us, what makes you think some farmer will?" Gunn asked.

"Those corncob pipe–smoking, piney woods senators back in East Texas think all you big ranchers are robber barons. The newspapers, too. They say you're making a fortune off of grazing your cattle on land the public rightly owns and that the little men of the state could use."

"Where the hell were they when we were fighting Indians

out here?" Gunn asked. "None of them would set a foot out here then."

"You don't have any idea the way things get when you get the government and a pack of lawyers involved. No, if we want to last we need to get in the first punch, before folks like Lowe even know they're in a fight."

"How much deeded land do you have?" the land man asked over his coffee.

"Two years ago, I bought forty-five thousand acres off of a veteran of the Battle of San Jacinto. It was one of those headrights the Republic gave to those who fought in the revolution, you know," Papa said. "That ground covers about seven miles on both banks of the Little Wichita."

"What?" Gunn and I both asked at the same time.

Papa got a twinkle in his eye. "Do you think I haven't seen this coming? Moon Lowe simply reminded me that I need to work faster."

"Is that all?" the land agent asked.

"The boys and I claimed a quarter section each under the state homestead act, and that pretty much covers the head-quarters where most of my improvements are. Had every one of my hands that would, file on a one-sixty themselves. Covered as much of the best water and graze I could."

"Standard practice," the land agent said.

When he said it was standard practice, he was right—the game being that the ranch owner paid the filing fee and the cowboys would sign their claim over to him when the five-year settlement and improvement clause was fulfilled. In truth, a lot of cowboys were kind of wandering sorts, but it didn't matter if they stayed around to "prove up" their claims. What mattered was that they tied up the land on the books and kept anyone else from filing a claim for it. You couldn't get a deed to everything that way, but in a country where water determined where you could live and where you couldn't, it was a good way to lock down a big chunk of country.

"And Clayton Lowe likes to tell everyone that moves in that we don't hold a deed to anything," Gunn said.

"We don't hold the deeds to enough," Papa said. "Not if we're going to keep it all together."

"I know some big operators who don't outright own much more than their headquarters. Hire enough cowboys and you can hold the range around you," Gunn said. "And none of our neighbors are pushing us."

"For how long? Are you willing to bet the future of this ranch on range customs and the goodwill of others?"

"We're the biggest outfit west of anywhere that matters."

"And we end up having more men on the payroll than we really need, simply because we need to keep up a presence. It's an expensive bluff, and our books would look a hell of a lot better if we could cut our payroll in half."

"That's what I'm here for," the land agent said. "To solve your problems."

"How much are you talking about buying?" Gunn asked.

Papa shrugged. "I'd like to buy it all."

I gave a low whistle.

"But unfortunately, I don't have the money for that," Papa said. "Me and Mr. Gunter here are talking about forty thousand acres, and that's going to break our bank account and then some."

"Where are you getting the rest of the money?" Gunn asked.

"You let me do the worrying about that. You never have worried about it before."

"That's taking a big risk."

"You don't get anywhere without taking some calculated chances."

"Forty thousand won't cut it," Gunn said. "I don't see

taking the risk when it doesn't totally solve our worries about somebody else coming in and filing on our ground or buying it out from under us."

"Your father thinks he has a plan for that," the land man said.

"We're going to add more along the Little Wichita and up to the south bank of the Big Wichita, along with a few choice other spots," Papa said. "I'm also buying all I can along our eastern line. That way, we can block access and easement to anybody moving west from the settlements. Fewer of those settlers are apt to spy something they want if they have to ride way to the south to get around behind us."

"It's going to be spotty, at best, and kind of patchwork," the land man said.

"It would work a lot better if it weren't for that school law." Papa saw the question on my face. "The state requires that every alternate section be left for school land in case someday somebody wants to build a school there."

"There ain't any schools out here," Gunn said.

"From the sound of you, I'd say that's a shame." Papa knew how to shut Gunn up. "What do you think, Joseph?"

I stumbled over that, not knowing what to say. Papa never asked me my opinion about anything, unless it was horses or cows. "You'll do what's best."

Gunn got up out of his chair and started down the porch steps.

"Where are you going?" Papa asked.

"You're going to do whatever you want to."

"I want you to take out the fence crew after dinner."

"The boys are about sick of building fence. None of them hired on to hold a set of posthole diggers."

"They'll do what I tell them to if they want paid."

"Listen to him," I said to Papa. "We won't keep good cowboys if you keep sending them out to build fence."

"In two years, maybe less, I want this ranch fenced in." Papa turned his attention back to the land agent, holding out his hand for a handshake. "Forty thousand acres at a dollar and a half an acre. You throw in the surveying, and give me a three-year option on another twenty thousand acres."

"Done." The land man shook Papa's hand.

"You could have done this cheaper without borrowing money and building fence. Give me a crew of cowboys and I'll guarantee you I can hold our lines," Gunn said.

"The deal is done. Do like I told you."

"As bad as I hate wire and fences, I'm riding to town to see if I can hire a fencing crew," Gunn said. "Only way I know to keep from having to build it myself."

"You're pretty loose with my money. In case you haven't noticed, this ranch isn't a democracy. And I don't see you have any room to complain," Papa said. "From what you spend on horses and fancy boots, and the tab that bartender in Destiny hits me up for every time I'm in town, I'd say you've been getting quite a bonus on your wages."

"Yes, master. I'll get back to the fields while you tend to the smart stuff."

"You listen and learn and this place might be something to be proud of when I'm through and hand it over to you."

"Come on, Little Joe." Gunn waved me down the steps.

"You two get on that fence like I said," Papa called out to us.

"Just act like you're going to do like he says," Gunn said. "Makes him feel better."

"You don't ever act like you're going to do what he says."

"Keeping him humble is my job."

Chapter Thirty-four

1881

"The old man has his way, we won't be able to ride three steps without getting off our horse and opening a gate." Gunn put his shoulder to the gatepost and leaned against it to get enough slack in the wire to lift the latch loop off it. "This used to be a good country until he went to fencing."

I looked up and down the line of barbwire stretching to the north and south as far as I could see—six strands and bull tight, just like Papa had said. It had taken him longer than he had wanted, but the whole ranch was finally fenced off, along with two other smaller pastures.

"The only thing I like about looking at that fence is knowing I didn't lift a finger to build it," Gunn added.

The road from the ranch to Destiny ran right through the gate Gunn was opening, and the trail up from Buffalo Springs joined it not far outside the gate. There was a big dust cloud coming up that trail.

"What are you looking at?" Gunn asked as he closed the gate behind me."

"See for yourself."

Gunn mounted and rode to the intersection and stopped. "Is that what I think it is?"

"That's Prince Lowe riding point, if I'm not mistaken."

"So old Clayton is getting into the cow business?"

"Looks like it. That's a big herd for one crew to handle."

"Those Lowes don't know their ass from a hole in the ground when it comes to cattle. Old Clayton ought to stick to his other ventures."

At a glance, there were at least three thousand head of cattle coming up the trail. We waited long enough for Prince Lowe to reach us.

"I wish you boys would move on," he said. "You're causing my leaders to scatter."

"Where'd you get that herd of wolf bait?" Gunn asked.

Prince bit his tongue and didn't let Gunn bait him too far. "They may not be fancy Herefords like you brag about, but they're good South Texas cattle."

Gunn was right. The Lowes didn't know anything about cattle. That mixed herd was a cull lot if I had ever seen one. Half of the cows were so old as to be smooth mouthed, the calves were coughy and runny-eyed, and the entire herd was in poor flesh.

"I guess you Lowes have taken it in your heads to get in the cow business," Gunn said.

"Pa's got another herd like this one coming up the trail behind us."

"It'll take a lot of grass to run them," Gunn said.

Prince looked smug. "Pa bought the Rafter J."

"Old man Dicketts didn't have enough range to run a thousand head."

"We know what we're doing."

"I bet you do."

"The city marshal's looking for you again, Gunn."

"Is he still sore that I knocked that sign over?"

"He's sore that you rode your horse up on the porch of the saloon and busted half the boards."

"A man's entitled to a good time."

"Tell that to the marshal if you've got the nerve to ride in there," Prince said. "I gotta get back to work. Can't say I ever enjoy talking to you."

"So long, Princey."

"You really ought not pick at him so," I said as we rode through their leaders to the far side of the herd, causing the Lowe hands to cuss us.

"Doing that is one of the few hobbies I can find out here to spend my spare time."

"You don't want to ride into town with the marshal looking for you, do you? Might be best to let it lay for a while. I heard you tore up that saloon pretty bad."

"The marshal will get over it. I'm sure he already sent Papa the bill for damages."

"What saloon was it?"

"Kaiser's."

"Kaiser don't own that anymore. Clayton Lowe bought it, from what I hear."

"And that's supposed to bother me. Hell, I would have ridden my horse inside if I had known that."

"Still, it might be a good idea to stay out of Destiny for a while."

"What's the matter with you? Used to be you rode into town every Saturday, rain sleet, snow, or shine. Doesn't have anything to do with that Lowe girl marrying that dry goods salesman, does it?"

"I'm not in the mood, that's all."

"There are other fish in the sea. That Cindy was too bony, anyway."

"You've got the years on me, and I don't see you sporting a wife."

"Wife?"

"Carmelita is sweet on you. You ought to marry her before you get too old and no girl will look at you."

"I admit I've thought about marrying her just to piss Papa off," Gunn said. "He's the only man I know that marries a Mexican woman, but warns his son to stay away from them. Wouldn't do for a Dollarhyde boy to stoop down with the peons. The man's a walking contradiction."

"Carmelita's a nice girl. She'd make you a good wife."

"I ain't looking for a wife. When I finally get tired of this outfit I'm going to ride out of here. Who knows? I might take a notion to see Montana."

"I don't believe you."

"At least I'm not pining over some skinny, bucktoothed snip that dumped me for a shirt salesman."

I looked back at the Lowe herd passing behind us. "You know what that means, don't you?"

Gunn looked at the herd. "Clayton ain't a patch on the seat of Papa's pants. Let him try to play the cattleman."

"Why do you think Clayton wants in the cow business when he owns most of Destiny? He's got his freight business, the store, his land office, and half a dozen farmers share-cropping for him."

"Be like him to take the opportunity to jab Papa in the eye with a sharp stick."

"That's what I mean. Looks like more trouble."

Gunn waved at the city marshal at the edge of town, and then twisted in the saddle and grinned at me. "What trouble?"

Chapter Thirty-five

"That's going to be the last time they cut our fence," Gunn whispered.

The moon was full, and we could see almost as well as if it were daylight. About a hundred yards from where we had taken a stand in a plum bush thicket, three riders were dismounted on the far side of the fence.

"What are you doing?" I asked.

Gunn was sitting in the grass with his Winchester rested on his knee. It was one of those new models, a '76, and shot a short, fat cartridge that would knock over a locomotive. Gunn had to order every new shooting toy that came out, no matter how Papa complained about the expenses.

"We've put the word out about what's going to happen to anybody that cuts our fence. Time we teach this bunch a lesson."

"You can't just shoot a man from ambush."

"Quiet. You spook them and I'm going to shoot you."

"It isn't right, Gunn."

"I'll show you right. The instant I hear that wire snap I'm going to put the fear in that bunch."

"We don't even know who that is out there."

"Damned fence cutters. I don't like wire any more than most of those free grassers, but you don't tear up what's ours. Probably the same bunch that stole those yearlings of ours. They could be fixing to cut our fence so they can ride in and moonlight a few more of our cows."

"You don't know that. I still think those yearlings found a gap in the fence and wandered off. Given time, we'll find them or they'll show up."

"You should have stayed home. You're a good hand. Maybe better than me, but this kind of stuff never has been your cup of tea. Leave the hard stuff to me."

"You don't want to do this. Not really."

Gunn looked to his right and left. Three more of our cowboys were squatting in the grass to either side of us. "When I shoot, you shoot. Aim high, but cut it close enough to them so that they get the message. Satisfied with that, Little Joe?"

"I say we ride down there and see who it is. We can get the law after them once we know who it is."

"That county sheriff is allergic to a horse. He wouldn't ride out of Destiny if you set his tail on fire."

"What about the Rangers?"

"They talk a big fight, but they haven't been able to do anything about this fence cutting, either."

All over the western half of Texas, night riders were cutting fences. As more and more barbed wire went up, the trouble grew worse. Some of the big cattlemen were for the wire, keeping other cattle from drifting on their range, grazing off their grass, and messing up their breeding programs. Most of the fence cutting sorts were smaller operators or men who depended on public lands to graze their cattle. The fact that people like us had fenced in land, consisting in a big part of those alternating school sections that still belonged to the state, was a fight that went all the way to the capital in Austin. While the politicians were trying to figure out what to do, the range country had split into two factions and things were about at a fever pitch.

"Don't do it, Gunn. Think."

"We keep what's ours."

The first strand of barbed wire snapped, and our cowboys' guns cracked at the same time. Gunn took a little longer to shoot, a full count after the rest of them. I thought he was being more careful to make sure he shot high. Full moon or not, shooting at night was an iffy proposition and a man couldn't really use his sights.

The men at the fence shouted something and fought to keep their horses under control. Only one of them managed to find his stirrup in a hurry.

"Give 'em another go," Gunn said.

The boys shot again, flame leaping from their gun barrels so bright it spotted my eyes. Something ripped through the grass between Gunn and me, and then I saw pistol flame from one of those men at the fence.

The fence cutters fired some more, and our boys didn't need to be told what to do. They shot back, that time not holding high. Two of the men at the fence had managed to get on their horses, but the third man was sagging against the barbed wire. In an instant, his horse was down and kicking out the last of its life beside him.

"Stop shooting, damn you," one of the fence cutters called out at us.

Either our hands heard him, or their magazines were dry. The two on horseback down at the fence managed to get their buddy untangled from the wire and up behind one of them.

"We letting them go?" one of our cowboys asked.

"I think they got the message," Gunn said.

When the fence cutters were gone, we rode down to the fence.

"That's Prince Lowe's horse," one of the men said. "Deader than a doorknob."

"Any of you boys hurt?" Gunn asked.

Muffled confirmations said that everybody on our side had come out unscathed.

"If that was Prince in the wire, I don't know that he fared so well," another said.

"This isn't good, Gunn," I said.

"Should have known it was those Lowes."

Chapter Thirty-six

It didn't surprise us when two Texas Rangers rode into the ranch a week later. It did surprise us some that one of them was our old acquaintance Lucius Pike. He looked a good bit older, but every bit as tough.

Papa came down from the big house and stood with his hands on his hips and watched the Rangers ride up the trail. Gunn was sitting in a chair in front of the bunkhouse, cleaning that rifle of his.

"Howdy, Lucius," Papa said when the two lawmen reached the bunkhouse. "You're early. Would have thought a man your age would sleep in a little later."

"Hard to believe it's past daylight and you don't have these boys out working," Pike said.

"This younger generation, you know. What brings you out this way?"

Pike lifted his hat and scratched his head. He hadn't been bald back the first time we met him. "Found a dead horse on your south line."

"Yeah?"

"Buzzards had been at him, but not so much that I couldn't tell he had been shot in the neck."

"So you came here looking for horse killers?"

"I came here because it was on your fence line. The top strand of your wire was cut, and I found a pair of pliers lying in the grass."

"This fence cutting is getting ridiculous."

Ranger Pike nodded. "Also found a whole mess of cartridge cases about a hundred yards on your side of the wire."

Gunn started to say something, but Papa cut him off. "Sounds like somebody got caught cutting wire."

"That's plain enough and why I'm here," Pike said. "Most of those cases were .44-40s, but one of you boys is packing bigger. Found a couple of these."

Pike held up a fat, short, bottlenecked brass case between his thumb and forefinger. It was a .45-75 hull, and the same as Gunn's '76 Winchester used. He cast a look at the rifle laid across Gunn's knees.

"Whose horse was it?" Papa asked.

"Don't know yet. What's worse is I found a big splash of dried blood that I don't think belonged to that horse."

"What can we do for you?"

"Argyle, I've known you too long to beat around the bush, so don't play cute with me. You know that was your boys shooting after they caught somebody cutting your fence."

"You here to arrest my hands for shooting that horse?"

"I'm here to give you a warning. Word is that Prince Lowe got careless cleaning his gun and shot himself in the thigh. Like to have bled to death before the doctor got to him."

"A man ought to know how to handle a gun if he's going to wear one. Maybe you ought to go clean it for him next time."

"Prince Lowe ain't going to say what really happened to him, but I can read between the lines. Saddle was gone from that dead horse, so one of them most have rode back and fetched it. But I swear I've seen Prince riding a gray horse like the one we found."

"Prince Lowe ought to take better care of his horse."

"Texas won't tolerate any more fence cutting. This night riding and pot-shooting is going to end. We don't care who we have to take in."

"Tell that to Prince Lowe."

"I will, but I'm telling it to you, too. Me and this here man beside me wear the badges. You do not."

"I'd hate to get cross with the Rangers."

Pike glared at Papa. "Gotta new state law about fence cutting. Somebody cuts your fence, you tell us and we'll handle it. Witnesses or not, no matter who's to blame, I'm going to be highly displeasured the next time I have to ride out here because you boys have taken it into your head to play vigilante."

"We'll yell out to you first thing," Gunn said.

Pike put his hand on his pistol holster and stretched a kink out of his hips. "Smirk all you want to, Gunn Dollarhyde, but you keep this up and I'm going to come back here. You don't want me to come back here. I saved your life once, and I'd hate for you to keep pushing me."

"Light and sit, Pike," Papa said. "No reason for all this bad medicine. How about we catch up on old times over a cup of coffee?"

Pike shook his head. "No, I've got more miles to go, and these old bones don't take the travel like they used to."

"I know what you mean."

Pike pitched the empty rifle case at Gunn as he turned his horse. "Bet that gun kicks like a bitch."

I was standing to one side, having walked up as the Rangers rode in. Pike's horse passed so close to me when he left that it brushed against me.

"Good to see you, Captain Pike," I said.

"No captain to it. It's Sergeant Pike now."

"Good to see you anyway."

Pike pulled up and looked down at me. "Are you still the praying sort?"

"I pray some."

Pike looked back over his shoulder at Gunn. "Might be a good idea to pray for that brother of yours if you've got any say with the man upstairs. If ever I saw a neck born for hanging, it's his."

Chapter Thirty-seven

Fourth of July, 1882

The railroad finally came to Destiny—seventy miles of new tracks laid from Fort Worth. And in honor of that occasion, the town held a bronc busting competition and a picnic. Every hand on the ranch turned out to see the train and celebrate the holiday. There were horse races, a pie auction for the Methodist church, and overall one whale of a good time.

I won the bronc riding contest, although I hate to sound like I'm bragging. I only mention it because it was one of those seldom, perfect days. I knew it from the instant I settled down in the saddle and they pulled the blindfold on that rank black horse I drew. From the first jump, I was right there square in the middle of him. I had my balance and I was in that perfect place were I belonged.

Gunn won second prize, and might have beat me if I hadn't've drawn a tougher horse. Thirty cowboys entered, and it says something about Gunn, that he could outride them all with not but one arm. But Gunn was a top hand. He might be too hotheaded and hard-handed to train a good horse, but nobody ever said he couldn't ride the hair off one.

Papa rarely went into Destiny anymore, but even he was smiling big and telling us that the $D had the best hands in Texas. We laughed our way down to the new depot house to see the train come in. A pretty big crowd was on the landing to do the same thing. It wasn't like anyone had never seen a train, but the arrival of the railroad was a pretty big deal. It made Destiny feel like a real town and like it was going places.

"You wait till next year, and we'll see who gets bragging rights." Gunn slapped me hard between the shoulder blades. There was already the slight smell of liquor on his breath.

I hefted the trophy saddle that I had won on my shoulder to remind him of it. There was a little brass plate nailed to the back of the cantle with a place to engrave my name. I was about to respond with some wisecrack of my own when I saw his attention was already elsewhere. His expression had changed in an instant.

Papa had the same look on his face.

"Well, I'll be," Gunn said. "Look what the dogs drug up."

Hamish stepped down from the forward-most passenger car and looked across the dock at us. It was better than ten years since I had seen him last, but I would have known him anywhere, even in that fancy suit and hat. Oh yes, he looked older, and the smooth, clean face I had once known now sported a mustache and a long set of sideburns. But it was him in the flesh. Anyone looking on could have spotted him for a Dollarhyde at once.

I started to call out to him, but he and Gunn were staring at each other so intently that saying anything would have felt like interrupting them. Gunn was the first to move, crossing the space between them in four long strides.

"Good to see you, brother," Hamish said.

"Is that all you've got to say?" Gunn asked.

Hamish stared at Gunn for a few seconds longer, and then held out his hand. "It's been a long time."

Gunn shook his brother's hand as if they were only old acquaintances. I knew them too good, and shouldn't have expected more. Long and tall and as fine-looking men as you will ever see. Both of them, the spitting image of their father; both of them marked by him in more than their looks. They could have been identical twins, except for the fact that Gunn was blond and Hamish was as dark headed as an Indian. Crazy stubborn.

"Didn't expect this," Gunn said. "What? Two or three letters since you've been gone?"

"You probably had to get someone to read them to you," Hamish said, unable to hide the grin slowly building across his face.

Before either of them could say anything else, a young lady stepped down beside Hamish and wrapped both hands about his elbow. She was wearing the fanciest dress I ever saw and a short top hat with a veil down the back of it and some kind of downy, purple feather plumed about the crown. She looked at Gunn and smiled like she had known him all her life.

"So this is the brother?" she asked.

"This is Gunn."

"Pleased to meet you Miss . . . ?"

"It's Missus," Hamish said.

"Huh?"

"It's Missus Dollarhyde. I'd like you to meet my wife," Hamish said. "Gunn, meet Tiffany. Tiffany, meet my brother Gunn."

She held out a lace-gloved hand and Gunn took it as

daintily as if he knew a thing about manners. "At your service, ma'am."

She laughed. "My, my. You didn't tell me he was so handsome."

"Keep your eye on him. He puts on a good act," Hamish said.

"And who's this dashing cowboy staring at you as if he knows you?" Her eyes latched on to me. "Is this the other legendary and long-lost brother?"

"That's Joseph in the flesh."

"Does he always carry a saddle around?"

"He's looking for a horse to steal," Gunn said.

"And is he always so shy?"

Hamish laughed. "There was a time when we thought he might be a mute."

I set my saddle down, rubbed my palms on my pants legs, and took her hand. "Pardon these two, if you will. Joseph Dollarhyde."

"Such a mannerly bunch," she said, still holding on to my hand. "I must say I'm a tad disappointed. After so many of Hamish's tales of the Texas frontier I expected to see wild men and buffalo herds the instant I stepped off the train."

"You shake off this ugly mug you've got hanging on your arm and I'll give you the grand tour," Gunn said.

"I have barely got off the train and you're already trying to steal my wife," Hamish said.

"I just don't want her to be disappointed. A man has to live up to his reputation." Gunn stepped in between the two of them.

Hamish's expression changed. With Gunn out of the way he saw Papa and Juanita standing against the depot wall. The staring match between him and Papa lasted even longer than the one between him and Gunn. This time, it was Hamish who had to make the first move.

"Papa." Hamish offered his hand.

Papa didn't answer him or take his hand, but Juanita quickly stepped forward and hugged Hamish.

"You look so handsome," she said. "*El guapo.*"

Hamish held her at arm's length. "You're as pretty as ever and I swear you haven't aged a day."

Juanita blushed and ducked her head. Papa cleared his throat and she quickly leaned back against him.

Hamish held out his hand again to Papa. "What's done is done."

"Not in my books. You stole from me. Quit me when I was counting on you."

"You don't think that. I never stole anything in my life."

"Argyle!" Juanita hissed under her breath and gave a quick nod of her chin at Tiffany, waiting behind Hamish and watching it all.

Papa straightened himself and stood a little taller. Slowly, he reached out and took his son's hand. "Welcome back."

An awkward quiet settled over us.

"Excuse me." Tiffany stepped up beside Hamish. "May I be introduced?"

"Forgive me, dear. This is my father, Argyle. Papa, this is my wife, Tiffany."

I never would have guessed Papa could do anything to surprise me. He was consistent if he was anything, and after all the years I thought I had a bit of a handle on him. But you never know.

Papa bowed slightly and doffed his hat in a wide sweep of one hand like I had heard about in the old days, but a practice so far outdated that it should have made him look silly. Instead, he pulled it off in a way that somehow made him look the grand gentleman instead of an old, dried-up cattleman.

"My pleasure, ma'am." Papa always had a strong Southern accent, but for some reason it poured out extra strong and as thick as cane syrup. "I see that my son has a fine eye for beauty."

"Why thank you, sir. You flatter me." Tiffany blushed. "Hamish, you never told me that your family were such charmers."

"Do I detect a bit of New England in your accent?" Papa asked.

"Connecticut, Mr. Dollarhyde."

"Let me introduce you to my wife, Juanita."

Juanita and Tiffany shared a quick hug.

"I see that you, too, have an eye for beauty, Mr. Dollar-hyde," Tiffany said.

"Call me Argyle."

"What say we all go get a bite to eat?" Gunn asked. "My stomach thinks my throat's been cut."

"Now you see my real brother," Hamish said. "Such delicate turns of phrase."

"What brings you back, Hamish?" Papa asked. The smile that he had put on for Tiffany was gone.

Hamish straightened his coat front. "Fort Worth is booming. I thought I might hang my shingle out there and see if I could do some business."

"What kind of business?"

Hamish seemed reluctant to say.

"He's a lawyer, Mr. Dollarhyde," Tiffany said, clutching Hamish's arm again. "A very good one."

"I worked for Tiffany's father's firm for five years," Hamish said.

"Uh-oh. This isn't going to be pretty." Gunn took Tiffany by the arm and whisked her away, throwing back over his shoulder at me, "See to her bags, my good man. Papa and Hamish might be still arguing come tomorrow morning."

"Lawyer, huh?" Papa asked after Gunn and Tiffany were gone. "Never thought I would raise one of those."

"I'm sure you share none of the blame, and we can't all be perfect."

"You haven't changed a bit."

"Not one damned bit, Papa. What say we catch up to Gunn and my wife, and you can chastise me over lunch?"

Chapter Thirty-eight

Hamish's homecoming lasted long into the afternoon. New stories were told and old stories rehashed. Good times, as if Hamish never left, and as if life were as easy and slow as that hot afternoon. Papa set aside his difficulties with Hamish and talked as if a new man. He seemed captivated by Hamish's lovely young wife, and I noticed that they were often holding side conversations of their own. Papa may have poked fun of Hamish for his love of books, but he too was a well-read man and had traveled much when younger. He and Tiffany spoke of New York and Paris—the Paris over in France and not the one in Texas—while Hamish and Gunn told stories from their youth in Alabama.

What knew I of plantations, riverboats, or what the newspapers were saying about the Cuban revolution? What knew I of Harvard and Boston elites and the latest fashions worn on the streets of a place so far away and foreign that I couldn't even imagine it? The longer they talked and the longer they laughed, the more lost I felt. Happy, yes, but nobody wanted to hear me talk about horses and cattle, or range conditions, or the coyote pup I had found and dug from its den the fall before to raise as a pet. Had I mentioned the funny feeling I got when I smelled a good wet wind blowing on the front of a spring storm, or how I liked the sound of the creak of saddle leather and the smell of horse sweat and wood smoke, all of them would have looked at me like I was daft. Not Gunn, maybe, but even he seemed almost a stranger to me in that moment.

They were all talking about things and places I'd never been or never knew, and reliving early times of which I was no part. Seeing them together was more than I ever hoped, but I sat to the side, listening more than speaking, feeling almost an outsider in my own family.

Juanita seemed almost as removed as I did, but twice I saw Tiffany notice that and make an effort to bring her into the conversation by asking questions of her. Juanita, the poor *campesino* and the widow of a vaquero who never owned more than his rope and his saddle, had a class of her own. She smiled like royalty and acted as if she understood everything that was being said. Maybe she understood more than I thought. She was always wise.

I don't know if any of them noticed when I slipped out of the restaurant. At least no one called after me.

It was almost dusk, and only a few families were left on the picnic grounds. Many were saddling horses or harnessing teams to return home. The gentlefolk were weary from a long day, but the young bachelors of the county were just getting going. Destiny now had three saloons, and the product they sold had the cowboys and farmer boys more than ready to celebrate the night away. A group of them had gone down to the edge of town, and I could hear them banging away with their pistols at an old anvil they had set on a tree stump. A dog tore by me at a dead run. Some of the kids had torn down a string of bunting and used it to tie a string of firecrackers to its tail.

I originally intended to go to the livery and check on my horse, but found myself wandering aimlessly down the street. I had nearly walked the length of it when I saw a shadow standing next to the big mound of buffalo bones at the edge of town. It was Cindy standing there, watching the fireworks somebody was launching into the air. I hadn't laid eyes on her in a long time.

"Hello, Joseph," she said when she noticed me.

"Hello, Cindy." I stared up at the looming mound of bones, glowing pale and ghostly under the fireworks exploding overhead. Various bone gatherers hauled them in from the prairie by the wagonload to sell to buyers who shipped them back East to make them into fertilizer or such. I wondered if those bone gatherers felt like grave robbers. Riding along and seeing one of those white bones sticking out of the grass felt to me like looking at a monument.

"The fireworks are pretty, aren't they?" she asked.

I knew she was giving me that impatient frown, even though it had grown too dark for me to see her good. For some reason, I usually frustrated her.

"You haven't been around to see me in almost two years," she said.

"Why, you're a . . ."

"Married woman?" She laughed. "And that means we still can't be friends? Lord knows I could use someone to talk to sometimes. You aren't much for talking, but at least you're usually a good listener."

I looked over my shoulder.

"Don't worry, Goggle Eye ate too much watermelon and went to bed early."

I couldn't believe she called him that. Everybody in town called him by that nickname behind his back, but I wouldn't have thought his wife would, no matter how funny his eyes looked. I wasn't the only one who had been shocked when she decided to marry him. True, he had a going business in town selling dry goods and shoes, but he didn't seem the kind to attract a woman's attention. The times I was around him, I found him a slovenly man, with his shirt always half-untucked, breathing through his mouth while he listened to what you wanted, and grunting when he could instead of talking to answer you.

"Let's take a walk," she said.

"I don't know that we ought to."

"Worried about my reputation or yours?"

"Don't talk like that."

"Come on. Let's take a walk down by the creek like we used to. It's too dark for anyone to see us."

"But . . ."

"My vows didn't say anything against taking a walk with an old friend."

We walked in silence until we made the water's edge. Cindy stumbled and balanced herself against me.

"Joseph, I swear you're even skinnier than ever."

Cindy was always a lean, bony girl herself and not one to talk, but I didn't offer that. If I did, she would want to argue about it, and I never could win an argument with her.

"What you need is to find you a good woman to feed you up. I fear if you don't you're going to end up some hermit like those old cowboys too banged up and crippled to ride a horse anymore and too far past their prime to start a family."

"I eat when I'm hungry. I don't think there's any worry that would require me to find a wife."

"Why haven't you found another sweetheart?"

"How do you know I haven't?"

"Don't lie to me. You aren't any good at it." She bent down and picked up a rock and skipped it across the water. "Are you still sweet on me?"

"What would your husband think about you asking me that?"

"I don't care what he thinks."

"Then why did you marry him?"

"Because he promised me he would sell his store and take me out of this one-horse town. If I had any sense I would have married you."

I didn't know what to say to that.

"Joseph, would you do me a favor?"

"You know I would." Nobody said my name like she did.

"Kiss me." She leaned against me before I had time to answer and kissed me so quick I couldn't get away from her. "All the years you sparked me, and that's, what, only the third or fourth time we ever kissed?"

"We should go back to town."

"'Should' has got nothing to do with it." Her palms were still on my chest and she kissed me again. Her breath tasted like green onions and barbeque sauce. "It's got nothing to do with anything."

I pulled away once more. "You shouldn't have married him if it was me you wanted to kiss."

"Oh, shut up. I take it back when I said you didn't talk too much." She gave me a hard shove in the chest, and it was so unexpected that I lost my balance and fell to a sitting position.

"I'm tired of waiting for something to happen," she said in a husky voice that didn't sound anything like her at all. "I'm tired of sweeping and cleaning after that sweaty goat I married. I'm tired of thinking and dreaming and nobody listening. I'm tired of it all."

"What?"

"You get out of those pants, cowboy."

"Cindy!"

She was unbuttoning my pants before I knew it, and

her grip was surprisingly strong. She broke the last two buttons, and dug her hands under me and gave the seat of my pants a tug. I landed flat on my back and she landed sitting astraddle of me after she gave my pants another tug that left them around my knees.

"I said hush. You owe me this much." She hiked her dress and grabbed one of my hands and shoved it between her legs. She wasn't wearing anything under that dress.

"You can thank me later." She was hot and wet against my hand and when she rubbed against me a hoarse little moan bubbled from her throat. "Don't you dare pull that hand away."

I'd like to say that I tried to talk her out of it, but I didn't. The temptations of the flesh are strong, and I was weak. Cindy always threw me off-balance.

"That's the way. Put your finger inside me." Her hips had a life of their own.

Before I could do anything she was jerking at the fly of my underwear.

"My, my, look what we've got here." Her fingers wrapped around me and I gasped. She shoved my hand from between her legs and scooted forward until she could slip me inside of her. "Oh yes!"

Wrong, wrong, wrong. So wrong. Fornicators and adulterers. Nothing was ever more right. Balance.

I thought she was going to pound me into the ground, but it felt too good to stop. The tangle of my pants wouldn't let me get my heels dug in, and I scrambled to keep us from sliding down the riverbank.

"Give it to me!" she cried.

I wanted nothing more than that. Nothing else mattered, but I was doing all I could do. Lord, help me. Shame and lust squirted out of me and her fingers dug into my chest until I thought she would rip my flesh. I felt my tool going limp, but she was going wilder than ever.

"Oh no, you don't." She ground into me harder and fumbled at the buttons on the top of her dress and shoved it back until her breasts swung free. My hands found them, kneading them and feeling the press of those hard, tight nipples against my palm. One of her hands reached under my neck and bent me forward until my mouth was pressed to her. I took a mouthful and she moaned even louder. I felt her insides shudder against me and her whole body began to tremble and her thighs squeezed me like she wanted to break me in two. After a long while, she fell atop me, breathing heavy and her mouth hot against my neck.

All I could do was lie there and stare up through the tree limbs, my heart hammering wildly in my chest and the sweat running down the crease of my back and tickling my tailbone. Another cluster of firecrackers burst overhead.

"Want to go again?" She raised up a little and looked back between her thighs at me, clucking her tongue and shaking her head. "Doesn't look like it."

As quick as that, she stood and began rearranging and buttoning her dress. "Best get your pants pulled up. It wouldn't do if someone came along and caught us like this. Goggle Eye is lazy, but even he might get his shotgun out from behind the counter and come after you if he knew you were diddling me."

I raised my hips and tugged my pants up, and she laughed again.

"What's the matter?"

She pointed at my feet. My boot heels had dug two holes in the soft ground of the riverbank.

"I think I might have spur marks on me," she snickered. "Trust a cowboy not to take his boots off."

She was a confounding woman.

"Run off with me," I said. "We could leave here and go somewhere else."

"You mean it?"

"I don't have much, but I've saved some."

"Much? Everybody knows your papa is the richest man in these parts."

"Maybe, but I'm not." I took note of the look on her face. "I make wages like every one of his hands. Thirty-five a month and found, and a string of company horses."

"You're kidding me."

"But I've saved some."

"How much?"

"Three hundred dollars, and I've got six good horses of my own that I could sell."

"How far do you think that will take us?" she butted in before I could answer. "I'll tell you where. Nowhere."

"Cindy."

"Didn't you hear me? I want out of here. I'm sick to death of wishing I was someone else, or somewhere else that mattered. There's got to be more and I want it."

"I'll work hard for us. You'll see."

"Too late for that. Too late for us."

"If you could wait."

"I've been waiting and waiting. Sometimes I feel I'm drying up inside and the wind will blow me away."

"I'm sorry."

"Don't be. It isn't your fault."

"I'm still sorry."

"For what?"

"For this. If I respected you I wouldn't have brought you down here and done what we did."

"You never cease to amaze me. That brother of yours

would root me around this riverbank like an old boar hog and never look back at me or say thank you when he was through."

"Gunn? You haven't?"

"No, that isn't my point. But you never fail to remind me that you aren't really a Dollarhyde. It's plain that you're adopted. You'll never make one of them, or a Lowe, either."

"What are you saying?"

"I'm saying you're acting like you've taken advantage of me, when nothing is farther from the truth."

"But . . ."

"But nothing. You think I haven't done this before? Do you think you're the first cowboy that I've crawled on when I got lonely?"

"Tell me that isn't true. You're just saying that to shock me."

"I didn't hear you complaining earlier."

"You've got to leave your husband."

She sighed. "It was fun. Settle for that. Who knows? Maybe we can do it again sometime. Fun's hard to come by, so don't ask so many questions the next time I ask you down to the river."

She pushed me away when I tried to follow her, and I waited for a while after she was gone before I headed back to town. I was lost in my thoughts, trying to recall everything Cindy had said to me, so I didn't notice the men who stepped in front of me until it was too late to run.

"Sneaking out with my sister, Dollarhyde?" Moon was a big man and he made a big shadow.

There were three of them. One of them I took to be Prince, but they didn't give me much time to consider who the third was.

"We're going to teach you not to be messing around with other men's wives."

"Leave him alone, Moon!" Cindy was somewhere behind them.

I had no doubt that I was about to hurt, and hurt very badly. That was how Moon tried to find his balance.

It had been such a perfect day.

Chapter Thirty-nine

Gunn found me not long after daylight the next morning. Somehow, I had managed to crawl my way to the bone pile at the end of the street. I guess I had passed out again. It was a fitting place. I was sure I was going to die or was already dead.

"Joseph, can you hear me?" Gunn asked.

I could hear him fine, although he sounded like he was far away.

"Take it easy with him. I'm guessing that he's got some busted ribs," another familiar voice said.

For some reason, I couldn't see except for a little out of one eye. The faces in the slit of vision left to me faded in and out of focus. I tried to show them that I could walk with some help, but trying to move sent agony through my whole body.

"Run, fetch a doctor," Gunn said.

I heard retreating footsteps and felt Gunn's hand on my shoulder. "Hang in there."

"It hurts. Bad."

"Who did this to you?"

* * *

"He's got three busted ribs, a broken arm, and I'm worried he'll lose that eye."

They thought I couldn't hear them, talking about me like I wasn't even there, until I tried to roll to my side and let out a groan.

"You save his eye. Do you hear me?" Papa said that like the doctor could do it simply because he told him to.

"I've patched him up the best I can. Let me know if he has any setbacks. I'll come back to look at him this evening. Might be a while before the swelling goes down enough for me to have a better look at his eye."

The doctor left, but that didn't mean there still wasn't a crowd in my hotel room. Gunn was standing there beside my bed, and Hamish, too.

I looked up at Gunn and tried a cocky grin like he would do. My face felt like it cracked when I tried it, and I gave up the effort. "Do I look that bad?"

"I've seen you better," Gunn said. "Lay still or you're going to bust your stitches."

My hand found my face, and my fingers lightly traced the row of stitches across my cheek and the other row from my nose to my upper lip. My face felt strange and swollen.

"Let me rest here a little and I'll be ready to ride back to the ranch," I said.

"You lay still. I think you're going to be here for more than a little while." Gunn put his hand on my shoulder again.

"Rest easy," Papa said.

"Water," I mumbled. The words wouldn't shape right. My tongue found a chunk missing from one front tooth.

"Get him some water," Papa said.

"Let him rest. I'll sit with him." Juanita was at the edge of the bed, holding out a glass of water.

The water looked good, but I was so tired.

"Was it Moon Lowe who did this to you?" Gunn asked.

I didn't answer him, but he knew.

"I saw Moon and some of his hands down at the livery corrals on my way here," someone else said.

I knew that second voice. It was Breed Collins, one of Papa's hands. We always thought he was on the run from the law up in the Indian Territory when he first hired on. Crazy fellow, and the one Gunn always took with him when he wanted to go spend a wild night on the town.

"Leave them alone," I said. "Forget about Moon."

"Gunn, don't go off half-cocked," Hamish said. "No good will come of this."

"Listen to your brother," Papa said. "Let's think this out. There's plenty of time to settle with Moon if it was him."

"Look what they did to him," Gunn said.

"It was my fault. I deserved it," I said.

I heard Gunn's boot heels on the floor, leaving.

"Breed's coming with me. Are you going to sit here and lecture me, or come with us and set this thing right?" Gunn asked.

"I'll go with you." Hamish's voice sounded tired, like it used to when we were boys.

"Stop them," I said to Papa. I didn't even know if he was still in the room.

Chapter Forty

I was so tired. I thought if I lay still enough I could sink into that feather mattress, and sink and sink until everything went away. But Gunn was gone out the door, and Breed Collins and Hamish with him. Hamish would try to talk some sense into Gunn, but that Breed wouldn't help. Breed was a fire-eater and would be all for a fight.

I took the water from Juanita and gulped it down, the sting of it waking me. Swallowing hurt my insides.

"Lay still, Joseph," Juanita said.

My right arm was in a splint and hindered by a sling, but I fended her off with my other hand and managed to sit up. My head spun badly, but I got to my feet after a bit.

"Where are my boots?"

Juanita tried to hold me there, but I staggered past her. There wasn't time for my boots. I went out the door in my bare feet and no shirt. Folks taking breakfast in the lobby stared at me when I came down the stairs clutching to the banister and making a slow go of it.

Juanita was behind me, begging me to stop, but she was too scared of knocking me off-balance and sending me tumbling down the stairs to stop me. I also saw Tiffany stand up from one of the tables. She seemed more shocked than anyone about the sight of me, and I must have looked bad. No telling what she was thinking about the family she had married into.

I don't know how long it took me to make my way down the street. I fell once or twice—maybe more, come to think of it. I was sure I wasn't going to get there fast enough. Gunn was going to kill Moon Lowe if I didn't, and then they would hang Gunn, all because of me. Me, the adulterer. Troublemaker. It's hard sometimes being a human.

When I was a boy I used to wish sometimes I was a horse. But horses don't have any more balance than we do. Running from shadows and spooking at the world around them. Lashing out with their hooves. Born scared before they know what to be scared of. Flighty, imperfect creatures. Unpredictable. Hurt you sometimes without meaning to.

Papa, Hamish, and Clayton Lowe were talking in front of Clayton's store. I could tell they were arguing about Moon. Prince and another man stood on the porch behind and above them. Gunn and Breed Collins stood off to one side, facing Prince and the other man, and Prince was already talking loud and nervous.

I fell against a hitching rail, trying to catch my breath. Hamish went at a run across the street, and I knew Papa had sent him to get the city marshal. He wasn't going to have time. Papa was too caught up in what he was saying to Clayton to see how Gunn and Breed were standing—spread wide apart from each other with their fists already wrapped around their gun butts.

"Where's Moon?" Gunn asked.

"He ain't around." Prince was standing in the door of the store with his left shoulder leaning against the doorjamb.

There was a toothpick in one corner of his mouth and a birdshead Colt stuffed behind his waistband.

"Make them stop, Pa!" Cindy Lowe was running down the boardwalk toward the store.

"Prince, you get back in there!" Clayton said.

The other man with Prince was sidling along the front wall, casual-like. People called him Wells, or something like that, one of Clayton's freighters. He wasn't wearing a belt gun, but he was trying really hard to act like he wasn't inching closer to the carbine stuffed in the saddle scabbard of the horse he had tied at the corner of the porch.

"Did you help beat my brother?" Gunn asked.

Papa started for Gunn, but he wasn't going to get there fast enough. Not with Prince sneering and mouthing like he was and all but daring Gunn to do something.

"We gave him what he deserved," Prince said.

Gunn's Colt swung up before the words even finished from Prince's mouth. Cindy was still running, but she wasn't going to get there in time, either. Prince never even got that birdshead Colt out of his pants before Gunn put a bullet in his gut and another in his chest as he was sliding down the doorjamb.

It all happened so fast—Gunn turned sideways to Prince with his pistol slowly lowering to hang beside his leg, and Cindy running and screaming across the porch. Prince's buddy, Wells, made a bad mistake, but he had no more time to work things out than I did. He lunged for his rifle, and Breed Collins didn't wait for him to get a hand on it. He thumbed two quick rounds at him.

It was all an accident. I'd seen Breed shoot, and the last thing he was likely to hit was what he was aiming at. He was lucky his first bullet hit that man in the ankle and knocked him down. He wasn't so lucky with his second bullet, because it hit Cindy the instant she ran between the two of them. She fell fast, and I knew she was dead the instant she hit the porch.

Papa and Clayton were both shouting something, and Cindy's mama was shrieking inside the store. A cluster of horses went by me at a run. It was one of our hands leading a pair of saddled horses for Gunn and Breed.

I must have passed out, for I don't remember anything after that. The family thinks I didn't even see any of it and that I went unconscious before it all happened. I don't tell them any different, but I saw it all. Wish I hadn't, because some things are hard to take.

They buried Cindy and Prince Lowe in the town cemetery two days later. I heard that Wells's wife and three children came down in a wagon all the way from Kansas and took him home. Breed's bullet had busted his ankle so bad that they said he was never going to walk right again.

I was in no shape to attend Cindy's funeral, even if Clayton Lowe would have let me.

Gunn and Breed went on the scout, with the county sheriff and Lucius Pike and a company of Rangers looking for them. There was a rumor that Clayton put a five-hundred-dollar bounty on Gunn's head on the sly, dead not alive. Hamish offered to defend Gunn in court, but none of us knew where Gunn was. Some said he went to Old Mexico and some said he went to Arizona. I never heard from him, but none of us were much for writing letters.

A week after that, I packed my bedroll, saddled my favorite horse, and drove the rest of my horses out of the trap and down the road until I passed them through the gate. Last I saw of them, they were running as loose and free as a herd of mustangs. I like to think they're still running.

I could have gone in any direction, but it didn't matter, so I let my horse take me where he would. It was a big world, and even a horse knows when it's time to run. Things can follow you, but running for the sake of running is sometimes good for the soul. I needed to find balance again.

PART III
ARGYLE

Chapter Forty-one

1894

Porches are something I never thought I would like, but you can see a long ways from a porch with a good view—things that are and things that only were, years from now or years before. The brandy helps.

There was a time I could never quit moving. I spent most of my life chasing one thing or another, but I found myself sitting more and more. I'd blame it on my aching joints, but I simply got lazy. There was no excuse for it. No man ever made anything of himself sitting. If I had to pick between smarts and ambition, I'll take the man with some drive every time. Living in the past isn't living. Moving is the only way to keep ahead, because life doesn't wait on anyone.

Drought, drought, and more drought, the worst I had ever seen. Two years' worth, and there was no end in sight. The country was so dry and burnt that I had almost forgotten the feel of rain. Heat lightning played across the evening sky to the west, only teasing me, but I hoped for a storm anyway. Call me a bullheaded old fool. I've been called that before.

I set my empty glass aside while I watched Paco moving a set of yearling heifers into the corrals. I wished there was somebody to help him besides his ten-year-old son, but I couldn't afford the help. Paco came up from the village from time to time when I needed him for a little day work.

It was hard to admit that I could barely afford to pay one old man every now and then, even to myself, but I despise sugarcoating things. No whining, no excuses, no saying you're sorry. Good enough to live by.

At least those Hereford heifers would bring me good money. Even the boys laughed at me when I started buying them, but I was right. A man intending to make money needs to think ahead, and a blind man could have seen the longhorn's day was going to come to an end. Those Herefords made money and would again. Half the ranches in West Texas owed their herds to the seed stock I sold them.

Gunn's parole had finally come through and they were letting him out of the Huntsville prison. Seven years was a long time for a man to be locked up. Them sending him there in the first place was the damnedest tragedy of justice in the history of Clay County. I don't care if Gunn went on the run and didn't turn himself in for two years. It wasn't right. He didn't kill that girl. Breed Collins did, and they hung him for it. Things should have been squared.

I did everything I could. Dragged that case out for two years and kept Gunn out of prison that much longer. It cost me five thousand dollars to hire good lawyers to defend him, but Clayton Lowe had that jury in his pocket. Half of them owed him money—damned cotton farmers and hayseeds, most of them. I should have never listened to Hamish and brought in those Dallas lawyers. Should have bought that jury myself instead.

I told Gunn not to go after those Lowes, but he wouldn't listen. Never would. But I don't blame him. God hates a coward, and a man doesn't let someone beat a family member half to death without doing something about it. The law wouldn't have done anything to Prince, just like they let Moon off with a pat on the wrist for what he did to Joseph.

My boys.

Joseph was always a strange one. He was the best hand with a horse I ever saw and knew range cattle in a way few men did, but that didn't mean I could ever figure him out. Did the best I could for him, but he never would take ahold of life. Then he quit me. Did my best for all of them. Juanita thinks that the Lowe girl getting killed broke Joseph up more than he could take, and that could be. He was always skittish and worried, and no fire in his belly. Too soft, and this country won't abide a soft man, no matter how good he was.

Somebody in a buggy was wheeling up the road. My eyes were still as good as ever, and I could tell it was Hamish before he even made it to the corrals. At least he didn't have Tiffany with him. That girl was a quite a gem, but he usually only brought her along so he could avoid the hard talk between us, counting on me to be the polite old man in her presence. It was about time we had a real talk. He had been hinting around of late about things I didn't like.

"Don't be stubborn, or you'll run him off again." Juanita brushed against me in passing. Men used to sneak glances at her when they thought I wasn't looking. She was once the prettiest woman in three counties, and if it weren't for Tiffany, she still would have been. Sarah was pretty like that. A man like me was lucky to have found two such beauties in one lifetime.

I didn't think of Sarah much, except sometimes when I can't sleep. I know the boys still blame me for that, but we all have to move on. Some say that time heals all wounds, but I don't know that it's true. I think such wounds never really heal, but some are tough enough to suffer them.

"I'll say whatever needs said."

"I've heard you tell your sons more than once not to give advice until someone asks for it."

"I'm his father. I don't need his leave to give my opinion."

"You know what he's come for."

"I've already given him my answer. That boy's a stubborn fool if he asks a second time."

"That boy is a forty-something-year-old man. People think highly of him. They say he could run for senator and probably win."

"I've always listened to him, but that doesn't mean I have to agree with him."

"All he wants is for you to see how good he has done. Don't you see he wants to show you that he can do things?"

Juanita went back inside before I could say anything else.

The hat Hamish was wearing was the silliest thing I ever saw. Town hat. The brim on it wouldn't shade enough sun to matter. It was a hat for a man that was rarely outdoors.

That's a Harvard man for you. He spent a fortune at that college to unlearn every smart thing I taught him, and spent all of his time and efforts politicking down in Fort Worth and trying to figure out what kind of business would make him money in the city when he should have stuck to cattle and land like I tried to teach him.

"Hello, Papa." Hamish took a little cast-iron weight with a rope on it from the floorboard of the buggy. He snapped the rope to the bit ring on the near horse and dropped the weight on the ground.

"That team acts green broke and spooky. I wouldn't trust them to stand tied to that little thing."

"I believe they'll stand fine."

"Suit yourself, but I've seen the time when a man was careful he didn't end up afoot."

Hamish took a seat on the edge of the porch far enough from me that he could twist around occasionally and look my way. "It sure is dry. I've never seen it like this."

"It's been bad before. You were gone a long time."

"When was it worse?"

"It will rain again. Always does."

"You don't have any more time. I talked to the bank. The foreclosure papers are going through."

"Gunn will be home this week, or maybe the week after. I've got Paco putting together a fancy set of heifers. Man up at Fort Hays, Kansas, said he would take two hundred of them for a good price."

"The price of two hundred heifers isn't a drop in the bucket compared to what you need. The ranch is broke. You're always so damned proud of your business sense, so why can't you admit that?"

"I didn't say it would solve everything. Just a start. I don't need you to tell me the predicament I'm in."

"You're broke and that's all there is to it."

"There's always something in your way if you want to amount to anything. First it was Indians and tornadoes and prairie fire, and now it's bankers and trainloads of farmers dumb enough to think they can make a living off a quarter section of free ground where it never rains.

"I started this ranch with nothing but what we could put in two wagons. Brought you out here when nobody in their right mind would set a foot in this country. Don't tell me about hard times. I've got the scars, boy."

"I was there, too." Hamish sighed.

I hated when he did that. My generation would never sigh at our elders. It was a sign of disrespect, and it was a sign of patronizing an old man.

"You owe almost a quarter of a million dollars to the bank, and you couldn't even make the interest payment this year. Everything you own is mortgaged," Hamish said. "That's the story I'm here to talk about."

"Those bankers were more than glad to take my money when I was making it hand over fist. Damn lot of crooks is what they are."

"I didn't hear you complaining every time you needed more money than you had and were wanting a loan."

"Is that what you came up here for, to tell me how nice my bankers are?"

"No, I came here to advise you. That's what you pay me for."

"I pay you because it grates on me to pay any lawyer, but it's some easier when it's my son."

"The Brits' offer is still on the table."

"I won't sell. I've already told them that. If I wanted to sell out I would have done it ten years ago. They aren't the first foreigners to try and buy me out."

"If I'm right, the bank is going to sell it to them anyway when the foreclosure is final. They don't even know that the syndicate is making this offer to you. The bank thinks they'll foreclose on you and make a little profit above your loans. The Brits think they can buy it cheaper off you than they can the bank."

I knocked my chair over getting up and stepped off the porch.

"There's a chance the bank might break up the ranch and sell it off piecemeal," Hamish added.

"It will be a cold day in hell when I see this place broken up and plowed into farms."

I thought better when I could pace, and it did me good to be able to kick the dirt once in a while when I was mad. Hamish didn't know much about the cow business, but he was right. Leave it to him to understand things when it came down to the books and pencil-pushing, tightfisted bankers. The only thing left was to make the best of the bad.

Back in the early '80s, every rich Englishman and Scotsman with the ability to sell some bonds or put a syndicate together wanted to own a ranch in the United States. Many of the old-time cattlemen, men that had never done much more than keep their heads above water in the cattle business, cashed in and sold out. Some of them made a killing. I turned down almost a half-million dollars for the ranch twice in those years.

But things were booming then and the ranch was growing. Over and over, after every good year, I took everything the ranch made and sunk it back into the business. A man has to think big if he wants to be big. You can't build anything unless you're willing to take some risks, and I took plenty.

I'll be the first to admit I blew through some money I shouldn't have. I like good brandy and a fine cigar, and those don't come cheap. I used to entertain the important folks from down at the capital and over to Fort Worth, cattle buyers, tycoon ranchers, bankers, and even a politician or two wanting my vote and my blessing, God forgive me. General Sherman even came to the house once and danced in the parlor with Juanita. Back in those days the ranch's future looked like a big bowl of gravy.

And then the blizzards came. I was better prepared than most, but I still lost stock. And then the cow market went to hell and the farmers and homesteaders came, crying for the state to open up the lease land. That meant buying more ground. Cows would only make a man so much, and the real estate men waiting at the trains for those farmers drove the cost of ground up so high that it was impossible to make a profit. Money, money, and more money, most of it pouring through my fingers like a sieve.

"Sell out. I got the Brits to make a new offer," Hamish said. "Same deal as before, except you keep the headquarters and its three sections and your choice of two sections on the river," Hamish said.

"Easy for you to say. You don't give a damn about this ranch."

Hamish held out an envelope. "It gets worse."

I took the envelope. It had the state seal stamped on it. "What is it?"

"The state ruled in Clayton Lowe's favor. You've got to give him easement through your fence. The law says that you can't block access to public lands."

"I lease those school sections for grazing. There's a damned gate to go through if they ever want to build a school inside the ranch."

"You didn't pay the lease, but it doesn't matter. The state's putting some of those school sections up for auction."

"Never thought it would come to this."

"Sell off everything but here and along the river. The Brits are counting on being able to outbid everyone for the state school sections. They think they can put together one of the biggest ranches in Texas. Selling to them might be the only way to keep Clayton Lowe's land office from moving farmers on our ground."

"Our ground?"

"I never said I didn't care about this place. I put a lot of years into it, right beside you," Hamish said. "And God knows I don't have any more use for Clayton Lowe than you do."

"First time I ever gave up."

"You always said that you have to fight with your brains and not just your fists. Selling off most of the ranch won't pay you totally out of debt, but it will buy you some time and give you a chance."

"Tell them to draw up the papers and I'll sign them," I said. "But I keep all of the old headright on the river and the headquarters. And I keep two hundred of my best heifers and ten bulls."

"They won't go for that. Place isn't worth it without access to the river. How about the headquarters and half the headright on the river? Say you keep the three sections immediately north of the headquarters and the same cut of the stock? I think they'll go for that."

"How much commission are you charging me for this deal? I know you lawyers don't work cheap."

"You haven't paid me your retainer fee in six months."

"Bill me again. I must have lost my mail."

"This one's on the house."

"Business must be good in Fort Worth."

"One of my first clients, a stubborn old cowman you might know, made everyone think I knew what I was doing. People did business with me on his say-so." Hamish went back to his buggy and undid the ground tie.

I wasn't about to let him have the last word. "You're lucky those horses didn't drag that weight off."

"You're going to have to ride the train down to Fort Worth to sign the papers. Be there next Monday."

"I'll be there. I can still find my way around."

Hamish climbed in the buggy and wheeled it around in the yard.

"The brand doesn't come with the place," I called after him. "They don't buy the brand. You tell them that."

I don't know if Hamish heard me. He raised one hand over his shoulder at me as he drove away, but that didn't mean anything. He never would listen.

Chapter Forty-two

I couldn't sleep that night. There was going to be a lot to do. I would have to make a range count of the herd to finalize the sale, and I needed to hire some help for Paco and me. Maybe old Miguel would help, if he could still ride a horse. And I would have to wire that man up in Kansas and tell him that the heifers weren't for sale anymore, because I was going to need them to start over.

Sixty-six years old and starting over. It could be done, but a man has only so much time. I was thirty-eight when I first came to this country and nothing to my name besides the thought that everything I left back in Alabama was gone. Years I had spent building up that plantation, and then all of it was lost to the war. I had all that indignity to drive me, and what seemed like forever to get it done. But it wasn't going to be like that again. The indignity was there, but time had finally caught up with me. That made me madder than anything could.

No whining, no excuses, no saying you're sorry. There were things to do, and I never counted on anyone else to do them for me. Get moving, even if you're old and tired and you've messed everything up.

I would have sat on the porch, but Juanita would get up and make me come back to bed. She thought I was getting too old to sit out in the night air, even if it was summertime and almost as hot as the daytime.

I took my pillow and walked out into the pasture beside the house. I could always think better without a ceiling blocking the sky. There was a little bit of a breeze blowing through the dry grass, and I found a likely spot and rested my head on the pillow, with nothing but the stars overhead to get in the way of my thinking.

I fell asleep. It was already turning gray when I woke up, but there was still time for me to be sitting at the kitchen table when Juanita came downstairs. I tried to shake the dirt and grass off the pillow. Juanita was picky about her household.

There was somebody sitting in a chair on the porch. It wasn't Juanita, for I could see the occasional glow of a cigarette when they drew on it.

"Do you always take a pillow with you when you go for a morning walk?" Gunn asked.

"Why didn't you telegraph me you were on your way?"

"Figured I could get here before you got around to going to town and picking up a telegraph."

It had grown light enough for me to make him out. He hadn't shaved in days.

"Good to have you back."

"You're not near as glad as I am to be out." There were crow's-feet at the corners of his eyes that I didn't remember and a scar on his chin that looked like the leftovers of a bad cut. That wasn't there when he went off.

"Take a few days to unwind. We've got plenty of time before I put you back to work."

"Sounds like you need some help. I saw Hamish at the depot house in Destiny. He was on his way to Fort Worth."

"We'll get things going again. I'm keeping the best of the stock. We'll high-grade them, and you can pick out a few of our top horses to hold out of the deal."

"Woman I saw in town stepped wide of me. I don't know how she knew, but she did. You'd have thought I had the plague. Maybe I've got some mark on me that don't show in the mirror, 'convict' written on my back."

"Lot of newcomers. It will take them a while to know who you are. The Dollarhyde name is still worth something around here."

"Not enough, apparently. Hamish says things have gone to hell in a hand basket."

"I never knew you to back down from a fight. We built it once, we can do it again."

We sat without talking for a while. I waited until he had rolled another cigarette before I spoke again. "Your saddle is in the barn. I oiled it up for you when I heard you were getting out."

"Chairs," he said.

"What?"

"That's what I did in prison. Wove chair seats."

"That's all over now. Put it behind you. It's going to take both of us to keep our stick afloat."

"First time I ever heard you sound like you needed help."

"You want any inheritance, you're going to have to fight for it. I taught you that much. Folks in town will be saying that we Dollarhydes are done."

"Maybe they're right."

"Boy, what did I always tell you?"

"We keep what we claim. We keep what's ours."

"That's right."

"Prison's the same way, but you don't always win."

"If it was easy, everyone would be winners. Life is dog-eat-dog, and I'll be damned if I would have it any other way."

"Anyone ever tell you that you're an optimist?"

"Is that a nice way of saying your father is one stubborn old son of a bitch?"

Chapter Forty-three

"I can't believe we're farming now." Gunn set aside the posthole diggers, lifting them high and stabbing them into the ground beside the hole we were working on. One-armed or not, he could dig like a badger.

"You didn't have to do the plowing." I looked at the neat, even rows of broken, fresh-turned ground while I lifted the tamping bar and beat at the hard-packed earth in the bottom of the hole. "I traded a fat beef for that plow work. First meat those farmers have probably had in months, and they were more than glad to break ground for us."

"Still, I never thought we would stoop to farming." Gunn's white shirt was stained and soaked with sweat, even though it was a cool fall day.

"It's livestock farming."

"Whatever name you give it, it's still farming. Ranching is where you turn out some cattle on grass and hire cowboys to handle them."

"No, that's cowboying you're talking about. Ranching is

growing beef and making money at it. Big pastures, little pastures, it doesn't matter."

"Matters to me."

I pointed to the eighty-acre perfect square of plowed ground, on the edge of which we were building the new fence. "Those men I hired are supposed to come back tomorrow and pull a harrow over this to smooth it out, and then they're going to plant it in wheat. Given the rain, this little patch of wheat will graze a bunch of yearlings until we have to pull them off in March. Come May or June, we can pay someone to harvest the wheat and maybe make a little money per bushel."

"Sounds like farming to me."

"I'm trying to figure out a way for us to make the living we used to make on four hundred thousand acres with twenty-four thousand acres."

"Why don't we ride up into the Indian Nations and see if we can lease some reservation ground from the Indians? That's the only open country left available that I know of."

"How many times do we have to go over this? We don't have the coin to play that game. If you've got a stash of money that I don't know about and want to spend all your time kissing up to Indians, Indian agents, and bribing politicians, go ahead."

"Never thought I would see the day when there isn't enough room for cowboys in Texas."

"People are hungry for land, like we were when we came out here."

"Most of those dirt farmers will starve out in another year. They're building half-assed towns where no towns should exist."

"Yes, most of them will starve out, but it will take a lot of them longer than that. And even when most of them are gone, it will be too late to help us."

"There are still big range operators. Burk Burnett is running more country than he ever did."

"Yes, but that won't last, not at the size they're used to operating at. Not the way we used to operate. They're running stock in places farmers are least likely to want to settle, or leasing Indian ground. They're playing a big-money game that is going to change when Congress busts up the last of the reservations up in the Territory. Instead of fighting a losing fight, I intend to be ahead of the game."

"Bobwire and stock farming, huh?" Gunn, like a lot of cowboys, referred to barbwire as "bobwire."

"And other things. A smart man sees what opportunities are coming and plans accordingly."

"Bobwire. I hated the stuff since the first wagonload you hauled in here. And here I am digging postholes and helping you string more of it," Gunn said. "No job at all for a good cowboy."

"Tough job for a one-armed complainer and an old man. Finish that hole and I'll get another post out of the wagon."

"I promise you this is the last fence I'm helping you build. In four years, I'd think you'd be sick of fencing and cross fencing this place."

"It the only way we can control what grazing we have. Take a look at the country we used to run cattle on, the same country you're pining so for. There isn't much grass left because we ran too many cows on it. Grazed it so hard we killed it out. There are weeds and sagebrush and mesquite taking over where there used to be good grass. This country was made to graze, but it needs a break to keep things growing. It needs backed off of when the rain doesn't come."

"There were more buffalo here than we ever had cattle."

"And those buffalo didn't stay on the same range all the

time. They grazed things short and then moved on. Gave the grass time to come back without hitting it too hard."

"Not everyone agrees with you. They say it's because it's been drier than normal."

"All the more reason to graze something a bit and then give it a break. You know, manage things. These smaller pastures we're fencing off give us a chance to do that."

"You sound like Hamish. Did you get all this from some book? All the cowmen in Texas, and I don't see them doing this."

"You haven't looked hard enough, but I admit there aren't many. And I admit I'm making this up as I go."

"I guess that means we're going to keep building fence and digging stock tanks for water."

"And we're going to cut a little hay to have around when we get a bad winter and the snow stays on the ground. And I'm going to have a few more water wells drilled. Those tanks we've been digging catch a little rain, but it's not enough. We need more windmills. That was one of the troubles we had running cattle on open range. There's not much standing or running water out here, and a cow will only graze so far from water. We couldn't even use all of the grass we had. Get out ten miles from water and see how much better shape the grass is in than closer."

"None of that explains how we are going to make money with our little herd, no matter what we do."

"I've told you this all before. We kept the best of our breeding stock, and I spent years breeding up those cows, mind you, crossing the best of our old longhorn and short-horn crosses with good Hereford stock. If we can't make money with numbers, we'll make it with quality. Give us a few more years, and everybody will want to buy our bulls and heifers to improve or start their own herds. One of our steers will make a man twice the money those old longhorns would on the same ground. Smaller ranches mean other cattlemen are going to be in the same dilemma we are. We'll sell them the cattle to make a go of it, and get premium prices doing it."

"Even if one of your fancy whitefaces makes twice the money a longhorn would, running a couple of hundred of them isn't going to make the same money as running twenty thousand longhorns."

"It isn't only the price difference. I used to have twenty to thirty cowboys on the payroll, and more during the spring and fall. Had cooks and blacksmiths and doctor bills when one of you fool cowboys busted himself up riding horses that never made me a dime. While you boys sat around bragging how you wouldn't do anything that couldn't be done from a saddle, I was losing calves to wolves, losing cattle because they drifted in the winter, and losing them because they were strung from hell to break-fast and anybody with a horse, a running iron, and some dishonest smarts could drive a bunch off and sell them and we'd never know what happened except that our count was low during roundup."

"Profit isn't everything. This ranch used to be something to be proud of. It used to be big. People knew our brand and it meant something."

"Keep helping me with the improvements I have in mind, and our brand will mean more than it ever did. We've got a railroad in our backyard and the means to ship our high-grade cattle anywhere."

"I miss the time when I could saddle a horse and ride all day and never hit a fence or quit seeing our cattle. I miss spring roundup and making a drive up the trail to market," he said. "I ride into town now, and there are more men talking about cotton prices than there are cowboys. I don't even recognize where I live anymore."

"Speaking of saloons, the city marshal was out here yesterday while you were gone."

"Was he looking for me?"

"Not like you're thinking. He only wanted to talk to you."

"That marshal doesn't like cowboys."

"He said he only wanted to talk to you and make sure you were getting along all right since you got out of prison. Destiny isn't quite as wide-open as it used to be, and he wanted you to know the rules when you come to his town."

"Checking up on the con, huh? Thinking I have to take that from him because I'll be too scared of going back to prison."

"Maybe so, but have the sense to consider that and don't make trouble in his town. You've got a prison record, and there are those that are going to judge you more harshly because of it. There are always those folks that like to see someone successful humbled—the high and mighty brought low, you know? We had a good run for a long time here and cut a pretty wide swath, and some are bound to be jealous."

"I remember when the city marshal didn't bother Dollarhyde hands."

"You sound like a child." I took a fence post from the wagon and brought it back and dropped it in the hole he'd finished. "There was a time when I didn't know anything but the cotton business and running a plantation. When I first came out here, did I try to do things like I did in Alabama? Did I know the first thing about cattle? All I knew is that things had changed for us, and I heard that the buyers up in Kansas might buy Texas steers. That was the situation then, and I adapted to it. This is the situation now. Adapt to it. You're forty-four years old. Time you grew up and took ahold."

"I could go to work riding for Burnett. The wages I could earn would help us out."

"Take your saddle up across the Big Wichita if you want to. Go be a thirty-five-dollar-a-month cowboy if you want to. Or, you can stay here and build something. Cowboying is for young fools. There's no future in it."

Gunn put his mind to tamping the dirt back in around the fence post with the tamping bar. Once finished, he gave the post a tug to make sure it was set tight and started for the next stake set in the long line stretching down the side of the new field.

"Tell me you're going to hang in there," I said.

"I haven't gone anywhere yet, but tell me you don't miss the old days."

"I don't miss all of it, but I miss the good parts worse every day," I said.

"I was thinking about Abilene the other day. Damned, there were some wild gals in that town."

I took the posthole diggers from him to take my turn for a spell. "I wonder what ever happened to Train Horn Sally, or Sal, or whatever they called her?"

"What did you ever know about her?"

I drove the diggers three inches into the hard ground, liking knowing that there was still a little steel in my shoulders and arms. "Boy, I wasn't always so damned old. No sir, I wasn't."

Chapter Forty-four

It was a cold, drizzly fall morning. I guess that was fitting, considering what we had to do. I had the wagon hitched by daylight, and didn't wait long for Gunn to saddle a horse. Neither of us said anything to each other when we rolled out of the ranch. The team plodded along the muddy road, and both of us tugged our hat brims down and kept our chins tucked into the collars of our yellow, India rubber slickers.

Hamish had built himself a house down the road a piece in the middle of the homestead quarter section I had him file on all those years before when he was but a boy. Hamish didn't talk about his business ventures with me, but I knew that he owned some hardware and lumber businesses scattered across central Texas, and there were hints that he was dabbling in other investments to go with his law office in Forth Worth. A month earlier, he had come to me to see what I thought about him and some other men opening a new bank in Destiny or up the tracks at Wichita Falls.

Whatever it was he was doing, he must have been minting coin, or else he was spending his wife's money, for he had a beautiful house. To add to that, he had bought another section of river-bottom ground north of his home and had planted fruit trees along the road through it and all the way up to the house. I could have told him that the country was too dry for fruit trees, unless you wanted to carry water to them, but he wouldn't have listened. Tiffany was a good woman, but she probably thought every house should have trees lining the lane up to it. Next thing would be that they put up white plank fences, acting like they were someplace else other than west of "it never rains enough" Texas. Hamish should have known better, but he had spent too much time back East.

He met us in the yard and climbed up on the seat beside me. Gunn wouldn't ride on a wagon when he had a choice, but Hamish had no such scruples. A wagon seat was as good as sitting astride a horse to him. No two brothers could have been so different.

Tiffany and her children were on the porch and waved to me—good-looking kids, a boy and a girl. That boy was about the age that Joseph was when I took him in. Gunn never had married, and it looked like I was going to have to count on Hamish for some grandsons.

Hamish didn't say anything, either; he only nodded at me then kept his gaze straight ahead. I turned the wagon around and drove out of the yard, putting the team to a trot once we hit the road into Destiny. The train usually made town by seven, and I didn't intend to be late.

The old bone pile at the edge of town was long gone, replaced by a cotton gin. Tiny bits of cotton were scattered all over the dead grass wherever you looked, the trash left over from the summer's harvest, like bits of snow that hadn't yet melted under the rain. Clay County had shipped three thousand pounds of cotton the year before. I never said it, but the irony wasn't lost on me. Me, a cotton man in my earlier years, ending up in the cattle business in prime Texas cotton country.

But they could have their cotton. That market was more up and down than the cattle business ever thought about being, and that was saying a lot. Cotton was at sixty-five cents a pound when I left Alabama, and it was at six cents a pound the last harvest the Destiny farmers made. That was a guaranteed way to starve, yet the damned fools were plowing more new ground every year.

It was hard to believe that I was looking at the same spot I had fought Indians on all those years before. The county courthouse was the biggest thing in town, three stories of red brick and a domed bell tower on top of it with a tiled roof. The new jailhouse down the street was two stories tall with yellow-washed stucco walls and white arches over the windows. I remembered when the city marshal had to chain his prisoners to a hitching rail.

There was an opera house that the town bragged would seat four hundred people, but I'd never been to see one of their shows. I counted once and there were six churches in town, and I guess you could find about any flavor of Jesus in Destiny if you were looking for such. Those preachers used to come out to the ranch to try and get me to attend. I knew they were really after money to build those churches, but I donated anyway. Spend enough money and they won't condemn you from the pulpit, even if you miss services.

We turned the corner at St. Elmo Hotel, another redbrick monster, and headed for the depot house. The train was pulling into the station, and I checked my watch to make sure it was running early and that I wasn't late. I hate a man who can't keep his appointments. I was never late to be where I was supposed to be, watch or no watch. When I told a man I would have a herd at such and such place on a certain day, I was there on that day. Your word is your bond and I don't break my word.

The express agent at the depot house guided us to the boxcar and slid the side door open while I backed the wagon up to it. I knew the man well, for there had been a time when he rode for me until a steer we were loading on a cattle car smashed him against the fence. He never was the same after that, and I was glad he had found a job with the railroad. But as good as we knew each other, he kept the small talk to a minimum.

Hamish and Gunn climbed in the car with the express agent. Once the wagon was parked I stepped over the seat and walked the bed and went inside with them. We found it among all the other express and freight in the boxcar. I thought it would have a place all to itself, but it was buried among the boxes and other things the railroad was hauling.

We sat the pine wood coffin gently in the wagon bed and tied it down with some grass rope. The rope was wet and hard to get to cinch down tight enough, much less tie it off. It screeched a little, sliding across the coffin lid. The grain in the yellow pine boards was already swelling, and you could feel it with your fingertips.

Gunn got back on his horse and Hamish and I started the wagon with Hamish twisted in the seat to make sure the coffin was going to ride okay. I thought about how far that coffin had come, and wondered if the way back to the ranch wasn't the longest leg of all.

"I never would have guessed Joseph for a soldier," Hamish said.

"I never could figure him, but I wouldn't have thought it, either."

"I remember when you had been riding him about not carrying a gun. Remember that pistol you gave him?" Hamish asked.

"I remember. He was digging around in that trunk he kept under his bed and I finally saw that pistol. I don't think he ever carried it and had it wrapped in a rag. Probably, he had forgotten about it, because it was freckled with rust," I said. "I scolded him and told him that I bought that pistol for him to make use of. Spent good money on it for him."

"Well, he put it to what he thought was good use."

We both chuckled, but it was only halfhearted. The story had passed among us for years and on another day it would have been as funny as ever. Joseph, maybe feeling bad about the money I had spent on that gun and intending to make good use of it, traded it to one of the fence-building crew for a boxful of blue quail chicks. He built some chicken wire hutches behind the bunkhouse and began raising quail. Before long, he had his own little menagerie. People would bring him all kinds of injured or orphaned wildlife. Folks rode all the way to the ranch to see his pet coyote. It almost broke his heart when that coyote pup ate from a cow carcass that a wolfer I'd hired baited with strychnine.

"Remember how he wouldn't kill a snake?" Hamish asked.

I could tell that Hamish was remembering out loud and not necessarily asking me anything, but I answered anyway. "Saw him get on top of a big rattlesnake once crawling under the floor of the bunkhouse looking for some kittens. He almost peeled his shirt off his back scrambling out from under there. He was getting his nerves back together and peering under the floor at the snake when I handed him my pistol to shoot it."

"Wouldn't shoot it, would he?"

"He said, 'No, that snake let me off easy and I'll do the same for him.'"

"Did you know he could pray in German?" Gunn asked.

"I used to hear him when we were boys, but I didn't know

if he was praying or reciting something from memory," Hamish said.

"Did you know he wrote some of his Quaker kin back East?"

"No. When was that?"

"A year or two after you left. He never heard back from them."

"Who would have thought our Joseph would want to go to war? Joseph the Rough Rider."

All the newspapers were singing the praises of Teddy Roosevelt and his Rough Riders charging hell-bent for leather up San Juan Hill and giving the Spanish the "what for" down in Cuba. I didn't even know what Cuba looked like. It was jungle, was all I knew.

What possessed Roosevelt to recruit a bunch of cowboys and Western men to take to the jungle, I don't know. They say men joined up from Texas, Arizona, New Mexico, and other parts far-flung, even up in the Indian Nations—a bunch of cowboys, freighters, miners, gamblers, and blooded Indians. Roosevelt was another one of those rich Yankees who liked to come out West and play with guns, but I guess he had enough sense to know he needed men with grit. Texas sons had plenty of that, and most of them knew how to shoot. Back in the war I had known, that was the only thing we had going for us. Lord knows, the Confederacy couldn't keep us equipped, but we never ran short of grit. Grit and spirit will sometimes carry you through when nothing else will.

Maybe it was the horses that made Joseph want to join. The papers say that the Rough Riders were meant to be just that—riders, cavalry. But the papers also said that most of their horses never made it to Cuba and those boys had to fight on foot. I could have told Joseph that war never turns out how it's supposed to.

He learned that too late, I guess. I didn't tell Hamish or Gunn—it was better that they might think their brother was shot in some gallant charge—but Joseph never made it to San Juan Hill. The malaria and yellow fever got the boy before his company ever left Florida. That's what the letter the government sent me said. Joseph had listed me as his next of kin, so they sent me a notice of his death, along with a letter from the President commending Joseph's service to the country. I wouldn't let them bury Joseph in Florida, and had them put him on the train. I wished I had thought to send more money for a better coffin. The one the government sent him home in was little better than a shipping box. Governments never can do anything right. Some politician was probably putting the cost of a good coffin down on his books and pocketing the extra money.

"They say Teddy led those Rough Riders up the hill cheering them on and keeping their courage up all the way," Hamish said. "They say he never got off of his horse, even though the Spaniards were laying down hot fire with their Mausers."

"I've never met the man."

"Those new German bolt-action Mausers are supposed to crack like a bullwhip," Gunn said. "They use that new smokeless powder."

"Tiffany's brother is an officer and still in Cuba. He says our boys' Krags still use black powder, and the Spaniards could see the powder smoke when they shot and used that to pick them out of the brush."

I wished Hamish and Gunn would quit talking. I doubted that charge up the hill would be anything like the newspapers said it was. War is never anything but ugly and dirty and harder to take than anything somebody would want to read about. Any reporting otherwise told me that somebody is trying to sell news. Besides, Joseph wasn't on that hill, and I preferred to remember him when he was still my best cowboy.

I saw Gunn looking sidelong at the coffin more than once. Gunn kept his feelings to himself about most things, unless you were trying to get him to do something he didn't want to. He got that from me. Hamish was more like their mother.

I hadn't thought about her in days. That's how it works when bad things happen. They put you in the mood to think about other bad things . . . things you've done and can't ever take back. I loved her so. I went crazy twice—once during the war and once when I lost her. My boys knew about the second time, and I couldn't fix that. Them knowing and what I did to them was hard to take, but me knowing was almost as hard. When you get numb like that you'll do things, looking for something to fill you back up on the inside, but that was no excuse. It was what it was and couldn't be undone.

"Is that who I think it is?" Gunn asked.

"Easy, Gunn. Let it lie," Hamish said.

I was so lost in my thoughts it took me a bit to realize what they were talking about. The rain had picked up some, but I could still see somebody standing in the door of the billiards hall up the street a ways. I was shocked that the kind of people who spent their time drinking beer and shooting pool would be up so early, much less such an establishment opening its doors for business before noon. Whoever it was closed the door before we were near enough for me to make him out.

"Who was it?" I asked.

"Moon Lowe," Hamish said. "I heard he was back."

"Gunn, don't you be thinking what I know you're thinking," I said.

"Clayton Lowe tells it that Moon has been working as a city policeman in Dallas," Hamish said.

"Who would hire him for a policeman?" I asked.

"I can believe it," Gunn said. "You ought to have seen some of the guards I had in Huntsville. Some of them were worse than the inmates."

"I can imagine," I said.

"No you can't, Papa. You don't have a clue," Gunn said. "Sorry, I shouldn't have said it that way."

"That's all right."

"That son of a bitch was waiting for us to come by. He knew that we were picking up Joseph's body," Gunn said.

"There's no way he could have known. Don't make trouble where there isn't any," Hamish said.

"Where there isn't any? I owe him about seven years' worth of trouble."

I saw Hamish about to say more than he should, but he kept it to himself. I'll give him that. Usually, Hamish puts too much faith in his ability to win people over with words, but arguing with Gunn would only make it worse.

"I think I'll go shoot some billiards," Gunn said.

"You do like I say." I sped the team up until I was beside Gunn where I could look him in the eyes. "We're going home to bury Joseph. Now."

Gunn was looking at the pool hall, but he kept his horse traveling beside the wagon. "It'll wait."

"And they'll stick you back in Huntsville. Forget Moon Lowe," I said.

We buried Joseph beside Sarah, Baby Beth, and Old Ben. The rain quit by the time we made it home. Paco and his boy had already dug a grave, but the bottom of it was standing in water. Gunn and Hamish shoveled some mud into the bottom of the grave to soak up some of the water, and then the three of us managed to lower the coffin in it.

We stood for a while, but none of us said anything in the way of a eulogy. I know Joseph would have liked some scripture read over him, and I regretted not having one of those preachers ride out and say a few words. The three of us took turns with the shovel, and we had the grave filled in by dinnertime.

"I'll order him a tombstone next time I'm in town," Hamish said.

"Have them put a horse on it, and some kind of scripture," Gunn said. "He would like that."

Hamish was good at picking out tombstones. The one he had picked out for Sarah and Baby Beth had a statue of an angel on it, and the marble slab that he had chosen for Old Ben was a pretty thing. Hamish had written the epitaph for Ben himself.

R. I. P.

BEN DOLLARHYDE

????—1866

Pioneer, beloved friend,
and bold companion;
Son of lion hunters and chiefs;
Saved the life of our father, and
Was always there for his children;
Served his family thirty years,
from Alabama to Texas;

LIVING PROOF THAT COURAGE AND
KINDNESS CAN GO HAND IN HAND.

Fine words, even if Ben's last name was never Dollarhyde, but I wished I had thought of those words. No matter, Ben would understand. Never had to say much to Ben, for he always knew what I was thinking. Knew me better than my own boys.

"Amen," I said, and started up the hill to the house.

Chapter Forty-five

1899

"Let me front you the money," Hamish said. "Pride goeth before a fall."

"You mean your wife's money." I regretted that as soon as I said it. Tiffany's parents were old money back East, but I knew that Hamish refused everything they tried to do for him and made his own way, even if it wasn't my way.

"This ranch is the only thing keeping Gunn straight."

"Straight?"

"You and I both know it. He's like you and needs something to fight," Hamish said. "Lose this place and it won't be long until he's in trouble."

"Don't talk like you're better than him."

"It has nothing to do with being better."

"Leave Gunn and I alone. Another year or two and the ranch will be paying again. Next year we'll have a good herd of young stuff for sale," I said. "That will get the wolf away from the door."

"Fine, but you're going to starve out before then. Look around. The place is falling down around you."

True, the house could use repainting, one corner of the porch was sagging, and a few roof shakes were lying in the yard. It was hard to keep up with only two of us to work. Keeping the headquarters in shape, by itself, was almost a full-time chore. I'd built big back in the day, and the place was made for a whole crew to run. The best Gunn and I had been able to do was try and keep up with what we still used, and it was hard to keep Gunn at any physical work that didn't require him to be on a horse.

"A pretty place doesn't make you any money," I said. "If I wanted a showplace I would sell out and buy one of those hot springs resorts and tend to tourists and lungers."

"I notice that you aren't drinking twenty-dollar brandy anymore."

"And because of that you think you need to come up here and tell me how to run things? Offer me charity?"

"Clayton Lowe bought your debt with Billings's store. He's filed for a lien on your property."

"Can he do that? I thought you were looking after my books and the legal end."

"Billings sold Lowe the note for thirty percent of what you owed him. I guess he thought that was more money than he was ever going to get out of you."

"I've never not paid a debt in my life. Billings was more than glad to make money off of me when times were good. He ought to have waited until I paid him off. Why, I loaned him money when he first put that store in."

"I imagine he has bills to pay, too. That old handshake stuff tends to go out the window when someone's fat is in the fire."

"So, Lowe can get a ruling for some of my property for a little three-hundred-dollar bill I owed Billings?"

"I can stop that, or at least drag it out. The judge isn't exactly an admirer of Clayton Lowe."

"That highbinder. He's had it in for us since the old days."

"It gets worse," Hamish said. "Moon Lowe is running for county sheriff."

"I heard."

"I sold my railroad stock last week. Made quite a killing."

"Is that what hanging out down at the capitol gets you? Sounds like the Austin politicians have been teaching you some of their tricks."

"I'm running for state representative, whether you like it or not, and I took that railroad stock as payment for some work I did years ago. If you will remember, I told you to buy some of it, but you wouldn't listen."

"If I let you loan me the money you'll be up here every day telling me how to run the place."

"No, that's not the deal. I'm not loaning you the money. I'll pay off your debt. You run the place until . . ."

"Until I'm dead."

"For as long as you want. Half the place goes in my name and the other half in Gunn's. You two keep all the profit or loss for yourself from the business. Cattle belong to you two."

"That's foolish. I thought I taught you more about business than that. You'll never make a dime with deals like that."

"I'm part of this family, too. I'll invest a little to see this thing held together," Hamish said, getting up from his chair. "Don't you think I like driving under that gate sign when I come home? And why have I got that damned brand painted on my office window in Fort Worth?"

"I guess because you're a Dollarhyde."

"Damned right. The Brits are breaking up part of the old ranch and auctioning it off sometime next year. Maybe I could pick up another section or two that join us."

"We could always use more land."

"Who do you think taught me that? I've already got the

papers drawn up. I'll bring them up tomorrow for you and Gunn to sign."

"I haven't said I'll do it."

"You will."

Juanita came out on the porch when Hamish was driving away. "Did you listen to him, or did you run over everything he had to say?"

"Didn't have any choice. He's trying to shove me out."

She rubbed my neck. "He's not shoving you out."

"I run this place. Those two would . . ."

She interrupted me. "Are you saying you raised two no-goods?"

"They're good men, but . . ."

"But what? You've told me more than once that a lot of people said you were crazy when you sunk all your money into this ranch. And the old-timers laughed at you when you brought in those first Herefords."

"They said I was a know-it-all and a big talker who would go broke because I didn't do things the way they did," I said. "I went broke, but a long time after most of them. Most of them that hung on were copying me."

"Hamish and Gunn may have different ideas than you do, but you're going to have to let them have their way sometimes. Listen to them, at least. You should have done that a long time ago."

"I know what Hamish is thinking, whether he says it or not. He's made some money and thinks he knows more than I do because of it."

"You always said you built the ranch for your sons."

"Hamish can say this is *our* ranch all he wants, but he's the one with the money."

"And that galls you that you have to have his help?"

"Takes more than money to run a ranch."

"Hamish knows that. I don't think he intends to shove you aside."

"He better not. He and Gunn can listen to me a few more years and it won't hurt them."

"I think Gunn is going to marry Carmelita."

"I thought she moved off. I haven't seen her since she was a teenager."

"She did, but she's been back for a while. Don't you ever go down to the village anymore?"

I hadn't done anything but ride past the village for two or three years. Rancho Poquito, the little village that was once the cluster of jacales my original hands had lived in with their families. There were only ten or twelve jacales left and the whole place was squalid. I would have forgotten it at times if I couldn't see it in the distance from my porch. Dirt-poor, yes, and none of them worked for me anymore, but that was no excuse. Those people still thought I was some kind of big shot, *el patrón*. The old men tipped their hats to me when I passed.

"Carmelita was always a pretty girl," I said. "I offered to send her to school once, but her father wouldn't take the money."

"I think you are going to have another Mexican married into the family."

"Hmmph."

"You don't care what people will say? Remember what some of the Anglos said when you married me?"

"Carmelita's daddy worked for me for better than fifteen years. Never a better man. Her mama, too. I don't guess Gunn marrying her will bring down the family bloodline."

"Won't stop people from talking."

"They will, but let them. Those kind don't matter as much as I once thought they did."

"She was married before. Her mother told me her husband was killed in an accident. She has a child."

I pulled Juanita into my lap. I hadn't done that in a long time.

"After all these years, and I still can't tell whether you like something or simply realize you can't do anything about it," she said. "Maybe you could put in one of your windmills down in the village . . . when you get the time and money."

"Gunn won't live in Poquito. He can build a house up here, or maybe we could remodel the old bunkhouse."

"That's not why you should build them a windmill. They are very poor."

"Poor folks everywhere."

"They have to carry their water from the river. The young people don't stay in the village anymore, not since you have no work for them. Most of those left are old."

"The young ones were spoiled, anyway. Is this you or Tiffany that wants this? She's always lecturing me on my philanthropic responsibilities and the plight of the poor Mexicans and how we mistreated them."

"Both of us, but mostly me. Most of those people were good to you. Good to me. They worked hard when you needed them."

"I let them live on my land and I've never asked for rent."

"I know it is not their land, at least legally, but they feel like this is their home, too. They built those jacales and raised three generations of babies there."

"I always paid them fair."

"They don't want your land. That's not what I'm saying. They didn't even ask for a windmill. Tiffany and I thought . . .

I thought that helping them with the water would be a good thing and a way to say thank you."

"Having a well drilled isn't cheap, and there's no guarantee you hit water the first time."

"Think on it."

"I've got plenty to think on."

"Come to bed. I don't like it when you make me sleep alone. It scares me when you go out in the night and wander around or do whatever it is you do."

"Habit from the old days."

"You have a warm bed now and a woman who loves you."

"I'm not sleepy."

"The ranch will still be here when you get up. Come to bed."

Chapter Forty-six

1905

Some crazy fool shot McKinley and that put his vice president, none other than Teddy Roosevelt, in the big chair. America reelected him in 1904. I could have cared less what that bunch of swindlers and pickpockets in Washington did, but when I received a letter from the Texas governor wanting me to attend a wolf hunt the President was holding not far north of me across the Red River in the Oklahoma Territory, I decided to go.

Gunn was still after me to try and get lease rights to run our cattle in the 480,000-acre chunk of the Comanche reservation that cowmen called the Big Pasture. We didn't have deep enough pockets to vie with the cattlemen grazing that lease, but to appease Gunn I said I would check it out. The thought that maybe I could talk to the President about the Rough Riders was the real reason I went.

The politicians had opened up most of the western half of the Indian Territory to settlement, the Oklahoma Territory they called it after that, and the President was campaigning his way through there on his way to a Rough

Rider reunion down in San Antonio. The culmination of his grand tour was to be when he returned to Oklahoma Territory for a wolf hunt with some dignitaries and a few of his friends. For some fool reason, the governor thought I needed to go. The President liked to meet cowboys and ranchers, and people had gotten it in their heads that I was some kind of pioneer or something. It was said that Roosevelt tried ranching himself up in the Dakotas, but the winter of '86 froze him out like it did the rest of us. Besides learning something about the outfit Joseph had joined up with, I was curious about a president that might know a little about ranching.

Gunn and I rode our saddle horses up to Frederick. I guess we could have taken the train, but no matter how my joints bothered me, I still preferred to travel by horseback. And it would do me good to ride over the country again.

Instead of following the railroad, we cut due north. I intended to look around the old Texas Ranger camp close to where I crossed the Red with my first trail herd back in '67. But they had built the town of Cottle, or what they were calling Salt Creek by then, nearby, and the people of that community had scavenged the old Ranger camp until you couldn't tell where it had been.

We rode a big loop to the northwest on our way to Frederick, winding through the Wichita Mountains and hitting the old Dodge City Trail that we had sent our last trail herds over years before. We camped one night beside a little mountain of bare, gray granite—more a round mound of rock standing alone in the midst of the flat country than anything. Gunn showed me the graves of two cowboys working under him who had shot each other to death in an argument on the trail.

Everywhere we went we ran across cattle, and we occasionally met friends from the old days that were still hanging on—not as many as I would have liked, but a place to stay overnight and someone to visit with. Like Texas, that country still had some open grazing, but it was a scattered patchwork mixed among the new towns and homesteads that had sprung up since the Territory was opened. Everywhere we went we saw people. It wasn't like that the first time I went over that trail in '78 or so. There wasn't anything back then but coyotes and Indians.

The papers said thousands lined up for the Oklahoma land rushes they held in those last years of the century—people hungry for land.

Even Gunn seemed to be enjoying himself. Give him a horse and some open country and he was as happy as a pig in mud.

When we finally made Frederick, it seemed like we were the last ones to the ball. The President's private train car was already parked on the siding, and he and his guides and retinue had taken over the town's only hotel as their headquarters. I saw the Texas governor with a group of men near Severs's Store, but avoided him. He had worn the gray during the war, but I couldn't abide by his politics. If I had ridden over there it wouldn't be five minutes until he was patting me on the back and asking me to tell Indian fighting stories or telling me how a state banking system was good for the people.

Good for the people. Government is inefficient by nature, has nothing to do with common sense, and is incapable of running a lemonade stand, much less banks. The governor and the rest of his ilk ought to tend to their cigars and leave us all to our own ends. But that's politicians and bureaucrats for you. Every damn one of them will tell you that they know something about business and the working man, but not many of them ever worked with their hands or ran a business, unless you count lawyering as a real trade.

When they say "for the good of the people" they mean something that will get them a vote or something that will line their pockets. I had all the politicians and government types I wanted back in Alabama. I came to Texas and still couldn't outrun them. You have a perfectly good place and then they show up, like hounds after scraps.

"Let's see if there's a room left in the hotel before we put up our horses," I said.

Gunn waved at the governor. "Try to be friendly, Papa."

"Your brother is more the kind to visit with the governor. You know how much use I have for those good old boys."

"Are you still sore because they made you pay a lease for the state land? What was that, four cents an acre and about fifteen years ago? And I thought I held a grudge. The governor there didn't have anything to do with that."

"I'm sore because they made me lease, and then tried to sell me what was already mine. I know his kind."

There was one room left in the hotel, and Gunn was going to have to sleep on the floor or find a hay pile down at the livery. Three days of sightseeing had me wanting a feather bed. Gunn took the horses and put them up for the night while I carried our things to the room.

I managed to dodge the crowd in the lobby on my way upstairs, but that so-called governor saw me when I came back down to hunt up a restaurant or someplace to eat. He was standing by a medium-sized man in glasses and a suit. I thought maybe he was the Oklahoma territorial governor or something. One governor was more than I could stand, much less two.

"Come over here, Argyle," the governor said.

Damn a man that doesn't know you or isn't your friend that will refer to you by your first name. Poor manners for a man who was once a Southern officer, but that's a politician for you—baby-kissers and white liars.

"Good evening, Governor," I said.

More men gathered around. The only one I recognized was Burk Burnett. To look at him, you would have thought he was another middle-aged cowboy, but Burk was one of the richest cattleman in Texas and the salt of the earth. At one time, his ranch neighbored ours to the north across the Big Wichita. When a lot of us were going broke, Burk was still growing his Four Sixes brand. Some of that may have had to do with him contracting with the Indians for a grazing lease, but a lot of it had to do with the fact that Burk had the good sense to marry the daughter of the president of the First National Bank of Fort Worth.

Those stories about Burk winning his first herd in a poker game with a hand of four sixes is a bunch of hogwash. Burk knew when to sell and when to hold, and figured out that banking was more profitable than cattle. I hadn't seen Burk in years, for he had left the ranch to his son and spent most of his time in Fort Worth. Burk's only problem was that he thought too much of the Kiowa and Comanche. But he wasn't around when the Indians were at their worst.

"Mr. President, I would like to introduce you to Argyle Dollarhyde, one of our earliest Texas cattlemen and pioneers," the governor said.

President? And there I was thinking the man in the glasses might be a territorial governor at best. I gave him a closer look, but he still didn't strike me as much.

"Old Argyle was out here before any of us," Burk said.

It grated on me when men called me old, but I guess that's the price of living too long. And Burk meant it as a mark of respect.

"Pleased to meet you, Mr. Dollarhyde." The President had a strange accent, somewhere between Blue Bastard Yankee and an English schoolmarm.

I shook his hand. "A pleasure, Mr. President."

"Call me Teddy. We're all good chaps here."

Chaps? "I'm sure we are."

"I see you wear a sidearm when not many do anymore, even out here. Is that a Smith Number 3 on your hip?" the President asked.

"It is. I guess I got in the habit of wearing one."

"Argyle drove one of the first trail herds to Kansas and is one of our most noted living Indian fighters," the governor said.

"It took exceptional men of rigor to settle the West," the President said, brushing his mustache absentmindedly with one hand.

I cleared my throat.

"Yes, the red man was a spirited antagonist. Wonderful savages," the President added.

"That's not how I recall them."

"The great chief Quanah Parker is somewhere around here. You must have Burk introduce you to him."

"I think I met him once."

"Oh?"

"Shouldn't say I actually met him, but we had a long-range disagreement."

The President laughed and slapped me on the shoulder. "You are a dry man."

The governor looked nervously from me to the President. "Don't mind Argyle. He's too humble to take credit for his deeds. Why, we've tried to have him down to the Austin several times to hold a banquet in his honor and to recognize his service to our great state."

"Don't make apologies for this man. I admire his bluntness," the President said with a smile. He raised a mug of beer in toast. "Bully to the rugged individualists who made this country great."

Bully?

"Argyle is most legendary for single-handedly routing an entire village of Kiowa back in the old days," the governor said.

"Tell me more," the President said.

"I'd prefer not to," I said.

"Come now, Argyle, don't be so humble. Tell us the story," the governor said. "I admit I have never heard it, except for third- or fourth-hand."

"That was long ago, and not worth telling."

"Argyle's wife was lost to the Kiowa." The governor tried to look squeamish as soon as he said it. "Forgive me. Perhaps it is rude on my part to bring up old memories."

"Forgive me, also," the President said.

"No apologies necessary. Like I said, that was a long time ago, and nothing to brag about."

"Needless to say, it's still something schoolboys will learn for years to come, and a good part of why your son will probably be elected to office," the governor said. "Texas does like her heroes and the sons of heroes."

"A round of drinks for the bully Indian fighter from Texas," the President said. "Let us proceed to the local watering hole and partake of some refreshments."

"Pardon me, Mr. President, but I had a long ride to get here. I think I will find a meal and then my bed," I said.

"Such Old South manners. Mississippi?"

"Alabama."

"Very well then, Argyle Dollarhyde, I'll see you in the morning. Perhaps then we can swap stories," the President said.

"One of my sons joined up with your Rough Riders."

"Glorious men. Glorious. Was he at the reunion in San Antonio, by chance?"

"He wasn't."

"Shame. It did my heart good to see so many of those I fought with. No bond is stronger than that shared by men who have faced death together." The President's voice rose higher and turned a little squeaky. "Do you know the American grizzly bear, Mr. Dollarhyde? Ferocious beast."

"We don't have them in Texas."

"No, sir, but terrible fighters anyway. Fast as a horse and with claws this long." The President held one hand about six inches from the mug of beer in his other. "I have hunted the grizzly, sir, and I promise you it is the finest big game animal in North America. Splendid animal. So full of spirit that a single bullet rarely takes it down."

"We have black bears in Texas," the governor said.

"Not the same," the President said.

The crowd around the President had grown larger. Most of the men were cowboys, and I guessed the novelty of a president telling hunting stories in the lobby had them curious.

The President turned to his audience. "I mention grizzlies because that is the only way I can describe those men who charged valiantly with me up Kettle Hill with the Spaniards pouring hateful fire on us so thick it felt like a swarm of hornets filled the air. Did those boys flinch or cower? No, sirs, no! No finer example of American spirit displayed since the Revolutionary War. Hearts like grizzly bears! Achilles and his Myrmidons would have been no match for those men. Such men haven't taken up arms since the walls of the Alamo!"

The crowd clapped, although somewhat awkwardly. The looks on the cowboys' faces said they thought the President had too much beer, but most of the men in the audience were Texans and mentioning the Alamo was a sure way to get their attention and to stoke up their fighting spirit.

"Good night, Mr. President," I said.

He looked put out that I didn't seem more impressed with his oration, and he asked, "I know you are a man of action, but did you ever command men in battle?"

"I've been to war," I said.

"So you understand what I speak of."

"I don't have your way with words."

"Memories were made that day on the hill."

"Soldiers call them nightmares."

"What's that? I could not hear you."

"Fine words, Mr. President."

Chapter Forty-seven

The Oklahoma wolf hunt really turned out to be a coyote hunt. There was a time when there were plenty of lobo wolves left over from the days when the buffalo were around, but the state put a bounty on them back in the '80s. That bounty got up to fifty dollars a wolf. All you had to do was show a pelt or a wolf scalp with both ears still on it. The cowboys and wolf hunters in Texas and the Territory had made short work of the wolves, and seeing one was a rarity.

I had assumed that the hunt would have consisted of a bunch of political types and city folks, and the sort that would tag along with a president trying to get his ear, but most of the crowd that showed up saddled and ready at daylight were cowboys and ranchers. The majority of the cowboys worked for Burk Burnett over in the Texas Panhandle. The governor and a couple of other sorts were the only dudes going with us.

We were still in front of the hotel when the President introduced me to the cowboy leading the hunt. He was a young man of average to middle height, with nothing exceptional-looking about him other than he seemed strong and knew how to look you in the eyes. The President was enamored with him.

"Mr. Dollarhyde, I want you to meet Jack Abernathy, wolf hunter extraordinaire."

"Pleased to meet you, Mr. Dollarhyde."

I shook Abernathy's hand.

"Jack here has the most unique way of catching wolves," the President said.

I studied the pack of dogs trailing from the leashes of several of the mounted cowboys. They were long, rangy mutts and no two of them looked alike. Some showed traces of greyhound and other breeds that I could not name. Some were slick haired and some were grizzled or shaggy. The one thing that they had in common was that they all looked built to run and every one of them was so excited that they were twisting and dancing on the ends of their leashes.

"I've seen wolves hunted with dogs before," I said. "Although that's an impressive string of dogs."

"Fine dogs, I assure you," the President said. "But it's Jack's way of catching a wolf that is of interest, and not so much how his dogs run them down."

The cowboy only smiled and nodded at the President. He seemed uncomfortable at the praise, but was bearing with it.

"Oh?" I asked.

"He catches them with his bare hands."

I remembered hearing about such a man, but expected him to be older. I immediately glanced at the cowboy's hands, but could see no scars on them.

A lobo wolf, or a buffalo wolf as some call them, could weigh as much as a man. Teeth like a steel trap. Even a forty-pound coyote wasn't something that I wanted to be bitten by. Most with good sense either poisoned wolves they wanted rid of, or shot them. An occasional cowboy risked running his horse to death to rope one.

"I'm sure you're going to enjoy the sport today," the President said. "I have the feeling it's going to be a bully hunt."

I had been interested to see what kind of man might have talked Joseph into joining the Rough Riders, but my interest in the President was wearing thin. I don't even know what I thought the President might tell me. The odds were he didn't even know Joseph.

The biggest Indian you ever saw rode through the crowd and stopped his horse by Burk Burnett. He was dressed like most of the cowboys, in tall-topped cowboy boots and a hat, but he wore his hair in two braids hanging down either side of his chest. Those braids were wrapped in some kind of fur.

He looked at me and I looked at him. I remembered him, even if it had been better than thirty-five years or so since I had seen him last. I didn't think he would remember me, but he did. I could tell it by the way he was looking at me.

He was riding a gray horse, but the last time I had seen him he was riding a black. I think it was him that had shot my horse Shiloh out from under me. Three times that day those Kiowa and Comanche tried to overrun me, and every time he was at the front of them.

"You are Dollarhyde. I remember you," he said.

"And I remember you."

They said that Quanah Parker had built a big house with stars painted on the roof of it, and was running cattle like the rich cattlemen his tribe leased land to. I remembered him differently, and when he wasn't so civilized. I never was sure whether it was Kiowa or Comanche who had raided my ranch. They often ran together in those days. Whether he was one of them or not, he was with Lone Wolf the day I fought them up on the Chisolm Trail, and he was that kind. Renegade and man burner.

"Easy, Papa," Gunn said.

Gunn didn't know who Quanah was, past the part that everybody in Texas knew about Quanah being the half-breed son of Cynthia Ann Parker, a white woman captured in a Comanche raid. Gunn knew more than Hamish did about how things were better left in the past, but he didn't know anything about what I had done when I had rode off and left those boys with the trail herd to go after Indians. And he didn't know Quanah could have been one of them that hit the ranch.

Burk Burnett must have seen how I was looking at his prize Indian. "Dollarhyde, today's a good day to let old things stay in the past."

I ignored Burnett and kept my eyes on the Comanche. "Maybe one day you and I will meet on the road somewhere and get a chance to talk about the old days."

The Comanche had eyes like brown flint. "I remember things, too, Dollarhyde. Maybe it would be good for us to meet alone and *talk*, as you say. We once started something that we never finished."

"I should have shot you then, but you were too hard to hit."

"Gentlemen," the President said, "I will have no trouble here."

"It was a good fight," Quanah Parker said. "If you hadn't had so many repeaters and that horse to hide behind, maybe it was you that would have gotten shot."

"Dollarhyde," the President said, "Chief Parker is an invited guest and a venerated member of the Comanche Nation. I would appreciate you showing him the courtesy you show the rest of these men."

The big Comanche waved a hand in front of him to

dismiss the President's words. "No trouble here. Dollarhyde and I go way back. I understand him."

I rode out of town at a long trot at the back of the group, headed northwest for the Big Pasture. The President rode at the head of the procession with the wolf hunter and Burk Burnett. Quanah Parker rode at the front with them, and he never looked back at me.

As I had thought, the first wolf the dogs ran down was nothing but a young coyote. The technique was to turn a few dogs loose to trail up or jump a coyote. They would either run it down, or if they tired and failed, a set of fresh dogs would be turned loose to give chase. A little coyote doesn't look fast, but the first one we jumped outran the dogs.

This coyote wasn't so lucky. Gunn and I were riding at the end of the long line of men trying to flush a coyote or wolf from the grass when a shout went up. By the time we rode over, Jack Abernathy was already off his horse and had his hands on the coyote.

I should have said he had his hand in the coyote. He walked proudly out of the cluster of barking, darting dogs with the coyote bit down on his right hand. The animal was still alive and clamped on him like a turtle. His other hand was gripping the coyote's upper jaw.

It didn't take long to see his trick. He had jammed his right hand so far in the coyote's mouth that it was behind the animal's back molars. Still, it took a nervy man with fast hands to stick his hand in there. One wrong move and you were liable to find yourself missing some fingers.

I was a little impressed, but not as much as the rest of the men. Once the coyote's legs were bound with string and his mouth tied shut, they all began to pat Abernathy on the back and question him about his technique.

"That's nervy enough, but I've got sense enough not to risk my fingers," Gunn said to me. "I guess he's got to show out to keep the President's business."

Gunn must have spoken too loudly, for everyone went quiet and gave us hard looks.

"It's not hard when you know what you're doing," Abernathy said. "I've never had but one bite me bad, and that was a big old loafer wolf."

"No offense intended," Gunn said.

"I sell them alive. Zoos and scientists and such. The only thing hard about it is that you can't go at it halfway. Lose your nerve and put your hand in there too timid or too slow and it won't work. Get your hand mangled is what you'll do."

"I imagine," Gunn said.

"Most men aren't fast enough or don't have the nerve."

"Oho!" said the President. "Do we have a challenge here? Is there any one of us who would like a try at Jack's technique?"

One of the cowboys tried when the dogs ran down the next coyote. By the time he got his nerve up the coyote was already mauled and bleeding from the fight with the dogs. It didn't seem like exactly a fair fight. I couldn't imagine wrestling a real wolf without the dogs taking some of the starch out of him first.

The cowboy was apparently too hesitant to stick his hand in the back of the coyote's jaws, or too slow. Oh, he was bold enough. He waded into the pack of milling, snapping dogs and got ahold of the coyote, but he got his hand severely bitten in the process.

Abernathy took over and soon had the coyote bound and muzzled, using the same technique as he had before. He acted like it was no big deal, and I wondered how many times he had done that.

The next coyote we jumped ran better than two miles before the dogs finally caught him and surrounded him. The riders held back to watch the fight between the dogs and the coyote. Most of the dogs darted in when the coyote's attention was on another dog, and took ahold of it. Several times they flipped it through the air or pulled it to the ground. Smaller than the dogs, maybe, but the coyote was a fighter and limber as a snake. Every time one of those dogs latched on to it, it would double back along itself and take a bite of them, its ears pinned flat to its head and its teeth bared in a grimace.

The President was positively beaming. He didn't seem to be overly coordinated or graceful, but I admit he rode pretty well for a city man.

"Who's next?" the President asked.

"Better be quick before they kill that coyote," Jack Abernathy said. "You have to get in there before they wool him too much."

Nobody immediately volunteered, and all of them were looking at Gunn.

"How about it, cowboy?" the President asked.

I could see Gunn getting ready to get off his horse, but I beat him to the punch.

"Oh, the Indian fighter from Texas!" the President said.

I handed my reins to Gunn and stamped my feet to try and limber my knees.

"Are you sure about this?" Gunn asked.

I started for the coyote that was spinning up a dust storm in the middle of the dogs.

"I know you don't like to hear this," Gunn said so that

only I could hear him. "But you aren't as spry as you once were."

"Jam that hand in there quick and hard. Don't hesitate," Abernathy called to me. "Pull on his top jaw with your other hand to help you adjust. Hurry."

I kicked the first dog out of my way. I couldn't even see the coyote for all the commotion. I was wading my way through the dogs and cussing them when the coyote broke free. He ran only about five yards before one of the dogs ran by him and rolled him in a ball.

I made a short run to the coyote and stopped just short of it.

"Get him!" the President shouted.

Several of the cowboys were hooting and cheering me on. Or maybe they were cheering for the coyote.

They all went quiet when I pulled my pistol out and shot the coyote between the eyes. None of them said anything when I walked back to my horse.

"Nothing to it," I said.

When Gunn and I rode off Quanah Parker was the last man we passed. His face was still hard as ever, but he nodded at me.

That says something when the only man left who can understand you is your enemy.

Chapter Forty-eight

1906

Gunn couldn't take it anymore. I guess he had fought his nature as long as he could, and needed to go see the elephant at least one more time.

People didn't make long drives with their cattle much anymore, with railroad tracks laid all over creation, but some ranch or another thought it would be cheaper to trail a small herd of steers from up in No Man's Land to their other ranch division in Wyoming. There hadn't been many herds driven far enough to matter in recent years. There was a chance that it would be the last drive. As it was, they were going to wind their way around every fence between here and Wyoming. That was a lot of fences and farmers. But Gunn wasn't about to miss out.

I don't blame Gunn. He was made like he was made, and he had hung around longer than I expected. I felt bad for Carmelita. A man shouldn't leave his pregnant wife like that, but she didn't seem worried at all. I didn't tell her that I wasn't sure he was coming back.

And I couldn't get her to come up to the big house and

stay with Juanita and me while Gunn was gone. She and
Gunn had rebuilt one of the jacales down in Poquito, no
matter how much I protested that the place was a pigsty.
She was four months along when Gunn left with the trail
herd, and it worried me, her being down there alone. She
had some family in the village, but they were too old to do
anything if she had trouble with the baby.

Carmelita was a sweet thing. She worked in Hamish's
new bank in Destiny for a while until her father became
sick and she had to move to the village to help mend him.
She was shy and quiet, but she had a smile for Gunn as
big as a rainbow. She took good care of the boy of hers
from her first husband, Pancho he was called, and I didn't
worry about her making a good mother for my next grand-
son. Juanita said I was silly for not considering Carmelita
might have a girl.

Juanita or I made it a practice to ride down to Poquito
and check on her every day or so. I intended to go that
morning, but I was running late. Two of my bulls got in a
fight in a fence corner and broke over a couple of posts and
tore down the wire. It shouldn't have taken as long as it did
but I finally had the fence fixed by late afternoon.

I put my fencing tools up in the shed when I got back
and rode down to Poquito, intending to wash up in the
windmill tank I had paid to have built at the end of the
village. I could see the galvanized metal wind wheel on top
of the wooden derrick spinning and the pump rod working
slowly up and down. The water flowing into the tank would
be cold and clear. A lot of the water on the ranch was
"gyppy," Texas talk for gypsum-laden water, but that well
was as sweet and tasty as any I had ever drank.

Good water or not, the windmill was one of the few
reasons I hated to ride down and check on Carmelita.
Every time I rode into the village some old woman was

thanking me by trying to give me a batch of tamales wrapped in a rag, or her husband was trying to give me a rawhide bridle he had braided or offering to do some work for me. I appreciated their gratitude, but I hadn't expected anything from them when I built the thing. If they enjoyed it, fine, but one day I intended to fence that section, and a windmill tank would water the stock in that pasture. At least that's what I told Juanita and Tiffany. I couldn't have them thinking I had gone soft in my old age.

Truth was, other than the overly grateful offers, I found that I enjoyed my time in Poquito. Miguel, Carmelita's father and one of my old hands, was still there, retired and too old for any kind of work, but somebody to swap stories with who remembered the old days.

I was thinking that I might talk to him as soon as I checked on Carmelita, when I saw there was trouble. Two white men were in front of Carmelita's jacal. One of them was still mounted and holding their horses, and the other one was beating on Miguel. I spurred my horse and slid him to a stop almost on top of the man on the ground. Their horses shied and the man holding them had his hands full trying to hang on to them.

Miguel looked up at me, blood trickling from his lip, and dust covering his hatless head. Moon Lowe stood over him, one fist drawn back to hit him again.

"Stay out of this, Dollarhyde," Moon said, letting go of Miguel and straightening. "This man was resisting arrest."

Moon Lowe stood well over six feet and weighed enough for two men. Miguel was so old and skinny he stood a chance of the wind blowing him away anytime he went outside.

"Arrest him for what?" I was already down off my horse, and I felt that old mad rising up in me. I hadn't felt that for a long, long time.

"I don't have to explain myself to you." Moon puffed his chest out, as if I couldn't see the sheriff's badge pinned on him.

"When you're on my ranch you do."

The other man, Moon's deputy, finally had their horses calmed down and he pointed at Miguel. "That old greaser tried to cut us with a knife."

I looked at Miguel, waiting. He told me what happened in Spanish. I didn't speak that language well, but good enough to get the gist of it.

"We came through here looking for a Mexican that stole a horse up in the north end of the county. Thought he might be hid out here with the rest of your greasers," Moon said. "Tried looking in this old man's house and he pulled a knife on me."

"He says you tried to molest his daughter."

"We never," the deputy said.

Carmelita was standing in the door, the waist of her skirt torn so that it sagged down over one hipbone. She held a knife and her eyes were hot. I presumed it was the same knife Miguel had tried to use. I remembered when Miguel was young and carried a knife that you could shave with. He always loved a good blade. If you had taken ten years off him, he would have gutted Moon and never broke a sweat doing it.

"If Miguel says you did, you did."

"Stop right there, you old fart. Don't make me take you in, too," Moon said.

"Like to bully old men and women, do you?"

Moon had his hand on his pistol, but I knew he wasn't going to draw. He never had that much guts. I fumbled my Smith out of its holster and he threw up one arm to block the blow I aimed at his head. He cried out when the pistol cracked him across the forearm, and I made another swing and felt the pistol barrel connect with his cheekbone. He fell like I'd stoned him, but tried to get up on one knee. I hit him over the top of the head, driving him down on his belly. My breath was coming in ragged gasps, or I might have hit him again.

Their horses were acting up again, and I slapped the deputy's horse across the nose with my hat before he could pull on me. I don't know if he was going to, but I was outnumbered and not taking any chances. The real truth was, I was mad and didn't give a damn.

I should have killed them both, but one of the first things to go with old age is your wind; I was too shaky to hit anything with my pistol.

"Get this sack of guts out of here," I said. "I ever see you on this place again and I'll bury the both of you."

The deputy had almost fallen off his horse, but he had righted himself. I covered him with my pistol and kicked Moon in the seat of the pants. "That's my daughter-in-law there. She or her father tells me you've been around here again, and I'll hunt you down. Hear me?"

The deputy held Moon's horse while Moon struggled into his saddle. He could barely hold his head up. I had hit him hard that last time. Served him right.

"You old . . ." Moon started to cuss me, but I let off a round into the sky and their horses turned tail and ran for town.

I holstered my pistol and leaned over with my hands on my knees. The mad was leaving me and I felt old and tuckered out. Miguel had got up and was standing by me, watching those sorry excuses for lawmen run their horses down the road.

"You make trouble for yourself," Miguel said.

"Moon Lowe never was worth a squirt of horse piss," I said and then remembered Carmelita was standing in the doorway. "Pardon me, Carmelita. I forgot you were standing there."

"That's all right," she said, and she was smiling at me and at those lawmen racing away.

Her smiling at me like that was the first really good feeling I had in a long time. Tired or not, it felt like giving Moon a whipping had taken ten years off me. It was probably going to cause me trouble, but it was worth it.

Chapter Forty-nine

Juanita was calling me to supper, but I wanted to sit a little longer and my chair on the porch felt good. I could see some of my cattle grazing in the pasture closest to the house. Good cattle—years of picking the best and grubbing and sweating and slaving away to build the ranch. Call me a proud old fool, but I was going to leave a mark in the world. People would remember that I did what I said I was going to do.

None of them understood that. Not Gunn, not Hamish, not Joseph. There were things I wished I could go back and tell them, but that might not have done any good. You can't put some things to words. If they couldn't sit with me on that porch seeing it all and understand, then there was nothing I could say to explain it. I wasn't perfect, but I did my best. Kept moving and trying.

"Come inside," Juanita called from inside the house.

I could smell the good meal on the table, but what I was looking at pleased me more. A cow bawled out there somewhere, and for a second it put me back thirty years or more. I could hear more cattle bawling and smell the dust rolling up beneath a trail herd, and me worried sick that there wouldn't be a market up in Kansas for them and not knowing what I was going to do to feed those boys or take care of them with their mother dead and us without a dime to try anything else. Worried and excited at the same time, and loving it all. Knowing I belonged and that I was building something special. That's all I ever wanted—not money so much as building something special.

That sun was like a bonfire on the horizon and like it was fighting to keep from sinking. Sometimes you see a sunset or a certain way the clouds look it's so special you want someone there to show it to. And sometimes you're content to keep it to yourself.

I remembered another such sunset when Gunn was lying in one of those jacales on a buffalo robe with his arm stump infected and me not knowing if he was going to live or die. Sitting and waiting and hoping. Hamish and Joseph scared and too shook up to talk unless I forced them to. José was gone to Mexico to try and hire his friends and there was nobody but me and the boys.

I closed my eyes and I could see the sun through my eyelids like an orange blanket and feel the warmth of that color hitting me in the face. And then I was sitting in the door of the jacal again, listening to Gunn babble in his fever when I saw Indians in the distance, a line of them passing between us and the sun, the squaws' peeled travois poles sticking up above the horses' backs like white bones. I thought those Indians had come to kill me for what I'd done and take my boys with them. But the warriors only sat their horses and watched the jacal until dark, and then they rode on. I sat up all night and listened and waited for them to come back.

Did you know that most of the Plains Indians had only one word for anyone outside their tribe? "Enemy." And if you translated their words for themselves it usually meant something like "the people." Savages, yes, a hundred years behind civilization, but they had that right. Your tribe was what mattered. Family. You looked after your own and those with a name. Your name. Dollarhyde.

That's what happens when you live too long. You spend more time in the past, until you can't tell which is which. I shook off the old memories and put my hands on the arms of my chair, intending to get up before Juanita started scolding me. The skin on the backs of my hands was liver spotted and paper-thin and there were red little bruises and tears that I couldn't remember doing. Where did the years go?

I caught a glint of sunlight on something down by the bunkhouse, and strained to see what it was. Who in the hell was down there? Maybe Gunn was back. It was about time. We had work to do, and that baby of his wasn't going to wait much longer to enter the world.

Something shoved me back in my chair. I felt funny— so light I didn't weigh anything. I tried to push up again but my boot heels slipped out from under me and my legs wouldn't work. Juanita was screaming. She never got that mad when I was late for supper. I started to answer her, but I couldn't speak. There was something wet all over the front of my shirt. Blood. Well, it wasn't the way I had expected it. Never is.

I tried and won't be judged for it. Never quit and gave it my best. If . . .

PART IV
GUNN

Chapter Fifty

"When did you get back?" Hamish knocked the snow from his hat as best he could before he entered the room.

"Last night. I was going to come see you earlier today, but I'm kind of under the weather."

Hamish glanced around the room. He didn't say anything about it, but I knew what he was thinking. I had put in real windows before I left for Wyoming, but little spurts of snow were blowing in through the cracks and gaps between the window frame and the picket-and-mud wall. Melting snow had run down the hot stovepipe and turned the packed-dirt floor under the stove into a small mud hole. I watched the water slowly soaking through and working its way across the rug under our feet. Hamish wouldn't have his family live in such a place, only his no-gumption brother.

"What happened to your leg?" he asked.

I shifted my casted leg on the stool in front of me and rearranged my blanket to cover it. "Horse fell on me."

"Why didn't you send word to me? I could have picked you up instead of Carmelita having to travel in this."

"Figured you were out campaigning."

"I lost the election."

"What have you done about Papa?"

"We buried him. I think half the cowboys and ranchers in Texas showed up for the funeral. The governor even gave a speech about him. I would have wired you, but nobody knew where you were."

"What about Moon Lowe?"

"We can't prove he did it."

Carmelita went behind the curtain that divided our sleeping quarters from the rest of the one-room jacal. She acted like she was going to check on Pancho, but I knew she would be listening behind the curtain.

"Carmelita said that Papa was shot the day after he pistol-whipped Moon," I said.

"True, but that still doesn't prove anything." Hamish looked tired. "Motive perhaps, but circumstantial at best. No court is going to convict him without more evidence, especially since he's the sheriff."

"I could care less about the court."

"Moon has got an alibi."

"I suppose it's his father."

"No, some woman over at Petrolia says he was with her that evening."

Another one of the coughing spells overtook me, and I doubled over and covered my mouth.

"You're sick."

"Just a cough."

"He walked here in the middle of the night," Carmelita said through the curtain.

"You walked all the way from Destiny in the middle of a snowstorm with a cast on your leg?"

"Rode in on the night freight run, and the livery wouldn't open up to rent me a horse. It's only six or seven miles, and I figured a stretch of the legs wouldn't hurt me."

"You could have got a hotel, instead of once again trying to prove how pigheaded and obstinate you can be."

"You and those big words."

"I don't know why I trouble with you."

Carmelita joined us again and picked up a damp cloth and dabbed my forehead with it. "*Tiene muy calor. Tiene fiebre.*" You're burning up.

"What did she say?" Hamish asked.

"She said I don't have a fever."

"Your face is as red as a beet."

"This chair is too close to the stove."

"If you go after Moon you're going to end up back in prison. You two are about to have a baby, and you've got that little boy back there in his bed to think about."

I had to fight through another round of coughing. My lungs rattled and my voice was raspy when I could finally speak again. "Papa's shot off his porch and that's all you can think of?"

"I've talked to the Rangers. They're checking into things."

"This ain't none of their business. It's family business."

"I'm going to get a doctor."

"Carmelita's taking care of me." The quack sawbones up in Wyoming had almost killed me trying to set my leg, and I'd had my fill of doctors.

I knew without looking that Carmelita was standing behind me and shaking her head. Hamish put his coat and hat on and started out the door, and Carmelita's fingers dug into my shoulder when I tried to get up to stop him.

Chapter Fifty-one

The snow got worse and it kept the doctor from making it out to the house for two days. He diagnosed me with pneumonia when he finally did get there. I was feeling too poorly to argue when they decided to move me up to the big house. Juanita wanted me to move my family in with her anyway, claiming that she needed the company and the house was too big for her to take care of alone. I knew a plot when I saw one. Juanita had been taking care of that house alone for years, but Carmelita took her side, for our soon-to-be family of four wasn't going to fit well in our jacal down in Poquito.

I lay in the bed for days, my lungs so full of phlegm and fluid it felt like I had a rock on my chest. And I had fitful, crazy dreams.

Carmelita and Juanita fussed over me like two hens, until I felt fit enough to get up the seventh day. I heard Tiffany's voice from the kitchen as I was coming down the stairs. I made a slow go of it with my crutch and I paused at the foot of the stairs to catch my wind. Tiffany was okay—a little too quick to point out how barbaric and backward we Texans were, but okay for all of that—but I didn't relish having to socialize with her feeling like I did. I didn't want to talk to anyone and I never minded being alone.

I noticed the photograph on a little table under the mirror on the wall at the end of the banister and picked it up. I had rarely been inside the big house since it was built, other than to take an occasional meal in the dining room with Papa. The bunkhouse was where I had my meals back when the ranch was in its prime, and I had batched and done my own cooking there until Carmelita and I were married.

So it was no wonder that I hadn't noticed the photograph before. The tintype was faded, but I recognized it. It was the one taken by that crazy Swede in Abilene the first year we went up the trail.

I studied the three faces staring back at me—Hamish sitting in his chair, with Joseph and me standing to either side of him, so long ago that we almost looked like strangers. I looked so pale and thin, with my eyes two times too big for my face. And where had I got that silly buckskin jacket and sash around my waist? I remembered thinking that day what a full-grown man I was, but I saw nothing in that photograph but a scared kid trying to turn slightly away from the camera so that his missing arm wasn't so plain to see.

Over time, I got used to my arm being gone, except for sometimes waking up at night and feeling it as if it were still there. I couldn't remember the last time I had dreamed I still had my arm, but I never did get over people looking at my stump. Until I married Carmelita, I never took my shirt off in front of anyone, even all the whores I'd bedded over the years. I'd rather stand in the middle of a crowded street with my pants around my ankles than to reveal the scarred stump left where my arm used to be. I don't know why it shames me so.

Nobody knows that, except for those few whores, who didn't think anything of a randy cowboy being in too big of a hurry to take off his shirt. Half those cowboys didn't even take off their boots. It wasn't something I talked about. Hamish wanted to talk about everything, like it made it better or solved something. I don't like people to see my scars.

The Swede photographer was better than I thought he was at the time. He'd exactly captured the way Joseph's eyes looked—caught it so that it was like Joseph was staring right at me then. I put the picture facedown on the table and left it.

"Look what the Devil drug in," Tiffany said. She was sitting at the kitchen table with their youngest on her lap. The girl was the spitting image of her, and a pretty little button. Papa used to say that you could see the good breeding in Tiffany at a glance, as if he could judge her like a horse or a cow.

"The prodigal son has returned, even if a little worse for the wear," I said.

Carmelita pulled out a chair for me while Juanita took a plate of leftovers from the oven, which they must have saved for me. From the sunlight coming through the window it was noon or later.

"You look better," Carmelita said.

I propped my crutch up against the table and took up a cup of coffee. Better, maybe, but I still didn't have any appetite.

"You should eat," Carmelita said.

Mexican women aren't happy unless they see their men eating and they'll fatten you like a veal calf in a crate if you aren't careful. Carmelita's belly was so big that she kept one hand under it to ease the discomfort, and her other hand braced against her lower back as she hovered over me. I wondered if it would be a boy or a girl.

"You haven't had anything but a little broth or soup in days," she added.

"I'm not hungry." I was watching the two boys playing on the porch. I could see them through one of the windows. Carmelita's boy—she got mad if I didn't call him "our" boy, but I hadn't got used to that—was shorter than Hamish's son, but they were close to the age that Hamish and I were when we first came to the ranch.

I never met Carmelita's first husband, but from what I can gather he was a no-good that beat on her some and ran off and left her when the boy was still an infant. Some border sheriff shot him for stealing horses, and that was the end of him.

The boy must have taken after Carmelita. He was a good kid, but I didn't know what you said to a boy that age. Hamish seemed to have the knack for it and his children adored him, but I was at a loss. Carmelita wanted me to spend more time with Pancho. He wasn't my own flesh and blood, but I was what he had. I thought maybe I would buy the kid a horse. A boy needs a horse.

The women tried to talk with me, but my mind was on other things. I finished my coffee and took up my crutch and went to the porch. The two boys almost knocked me over, chasing each other through the front door.

Papa's chair was still there, looking no different than ever, except that it made me feel empty. I hadn't felt so empty in a long time.

I noticed a dark spot on the porch boards that might have been a bloodstain. Somebody had tried to scrub it away, but it was still there. I looked down the hill and tried to imagine where the shooter had been.

I don't know how long I stood there before I recognized

that Juanita was in the doorway behind me. The coughing hit me again, and when I was through I had to sit in Papa's chair. The cold air felt good on my bare toes sticking out of my cast. Never trust a half-broke horse on slippery ground. Story of my life—slippery ground and one wreck after another.

I thought Juanita might sit with me. She obviously had something on her mind, but she stayed leaning against the doorjamb. You wouldn't have looked at her and guessed she was older than me. Prettiest woman I ever saw.

The silence between us felt as awkward as ever. I cleared my throat, but could think of nothing to say to her. How long had it been?

There had been a time when I thought of little else but her. All those years, and I had never found another like her. Carmelita reminded me of her a little sometimes, and I wondered if that was why I married her. It shamed me, but I didn't feel about Carmelita like I used to about Juanita.

It was the first time I had been alone with Juanita in years. I had made a point of that; she had made a point of that. Papa was always around, and that was best. I knew she hadn't forgotten the last time we were alone together when I had tried to kiss her. What was I, twenty-five then? It wasn't a planned thing. I had come up to the house looking for Papa and she had been there alone, standing so close to me that I could feel her breath and those smoky eyes looking like something you could swim in. She had shoved me away before I barely touched those lips, and waved her pointer finger slowly at me and shook her head.

"*No bueno. Es no bueno. No somos malas personas,*" she had said. We aren't bad people.

And I went away. I know she never told Papa. It was our bad secret; my bad secret. We never spoke more than a few words to each other after that.

"I miss him, too," she said behind me.

"Did you see who it was?"

"I was inside. All I heard was the shot. Miguel found boot tracks down at the corner of the bunkhouse. Big tracks."

It wouldn't have been an easy shot, but not a difficult one, either. It was only maybe two hundred yards from the bunkhouse to the porch. I was no rifle shot, but I had hit targets farther away than that, especially if I had something to rest my gun on, like one of those logs ends at the corner of the bunkhouse. No shot at all, especially for someone with one of those old buffalo guns with a telescopic German sight on it like Moon used to use.

"Do you think it was Moon?" she asked.

"It was him."

She stepped beside me, but I didn't look up at her.

"Take care of Carmelita," I said. "She'll need some help with the new baby when it comes. Hamish and Tiffany will help. You won't have to ask them."

"I will look out for your family."

"I can't let it lie."

"I know," she whispered. "Kill him. Kill him for your papa. Kill him for me."

Her hand was hanging beside mine on the arm of the chair. For an instant, our fingers clasped each other's and then she let go and went back into the house.

Chapter Fifty-two

Hamish's horseless carriage, "automobiles" those that had them called them, raised a trail of dust that I could see for two miles. I was holding the bay while Miguel did a bad job of nailing a horseshoe on. The horse didn't want to stand still, and my father-in-law was too old to be standing under a horse.

Hamish didn't slow down until he was right on top of us, covering us in dust and causing the horse to shy sideways and jerk its back leg loose from Miguel. Hamish should have known better, and there should have been a law against those horseless carriages. Anything that will scare a horse like that was a danger to society.

Hamish sat in the automobile long enough for us to admire it. It was one of those open-topped Oldsmobiles with a curved dashboard like a buggy and a brass carriage light on either front corner of it. He steered it with some kind of rod sticking up out of the floorboard, but watching him come up the rutted track to the corrals, the front wheels ducked back and forth and the whole thing looked like it rode rougher than a cob. Hamish bounced so high over a couple of bumps that I saw daylight between his rear end and the seat. Tiffany said Hamish couldn't go two miles without having to dig it out of some rut or mud hole, and carried a shovel and a pry pole tied on the back for those occasions.

I waited for him to shut the noisy, stinking thing off. I never could stand even the sound of a steam engine, much less a gasoline contraption like that. Horses are quiet and give a man time to think.

"That leg of yours looks like it still hasn't healed," Hamish said as he climbed out of the automobile, leaving it running. "And you've been out of that cast for a month."

"It's getting better." I leaned against a fence post, my leg throbbing like it had been hit with a hammer.

"That's not what Carmelita told Tiffany. She said you can barely get around on it, and that you haven't been sleeping an hour or two a night. You ought to have the doctor look at that again."

"He's looked at it three times. Break your leg and see how you hobble around."

He noticed the crutch that I had left leaning against the side of the barn while I tried to help shoe the horse. "I'd say something's keeping the bone from knitting right, or that you tore some muscles or something."

"You're a doctor now, are you?"

"How's the new baby?"

"Joseph's fine. Fit as a fiddle."

"Good." Hamish seemed to have something on his mind other than my leg and my new son, but he never went straight at a thing.

I knew it had something to do with the other dust cloud worming its way to the ranch, coming from town.

He saw me looking. "That's some freight wagons I've got hauling equipment."

"Five freight wagons' full of equipment? Has Tiffany got you adding on to the house again?"

"It stuff for a drilling rig."

"You're kidding me."

Hamish brushed at a something on his khaki pants and frowned. I noticed that he was wearing a pair of brogan, lace-up work boots like those oil field workers wore.

The whole damned country had gone crazy over oil, ever since that Spindletop strike down on the Gulf at Beaumont. "Black gold" they called it. Then some fool had to go and drill an oil well north of Destiny. They said they hit a gusher, whatever that was. It was big money, and that was all it took to have wooden rig derricks sprouting up all over the northern end of the county.

"I would have thought you were busy enough without wildcatting for oil," I said.

"We might be sitting on a fortune," Hamish said. "You're always saying how you want to see this ranch built back up."

I'd seen all I wanted of the oil business. Petrolia was only a bit north of us, the little town practically booming overnight and full of men wearing stained work clothes and smelling of tar and grease. Not only were the noisy drilling rigs everywhere you looked, sometimes five or six of them in a single quarter section, but you could sit on the porch at night and hear the steam and gasoline engines running and the creak of drilling cables working up and down.

"I'm going to try a test hole on the north end of the ranch," Hamish said. "Straight across the river from where that big buffalo wallow used to be."

"In that cottonwood grove?"

"Close to it."

"Leave those trees alone. That's always been my favorite place on the ranch."

"I won't bother them."

The wagons pulled to a stop, great big things, hauling lumber and equipment that I didn't even recognize. A stocky man on the front seat of the lead wagon got down and came over to us. He was wearing those lace-up boots like Hamish's and a pair of overalls, but he had on a clean white shirt and a tie, of all things, cinched around his collar. He took hold of the short, pencil-rolled brim of his hat and lifted it away and mopped at his brow with a red handkerchief he pulled from his bib pocket.

"DB Jackson, I want you to meet my brother, Gunn," Hamish said.

The man had a grip like a vise when I shook his hand. I'd seen his kind before when I had gone to see a doctor in Petrolia to get a second opinion on my leg the week before. The whole town was a madhouse, the streets crowded with wagons, and the combination of spring rains and traffic had turned the place into a shin-deep mud hole. Two crews of those oil field boys, roughnecks they liked to call themselves, were drunk and fist fighting in the street. Straight-up fist and skull didn't last for long, and they were soon using pipe wrenches or anything else they could lay their hands on. I'd seen wild cow towns, but that oil town was more wide-open than any of those. Word had spread that money was flowing out of the ground, and the whores and gamblers and a host of shady sorts had flocked to the town like flies on a cow patty. I had heard stories of mining boomtowns back in the old days that were like that, but never laid eyes on anything of its kind.

"I had DB out last month to look over our ground," Hamish said. "He likes the look of things."

"Pay a fellow enough and he's liable to tell you anything," I said.

The roughneck didn't like what I had to say, but Hamish

cut him off before he could get started. "DB comes highly recommended, and I stole him away from Texaco."

I never did trust a man who went by his initials. My experience was that they usually thought too much of themselves. And poking holes in the ground was no recommendation to me.

"You didn't ask me about this," I said.

"We'll drill one test hole and see how it looks."

"This is a ranch, last time I looked. I don't recall you ever mentioning that we were going into the oil business."

"You don't have to be like that."

"I don't like you sneaking up on me with this."

"If you had been here instead of going off on some cattle drive like a kid cowboy, I would have talked to you about it."

"I don't guess I have any say. My name may be on the deed with you, but you're the moneyman."

"I saved this ranch. If it wasn't for my money somebody else would own this place."

"Does that make you feel good?"

"We aren't arguing about oil wells, are we?"

"Dig where you want to. Hell, drill a hole right in the front yard if you want to, but don't tear up that cottonwood grove. I like to lay under the shade of one of those trees when I'm feeling lazy."

Hamish's driller and the line of wagons continued north through the headquarters. Hamish started to get in his automobile, but paused there. "You really ought to get that leg looked at again. I know a good doctor in Dallas."

"I've been to Dallas, and I didn't like it."

"I never knew you to wear a beard," he said. "Never recall you going a day without shaving."

"Anything else you want to change about me?"

"You ought to eat more. You look puny."

"I had a full glass of whiskey for breakfast. Forgot to pack a lunch, so I'll have two for supper when I get home tonight."

"Joke all you want, but that leg worries me. I'd hate to see you . . ." Hamish hung up on what he had started to say.

"What? You'd hate to see me a cripple?"

Hamish climbed in and throttled up his motor, but didn't take off. I could tell he was weighing what he was about to say.

"The grand jury looked at Papa's murder, but they didn't charge anyone," he said. "The county prosecutor won't bring charges against Moon, either."

"That's too bad."

Chapter Fifty-three

Hamish's driller and a crew of two other men had the rig up and running in a week. I still couldn't ride a horse, so I told Carmelita we were going for a picnic on the river. I hitched a team to Papa's buggy and drove her and the kids up to the cottonwood grove and we had lunch on a blanket. Of course, I made a point to swing by Hamish's well site on our way back home. I was curious to see what Hamish was wasting his money on and what all the racket they were making was about.

The crew had built a wooden derrick that looked like a windmill tower, only bigger. The thing must have been eighty or ninety feet tall. There were all kinds of pulleys and cables and a steam engine powering the whole thing.

Hamish was standing on the plank floor beneath the derrick, talking to that driller and looking down the hole they were drilling. He saw me before I could leave and waved at me to hold up while he walked to the buggy.

"Hello, Carmelita. Hello, Pancho." He ruffled the boy's hair and lifted the blanket Carmelita had Joseph wrapped in and tickled his cheek with one finger. "Fine-looking family, Gunn."

"Struck it rich yet?" I asked.

"Get down and come take a look."

I tried to dodge out, but he wouldn't hear of it. He was prouder of that rig than anything I had ever seen him own. I took up the mesquite stick that I had peeled for a walking cane and followed him to where the crew was working. I could get along without the crutch anymore, but my leg was still iffy and apt to buckle on me.

Hamish glanced at my improvised cane. "You look better. How's the leg?"

"Tolerable. I'll be running footraces with the kids in another week," I said. "Quite a job you've got going here."

"See that big wheel there in front of the engine? That's the band wheel. And see that crossbeam on top of that samson post that's rocking like a teeter-totter? That's what works the drilling line up and down." He sounded like a kid in a candy shop. It was the same look on his face he got when we were kids and he was reading a book he liked or talking about what he'd read.

I had seen water well drilling rigs, but never really paid attention to how they worked. "How do you drill a hole with nothing but that cable?"

"We've got a bit on the end of that cable."

"Bit?"

"It's really just a big heavy chisel. Lift it and drop it over and over and the point on it pulverizes what's below it. See that sheave or big pulley on the opposite side of the drill floor? That's the sand wheel." He shaded his eyes with one hand and pointed up at the top of the derrick with the other. "Got another cable that runs through the sand wheel and up through the crown block there on top of the derrick. There's a bail on the end of that sand wheel line that we can lower down in the hole and pull out the cuttings and clean out the well."

"Cuttings?"

"Bits of rock and debris, shale and sand. We have to do that about every two or three feet, depending on the formation we're drilling in. DB keeps a close eye on the cuttings to tell what kind of formation we're drilling in."

"Must be a slow way to dig a hole. How deep are you?"

"Six hundred feet, but we've hit some hard stuff. We've wore out two bits this morning, and we're about to work our tool hand to death sharpening them." He pointed to one of his crew working with a portable blacksmith forge and hammering on the point of a chunk of red-hot steel with a shop hammer.

"Why has that driller got his hand on the drilling cable while he's looking down in the well?"

"He's feeling for when there isn't any slack in the line. That will let him know when he needs to let out a little more cable. If he lets out too much the cable can get a kink in it."

"What do you need with those other guys, if that's all there is to it?"

"One of them is the motorman. He tends the engine," Hamish said. "And we're about to run our first string of casing, and that's a job for three men."

I looked a question at him.

"Casing—steel pipe barely smaller than the hole that we put down to line the walls. You lower one joint of it down the hole with that set of blocks hanging inside the derrick, and thread the next joint of casing to it and lower again."

"Quite a toy you've got."

The crew was taking a lunch break, and the driller walked over to join us. He wasn't wearing his tie anymore and was filthy from head to toe. He pulled off his gloves and offered a handshake. He was the handshakingest man I ever saw.

"What's it looking like?" Hamish asked.

"No sand yet," the driller said. "But I don't expect it for another hundred feet. Maybe a little more."

"What's the deal with sand?" I asked.

"The oil doesn't flow out of rock very well, and most pools lie in sand," Hamish said. "Find black sand and you might be onto something."

"How many of these oil wells have you drilled?" I asked the driller.

"I've lost count," the driller said. "Started when I was a boy in the Corsicana field. Drilled my first well when I was nineteen up in the Bartlesville pool in the Indian Territory. Gulf Oil hired me and I went to Beaumont and then to Jennings, Louisiana. Been working for one company and then the other since, and wildcatting in between when I couldn't find the backers."

"And how many times have you found oil?"

"Brought in a well down at Beaumont that produced a thousand barrels a day."

"That's not what I asked."

The driller looked a little bothered by my question. "Three times. The rest of them were dusters."

"Long odds." I looked at Hamish.

Hamish shrugged. "Remember what Papa used to say? You don't get eggs without spending the money to buy the hens."

"Papa had the good sense to know that the only real riches are land and cattle."

"Papa could have used a few oil wells. Oil is sixty cents a barrel and climbing."

"Don't spend your money before you make it." I waved good-bye and went back to my buggy.

I snuck a snort of whiskey from the flask in my vest

pocket as I was going around the back of the buggy. I smiled at Carmelita when I climbed onto the seat beside her.

"You look in fine spirits," she said.

"I was thinking I might drive into Destiny."

"Joseph is getting cranky. I think he's got the colic again."

Joseph was squirming against her chest and fighting his blanket. His little face was red and twisted in a fury that told me he was about to cry.

"Boy's got a temper."

"His belly hurts. That's all."

"No, he's definitely a Dollarhyde. Temper like a long-horn bull."

"You won't mind if I don't go to town with you? Joseph kept me up all night, and I could use a nap."

"I'll drop you off at the house. I was thinking I might go look up somebody in town."

"An old friend?"

"I wouldn't say that. Just somebody I need to have a few words with." We drove a little farther. "Honey, if something ever happens to me, trust Hamish. He'll look after you. He's a good man."

She gave me a worried look. "Is your leg hurting again?"

"No, I'm fine. Don't know why I mentioned it."

I dropped her off at the house and made sure to kiss her before she went in the house with the kids. I waited until I had driven out of sight before I took another sip from my flask and reached under the seat and pulled out my pistol that I had wrapped up in my coat. Whiskey always made me mean or sad. By the time I hit the edge of town the flask was empty and I was feeling mean.

Chapter Fifty-four

I chose a corner under a barber pole straight across the street from the county jail. I had been standing there over an hour and knew good and well that Moon saw me if he was in there. But I could play the waiting game as long as he could.

Like I figured, his nerve finally broke, or he got up enough of a mad to overcome the yellow streak that ran through him. He came out the door, hitching his pants up and studying the street like it was a normal day.

I wasn't as smart as Hamish, but I was a whole lot smarter than Moon Lowe. It was time I jerked his chain a little.

A deputy came out the door behind Moon, but stayed on the porch, acting like he didn't know I was around. I didn't know him, but from Carmelita's description, I was guessing that he was Deputy Long, and the very same fellow that had roughed her up with Moon.

"Not many wear a sidearm in town anymore," Moon said.

"Some law against it?"

"No, but there ought to be."

"I hear you make your own laws."

"You're looking for trouble."

"I'm looking at a badge with a tub of guts pinned on it."

"Give me that pistol. We're going over to the jailhouse."

"Take it from me, Moon. Take it from me."

"You arrogant bastard," Moon said. "Think you can come into my county, my town, and threaten me? Nobody's going to care if I lock up an ex-con like you."

"Don't look over your shoulder at your deputy. He can't help you. I could shoot you full of holes before he gets his finger out of his nose."

"You're drunk."

"Go ahead, pull that pistol on your hip. I see you wanting to. Make it easy for me."

"I didn't shoot your old man."

"Liar."

"I don't have to take that off of a drunk cripple like you."

"You're taking it. You always were a coward. Beat any old men or women lately? No? Probably some old cowboy kicked your ass up between your shoulder blades."

"Deputy Long, come over here and lend a hand." Moon said it louder than he needed to, probably hoping anyone on the street would hear him. He was trying to set up an alibi and make it look like the good sheriff was doing his duty. "This man is resisting arrest."

"Shame, or I would have got you when I got Prince. Prince was a no-good, but at least he had some sand."

"Don't you mention my brother."

For a brief instant, I thought he was going to pull on me. But that wasn't the way Moon did things. He was like some of those coyote dogs I had seen on that hunt with Papa. You had some dogs that would go right for the coyote's throat, risking being bitten to go for the kill. And while the coyote was busy with that dog, the other kind dove in from behind and got in a bite. Ass-biters were what coyote hunters called them.

"How'd that make you feel? You got Prince to help you beat up Joseph and then you ran off and let Prince take your medicine?"

Moon was shaking. Even an ass-biter like him had a limit to how far you could push him. Deputy Long was halfway across the street, and I had taken things about as far as I could go.

"Prince was . . ."

I cut him off. "How about you come see me sometime? Let's settle this without an audience."

"You don't . . ."

"See you later, Sheriff."

"Did I just hear you threaten an officer of the law?" Moon called after me. "You don't know the trouble I can bring down on you!"

I was counting on that.

Chapter Fifty-five

I thought Moon had finally worked his courage up and decided to make an issue of my tough talk when I looked in the bar mirror and saw one of his deputies look at me and start across the room. I would have seen him when he came in the door, instead of when he was almost on top of me, but I had belted back a few since I met Moon on the street.

It wasn't Deputy Long, who I had seen with Moon at the jailhouse. This new deputy took a place at the bar beside me, obviously not wanting a drink, for he was facing me and paying the bartender no mind.

"He wants to see you."

"Tell Moon to go to hell. If he wants me shot resisting arrest he can come do it himself."

"Ain't Moon that wants to see you. Mr. Lowe is waiting in his office to talk with you."

"Clayton? I would have thought he choked on a sour pickle and died years ago."

"He doesn't like to be kept waiting."

Did Clayton think I would actually go in his office and step right into whatever he and that sheriff son of his had set up for me? They must have thought I was stupid or crazy.

I drained my glass and took up my cane and hobbled after the deputy. The bottle I had been nursing on was ninety-five-proof stupid and crazy and the rest of it was bitter branch water.

"I didn't know a county deputy's duty was to run and fetch for Clayton Lowe," I said, unable to resist jabbing the deputy a little.

The deputy kept walking. "Are you sure you're sober enough to walk?"

"Whiskey doesn't have that effect on me. This bum leg's what has me hobbling."

"What does whiskey do to you?"

"First I get charming. Then I turn bulletproof. And then I turn invisible."

"Which one are you now?" the deputy asked. "No, let me guess. You're bulletproof?"

"No, charming. Can't you tell?"

"You talk too much," the deputy said.

We reached Clayton's office before I could antagonize him more. The old store had been replaced by a brick affair. The upper story contained Clayton's land and shipping business and a set of side stairs led up to it from an alley at one end of the building. The deputy stepped aside for me, but I shook my head and pointed up the stairs, directing him to go first.

"I'll take my bullets in the front, thank you."

He didn't like that any more than he did me, but he went up the stairs ahead of me, knocking on the door at the top before entering. When I stepped in the doorway behind the deputy, Clayton Lowe was sitting behind a desk on the far side of the room. Either that man didn't like me, or he had been sucking on those sour pickles again.

"Sit down, Gunn, and take a load off that leg."

"I believe I'll stay standing. This ought not take long."

"You always were a trying one. I don't see what it would hurt to have a drink with me and talk like civilized men." He tried to smile, but I noticed his hand shaking on the tabletop. I also noticed that one side of his mouth didn't seem to work right, that whole side of his face kind of sagging. A little white froth of drool worked like a spider-web at that corner of his mouth. The way he was keeping the other arm below the table, I thought he might have a gun on me, but that arm was on the same side of his body as that sagging face. I got the impression that his arm didn't work too good.

"Nice office you have here. Land business must be good," I said.

"I won't let you kill Moon," Clayton said. "You've taken one of my boys, and I won't see it happen again."

"Moon shot Papa."

He gave an odd shrug of his shoulders. "What if I were to send Moon out of the country, and he never came back?"

"I'd hunt him until I found him."

"Why do you hate us so?"

"Your family has always been the one making trouble. You picked fight after fight with us, even when you couldn't win. We warned you time and again."

"Do you think I hate you Dollarhydes?"

"I never cared enough to think on it."

"I didn't hate your father. I tried every way in the world to get along with him," Clayton said. "But you couldn't tell him anything."

"Papa was twice the man you are."

"Do you know what I did hate? I hated that your papa thought he was better than me. Men like that can't share. It isn't in them. He thought he was so big that other folks didn't matter. Didn't realize that it takes a lot of folks working together to make a place matter, and not one man."

"You mean he wouldn't let you make the rules," I said. "You had the whole wide world open to you, but you couldn't stand it because our ranch was the one place where you weren't ever going to matter. Outside this pissant town, you never could measure up to Papa, and you knew it. That's what bothered you most, wasn't it?"

Clayton's hand on the table was shaking worse. From the look of him, I guessed a stroke had got him sometime back. I remembered him as the tall, immaculately dressed man he had once been, but the bald, scarecrow thing in front of me was only a shell of that old memory.

"Clayton, I'm giving you the benefit of the doubt. That other hand of yours might be under the table because it doesn't work so well anymore, but then again, you might be thinking on pulling a pistol you've got stashed in that desk and counting on this deputy here to finish me if you don't get me."

Clayton's eye threw hellfire at me, and his mouth sprayed spit. "You Dollarhydes!"

"Good night." I backed out the door, keeping a closer eye on the deputy than I was on Clayton.

"I won't let you kill my boy!" Clayton yelled after me as I headed down the stairs.

Chapter Fifty-six

Maybe it was because I was too drunk to go home, or maybe it was because my whiskey flask was empty and I had a partial bottle stashed in the dugout. For a time, Papa had used it to store junk, but it hadn't been fit for even that in years. The roof had caved in, along with a good part of the front wall, and the weeds and grass almost hid it from a casual glance.

I took a seat on a crate I drug out of the dugout and nursed my whiskey, staring at the ruins of what had been our first home in Texas. Only, it never was.

Sometime later, I sloshed kerosene into the tumble of fallen rafters and threw the can in after it. A clump of dry grass was enough tinder to get a fire going and I pitched it in the ruins with the kerosene. There was enough refuse inside to get the flames going high, and the rafters and rotten decking were burning before I returned to my seat and took my whiskey bottle back up.

Somebody yelled at me from the big house. It was a woman's voice, but it was Hamish who showed up first. Carmelita or Juanita must have gone to get him.

He killed the Oldsmobile's engine and turned off its

lights. The flames were almost hot enough to singe my face by the time he came to stand beside me. I could see Mama's mahogany dresser burning in the center of the fire.

"Are you about to tell me that I'm drunk or crazy?"

Hamish shook his head in the firelight. "No, we should have burned it a long time ago. Remember how Mama cried when she saw what Papa wanted her to live in?"

"Go get some boards off of that rotten lumber pile over there and let's burn her up."

"You loved Mama, too."

"Mama quit us."

"Mama was strong as Papa. Maybe stronger," he said. "The Kiowa took her. How can she have any blame in that?"

I laughed bitterly. "Mama shot Baby Beth and then shot herself. You didn't go in the dugout, but I got close enough before Papa stopped me. Saw the hole in her head and that little pistol Papa gave her lying there off the end of her hand."

"You lie."

"You've got that pistol still, don't you? Why do you think the Kiowa didn't take it if they killed her? They never left a gun lying around after a raid."

"They overlooked it. It was Kiowa, and they were out for revenge because we had fought them and killed a couple of them when we helped those Quakers."

"Who knows what those Kiowa were up to, or even if it was Kiowa. Could have been Comanche or any kind of Indian, no matter what Jose thought. He didn't know much about Indians, and never said he did. It was Papa grilling him hard that made him give an opinion that it was Kiowa. That, and the fact that me and Papa had killed two of them the day Papa traded for Joseph." I could tell Hamish was listening to me, even though he didn't want to. "Maybe those Indians were only riding by, curious like, and Old Ben wasn't taking any chances and was going to get in a first shot. Maybe she saw them kill Old Ben and did it then. Something like that is the only thing that explains why they didn't take her gun, nor Old Ben's either. I carried his pistol for years myself."

"They set fire to one of our wagons and stole some of the stock."

"Could have had their mad up by then. How come you think Joseph was able to hide from them so easy, and Juanita, too? I think they weren't dead set on raiding us, but something went bad. After that, they took what was handy and moved on quick. Indians don't like suicides. Maybe Mama was what caused them to go without taking the time to carry off everything on the place."

"You are crazy."

"Doesn't matter if they came raiding or not, there's one thing I know." Hamish was about to interrupt me, but I cut him off. "Instead of forting up and trying to make a go of it, Mama lost her nerve and wasn't going to let them get her or Baby Beth. All those horror stories of what Indians did to white women and that 'save the last bullet' stuff was too much."

"What's wrong with you to make up such things?"

"If Papa was still here you could ask him."

The air went out of him and he sat against the bottom rail of the corral fence with his hands on his knees and his head hung. The flames were dying down.

I let Hamish think on it while I stared at my whiskey flask until I threw the empty thing in the coals. I never should have told him. I had kept it from him all those years, but whiskey is full of regrets.

"Sometimes I hate you," he said. "Sometimes I don't know how we can be brothers."

"They say you can pick your friends but you can't pick your family."

"You and Papa. I used to try to be like you, all the time feeling bad because I couldn't. Took me years to figure out I could be something else."

"You got her smarts."

He stood like he was going to his car, but held where he was. "You know when I knew I wasn't like you and Papa? I knew it that morning in that Wichita village."

"That was a bad morning."

"As far as I know, he never said a word about what he did that morning for the rest of his life. It was like he could forget it happened, but who could do that?"

"Papa had his own ways. Walk a mile in his moccasins before you go to judging him."

"He shot Emilio right in front of us. I loved Papa as much as you did, but I never could forget that."

"We've all done things. You always want to pick which part of Papa you liked. He had his faults, but I took him on the whole, like I take you on the whole, the good and the bad."

"I'm going to make something big so that all that wasn't for nothing. I'm going to make it good."

"Fix it all? Make it bigger than Papa did? You sound a lot like him, whether you'll admit it or not."

"I'm nothing like him. I loved him, but God strike me down if I ever become him." Hamish went to his car and I listened to him drive away.

"Don't toy with God, brother," I said to myself. "He's got a wicked sense of humor."

Chapter Fifty-seven

Tiffany came by the house and told us that Hamish was about to bring in his oil well, and she wanted us to be there to see it. She was driving Hamish's automobile, wearing a canvas driving duster over her dress, a pair of goggles, and had her hair tucked up inside a cap. The sight of a woman driving such a contraption struck me odd, especially in that getup, but Tiffany was an Eastern woman and what Hamish called a freethinker. Next thing you know she would be wearing pants.

I went to the barn and hitched a team to our buggy, while Carmelita got the kids ready and Juanita packed a basket with a lunch. I picked them all up in front of the house and we drove to Hamish's well site.

I quickly saw that we weren't the only sightseers to have heard the word, for there must have been fifty people already there, with their wagons scattered back a hundred yards or so from the rig and sitting in the wagon beds like bleachers or spreading blankets on the ground. The ladies spread our blanket, and by the time Juanita broke out our lunch more people were arriving. And they kept coming and coming.

Hamish's driller and his crew were busy tending to

things that I had no idea about, but what struck me most is that they were nervous. You could see it even from a distance. I saw the driller pull Hamish aside several times, and the discussion between them was intense. I assumed they were simply on edge as to whether or not they were going to bring a well in. The majority of the holes the crazy oil field wildcatters in the county were drilling turned out to be nothing but dusters or shallow and short-lived low producers, and Hamish was probably sweating bullets, considering the money he had spent trying to become the next Rockefeller.

"Rumor is, DB has found himself one hundred feet of black sand," a man standing near our picnic blanket said.

"They might have something, then, but don't count on it," the man with him said. "If rumors and hope were barrels of oil, we'd all be rich by now."

From the look of the two, I guessed they were roughnecks or oil field types themselves. In fact, many of the crews from rigs working in the area had shown up to see how things played out. Maybe it was professional courtesy, but I imagine they were trying to get the scout on where the next hot area would be. The big shots back East, the Texacos, Gulf Oils, and Standard Oils, all had their lease men traveling the country trying to buy mineral rights to whatever ground interested them. Coupled with those big-money lease agents, there were just as many shady, pie-in-the-sky wildcatters doing the same thing. I had asked Hamish why we didn't lease the ranch, bank the money, and let some other fools worrying about drilling holes, but he was convinced that a fortune was buried below us and was dead set on keeping the lion's share instead of leasing out our ground for a royalty percentage.

Everybody had the oil fever. That was the only reason I could see for the size of Hamish's audience. Unless you were an oilman, sitting in the sun watching Hamish's crew was like watching grass grow. But, no matter, the crowd hung around throughout the day. Whispered rumors went through the crowd about what Hamish's crew were doing.

"I worked with DB down in Beaumont, and he knows what he's about," a man said, pointing to where Hamish's driller was leaned over the hole in the middle of the drill floor, staring intently down it with one hand on the drilling cable. "He thinks he's about there and getting nervous. When you see old DB get nervous you had better look out! The whole dam rig's about to blow sky-high or it's a gusher for sure!"

"Should have got him one of those new rotary rigs," another said. "I wouldn't dig a hole with one of those cable antiques."

"I hear the well on the Johnson's place is making a hundred barrels a day," a woman said to the woman beside her, keeping her hand to one side of her mouth as if the gossip was too juicy for the rest of the crowd. "Harriet Roberson down at the store told me that Lydia Johnson was spending money like it would never end and bought five yards of new dress material like it didn't cost anything. Said Lydia's husband had bought him one of those new go-devils to plow his fields, but couldn't get any work done because he was too busy driving it up and down the roads and showing it off to his neighbors."

"I saw Lydia yesterday," the other woman said. "She wouldn't even talk to me, with her nose up in the air. I guess now that she's rich she's too good for us."

I listened closely, but nobody seemed to know what they were talking about, other than sharing rumors about who had gotten rich with oil in their backyard or who had gone broke trying to drill for it.

It was nearing sundown, and still nothing happened.

Hamish's crew ran several different kinds of tools down the well bore, and that was about as exciting as it got. The only thing of interest to me was that the driller left his work once and went over and chewed out one of his men. When he went back to looking down his hole, the man he had tore into threw his cigarette on the ground and ground it out with his foot.

"DB is worried about getting gas back. If I was him I would fire that damn fool for smoking a cigarette. Stunt like that could blow us all to hell," the same oil field man who had spoken earlier said. "Could be a gusher. Could be, but I remember that Heywood well at Jennings. That thing burned for a week. Smoke so thick you couldn't see for miles. I thought we were all dead."

The driller and his crew spent an hour pulling the drilling cable up out of the hole, attaching another tool on the end of it, and running it back to the bottom.

"He's going to swab it," one of the men said. "If he's swabbing it that means he thinks she might flow."

"What's 'swabbing it' mean?" I asked them.

"Going to work that swab tool up and down inside the casing like a pump on a windmill to make a little suction. Old DB has run some casing pipe down the hole to line it, but he's left a little stretch unlined at the bottom where that black sand is. If there's oil there, sometimes it's stuck back in the formation and doesn't want to come out."

"If the oil does start to come out, is he going to have to rig up some kind of pump and engine to get the oil out of the hole?"

"Later, maybe, but not at first, at least if he's got himself a well that's any account."

"That's why everyone is down here to watch," the other man said.

"Why are all these people here?" I asked. I was there

because I was curious, but I didn't understand why so many people had shown up to watch something so boring. Maybe they were simply curious like me. Maybe they wanted to see who the next rich man or the next broke fool in the county would be.

"Sometimes it comes out of the hole in a hurry. Know what I mean?" A roughneck nearby that had overheard our conversation laughed.

"You mean a gusher?"

"That's exactly what I mean."

I still wasn't sure what to expect. From all accounts a gusher was when oil started shooting up out of the hole, and that was what every oilman in Texas dreamed about. I watched as the drilling cable worked up and down. The driller said something to Hamish, and Hamish jumped off the rig floor and started toward the crowd, waving his hands and shouting for everyone to move farther away from his rig.

The crowd began to move back reluctantly, but before they had moved far enough to matter, Hamish's driller bailed off the rig floor and ran toward the crowd. His crew was right on his heels.

A waist-high stump of the casing that lined the well was sticking up in the middle of the drill floor and it began to shake and rattle. You could hear it all the way back where we were. And then we heard something else that I can't describe, and then black oil shot out of that casing in a six-inch stream. It hit the crown on top of the wooden derrick and spread into a fountain some one hundred feet high. Within seconds, everything within a seventy-yard radius of the rig was covered in oil. People cheered like they had seen the Messiah himself riding down out of the clouds in a golden chariot pulled by angels.

"Look at your brother!" Carmelita shouted above the

noise of the crowd with her eyes as big as saucers and a smile on her face.

Hamish and his driller were soaked in oil and dancing some kind of jig together and shouting at each other like wild men, while the oil continued to fall over everything.

"Looks like a good well," one of the roughnecks I had been talking to earlier said. "That Dollarhyde is going to have to get her shut in and some storage pits dug or hire some tanks built. Iffen it was me, I would have shut her in earlier, instead of letting all that money blow out on the ground."

His partner slapped him on the back. "Henry, you been working pools long enough to know that you ain't an oil man unless you can show off a gusher. Besides, it looks like old DB and that Dollarhyde can afford to waste a little. That's a ringtailed tooter of a well if I ever saw one."

Hamish came running through the crowd, casting about with his eyes until he spied us. He grabbed up Tiffany and hugged her, even though she playfully chided him for getting oil all over her clothes.

Hamish swung Tiffany around in circles and then let her go and began to chase his boy around and around her, his outstretched arms covered in the black slime making the boy giggle and dodge.

When Hamish finally stopped and looked up at me the only bit of his face that wasn't black was two white rings around his eyes and a pale smear on one cheek where he had swiped at it with a rag Juanita offered him.

"I did it," Hamish said, smiling like a madman.

I sniffed the air. The stench of oil was everywhere.

He saw me do that. "That's money you're smelling. Lots of it. This well will make us a fortune, and the next ones even more."

"You're going to drill more of them?" Juanita asked.

"Oh yes! This is only the start. We own all this ground, and if the rest of it is like I think it is, we're going to have our very own oil pool."

"Congratulations," I said. "Looks like you're going to be rich."

"We're going to be rich, brother. Think of what you can do to the ranch."

"You were right, Hamish. Papa would be proud."

Chapter Fifty-eight

It was a little after daylight and I was feeding the horses when I saw them coming four abreast down the road. I could see the twinkle of sunlight on Moon Lowe's badge, and the skinny man beside him was that Deputy Long, the one who had helped Moon beat on Miguel and had tried to have a go at Carmelita. I hadn't seen Zeke in years, but he was with them, too, riding on the other side of Moon. Moon wasn't playing games when he brought Zeke with him.

And that wasn't all that let me know that they weren't showing up to arrest me. No, the old man himself, Clayton, was out wide of Zeke, his horse dragging behind a little. I wouldn't have thought he could even sit a horse anymore, but there he was, no matter how he slumped in the saddle. It took a lot of hate for a man in his condition to have ridden to find me.

I gauged the distance to the barn, but they were already too close. Zeke spurred his horse up on my left, stopping between me and the barn. There was gray in Zeke's hair that hadn't been there once upon a time, but older or not, he looked as mean as ever.

Moon and Deputy Long parked their horses directly in

front of me, about ten yards away. Clayton hung back a little, more to my right. I could see in their faces that they thought they had me like a duck in a shooting gallery.

I stuck the pitchfork I had been using in the ground and tugged the glove on my hand off with my teeth. It was a cold, windy day, and I was going to be slow getting my Colt out from under my coat.

Moon Lowe smiled. Leave it to him to gloat. "Where's all the tough talk now, Dollarhyde?"

I moved my right hand slowly and gingerly worked at unbuttoning the one button that held the front of my coat closed, expecting them not to let me get that far.

"I'm here to arrest you for threatening a duly appointed officer of the law," Moon said.

"You'll get safe passage to jail," Clayton threw in quickly, his voice as trembling and slurred as it had been when I last saw him in his office. "You have my word."

Standing there with my back to the corral fence and facing them, I knew a lie when I heard it. Taking my chances there and then was better than being shot in the back on the road and Moon's posse claiming I had resisted arrest or tried to run. If they wanted me to beg or plead, they were going to have a long wait.

"I don't think he believes you, Pa," Moon said.

Deputy Long already had his Winchester lying across his saddle swells, and he held it one-handed and poked it in my direction. "No, not a desperate man like Gunn Dollarhyde."

Only Clayton and I didn't laugh.

"Shut up!" Clayton said. "Gunn, if you're packing a pistol, pull it easy and throw it on the ground."

I got my coat unbuttoned and let my arm lower.

"Go ahead and give me an excuse. I been waiting for this for a lot of years," Zeke said.

Moon's horse was turned a little to my left, and he thought I didn't see him slipping his pistol out of his holster on the side away from me. I threw back my head and laughed.

"What are you laughing at?" Moon had that pistol almost clear of his holster.

"I'd about given up on you boys ever showing up," I said.

"What's that?" Clayton cocked his head at me to hear over the wind.

"What took you sons a bitches so long?"

My words threw them off a little and made them all hesitate, and I took advantage of that split second that I had bought myself. I raked back the right side of my coat and my hand found the butt of my Colt far faster than I had dared hope. Moon tried to bring his pistol to bear on me under his left arm but he bobbled the barrel of it against his saddle horn and his shot went off wide of me.

I shot Moon twice in his side, telling myself if I got one of them it was going to be him. He grunted when the second bullet hit him, and his horse took a high lunge with him slumped over its neck.

By that time guns were going off like a cannon volley. I was vaguely aware of Deputy Long's rifle shot busting splinters from a fence rail beside me, and I felt something else tug at the side of my coat. There was a wooden water tank in front of the windmill tower three steps to my left, and I dove against it, hoping to put it between me and Zeke over by the barn. The sides of the tank were only waist-high, but it was the only cover I had.

I sat on the ground with my back to it and took aim at Clayton, the only one of them with a clear shot at me. His horse was dancing sideways and fighting the bit, and my first shot missed him badly. I thumbed back my hammer for another round just as Deputy Long came around the water tank from my left with his Winchester to his shoulder and working the lever like he was fanning a fire. One of his bullets spanged off the ground between my outstretched legs and ricocheted off a nearby fence post. I shoved my Colt at him at arm's length and let him have one. From the way his hat flew off and the way he reeled limply backward I must have shot him in the head. His body stayed on his runaway horse for a few strides before it toppled slowly from the saddle.

Clayton's horse had gone so wild that it had him out of the fight for the moment, and I got to my knees, thinking I would try to spot Zeke where he had been by the barn. It would be like him to be circling around the corrals looking for a shot at my back.

I poked my head up over the waist-high side of the tank just in time to catch a glimpse of him still in front of the barn door with a shotgun leveled on me. Before I could duck, a load of buckshot slapped the water right in front of me. I fell on my side behind the tank barely in time to avoid the second charge from Zeke's gun.

Thinking his double-barrel was empty, I lunged to my feet and threw a wild shot at him. He was bumbling his reload badly, and I was taking more time with my second attempt at him when something knocked my bad leg from under me before I could get my aim. I went down on the seat of my pants, with only a fence post at my back keeping me halfway propped up. My knee felt like it was torn off and the pain was so bad it took me a bit to realize that Clayton Lowe had gotten his horse under control and was walking it right at me and blazing away with a little pocket revolver.

There was no time but to snap a shot at him from my hip. Shooting like that is no way to hit anything, but I did manage to hit his horse or close enough to it to cause it to rear high on its hind legs, pawing the air like a circus horse.

I worked my hammer and tried another shot, but my Colt snapped on an empty chamber. I didn't even remember having fired that many times, but that's the way it is when things get crazy. Everything is happening so fast you can't remember half of it when it's over, much less when it's happening.

I looked up into the shadow of the horse rearing over me and hurled my pistol at its head. The horse walked backward on its hind legs, so straight up in the sky that it looked ten times its size. As if in slow motion, it fell over backward and I heard the thump of the saddle horn hitting the ground and Clayton's bones snapping beneath it. He screamed in such agony that the sound of it made the hair on the back of my neck stand up.

The horse kicked out frantically and squirmed and twisted on its back in an attempt to get rolled over and find its feet. It left out in a dead run when it finally managed to get up, the whites of its eyes showing as it stared back at Clayton's body bouncing off the road beside it, limp and lifeless and flopping so that it looked like no real man at all.

Another buckshot charge hit the side of the water tank, and I knew Zeke was coming to finish me off. I caught a glimpse of his hat above the tank as he walked his horse around it. And me without anything to defend myself with, and too shot up to even stand and take it like a man.

I looked up at Zeke when he rode into sight, staring down at me and grinning with the double bores of that 12-gauge staring at my face like another set of eyes. I could already feel the hole in my chest he was about to open up.

I had gotten more of them than I had thought I would. Even old Wild Bill Hickok himself couldn't have done better, unless you count those penny dreadfuls they write about him. A man doesn't face down four men and expect to get them all, much less live. Not out in the open with nothing but a Colt pistol and guts.

It had been a good life.

Who was I kidding? There was a time when I didn't care if I died, and a time when I felt like I was already dead. But I wanted to live. There was Carmelita and baby Joseph, and the boy, Pancho, who liked me for no reason that I could put a finger on, and smiled and laughed at the things I said to him, although nobody ever considered me a funny man. That felt good, and thinking on those things made me wish to hell I still had my Colt and one more bullet to fight with.

That sorry Zeke had me dead to rights, and I spat on the ground at his horse's feet, glaring at him and not wanting to give him the satisfaction of seeing me scared.

"This is gonna hurt, Dollarhyde," Zeke said.

A gun went off before he could pull his trigger, a big one, and then again. The air went out of him in a grunt and he fell from the saddle like he was poleaxed. I stared at him lying facedown at my feet, not a twitch of life left in him.

And then someone else was coming around the water tank. It was Hamish and he looked down at Zeke's body and then at me while he thumbed another paper cartridge in Papa's old Sharps.

"Never expected to see you," I said.

"That's why I've always told you to let me do the thinking." Hamish squatted down and winced when he looked closer at my knee. "I swear, you're bound and determined to lose all your limbs."

My pants leg was soaked through so much that there was already blood growing a circle in the dust beneath my knee. "You watch out. I don't know if Moon's finished off."

Hamish looked back over his shoulder and winced. "No worries about him."

I undid my bandanna from around my neck and Hamish tied it above my knee as tight as he could to try and slow the bleeding. It was the same knee on my game leg. I never had any luck.

"That looks bad," Hamish said.

"It's too far from my heart to kill me." I tried to laugh to lift some of the worry from him, but it hurt too bad and I gave it up. "This wasn't your fight."

"To hell it wasn't."

"You took your sweet time, if it was."

"I had just gotten to the house from the rig, and saw them coming down the road. I expected you to have the good sense to hole up in the barn and keep them back until I could get down here."

"I like to hog all the fun."

Hamish helped me to my feet and I threw my arm across his shoulders, glancing at the three bodies as we walked among them, and it was hard to believe that less than a minute before all of them had been alive. I wondered if any of them had expected that they would end up like that when they rode out of town, but I guess nobody ever expects exactly what they end up getting.

"I thought you gave up guns when you gave me your pistol back at that train station when you ran off back East to go to college," I said.

Hamish looked down at Moon Lowe's body. "I did, but I made an exception this morning. In law work, we call it jurisprudence."

"Speaking of the law. You tell them I was the only one in on this."

He shook his head. "We'll tell the truth."

"Always got to be difficult, don't you?"

"I'm the big brother."

"They might hang us both, and if they don't, you don't

want any part of prison. I'd take a hundred days like this morning instead of one more day in Huntsville."

"Don't forget, I'm a pretty good lawyer."

"You're taking a risk. They find out you were in on this shooting and you aren't ever going to get elected to office."

"I've given up on politics. You and I are going to be oilmen."

"I'm a rancher. You can keep your oil to yourself."

"All right, I'll be an oilman and you play cowboy."

"I'm not taking any orders from you."

"All right."

"And if you let that sawbones in Destiny take off my leg I'm going to shoot you, brother or not."

"Fair enough."

"Quit being so agreeable. It throws me off."

Hamish loaded me in his car and drove us toward Destiny. The thing bounced and bucked like a bad horse and I only thought my leg had been hurting before.

"First time I ever rode in one of these," I said.

"You better hope it isn't the last. You're bleeding like a stuck pig."

I grabbed at my hat when he sped up to keep it from blowing off. It was bad enough that I was going to have to ride into town in an automobile, but I would be damned if I would go bareheaded. A man has to keep a little pride.

We went through the gate at the east edge of the ranch and passed under the plank overhead with the $D burned deep into it.

"Hamish," I said. "Are we good men?"

Hamish pondered that while he dodged a hole in the road. "I don't know. There are a lot that are worse. No whining, no excuses . . ."

"And no saying you're sorry."